THE LEGEND

A MEDIEVAL ROMANCE

BY KATHRYN LE VEQUE

Print Edition

Printed by Dragonblade Publishing in the United States of America

Library of Congress Control Number 2014-004
ISBN 1495291022

Kathryn Le Veque Novels

Medieval Romance:

The de Russe Legacy:
The White Lord of Wellesbourne
The Dark One: Dark Knight
Beast
Lord of War: Black Angel
The Falls of Erith

The de Lohr Dynasty:
While Angels Slept (Lords of East Anglia)
Rise of the Defender
Steelheart
Spectre of the Sword
Archangel
Unending Love
Shadowmoor
Silversword

Great Lords of le Bec:
Great Protector
To the Lady Born (House of de Royans)

Lords of Eire:
The Darkland (Master Knights of Connaught)
Black Sword
Echoes of Ancient Dreams (time travel)

De Wolfe Pack Series:
The Wolfe
Serpent
Scorpion (Saxon Lords of Hage – Also related to The Questing)
Walls of Babylon
The Lion of the North
Dark Destroyer

Ancient Kings of Anglecynn:
The Whispering Night
Netherworld

Battle Lords of de Velt:
The Dark Lord
Devil's Dominion

Reign of the House of de Winter:
Lespada
Swords and Shields (also related to The Questing, While Angels Slept)

De Reyne Domination:
Guardian of Darkness
The Fallen One (part of Dragonblade Series)

Unrelated characters or family groups:
The Gorgon (Also related to Lords of Thunder)
The Warrior Poet (St. John and de Gare)
Tender is the Knight (House of d'Vant)
Lord of Light
The Questing (related to The Dark Lord, Scorpion)
The Legend (House of Summerlin)

The Dragonblade Series: (Great Marcher Lords of de Lara)
Dragonblade
Island of Glass (House of St. Hever)
The Savage Curtain (Lords of Pembury)
The Fallen One (De Reyne Domination)
Fragments of Grace (House of St. Hever)
Lord of the Shadows
Queen of Lost Stars (House of St. Hever)

Lords of Thunder: The de Shera Brotherhood Trilogy
The Thunder Lord
The Thunder Warrior
The Thunder Knight

Time Travel Romance: (Saxon Lords of Hage)
The Crusader
Kingdom Come

Contemporary Romance:

Kathlyn Trent/Marcus Burton Series:
Valley of the Shadow
The Eden Factor
Canyon of the Sphinx

The American Heroes Series:
Resurrection
Fires of Autumn
Evenshade
Sea of Dreams
Purgatory

Other Contemporary Romance:
Lady of Heaven
Darkling, I Listen

Multi-author Collections/Anthologies:
With Dreams Only of You (USA Today bestseller)
Sirens of the Northern Seas (Viking romance)
Ever My Love (sequel to With Dreams Only Of You) July 2016

Note: All Kathryn's novels are designed to be read as stand-alones, although many have cross-over characters or cross-over family groups. Novels that are grouped together have related characters or family groups.

Series are clearly marked. All series contain the same characters or family groups except the American Heroes Series, which is an anthology with unrelated characters.

There is NO particular chronological order for any of the novels because they can all be read as stand-alones, even the series.

For more information, find it in **A Reader's Guide to the Medieval World of Le Veque**.

To my son, James

A tall, blond hero in the making

TABLE OF CONTENTS

PROLOGUE

1270 A.D.
The Holy Land

"HE IS DEAD, Alec! Let him go!"

Two men were huddled on the sand in a heap, one man clutching the other to him fiercely as blood coated the both of them.

A tall, superbly muscled African again nudged the one of the pair who happened to be alive. "Let him go! We must leave this place!"

The man raised his face from where it had been buried against the head of the other, his sunburned skin coated with tears. "I did this. God help me, Ali, I did this!"

Ali crouched next to the white man, his black hands grasping at the hard English armor. "'Twas an accident, my friend. He came from the shadows and you had no way of knowing it was…."

"God, no!" Alec screamed his anguish. "Christ, Peter, wake up! Wake up and walk from this place with me!"

Ali's onyx eyes darted about the abandoned fortress, searching for the approaching enemy. They had been concealed among the crumbling ruins for nearly two weeks until the Muslims had discovered the refuge of thirty English knights. English who had been raiding villages, killing Muslim enemies and causing heavy losses to weaken the area for the glorious arrival of Prince Edward. It was the prelude to another siege of Acre and the Seventh Crusade was at hand.

But their hideaway had been discovered and even now nearly three hundred Muslims lay siege to the English warriors. Hope for escape was dim, but there was still time if only….

"Alec," the black man yanked him harshly, dislodging the dead man and causing him to fall in a heap. "We must leave. *Now*!"

Alec groaned when the body fell away from him, struggling against his friend. But the grappling ceased when they heard the clash of weapons in the distance.

"Oh, Christ," Alec mumbled, torn between the body on the floor and knowing that he should vacate. His breathing was ragged, harsh. "Oh, Christ, Ali, I cannot leave Peter's body to be destroyed. My father will never forgive me."

"Your father will understand," Ali insisted, tugging desperately. "If we do not leave now, Lord Brian will have lost two sons."

Rapidly, shakily, Alec knelt over the body of his brother and kissed him on both cheeks. Tears sprang to his eyes again, pelting warm droplets on the cooling corpse as he touched his brother's face for the last time.

"Forgive me, Peter," he whispered in a strangled voice. "'Twas dim and you wore no armor and I…. I thought you were an assassin."

Ali waited as long as he could before yanking at Alec again. "Now, Alec, or we both die!"

Alec knew it to be true; he could hear the screams of his fellow knights and the clash of weapons drawing closer. Unsteadily he rose, taking Peter's sword with him.

Ali was already running, pulling Alec with him. Alec's legs were moving as ordered but he continued to look back at the prostrate body of his brother, nearly cut in half, bathed in his own blood. Blood that Alec had spilled from him.

Agony clawed at him as he beat a hasty retreat down the escape tunnels carved beneath the hot desert sands. His breathing was rapid and uneven, pain filling every corner of his mind. *Dear God, how could I have killed my own brother? How could such a thing have happened?* It had been a senseless mistake; his sense of self-preservation acting before his reasoning mind questioned the action, and then....

Alec knew God would forgive him, just as his father would be gracious with his mercy. But Alec was not concerned with the forgiving nature of those not guilty of fratricide. It was his own quality of self-forgiveness he was concerned with.

Aye, it had been dark. The interior of the deserted garrison was always dark. Peter and Alec and the other Christians met the Muslim siege bravely. In command of the advance party for Prince Edward, Alec held off the siege for as long as he could until one of the crumbling mud walls had given way and a multitude of Muslim warriors had poured in through the breach.

After that, there had no longer been a chain of command. The English had panicked, and chaos ruled.

Alec had ordered a few of those still retaining their senses to seek the interior and escape through the secret tunnels carved out by the Saracens many years before. The Muslims had been everywhere, killing anything with white skin, filtering into the abandoned garrison in chase of the Christians. In the madness, somehow he and Peter had been separated.

The enemy was, literally, everywhere. Alec and Ali had found their way into the depths of the sublevel, awaiting other English knights to direct them to safety. Amidst the chaos and darkness they heard footfalls. Alec tensed; his broadsword ready to gut the unsuspecting intruder, for no clarifying signals had yet been given. Every knight knew to emit an identifying signal whilst traversing the tunnels to assure allies within earshot that a friend, and not foe, approached. The signal, given every five or six steps, was a single grunt.

Alec had waited for the rhythmic grunting, but there had been none forthcoming. When he saw the flash of a sword and a naked hand holding it, he hadn't given a second thought as he lashed out and caught the intruder mid-section, severing him cleanly.

His ever-cool manner did not faltered even as he stood over the slain body, incognizant of the fact that his victim was his brother until a slow realization gripped him. Then Alec found himself living and breathing the blackest of nightmares.

He damned Peter, even as he ran to preserve his own hide. Why hadn't he given the signal? Why wasn't he wearing his armor? Why, in God's name, did not he simply call out his brother's name, knowing that Alec would be hiding in the catacombs waiting for him? Alec never went anywhere without Peter; everyone knew that.

Until now. Alec was running alone.

CHAPTER ONE

Baron Rothwell;

As you are a man with little time to spare, I shall come to the point. As you are well aware, there has been continuing discord between St. Cloven and Wisseyham Keep. The actions which preceded this unrest had to do with land rights upon which Sir Albert de Fluornoy was most inequitable. In truth, my lord, he stole lands which did not belong to him. The dissension has been rampant now for many years, an environment which, sadly, my son and Sir Albert's children have grown accustomed to.

It is my understanding that since Sir Albert's death six months ago, St. Cloven is without a lord and the prosperous business has been left to the minimal capabilities of his young daughters. Therefore, I am proposing that my son and the eldest de Fluornoy daughter be joined in matrimony. It is my sincere wish that the dispute clouding our daily existence be quelled with the marriage of our respective heirs, bringing peace to a province that has known little harmony for nearly thirty years.

I know that your infinite wisdom will triumph in this most serious matter. We trust your decision will be the correct one.

Written at Wisseyham Keep
Sir Nigel Warrington
20 June 1282

ଓ

"WHAT DO YOU think? Is it respectful enough?"

Colin Warrington smiled at his father, his eyes resting on the freshly sanded missive. "If it were any more respectful, you would be licking his arse," he snorted softly. "Summerlin is no fool, you know."

"Nay, he is not a fool, but he is eager to maintain a peaceful barony and he will do what is necessary. Besides, I would bed with the man himself if it meant acquiring St. Cloven, and I have already damn near made a pact with the Devil to gain you what you deserve. St. Cloven is famous from Edinburgh to London and more than loaded with suitable wealth for Warrington coffers."

Colin cocked a slow eyebrow. "'Twill be my wealth, father. Mine alone."

Nigel eyed his son and rose stiffly; his joints were growing stiffer and more painful by the day and there were times when it was difficult to walk.

"As you say," he replied. "But you will recollect who obtained for you that wealth and you will return the proper respect due."

Colin looked away from his father, pondering his immediate future. They were closer to St. Cloven's wealth than they had ever come and his impatience was growing. Lord, it had been a long, long road and he was thankful that the end was finally in sight.

To have St. Cloven for his own was a dream he and his father had always shared, a dream that had known its setbacks and disappointments. The dream continued to lurk in the recesses of their minds, even as the years passed and time faded the urgency. But the dream never died, remaining dormant for the opportunity of an open chance to act.

Nigel thought he saw a chance, once. In spite of the land dispute, he had petitioned Sir Albert for the eldest daughter's hand, hoping to marry the young heiress to Colin. Sir Albert had responded strongly to the impropriety of the request, adding further insult by promptly pledging ten-year-old Lady Peyton to fifteen-year-old James Deveraux of King's Lynn.

It had been a setback, but not the end of the dream. Years passed and Nigel was content to bide his time until another opportunity presented itself. And he knew, without a doubt, that another chance would happen across his path. He would simply have to be wise enough to interpret it.

At a tournament in Norwich, the long-awaited opportunity came in the form of a poor knight who advanced to the final rounds of the joust competition against Lady Peyton de Fluornoy's arrogant fiance. A poor knight coerced into an evil action, lured by his desperate need for money. A poor knight forced into a murderous act in exchange for the welfare of his family, and Nigel had taken full advantage of the warrior's destitute state and had been wise enough to interpret the chance.

Twenty gold coins had bought Deveraux's death. Fitting, considering it had only taken thirty pieces of silver to betray Jesus Christ. Betrayal means the same in any monetary denomination.

"She never did suspect anything, did she?" Colin asked after a moment, passing a glance at his father.

"Who? The Lady Peyton?" Nigel shook his head. "A witless bitch, like all the rest. She shall never come to know how she has been manipulated."

"It wasn't difficult to orchestrate Deveraux's death," Colin picked at his yellowed teeth. "'Twas a perfectly believable plot, maneuvering the break of a crows-foot joust pole only to have it replaced by the spare, which happened to be spear-tipped. Twenty gold coins will buy just about anything, including an honorable knight to do away with an opponent."

"I thought we were going to have trouble with de Fortlage. He is so damned ethical that when you suggested he eliminate Sir James, I thought he would run straight to the field marshals and inform them of your proposal. 'Tis amazing what money can buy, including silence."

"And it certainly did not hurt matters that you were sitting behind his wife in the lists pointing a dagger at her back," Colin chuckled at the memory of particularly ugly blackmail. "No one ever suspected that

Deveraux's death was planned. De Fortlage said it was an accident and his word was believed without question."

Nigel smiled, entirely pleased that his plans to procure St. Cloven for his son were moving along so admirably. Now, to wed his son to the heiress and all would be complete. The wealthiest ale empire in all of southern England would belong to Colin.

"Now, we will send this message to Summerlin and wait for his reply which, I am sure, will be in the affirmative. What better way to assure peace than to marry two enemies?" his eyes grazed the sanded missive as the ink dried, re-reading his words. "There is virtually no possibility that Brian Summerlin will refuse such a submissive and polite request."

Colin rose on his long legs; he was a muscular man. "And I look forward to acquiring my new wife. God only knows, she is a beauty to behold."

"And a virgin, I am sure," Nigel snorted. "Albert kept both she and her sister secluded from the world. Outside of James, I do not believe they had many visitors to St. Cloven. You know what a recluse Albert was."

"Indeed I do," Colin moved for the door, pausing a moment in thought. "Other than marrying the Lady Peyton, we have never truly discussed what would become of her once I took possession of St. Cloven. You do not really expect me to treat her as a wife, do you?"

"I care not what you do with her once you obtain the manor. Keep her abed day and night if it pleases you, or throw her down the stairs and be done with it. 'Tis your decision."

Colin smiled, a sinister gesture laced with the promise of pure evil. "I shall consider those options. Both of them."

Nigel smiled darkly, a gesture reminiscent of his son. Lady Peyton de Fluornoy was a very minor player in his grand game, a pawn to be used and disposed of.

The main objective, of course, was revenge; revenge for lands stolen, for wealth earned by St. Cloven from those lands upon which fields of barley thrived, and indirectly, revenge upon Baron Rothwell. Wealth the Warringtons claimed, considering the land which fed St. Cloven's brewery belonged to them. Selective in memory, of course, they conveniently neglected to recollect that the House of Warrington never showed much interest in the overgrown meadows until Albert de Fluornoy's father claimed them for his own use.

After thirty years, the family honor was still at stake and Nigel considered it just compensation that St. Cloven was finally within his grasp.

Baron Rothwell fit into these plans rather nicely. As Brian Summerlin sat majestically atop the throne of the Rothwell barony, the power of a substantial province in his palm, Nigel would gain power beneath his nose. With Wisseyham Keep and St. Cloven joined by marriage, the link would prove extremely powerful and their rising force would be a power Summerlin would be compelled to reckon with.

Alone in his solar, Nigel continued to smile as his thoughts shifted from his liege to the object of his hatred. How considerate that Albert should die without finding another suitor for Lady Peyton. St. Cloven was without a capable man to administer her wealth, and Nigel silently thanked Albert for his thoughtfulness. He could not have planned events better himself.

All that was left was for Nigel to solicit the liege of the province for Lady Peyton's hand. With Albert dead, there would be no one to oppose his request. And surely Baron Rothwell would do anything to maintain peace and serenity within his barony; a wedding between warring clans would be an acceptable solution. Moreover, Brian would do anything Nigel asked of him. It was a dark secret they shared.

Sighing with relief, he drew himself a chalice of St. Cloven pale ale. Swirling the sweet liquid in his mouth, he swallowed and erupted into sinister laughter.

All of it would soon be his.

St. Cloven
Cambridgeshire, England

LADY PEYTON DE Fluornoy swirled the last drop of red ale, breathing through her nose to fully extract the flavors as her father had taught her. She had been doing this since childhood and had a better palate for ale than most seasoned men. A most useful talent, considering her family had been in the ale business for four generations.

"Too much wood," she sniffed. "This batch has taken on too much of the barrel. Give it to the villeins. I would taste the batch of red ale that is not quite as aged. If it is not ruined, then we will transfer the contents to beechwood barrels. This oak is too strong. I never have been fond of oak, even though father insisted it adds flavor."

Lady Ivy de Fluornoy relayed the orders to a hovering servant. When the man disappeared, she turned to her elder sister. "The taste was normal to me. How can you taste the wood so strongly?"

"I just do. Why must you question my palate? I am never wrong."

Ivy made a face at her sister's arrogant declaration. "And I say it tasted fine. As long as it is good enough to get drunk by, what do the innkeepers care?"

Peyton shot her sister an intolerant look. "We sell to more than just innkeepers, as you well know. Now, leave me alone. Go bother someone else."

"There *is* no one else," Ivy said, plopping down in a leather chair that had once belonged to their father. "We are quite alone, you and I."

Peyton gave her sister a long glance, some of her irritation fading. "You need not remind me. I have been well aware of the fact for six months now."

"And well aware of the fact that St. Cloven is a goldmine to the man who marries you," Ivy shot back with soft intensity. She gazed at her sister, watching the emotions ripple across her beautiful face. "Your fate is in the hands of our liege, as much as you loathe the fact. You do not control your destiny and your daily moods reflect your frustration."

Peyton's sapphire-blue eyes flashed angrily for a split second before banking with equal rapidity. "As our liege controls your fate, as well," she reminded her. "It is the man's duty to select husbands for both of us since…."

Peyton's voice trailed away and Ivy knew exactly what she was going to say; since my betrothed saw fit to get himself killed on the tournament circuit and since father died before he could complete a contract on you.

"I do not want to marry anyone," Ivy bemoaned quietly. "I am too young. Seventeen is far too young."

"Mother was married at fourteen," Peyton reminded her, inadvertently pondering the man to whom she was betrothed. The man she should have married.

"I did not mean to bring up James." Ivy knew what her sister was thinking. In fact, she thought of little else.

Peyton shrugged, her luxurious cascade of golden-red curls shimmering in the weak light. "Whether or not you mention him, he is always on the surface of my mind. It takes very little for me to think of him."

Ivy felt the stab of pain for her sister, remembering too well the loss of Sir James Deveraux nine months prior. The anguish still clouded Peyton's face. She hadn't been the same since dashing blond James was gored by a spear-tipped joust pole in full view of his fiancée.

Ivy rose, not wanting to linger on the private memories. "I shall see to sup. It is my turn, is it not?"

"It is," Peyton nodded. "I would prefer fowl this night. Or mayhap lamb. No mutton, if you please."

"Venison?"

"Disgusting, wretched stuff."

Ivy smiled, her pale coloring in sharp contrast to her sister's radiant beauty. "You used to like it well enough."

"I have changed my mind. Nothing heavy. Or slicked with grease."

"What gall! When it is your turn to see to meals, you serve items that are literally floating in slime."

Peyton smiled deviously. "Because you like it that way, darling. Admit it."

"I shall admit that you are intent on making me fat so that no man will have me."

"I thought you did not want a husband?"

"I never said that. Stop twisting my words."

Peyton laughed again, patting her sister's blond head affectionately. "Stop fretting, Ivy. 'Tis out of our hands, I am afraid."

Ivy wandered to the solar door, her fingers probing the scrubbed jamb absently. Behind her, Peyton stood staring into space, no doubt with James on her mind. The pain, although somewhat faded, still clutched at her heart. It took her months before she could right herself after his death.

"Do you think Lord Brian will choose Colin?" Ivy's voice was faint with dread.

Peyton was jolted from her train of thought, her expression contemptuous. "Not unless he is willing to be an active party to murder, for that is what will surely happen if he betroths me to Colin Warrington. I shall kill the beast before I shall allow a marriage to take place."

Ivy thought a moment. "Mayhap the union would ease the feud. After all, the Warringtons and the de Fluornoys have been fighting for decades, and…."

Peyton put up a hand. "Say no more. I will not even hear of the possibility. Now go order me a round of slop, sister."

Ivy cocked a slow eyebrow. "Slop, did you say? That, darling Peyton, can be arranged."

Peyton waved her sister on with a grin. Outside, the sun was setting over the golden-pale fields of grain that kept St. Cloven firmly established in her trade as the sisters made their way to the manor.

Dinner was an unexpectedly flavorful affair and Peyton enjoyed the rewards of her sister's uncanny sense of table with nary a greasy dish in sight. Fowl, boiled vegetables and a pale yellow ale graced the table. And, to match the yellow ale, Ivy had instructed the cook to dye everything saffron yellow. So Peyton ate yellow meat, yellow vegetables, and only half of her bright yellow custard. In truth, she was stuffed full from the main courses and sat back in her chair, sipping her ale with satisfaction.

Across the table sat Ivy, eating everything in sight. She was a large girl, round and curvaceous with a tendency for fat. Fortunately, she fatted in all of the right places and drew many a man's stare with her buxom profile and generous hips. Formed like their father's side of the family, she was in sharp divergence to Peyton's slender beauty.

Although Peyton was no fragile, delicate hybrid; average in stature and height, she was inordinately strong for a female. But her graceful limbs and creamy skin gave her a soft, dainty appearance, and her beauty was absolutely unequaled. James always told her that she reminded him of a porcelain doll, perfect and sculpted in every way.

She and Ivy were very different in appearance, but not in personality. Their father used to call them magpies, for they chattered incessantly. And fought like Lucifer and Gabriel when the mood hit them.

Aye, they missed their father terribly. For a man who had been hardy and robust all of his life, his death from a heart attack six months prior had come as a deep shock. After their mother had died when the girls were very young, Albert de Fluornoy had coddled and spoiled his children. He had been their only family with exception of the creature currently seated at the far end of the table.

Jubil de Fluornoy was an enigma of sorts. A self-proclaimed witch, she was a peculiar woman with even more peculiar habits. Bizarre did not quite encompass the exact description of Aunt Jubil; in fact, Peyton had yet to come up with the exact terms to describe her father's younger sister. Weird certainly seemed appropriate most of the time and Peyton and Ivy spent a good deal of time ignoring their only living relation.

"There's a cock's foot in here," Jubil hissed, picking at her trencher.

Ivy glanced at Peyton. "Aye, there is, Jubil, just for you," she replied sarcastically.

"A big bloody one!" Jubil suddenly declared, although neither girl could see what she was talking about. "It's preparing to fly away!"

Peyton rolled her eyes irritably. Her aunt was known to ingest concoctions distilled from native plants and roots to aid her in her "visions". Sometimes it took days for the potions to wear off, leaving Jubil insane for that particular length in time.

"Jubil, there's no cock's foot in your dish," she said with little patience. "If you are finished with your meal, then you are excused."

Jubil began to shovel clumps of food all over the table in her attempt to single out the elusive cock's foot. Peyton ducked as a piece of roast fowl flew particularly close.

"Cock's foot! Cock's foot!" Jubil cried, jamming her fingers into her trencher and withdrawing an object pinched between her index finger and thumb. Her eyes were wild as she scrutinized whatever it was. "An eyeball! I knew it! I thought I smelled the essence!"

Ivy closed her eyes, silently beseeching God for patience. "Oh, Christ."

Peyton watched with morbid curiosity as Jubil bound from her chair, still squeezing the bit of "eyeball". "I can use this, I can," she smiled at Peyton. "I shall use this to divine your future, sweetheart. We will see what Lord Brian Summerlin has in store for you."

Peyton shook her head as Ivy looked bored. "I do not want to know, Jubil. Truly."

Jubil did not hear her. She shuffled off, clutching her prize and mumbling to herself.

"My God, Peyton. What are we going to do with her?" Ivy demanded softly. "My appetite is gone."

"Your appetite is gone because you ate everything but the bowls," Peyton said. They had long since stopped figuring out what to do with Aunt Jubil.

In the warm dining hall this night, Peyton and her sister were alone save a few serving women and two household guards. Since their father had been somewhat of a recluse, positive any stranger or traveler had come to his doorstep for the sole purpose of extracting his ale secrets, there had never been an overabundant amount of activity at St. Cloven and the women were not lonely. They simply learned to entertain themselves.

"What is it tonight, Peyton? Cards? Chess? Backgammon?" Ivy leaned back in her chair, stretching her arms over her head.

Peyton sat silently, listening to the faint howl of a dog somewhere, the crackle of the fire in the massive stone hearth.

"Nothing, I think. I am tired tonight."

"And you are worried, as well. Lord Brian promised you that he would decide your future by the end of the month and that is in two days," she sat straight. "Mayhap when the messenger comes, we will tell him you died in your sleep."

Peyton smirked, running her hand wearily over her face. "Not a bad idea, methinks. Oh, why can he not simply leave us be? Why must we be wed? I do not want a husband."

It was a plea, not a question. Ivy shrugged. "Because St. Cloven needs a man to protect her," she said. "Mayhap your husband will come with an army of a thousand."

"We do not need protection," Peyton snapped softly. "Father's household troops have proven quite adequate for many years. In fact, we did not even have soldiers until twenty years ago when Warrington began making threats. 'Tis only because of Nigel Warrington and his idiot son that we need men here at all. And as for an army that would come attached to any future husband, they'll probably spend all of their time in the ale barn drinking us into the poorhouse."

"Tsk, tsk," her sister admonished mockingly. "A prospective husband will not tolerate your nasty temper."

"Then that is his misfortune," Peyton sniffed, rising wearily. "As for me, I shall retire to bed and await my sentence.... I mean, ponder my destiny. Surely a missive will come from Blackstone tomorrow. Lord Brian has had nearly a month to decide what is to become of me."

"Become of *us*," Ivy reminded her.

"Us," Peyton corrected. "Good sleep, darling."

"Good sleep," Ivy watched her sister mount the stairs, her heart going out to the eldest de Fluornoy sibling. She wasn't worried so much for herself, because a husband meant very little in an emotional sense. But Peyton was still recovering from the fierce loss of James, and was very vulnerable. Ivy still heard her crying at night, bemoaning her loss.

Ivy knew from watching her sister that love was a terrible, sorrowful emotion and she herself vowed to never succumb to the devastating weakness.

ଔ

Blackstone Castle

LORD BRIAN SUMMERLIN sat hunched over his carved oaken desk, pondering what he considered a most weighty subject. Two contracts sat before him, drawn out and awaiting approval. He sat back and scratched his head; approval would not come easily.

A rap sounded on his heavy oak door, and the caller did not wait to be hailed entrance. Brian heard the familiar footsteps, not bothering to glance up from his business. He knew who it was without looking.

"Do you have the tally for the horse sales?" Brian asked softly.

"Four colts sold, two fillies," the man replied. "And a further promise to breed my Saracen stallion to two brood mares at 25 gold marks a piece. Quite handsome."

"Quite," Brian agreed. "Sit down, Alec. We have more business to attend to."

Alec Summerlin sat opposite his father. Intense blue eyes, as bright and pure as the summer sky gazed steadily at the older man. When Brian looked up from his parchment, he met his youngest son's gaze. For a brief moment, his eyes grazed his son's features, the familiar lines. Surely no handsomer man had ever lived, Brian was sure, for the man favored his mother to a fault. And Celine was most certainly the most beautiful woman he had ever seen.

As dark as Brian was, Alec was equally as fair. His blond hair, bleached from time spent in the sun, was cropped close to his scalp so that it stood straight up on the top. A granite jaw and cleft chin seated a full-lipped mouth and straight nose. Aye, he was indeed a fine example of a man and Brian was proud of the accomplishments he had achieved in his lifetime. It was almost enough to overshadow the tragedies and the disappointments.

His eyes left his son and returned to the contracts before him. There was no use in skirting the impending issue and he folded his hands thoughtfully as he searched for the proper words.

"Alec, I have made a crucial decision this night. As you know, St. Cloven has been without Albert de Fluornoy for six months now, leaving his two daughters in charge of a valuable keep. You have been to St. Cloven, have you not?"

"Years ago when I went with you. I hardly remember the place, except that it smelled of wood. Like cedar."

Brian nodded. "Albert was fond of the smell. There is more cedar from Lebanon in that place than hearty English oak. In any case, as de Fluornoy's liege, the duty falls on me to wed the daughters. Albert failed to do that before his demise, unfortunately, and I have had a devil of a time with the problem. The girls are past prime marriageable age."

Alec sat back, absorbing his father's words, a flicker of horror igniting in his mind. But he doused it quickly, hoping his suspicions were incorrect.

Brian began to speak more rapidly, becoming animated as he went along. "As I see it, St. Cloven is in need of a wise man to administer her business. Strength, knightly skill, are unnecessary in the management of the keep. Although there has been a dispute with Nigel Warrington for many years, there has never truly been any bloodshed. For the most part, a bloodless war," he brought his eyes to rest on his son, guarded brown orbs meeting pure blue. "Which is why I believe you will be perfect for the position as lord of St. Cloven. I am pledging you in marriage to the eldest daughter."

Alec did not react. He rarely reacted to anything, good or bad. His emotions were nonexistent for the most part, a fact which oft drove Brian to the brink of madness. He could never anticipate his son in any way.

"I do not want the position," Alec finally said.

"It is not a matter for discussion. You will wed Lady Peyton de Fluornoy and assume your post."

Alec paused a moment, still unreadable. "I am quite content here. I have no desire for a wife or a keep of my own. Blackstone keeps me busy and…."

"Alec!" his father boomed, bolting from his chair. "Your brother Paul will inherit Blackstone, not you. And St. Cloven is by far the richest house in the province. Doesn't that mean anything to you? I am handing you a fortune, lad! Besides, this is your best chance for a marriage of any importance considering…." he suddenly broke off, looking to his son apologetically. "I am sorry, Alec. I did not mean to sound demeaning."

Alec's gaze was open, steady. "What you were going to say is that this is my best chance for a powerful marriage considering no one wants a coward for a groom. Since the de Courtenays broke my engagement, there hasn't been another offer. No one wants a husband who refuses to bear arms. Isn't that what you were leading to?"

Brian turned away. "I have never chastened you your decision, lad."

"But I was a supreme disappointment," Alec said softly. "I was your shining star, your proudest achievement until I killed Peter. I have never regretted my decision not to ever again wield a sword, Da."

"I know," Brian said softly. "But your brother's death was an accident, Alec. Ali was there; even he says it was an accident. There was no reason why you should make such a vow of restraint. 'Tis every man's duty to bear arms to defend what is his, to protect his interests. Surely you…."

"We have had this discussion before," Alec said quietly. "I shall never bear a sword again. Ever. Now, back to Lady Patton...."

"Lady Peyton," Brian corrected him. "She is twenty-one years old, betrothed once before to a knight who was killed nearly a year ago."

"Peyton, Patton, whatever. I have no interest in marriage."

"Not even to the wealth of St. Cloven?" Brian knew that Alec had a mind for money and investments; surely the thought of wealth could lure him.

Alec stood up, all six and a half feet of him. He was Brian's largest son, the most powerful man he had ever seen. His sheer height was compounded by enormous muscles, the result of years of physical work and training. When Alec had wielded a sword, there was not a man who could defeat him. King Edward knew it, else he would not have appointed Alec as one of his premier warriors. There was not a man in the civilized world who could have bested Alec Summerlin in a sword fight. When the man swore off fighting, it had been a tremendous blow to the Christian army of Edward.

Brian watched his son stroll leisurely to the window, once so proud of the man. He still loved him dearly; he was the only normal son he had left. Paul, the eldest, had the mental capacity of a child. With his second eldest son dead, Alec was his salvation.

"Her wealth is so great?" Alec asked.

"St. Cloven pulls in nearly 5,000 marks of gold each year for her ale sales. Her coffers are overloaded."

Alec looked at his father, a lifted eyebrow indicating interest. "But I have to marry Lady Patton to obtain this money."

"Aye, you do," his father said firmly. "We will not bargain over this, Alec. You will do as I ask, for once. You will marry Lady Peyton and administer St. Cloven's ale stores."

Alec's pure blue eyes were cool. Brian gazed back, trying to anticipate the next barrage of refusals, but in truth, there was nothing more to say. He had been quite plain with his wants; they both had.

God only knew how stubborn Alec could be; Brian had never seen a more stubborn man, nor willful, nor controlled. All of these things were his son, a man who had once been the greatest swordsman in the realm. *The Legend*, they had called him. Legendary skill, strength, size, power…. all of it was his.

Alec was an intellect, but there were those who were greater tacticians. He could joust and ride and combat with the very finest in England, as he had proven time and time again. But it was his swordsmanship that distinguished him from all the rest. Edward once said Gabriel himself had given Alec his divine gift, so talented with a broadsword that surely God himself was jealous of the skill. There was no man more known for his swordsmanship in Edward's realm than Alec. He was The Legend. And he had given it all up.

Aye, Brian was disappointed, but only for Alec's sake. The man could have been the greatest warrior England had ever seen. Alec's fate was a sad, noble thing indeed.

"If I am to marry Lady Patton, and I have not yet said that I agree, I would see her first," Alec finally said. "Give a grand party and invite her. I would look over the prospective mother of my heirs."

Brian sighed irritably. "Alec, one does not look over a woman as one would a brood mare, to determine if she is good breeding stock. There is far more involved, lad. Bloodlines, heritage, family ties, disposition. All of these things contribute to a satisfactory marriage."

"And money," Alec's eyes twinkled slightly, taunting his father. "You yourself have tried to convince me that I should marry Lady Patton simply because of the wealth of St. Cloven. And now you tell me that there is more to a marriage than that?"

Brian shrugged, cornered, and turned away. "Stop being so smart, Alec, I do not think I like it. You know very well what I am saying."

Alec moved to a carved pine table and poured himself a full goblet of liquor. He took a healthy drink, looked at the cup as if to ponder the contents, and drank again. Brian watched him with a faint smile.

"St. Cloven Red Ale," he informed his son. "You have tasted it on many occasions."

Alec studied the red liquid. "And if I am lord of St. Cloven, I will not have to pay for it any longer. And neither shall you."

"Ah, so you see? We will both be gaining much from this union," his father encouraged firmly, still smiling. His mirth faded after a moment. "I do not want to force you into this, Alec. I want this to be a mutual agreement. This very well may be your last chance for a marriage into a decent family."

Alec was still regarding his chalice, swirling the liquid absently. He was so very unreadable.

"I understand that perfectly," he said softly. "And in faith, 'tis not that I do not wish to marry; certainly I want a wife and heirs at some point. But I have given the matter little thought. Your suggestion comes as somewhat of a surprise."

Brian meandered over to his son, putting a gentle hand on his broad back. "All I will ask, then, is that you consider it. And do not take too long, for I promised Lady Peyton that I would present a prospective bridegroom before the end of the month."

"You give me a mere two days to contemplate my future?" Alec lifted an eyebrow at his father. "Will you then give a party and invite my prospective wife?"

Brian threw up his hands. "If that is what it will take for you to make up your mind, by all means. I shall have the steward write the necessary missives and invite all of our local allies. We will make it a grand social event."

Alec nodded, finishing off the ale. Brian moved back to his desk, contemplating the two contracts before him. Alec, meanwhile, poured himself a second cup of ale.

"There are two sisters, you know," Brian said softly. "Peyton and her sister, Ivy. I must still find a husband for Ivy."

Alec turned to his father, ale in hand. "Can I choose between the two? What if Ivy is the more desirable sister?"

"Then that is your misfortune. You will not inherit the keep if you marry the youngest sister."

Alec grinned into his cup. "Can I have them both, then?"

Brian shot his son an exasperated look. "Enough, Alec. One woman will be quite sufficient."

Brian turned to his contracts and Alec hung by the desk, enjoying the fine ale and pondering his apparent destiny. He glanced over at his father, who was seemingly lost in thought.

"Have you a husband in mind for the second sister?"

Brian snapped from his thoughts and picked up a quill. "I was thinking on Ali."

Alec showed more emotion than Brian had seen in a long while; his eyes widened and his jaw hung slack. "Ali? Christ, he shall never agree to that. And what of Olphampa? Surely you must discuss it with his father first."

"Ali's welfare is my concern, as it has always been," Brian replied steadily, turning to see his truly astonished son. "He must be wed, Alec. And since there is not a Nubian princess within ten thousand miles of Blackstone, an English princess will do quite nicely."

Alec was shocked. Then, the shock evaporated into anger. "You know how women react to him. They look at Ali and see a man with black skin, a man who is unlike the conventional norm. Women have been very cruel to him and I forbid you to…."

"I know, I know," Brian cut him off quietly but firmly. "But mayhap if I provide him with a substantial dowry, mayhap if I make him quite appealing financially to a prospective bride, she will be more willing to…. accept him, as it were."

Alec's face was like stone; hard and immobile. He had always been fiercely protective of Ali, ever since he had been old enough to realize that some people were not inclined to accept him as a human being. Ali was more a brother to him than his only surviving brother.

However, his father was correct. There were no black females available for marriage in England. In fact, outside of the Holy Land, Alec had never even seen a black female. It was only logical that Ali marry an English girl, someone he could feel affection for and bear him sons. A woman who could accept him for what he was, but the hope was unrealistic at best; Alec had never known a woman to approve of Ali's color. Yet in spite of his obvious difference, why should his dark friend be excluded from the normal rites of an English male?

Alec sighed, setting down his chalice. "Say nothing to him for the moment. At the festivity, I shall make sure to point out the younger sister and see if he expresses any interest."

"Fair enough," Brian agreed. "I suppose proceeding on the basis of attraction is acceptable. If Ali likes what he sees, I shall broach the subject."

Alec moved for the door. "What about me? What if I do not like what I see?"

Brian shook his head faintly, exhausted with the arguing. "We will cross that bridge when we come to it. Go now, your mother should be serving afternoon refreshments."

Alec quit the room, leaving Brian drained and thoughtful. Whether or not Alec found his prospective bride agreeable, Brian's mind was made up. Pleasant or not, Alec would marry the lady of St. Cloven and reap the rewards of the keep.

But, of course, there was the little matter which Brian had neglected to inform him, and that was the Warrington petition for the lady's hand. He'd never tell Alec, of course; it would be one more excuse to refuse the betrothal.

Brian was no fool; he knew that Nigel Warrington had set his sights on obtaining what he believed rightfully belonged to him, and St. Cloven was an auspicious beginning. He had no intention of seeing a Warrington as lord of St. Cloven; it would be a Summerlin, no matter if he had to tie his mulish son to the front gates to keep him there. Alec would be lord of an ale empire and damn well be pleased about it.

In faith, he wished he could tell his son the whole of it. But some things in life were better left unsaid, some things better left buried.

CHAPTER TWO

THREE LADIES AND seven soldiers made up the party from St. Cloven. Behind them, a wagon carted six barrels of their finest dark ale as a gift to their liege, Baron Rothwell. Traveling to a celebration, the mood should have been light and gay. The weather of late summer was delightful and the sky bright, but there was little talk and even less joviality.

To Peyton, it felt like a death march. A forced trek into the gaping jaws of fate. Lord Brian had summoned her and Ivy to discuss their betrothals under the guise of inviting them to a grand party in honor of his wife's birthday. The birthday was a convenient excuse, Peyton was positive. It was all a ploy to force her into doing what she so desperately loathed; to accept a husband.

Dressed in a lovely turquoise blue silk that complimented her golden red tresses perfectly, she looked entirely delicious seated atop her brown palfrey. But her mood was anything but delicious; it was bitter and distasteful. She hated the fact that she and Ivy had been forced to dress like fine horses for the auction block so that Lord Brian could get a good look at them. The prettier the girl, the wider range of suitors there would be.

A thought suddenly struck her as she mulled over her fine appearance and she turned to catch her sister's attention. Ivy was mounted astride a dark gray warmblood, a difficult animal that would have given most men a good deal of trouble. But Ivy rode the beast effortlessly and Peyton waved her forward.

Ivy reined her horse next to the delicate brown palfrey. "Let me guess; you have finally come to your senses. We are going to turn for home and pretend we never received the invitation."

Peyton gave her an impatient look. "Be serious. I have a plan."

Ivy grinned with the prospect. "As I said, you have finally come to your senses. What sort of plan?"

Her impatient expression turned sly. "Are you a brave girl, Ivy? What I am about to suggest might shock you."

Ivy snorted very un-ladylike. "You could never shock me. What is it you have in mind?"

"Bring Jubil forward. She shall want to help us."

After a brief conference, the caravan came to a halt as the ladies dismounted and moved to the rear of the wagon where their baggage was stored. The curious household soldiers tried to catch a glimpse of the activity but, other than a good deal of giggling and commotion, were unable to determine what the women were up to. Resigned to an impatient wait, they busied themselves with such things as picking noses and chewing fingernails, keeping vigilant watch for any criminal activity that might prey upon their valuable caravan.

It was an excessive wait; nearly an hour later, the party resumed their journey. Peyton and Ivy rode at the head of the column, joking and laughing softly between them. Something seemed to be quite humorous, but the soldiers were at a loss to understand the cause and were furthermore concerned with keeping alert for bandits or thieves. The roads north of London abound with the worst type of element and protecting the de Fluornoy women was of the utmost priority. With a piqued sense of urgency, the column proceeded onward to the seat of Baron Rothwell.

Blackstone Castle was a massive fortress built for protection and strength. Nestled in the serene lands east of Daventry, the barony encompassed the bustling city and several other lesser bergs. Peyton had never been to Blackstone, although she had heard tale that the Summerlins had occupied the bastion since the days of King Harold. They had been one of the very few noble Saxon families left intact after Duke William's invasion, wealthy with their ventures in equine and cattle.

As the party drew closer to Blackstone, Peyton could deduce how the bastion acquired its name; it was built entirely with black stone. The dark aura gave the castle a most sinister countenance and Peyton felt a sharp discomfort as her sapphire blue eyes scanned the edifice. She shivered involuntarily, passing a glance at Ivy over her right shoulder. Ivy, too, looked uncertain of the structure and they passed uneasy glances.

The party rounded a small crest and the full impact of Blackstone loomed into view. Huge banners that were easily ten feet in length streamed from three massive turrets, bright red and silver with the Summerlin dragon. The gates were extended in a welcoming gesture and there was quite a bit of activity going on around the place, although Peyton saw few guests and mostly soldiers.

"Look at all of the soldiers," Ivy said in awe, as if reading her sister's mind. "Armed to the teeth."

Peyton swallowed her apprehension. "Be brave, Ivy. We must not fail."

"We won't."

Ivy suddenly smiled a huge, gaping smile and Peyton was jolted from her anxiety at the sight; four front teeth were blacked-out with a paste made of charcoal and beeswax from Jubil's medicinal stores. She returned her sister's smile, displaying several blacked-out teeth that gave her own beautiful smile a most snaggle-toothed appearance.

Upon closer inspection, the women had smudged great dark circles under their eyes and had taken liberty with Jubil's arsenic powder, giving them an extremely sickly countenance, at least enough to deter any prospective husband.

"Thank God for Jubil's supplies," Ivy said, sticking out her tongue for good measure. It, too, was black as sin. "The uglier we are, the less likely we will be forced to wed."

Peyton nodded sincerely. "I hope so. I only pray that I can keep from laughing when Lord Brian sees what a treasure he has in the de Fluornoy women. You must stick to the scheme, Ivy. Follow my lead and do what I do."

Ivy continued to giggle as they rode up on the gate. They were met by several soldiers, led by three knights. One knight on a great brown destrier reached out to halt Peyton's mount.

"Announce yourself, my lady," he asked politely.

No time like the present to begin their act. Peyton smiled brightly and was positive she could hear a collective gasp of horror go up among the men.

"Lady Peyton de Fluornoy and party," she said brightly. "We are expected."

"Aye, you are," the knight replied in a peculiar voice. "Move forward into the bailey and you shall be met by a steward who will direct you."

She batted her dark-circled eyes at the knight and spurred her horse forward, followed by the rest of the group. Ivy made sure to smile at the knight as she rode past. Visor down, she couldn't see his face but hoped he was disgusted with her appearance.

The knight turned to watch them as they rode into the open mouth of the courtyard. Ali did not know what to think.

The bailey was a vast thing, extremely well kept. It appeared more as a manicured drive than a bailey, servants with decorated dogs standing at spaced intervals and shaped dogwood trees flanking the main entrance to the castle. It was a busy courtyard, servants and residents alike moving about in chaotic order in anticipation of the impending arrivals. The excitement of a celebration filled the air and it was difficult not to catch on to the thrill. Even for the most recent reluctant guests, the excitement was intriguing.

A brightly colored steward in the Summerlin colors of red and silver stepped forward to greet them. Dressed in a satin tunic and hose with a satin cap, he bowed deeply.

"Might I have your house name, my lady?" he asked politely.

"De Fluornoy," Peyton handed her reins to a servant and dismounted with help from one of her soldiers. The St. Cloven man peered at her most strangely and Peyton suspected that her cover would be blown before she had a chance to complete her objective. Pursing her lips threateningly at the dense soldier, the man hastily moved away from her.

"Ah yes! We have prepared a suite of rooms for you and your sister," he turned sharply and snapped orders to a group of soldiers hovering a few feet away. Immediately, the men moved forward to collect the baggage.

As their parcels were efficiently removed, the steward returned his attention to Peyton. His eyes widening as he received a second, closer look at the lady; outrageously pale with black-shadowed eyes, he took an unconscious step away from her as if she carried the plague.

Peyton played into the man's shock, beaming foolishly at him. "Thank you, sirrah. Would you be so kind as to show us to our rooms?"

"Are there going to be lots o' men at the party?" Ivy chimed in loudly, making sure to exhibit her disgraceful teeth.

"Indeed! Men!" Peyton agreed eagerly, and the two of them cackled like witches before a cauldron.

The steward visibly flinched. "Aye, my ladies. There will be many.... uh, men," he swallowed hard. "But.... but *married* men. There will be very few single men, or those who are unbetrothed. In fact,..."

Ivy cut him off. "Who cares if they are unwed or not. Just give me a good arse to pinch and...."

"Ivy!" Peyton admonished, half-serious. "Surely you must not think of a man as a fleeting pinch. After all – 'tis that very attitude that has driven two men to their grave already."

Ivy sniffed, tossing hair that she had purposely mussed with leaves for a completely squalid effect. "Old badgers, both of them, with the potency of custard."

"You made them old before their time," Peyton retorted, laughing silently at the steward's horrified expression.

Ivy put her hands on her round hips. "Do not portray yourself as an innocent, Peyton. Certainly, you are no saint."

Peyton's mouth opened in outrage and she shoved her sister boldly. "How dare you intimate that I am a whore!"

"Your words, darling, not mine," Ivy advanced on her sister, pleased with the turn the act was taking.

"Oh!" Peyton shouted, incensed. "You pox-ridden, self-absorbed wench! How dare you insult me!"

She charged Ivy, a girl considerably larger than herself, and the two went tumbling to the ground in a great pile of silks and satins. The steward, appalled at the turn of events, loudly demanded for them to cease as the shocking situation exploded before his disbelieving eyes.

Grunting and screeching, Peyton and Ivy rolled about in the dusty bailey and slung insults that would have made a whore blush. Content with their play-acting, they wrapped their hands around each other's necks and screamed louder. But the more they yelled and insulted each other, the more laughter threatened to jeopardize their scheme. Over and over they rolled until Peyton bumped into the wheels of the wagon. Jubil, a vacant expression on her face, stood by and watched without concern.

"Stick your fingers up her nose, Peyton," Jubil called helpfully. "She shall stop soon enough."

Peyton heard the encouragement and almost dissolved into hysterical giggles. Jubil was quite sane this day, an unusual state for their aunt, and had meant the comment to enhance their act. Jubil was most likable when she was rational.

In their struggles they managed to twist themselves underneath the wagon and Ivy bumped her head to a grunt of curses. Peyton lost her control and started to giggle until Ivy rubbed dust in her face and once again the struggle was on, only this time Peyton's irritation was genuine. She was preparing to grab her own handful of dust when someone abruptly grabbed hold of her feet and, with a hard tug, unceremoniously yanked her from underneath the wagon. Emitting a loud yelp, Ivy followed her sister in the same fashion.

Blinking dirt out of her eyes, Peyton's gaze met with knees. Clearing her eyes again and refocusing, she found herself facing the largest legs she had ever seen, bulging with muscles underneath the black breeches. The circumference of the thighs alone was substantially larger than her waist. Puzzled, she craned her neck back to look into the face of the referee as Ivy struggled to stand.

"Why did you do that?" Ivy demanded loudly, brushing dirt from her skirt irritably. "By what right do you lay hands upon us?"

Peyton was still sitting on her bottom, blinking up at the collection of male figures that were surrounding them. The sun was shining brightly in the noon sky, blinding her to the facial features of the group. She put up a hand to shield the sun's glare as Ivy worked herself into a rage.

"By right as lord of Blackstone," came a deep, booming voice. "Who are you, girl?"

"Lady Ivy de Fluornoy!" Ivy snapped. Then, the impact of the man's words settled and her pale face turned a peculiar sickly color. "Lord of Bla.... Baron Rothwell?"

Peyton struggled to stand up, feeling the least bit apprehensive that the baron himself had broken up their fight. She did not realize their tussle had gotten out of hand; she'd only meant to give the gossips something to chew over in the hope that the appalling rumors would reach Lord Summerlin. It had never been her intention to outright disturb the man.

"Aye, Baron Rothwell," Brian put his hands on his beefy hips, eyeing Ivy. "So you are Lady Ivy, are you? Well, I must say I expected better behavior from Albert's daughter. Who is your sparring partner?"

"My sister, Lady Peyton," Ivy said lamely, glancing at her sibling as she regained her feet.

Brian's brown eyes focused on Peyton and she felt her courage wan. *Be brave!* She scolded herself strongly. *You must continue what you started!*

In a show of both forced and foolish boldness, she put her arm companionably around Ivy's shoulders and smiled her gaping smile. "'Tis a pleasure, my lord," she said gaily. "Do not mind Ivy and me; we do this habitually. Always room for another bruise, I always say, especially from my own sister. How do you think I lost all of these teeth?" She pointed to her sniggled smile.

Ivy looked at her in shock, faltering a moment before following her sister's lead. She had been fully prepared to beg forgiveness from the baron but reconsidered when she saw that Peyton was willing to continue the charade. Weakly, she smiled in agreement.

"Beauties, are they not, my lord?" Jubil smiled brightly from her perch on the wagon. "Fine, fine breeding stock for the nobility of England."

Brian ignored Jubil, eyeing both sisters critically. He did not dare look at Alec; standing directly in front of Lady Peyton, he could only imagine his son's reaction. Looking into the gray faces and craggle-toothed grins, he was sure they were all having the same horrified responses. And he found he was extremely disappointed to discover that the de Fluornoy sisters were hags, for it would make finding them husbands close to impossible.

He would not dream of saddling Alec with the eldest, no matter how wealthy she was. It would seem that the grand party had been unnecessary to inspect the prospective brides; the determination was already made.

He could scarce believe the ugliness before him. "Good Christ," he muttered before he could stop himself. Clearing his throat, he spoke louder. "You may act as you choose at St. Cloven. However, I expect refined conduct at my home. Rolling in the dirt as common villeins is unacceptable."

Peyton looked at him as if she hadn't understood a word he said while Ivy picked her nose, much to the disbelief of the Summerlin men. "We.... we are unacceptable, my lord?" Peyton queried with feigned distress. "How so?"

Brian watched as Ivy looked at her fingers, sniffed them, and then wiped them on her gown. Clearing his throat again to cover his disgust, he stepped back. "We will not tolerate ruffian behavior, ladies. Regain your trunks and return to St. Cloven this day."

With a final, mayhap disappointed glance, Brian returned to the castle. Peyton and Ivy watched him disappear into the innards of Blackstone, thrilled with their fortune. They fought down their glee and immediately turned to their servants, ordering any offloaded baggage to be retrieved. Ignoring the astonished Summerlin men that were still standing about, Peyton motioned to St. Cloven soldiers.

"Remove the ale," she instructed. "Tell the steward it is a gift from the de Fluornoy sisters."

In a brief few moments, Peyton and Ivy had forgotten about their successful masquerade in anticipation of returning home without a betrothal. The sooner they unload the ale and retrieve their things, the sooner they would return to St. Cloven.

Alec and Ali stood together several feet away, watching the two women curiously. Brian had not made any mention of a betrothal to Ali, but Alec had taken it upon himself to inform his friend and the two of them studied the de Fluornoy sisters with a strange mixture of emotions.

"Christ, Ali, have you ever seen anything so horrible in your life?" Alec mumbled.

Ali raised his faceplate, his black eyes focused on the red and blond heads. "Which one was supposed to be for you?"

"Lady Patton. The redhead, I believe. Her hair is acceptable enough if she were to wash it, but her face...." he shook his head, unable to continue and thanking God that he had not agreed to a betrothal before he had laid eyes on his potential wife. In a sense he was disappointed but, as he watched them leave, he was mostly relieved.

Ali watched Ivy as she helped a soldier with a barrel of ale. "I think the blond could probably take me on in a fist fight and win," he snorted with the mental picture of a wife who could best him in a duel. "'Twould not be pleasant to be married to a woman I was afraid of."

Alec laughed softly. "Agreed. I am afraid to continue gazing at them lest I turn to stone." With a final glance, Alec turned for the castle. "See that they leave promptly. I want them well away so we can enjoy the party without bitter flashbacks of the witch sisters."

It took very little time to reload the wagon with their baggage once the barrels of ale were offloaded. Peyton was thrilled that their deception had worked so well and was eager to return to the keep.

She was positive that Lord Brian would not force them into betrothals and she felt a giddy sense of freedom. Although she was disappointed that she would not be attending the party that night, for they rarely attended such gaiety, her feelings were quelled by the fact that she and her sister would not be coerced into marriages against their will. After their display of bad manners and even worse hygiene, Lord Brian would undoubtedly forget about the distasteful de Fluornoy women.

An escort of Summerlin soldiers was waiting for them as they exited the gates, guiding them from the compound to the road beyond. The march was silent and she could feel the critical stares of the Summerlin men as they rode in uncomfortable quiet. Almost two miles out, the Summerlin guard turned back for the fortress, leaving the St. Cloven party to continue alone. Another three hours would see them home and Peyton relaxed.

"I thought they would never leave," she exclaimed as she reined her horse to a halt.

Dismounted her palfrey, she went to the wagon and dug into one of the smaller satchels bearing linens. Immediately, she began to rub the black off her teeth. Ivy joined her and together they cleaned their teeth and laughed at their cleverness. Jubil dismounted her nag and brought forth her considerable case of medicines. Rummaging about, she drew out an alabaster jar of ointment and smeared it on Ivy's face.

"Jubil!" Ivy sputtered as her aunt rubbed on the paste. "What are you doing?"

"This will take the powder and charcoal off your skin easily," she said, taking the linen her niece held and wiping at her cheek. "'Tis a mixture of calendula and chamomile in lard base. I also have a mud and honey mask that will thoroughly cleanse your skin."

"Let's get this powder off and return home," Peyton put her fingers into the cleansing cream. "Then we will submit to your mud and honey mask."

The scrubbing and rubbing went on for the better part of an hour until both girls were fresh-scoured and bright as gold. Peyton brushed the leaves and dirt out of her hair before securing it at the nape of her neck with a pretty ribbon. Feeling infinitely cleaner and light of mood, she demanded her sister make haste and finish her toilette so that they could make it home by nightfall. Ivy stuck her tongue out at her sister as Jubil combed at a particularly nasty snarl in her blond hair.

Peyton laughed at her sister's discomfort, taking the time to glance about the Cambridgeshire countryside and breathing in the freshness of summer. The scent of indigenous blossoms filled the air; wild jasmine, foxgloves and hemlock lined the road. Mustard was abundant as well as wild primroses. Yellow wild dill grew in great clusters and Peyton turned her eyes upward to the cotton-puff clouds that skirted across the blue sky. Aye, it had turned into a fine day.

"I could scarce believe when Lord Brian told us to return home," she remarked to Ivy.

Ivy laughed, running her fingers through her newly-silken blond hair. "Did you see the expression on his face when I picked at my nose? I almost burst into hysterics."

Peyton laughed again. "It was worth all of the embarrassment to see his reaction. We are fine actresses, darling."

Ivy nodded in agreement and moved for her leggy horse. Jubil, meanwhile, was still fussing with her medicines.

"I must know if there will be any retribution," Jubil was mumbling. "Lord Brian may see fit to punish us for our behavior. Or he might see to kill us all together and annex St. Cloven."

"There will be no reparation, Jubil," Peyton said calmly. "He shall simply forget about his appalling vassals."

But Jubil busied herself with her medicaments while the party waited impatiently. "Did you see Alec? He has grown since the last I saw him."

"Who is Alec?" Peyton asked.

"Why, Alec Summerlin, of course," Jubil exclaimed, holding a vial aloft as she inspected the contents. "The Legend himself."

Peyton and Ivy glanced at each other. "What are you talking about, Jubil?" Peyton asked with growing annoyance.

Jubil apparently found what she was looking for and set to stirring the mixture into a small pewter bowl. "King Edward labeled Alec Summerlin 'The Legend' because of his skill with a broadsword," she said as she stirred. "He saw action in the Seventh Crusade with his father and Edward when he was still a prince. But he returned from Jerusalem prematurely and it is said he has not wielded a sword since, although I have not heard why. 'Twas said the man could cut an enemy in two with one clean stroke."

"And just where did you hear that wild tale?" Peyton lifted an eyebrow.

"Out collecting," Jubil informed her. "I have met up with villeins and squatters who've told tale of The Legend. He would have been the greatest warrior England had ever seen had he not surrendered his arms."

Her aunt called it "collecting"; gathering ingredients for her witches brews and potions. Henbane, periwinkle, foxgloves and ground ivy for a variety of medicinal and clairvoyant needs. Thorn apples, nightshade, monkshood, white water lily and hemlock for magical purposes. Jubil also kept a garden in which she grew verrain, an herb, and ryegrass for the purpose of medicinal ergot, a fungus which grew on the grass.

Jubil glanced at her eldest niece as she prepared her potion. "He was standing 'fore you, Peyton. He is the one who pulled you out from underneath the wagon. Did you not see him?"

Peyton thought a moment, and then shrugged. "The sun was in my eyes, but I saw his legs.... I think. I saw legs as big around as my entire body."

"That was him," Jubil nodded confidently. "A big brute, he is."

Peyton snorted. "Big, indeed. He must be a monster."

"But did you look at his face, Peyton?" Jubil looked up from her implements insistently. "He is a beautiful man indeed. Beautiful!"

Peyton and Ivy looked at each other, smiling at Jubil's declaration. Peyton leaned forward on the pommel of her saddle, a mischievous twinkle in her eye. "My, my, Jubil. He warms your blood, does he not?"

Jubil snorted, shaking her faded blond head. "No man warms my blood or my body, little goats."

Peyton and Ivy laughed heartily at Jubil's expense, but their aunt ignored them as she finished merging her potion. Satisfied she had the proper parts and elements, the ladies watched with fading mirth as Jubil downed the contents in a pewter cup.

"There!" Jubil smacked her lips and put away her things. "By tonight we will know what the future holds."

Ivy shook her head. "More visions."

Peyton gathered the reins on her palfrey, her attention turning for home and eager to make haste before Jubil veered out of control.

ଓ

ALEC HAD FORGOTTEN about the de Fluornoy horror and was engrossed in conversation with Lord Whittlesee and his son Arthur. Blackstone was full of friends and allies that Alec hadn't seen in quite some time and he was becoming swept up with the festive atmosphere, completely disregarding the original purpose of the party.

It had been meant for him to meet and approve of his future wife; instead, the pressure was off of him and he could look forward to the celebration with relief. Ali, too, seemed much more congenial knowing he would not have to accept a wife this night.

Ali was in charge of the arriving company while Alec was overseeing the guests that had already situated themselves and were wandering the halls of Blackstone waiting for the celebration to begin. Alec had been corralled inside the castle since before dawn, the only exception being when he had gone outside to break up the tussle between the de Fluornoy sisters, and he was frankly eager to catch a breath of fresh air before delving into the social presentation of the evening's festivities.

Alec liked social events, providing he was not required to attend more than twice a year, but he was hard-pressed to keep conversations going and act the perfect host. His nature was far more reserved, bordering on shy, and twice his mother had shot him reproving glances from across the room when he appeared to be neglecting his duties.

Excusing himself from Lord Whittlesee and his mother's piercing gaze, he made his way out to the manicured bailey and drew in a deep breath of July. Dressed in fine black breeches, black leather boots and a tastefully embroidered brilliant blue tunic, he resisted the urge to rip off his fancy clothing as he entered the familiar courtyard. Silks and satins were not his taste in dress, simply his mother's command during this social event. He felt like a court dandy.

"I have not had a chance to tell you how lovely you look," Ali purred seductively, strolling up behind him.

Alec raised a dark blond brow. "Thank you, lover. Might I say I find men in armor most arousing. Come closer; I must have you now."

"Stop it, Alec, you will have me blushing," Ali raised his visor, grinning a full smile of brilliant white teeth.

They smirked at each other, mutually trained gazes roving the bailey to make sure all was running smoothly. Nearly all the guests invited had arrived and soon they would close the gates, protecting the valuable houses inside. With parties as large as this, thieves were not far off and a full complement of soldiers would be mounted on the wall to discourage raiders.

"Did you see Isabeau?" Ali asked softly. "Why did not you tell me she was invited?"

Alec did not look at him, lifting his massive shoulders carelessly. "Because it would have upset you prematurely. As it is, you have only been unnerved since you saw her but an hour ago."

Ali drew in a deep, steady breath. "Her father actually spoke to me. What a surprise."

Alec glanced at his friend. Ali had been in love with the fair Lady Isabeau for as long as he could remember. But her father, a lesser baron with a large grain mill, had forbid Ali any contact with his only daughter. Isabeau was promised to be married come the fall and Ali was still having difficulty coming to grips with the fact. In a land of whites, his suit had been outright rejected because of his color and although the refusal had not been a surprise, the knowledge of prejudice did nothing to ease the ache.

Young Ali Boratu grew up the only black child among whites, reminded every day of his life of his stark difference. The English looked at the black boy as somewhat of a great curiosity, something to be scrutinized and studied. Some accounted him little more than an animal. To this day, he continued to struggle with the prejudice that plagued him from those too ignorant to realize he was a man, like any other.

In spite of his distinction, Ali went the usual route of a noble-bred lad. Brian had managed to convince a relative, the Earl of Havenwood, that the young black lad was intelligent and capable of learning and should be allowed his education. Reluctantly, Ali had been able to foster along with Alec and Peter, but growing up amongst arrogant English lads had been a daily struggle against intolerance and hatred. It had been more of an education than he could have possibly imagined. But as the years passed, he managed to prove his worth somewhat and had even squired for a very fine knight.

Still, he was different. Even if Alec and Peter accepted him regardless of the color of his skin, the same could not be said for the other

Englishmen he worked, lived, and slept with. Once, Ali had grown frantic with the bigotry and had tried to lighten his skin by applying an arsenic paste. The only result had been a terrible sickness, and Alec had forced him to promise that he would never try anything so foolish again.

It had been a promise not easily extracted. Even if the paste hadn't worked, he refused to give up. England was, after all, his home and he desperately wanted to be sanctioned by those around him. All he had ever wanted was to be accepted.

Even as his color hindered the process of growing from a lad into a young man, he tried his best to maintain his dignity. But when it came time for him to be inducted into the knighthood, the deepest blow was yet to come. The church would not overlook the color of his skin and since Ali was not white, he bordered on bestial. Animals and apes were not intelligent enough to be knights.

Brian had battled viciously on Ali's behalf. So had the knight for whom he had squired and his liege where he had fostered. But the church was firm, and the apostolic delegate reaffirmed the original decision. Ali was not man enough to be a knight.

Twelve years later, he was still bitter. Especially in lieu of the fact that King Edward had considered him a fine enough soldier to accompany Alec on the advance team to Acre, clearing the way for the monarch's approach. A man with no true country, no true people, faced the biting truth of his difference every day of his life.

Alec broke into his thoughts, jolting him from the all too familiar anguish. "Mayhap Isabeau's father will allow you to dance with her this eve. What harm can one dance do?"

Ali sighed, wrestling against the habitual depression that usually accompanied his deeper reflections of dissimilarity. "It can destroy my soul. To hold in my arms what I can never have? Nay, my friend, I do not believe Lady Isabeau and I will be doing any dancing tonight."

A small black man emerged from the innards of the castle, making his way towards the two inordinately tall young men. He smiled amiably as he caught sight of his son and the youngest Summerlin male.

"Olphampa," Alec scolded. "Father will have fits if he sees you are not properly dressed for his orgy."

"Party, Alec," Ali reminded him, forcing himself from his gloom.

"Sorry. I meant party," Alec corrected himself, winking at Ali as he gestured at Olphampa. "Why are you not dressed in the ordered colors?"

"You are not in the commanded colors either," Olphampa pointed to Alec's sapphire blue tunic. "What did your mother say when she saw that you had refused to wear red?"

"She hasn't said anything – yet. When she comes toward me, I make haste and run the other way."

Olphampa laughed deeply. "She shall box your ears when she catches you," he turned his attention to his son. "Which brings me to the point, Ali. The de Fluornoy's left a satchel in their rooms and it is full of belts and other valuable accessories. I suspect it will be sorely missed when discovered."

"Indeed," Ali agreed. "I suppose I should return it to them before the celebration begins."

"Absolutely," Alec agreed. "If you do not, they might be forced to turn about and seeing them within my beloved bailey one time was quite enough. I have no desire to experience a second encounter."

Ali made a wry face. "Good lord, no. I shall return it right away."

A figure in scarlet silk appeared in the castle entrance and Alec caught sight of his mother's displeased face immediately. Rather than face her wrath as a result of his negligent host duties, he gave Ali a shove in the direction of the stables.

"I shall go with you," he told his friend. When Ali looked puzzled, Alec gave him another shove. "For protection."

Ali caught sight of Lady Celine and understood. "And in return, I shall protect you from your mother? Hardly a fair trade."

Olphampa turned to see Lady Celine scowling at her son. "I shall retrieve the satchel and meet you at the gate!" he called to the retreating men. "Cowards," he muttered as they fled.

Alec, mounted aboard his magnificent silver destrier, accompanied Ali and four soldiers down the road St. Cloven's party had taken. The warmth of the weather brought out the fragrance of the summer flowers and they rode through heady pockets of jasmine and primrose. The ride to St. Cloven was at least three hours, but Alec estimated they would catch up within the hour for as slow as the party was traveling. A minor errand, and then a night filled with drinking and merriment to follow.

After only a half hour, St. Cloven's group was sighted and Alec spurred his horse faster. The sooner they dealt with the unpleasantries of the de Fluornoy sisters, the sooner they could return. Ali shouted to the caravan and slowly, the wagon ground to a halt as the chargers closed in.

Alec reined his horse toward the wagon, his eyes finding the turquoise blue gown of the older sister. The woman that had once been considered to be a prospective wife until, thankfully, he and his father had been slapped to their senses. With a deep breath for courage, he reined his horse in the direction of the blue dress.

"My lady," he began in his deep, melodious voice. "When you left Blackstone, this valuable bag was left behind and…."

His eyes came up reluctantly to meet her face and when their gazes locked, he almost choked on his tongue. His eyes widened in surprise as he stared into sapphire blue eyes of such intensity that they took his breath away.

But it wasn't merely the eyes; the porcelain face of curvaceous lips and pinkened cheeks was utterly beautiful and he heard an appreciative sigh, unaware that it had come from his own throat. The woman before him possessed beauty only given credence to in myth; she certainly wasn't the hideous hag that he had met up with at Blackstone. But he had been understandably lured by the blue dress…. the red hair…. Alec was suddenly very confused.

"I apologize, my lady," his brow furrowed. "I was looking for St.

Cloven's party. Is this not..?" he glanced at the wagon; aye, it was the same wagon. And the soldiers were familiar, clad in fine tunics of St. Cloven gold and black. And the sister, dressed in yellow…. he observed a very pretty face of clear skin and blue eyes and was deeply puzzled. He found himself turning back to the woman in the turquoise gown, once again enraptured by her utterly divine features. "Is this not St. Cloven's party?" he asked.

Peyton's gaze was fastened to him firmly; she could not have torn her eyes away had she tried. Blond hair, a granite jaw and piercing sky-blue eyes left her gasping for every breath. Had he not been so tremendously large, she would have considered him extremely handsome. Masculine, powerful, virile…. everything a man should be. It was a magnificent combination and she would have been completely enchanted had she not been swept with darker, guiltier thoughts.

She couldn't consider him handsome. Only James was handsome.

Peyton struggled against her bafflement to form a reply. "It is," she responded as evenly as she could. "Where is our bag?"

Alec motioned lamely to Ali, who rode up beside the wagon and deposited the satchel neatly amongst the packs. Moving beyond puzzlement to suspicion, Alec returned his attention to Peyton.

"Who *are* you?"

She hesitated a moment. "You will tell me your name first, my lord. I do not speak with strangers."

"Sir Alec Summerlin."

Peyton's eyes widened. *Jubil's Sir Alec!* Good lord, their brilliant scheme would be ruined if she revealed her name! She could feel a nervous sweat glossing her back as she glanced to Ivy's anxious face; even her sister knew there was no possibility out of their predicament. Being an intelligent man, he had most likely surmised his own answer and she suspected additional falsehoods would not be well received.

He heard her sigh heavily. "Lady Peyton de Fluornoy."

Alec eyed her a moment before leaning against the pommel of his saddle, scratching his head with confusion. "But…. what in the hell was all of that back at Blackstone? The fighting, the grotesque appearance?" His confusion suddenly gave way to annoyance and he cocked a stern eyebrow. "I would hear a plausible explanation, lady."

Peyton's nervousness moved to her hands and caused them to shake. "I….I know not what you mean, my lord."

Alec's irritation became full-blown with her evasive answer. In the blink of an eye, he dismounted his destrier and moved to Peyton's small palfrey. In a great whoosh of turquoise silk, Peyton was removed from the animal and she yelped in surprise.

"Unhand me, beast!" she found herself in the most powerful grip she had ever experienced.

"Not until I have had an explanation," his voice was calm and characteristically controlled.

Ivy bolted from her horse to aid her sister but was immediately halted by an armored figure. Ali had hold of the big woman and was not surprised to discover her to be extremely strong. "Hold, demoiselle," he commanded quietly.

Infuriated and frightened, Ivy took a swing at his helm and cried out when the metal bruised her fist. Undaunted, she took to kicking and twisting in his grasp, but he simply tightened his grip.

Around them, the St. Cloven soldiers tensed but were quickly quelled by well-armed Summerlin men. And through it all, Jubil sat atop the wagon and smiled foolishly.

"Spank her, sweet Alec," she murmured. "She is a naughty girl at times."

Alec heard the purred words but did not give the older woman a second glance as he pulled Peyton into the trees, away from the party. Peyton screeched and struggled, fought and grunted as he hauled her through the undergrowth for several yards before coming to rest.

He loosened his grip and Peyton slapped his hands away, managing to yank herself free. Once loose, she attempted to turn away from him, but he grabbed her with hands of steel and trapped her against his massive chest.

Frightened sapphire eyes met the blue of the sky. "Now," Alec's voice was a growl, "you will tell me what prompted your little performance back at Blackstone. And no lies, else I will take you over my knee."

His size was overwhelming. Peyton blinked nervously at him, the mental picture of his trencher-sized hand meeting with her backside nearly bringing tears to her eyes. But she would not give in to her fear; not yet, at least.

"I shall not tell you anything!"

His face remained expressionless as he lowered his great head until it hovered a mere inch from her own. She was quivering with fear and fury, feeling the heat from his body as if the sun were scorching her tender white flesh. He was incredibly large and powerful and fearsome, yet his expression was anything but hard. She'd seen the look in James' eyes many a time. Always before he kissed her.

"You will," he growled. "Shall I pry it from your delicious lips?"

Instinctively, she knew he meant to kiss her and she tried to pull away. But his hand moved into her hair, holding her tight. His face dipped even lower until she could feel his breath on her lips.

"Tell me, Patton, or I shall force it from you."

She was trembling, but not entirely from fear. His closeness somehow brought a fire to her limbs like nothing she had ever experienced. Her mouth was dry from her heavy breathing and she reflexively licked her lips to moisten them.

Alec caught the flicker of pink tongue and painful lust bolted through his limbs. Honestly, he had only meant to intimidate her, but the erotic action inflamed his senses and he was dangerously close to losing his control. The urge to suckle the tender pink morsel was overwhelming.

"M-my name is Peyton," she breathed, knowing she should pull away from him but strangely not wanting to.

"As you say. Explain yourself and I may be merciful."

Merciful? What did that mean? That he would let her go, or that he would put her over his knee regardless? She struggled against her fear, against her confusing giddiness, against herself. Why did he seem to scald her at every point where their bodies touched?

"We…. my sister and I, that is, have no desire to be married," she stumbled through her explanation. "We thought…. we hoped to discourage Lord Brian against seeking betrothals."

Alec gazed at her a moment before loosening his hold. Peyton yanked free and stumbled back, eyeing him warily.

"So you made yourselves up to look like ghouls?" he asked.

"Aye," she whispered, then swallowed hard and forced her courage. "We will not be married, to anyone. We do not want to marry."

Alec crossed his arms and Peyton's breathing began to come in peculiar gasps again; they were the biggest arms she had ever seen, every magnificent muscle straining against the restrictive silk. "Why not?" he asked.

She had expected a reprimand or a lecture; certainly not a question and was caught off guard. "Because…. because we do not need men. We do fine by ourselves and we do not need the nuisance of men dictating our every move."

"I see. So you sought to make your own decision by deterring my father from selecting husbands for you?"

"Exactly," her initial fear faded, replaced by her standard boldness. "I would wager to say that after what he has seen this afternoon, we will not have to worry about husbands any longer."

Alec looked at her, long and hard, before depositing his considerable weight on a stump. Thoughtfully, his eyes grazed her. "'Tis your duty to marry and provide heirs to carry on the tradition of St. Cloven," he said. "What will happen if you and your sister die old maids, with no children to continue the legacy? The tradition of St. Cloven ale will die."

Peyton's brow furrowed and she lowered her gaze. She opened her mouth to retort but found she could not find a suitable argument to his calm rationale. "I…. I did not say we did not ever wish to be married," she replied quietly. "We simply do not want to be married any time soon. Eventually, we will marry and bear children and pass the tradition on."

As she said it, she thought of marrying and of betraying James' memory. A wave of pain rippled across her delicate features.

Alec saw it. "Why does the thought of marriage distress you?"

"It doesn't," she snapped, fighting off the melancholy and focusing on her annoyance instead. She faced him and put her hands on her hips. "Are you going to return to your father and tell him what we have done?"

He raised a slow eyebrow. "Nay. You are going to tell him."

Her jaw hung slack with surprise. "What?"

He rose and she was startled anew by his size. "You will be my guest at the party tonight and will be given the chance to explain your actions to my father personally."

"I will not!" she retorted hotly as he moved toward her. "If I return to Blackstone, it will be kicking and screaming all the way!"

"If you so choose." He was still moving toward her.

She backed away from him, frightened and angered. "You will not lay a hand on me, Alec Summerlin! You will be sorry!"

He actually smiled. "Nay, lady, I guarantee I will not be sorry. But you will be."

"How dare you threaten me! If you so much as..!"

He suddenly bent over and grabbed her about the waist, throwing her over his shoulder as if she weighed no more than a child. Grinning, he carried his struggling burden back to the waiting party.

"Ali, the ladies will be returning with us to Blackstone," he said pleasantly, eyeing Ivy. "Lady Ivy will be your guest at tonight's party."

Ali turned his helmed head to the blond sister, thinking her to be quite lovely without the dark circles and gray skin. "My pleasure, my lord."

But Ivy scowled at him. "I shall not be anyone's guest! We are going home!"

On Alec's shoulder, Peyton's struggles increased. "Defend yourself, Ivy! Do not let him force you!"

Ivy took her sister's advice and shoved Ali hard enough to cause him to lose his balance. Another kick to the stomach had him stumbling off the road, almost falling down a slight decline. She dashed toward the wagon to spur the team onward, but Ali regained his footing and was upon her before she could carry out her mission.

Clutching the struggling buxom woman against him, he turned to Alec. "This will prove to be an interesting evening."

Alec smirked in humorous agreement and turned to his destrier, preparing to mount with Peyton slung across his shoulder. Peyton, however, had managed to upright herself somewhat and boxed his left ear sharply. Alec winced. "Unwise, lady. Another infraction and I shall tie your hands together."

Jubil was staring at him quite dreamily, unconcerned that her nieces were being abducted. "Plant your hand on her bottom, my lord. She shall stop soon enough."

This time, Alec listened to her. He raised his eyebrows. "Is that so?" Without hesitation, he smacked Peyton soundly on the behind and she yelped. But, true to Jubil's word, she ceased her struggles purely out of shock.

"Jubil!" she cried miserably. "You traitorous cow! Stop helping him!"

"Do not listen to her, Jubil," Alec said, his lips twitching with mirth. "I demand you continue to aid me."

"As ordered, my lord," Jubil sighed.

Peyton's struggles commenced once again as Alec mounted and she accidentally kicked the charger in the neck, causing the animal to bolt. Alec's attention was diverted as he fought to control the steed and Peyton saw the opportunity she had been waiting for; prying herself free of his confining embrace, she managed to twist from his grip. But momentary glee met with harsh reality when she realized the horse was extremely tall. There was nowhere for her to go but down.

Peyton fell like a stone before Alec could grab hold of her. In a burst of stars and sharp pain, the world abruptly went black.

CHAPTER THREE

IT WAS NEARLY dusk by the time Alec returned to Blackstone. The celebration had already begun and Olphampa waited in the bailey nervously as the great gates swung open to admit the incoming party. He rushed forward to meet them.

"Alec! Ali! What happened?"

Alec did not answer; his face was emotionless as he dismounted his steed and moved to the wagon. Ali dismounted as well, instructing the servants to stable the horses and store the wagon when it was emptied. Olphampa watched the orderly chaos around him, baffled by what was going on. Curiously, he peered into the rig.

Ivy was perched like a lioness over the prostrate form of her sister. Alec stood at the foot of the wagon, his great hands on his hips.

"Has she regained consciousness?" he asked.

"Nay," Ivy said glumly. "She has not moved a muscle."

Alec's jaw twitched, unusual for the usually controlled man. "I shall move her inside."

"Do not touch her!" Ivy spat, throwing her arm over her sister possessively. "This is your fault! If you had not…!"

"We have been through this, demoiselle," Ali said calmly, grasping Ivy by the arm. "Move aside so that we may remove your sister."

Ivy grunted and cursed as Ali pulled her from the bed of the wagon. Alec leapt into the vacated spot and gazed down at Peyton's sleeping face. A peculiar stab clutched at him, something he was unable to interpret as he studied the fine features and creamy skin. Irritated with unfamiliar feelings, he scooped Peyton into his massive arms and climbed down from the rig.

Olphampa peered at the burden in his arms. "Who is this, Alec?"

Alec glanced down at the perfect, porcelain face. "This is the Lady Peyton de Fluornoy. Send Pauly to her room and tell him that…."

"She doesn't need your help," Ivy burst angrily, in Ali's grasp. "Jubil can take care of her."

As the name was mentioned, all eyes turned to look at the older woman seated on the wagon bench. Jubil sat in a haze of glory, her eyes unfocused and a foolish smile on her lips. Ivy, sheepish as well as angry, slanted Alec a reluctant gaze.

"Well…. she will tend her when she is feeling better," she mumbled. "I shall care for Peyton until that time."

Alec ignored Ivy and turned to Ali. "Find Pauly. Tell him that the lady has struck her head and has been unconscious for an hour, at least. Make haste, man."

Ali handed Ivy over to another knight and went on his way. Alec turned to Olphampa. "See that the woman in the wagon is brought to the de Fluornoy suite." Passing a final questioning glance at trance-like Jubil, he hurried on his way.

Inside, the castle was warm and fragrant, full of laughing people and gay music. Directly in front of him loomed the wide arch to the main hall, decorated with fresh rushes and fragrant flowers. Beyond was a roomful of merry revelers.

But Alec paid the party little heed as he headed for the wide staircase to his left, shifting Peyton in his arms as he neared the steps. He kept glancing at her still face, looking for a glimmer of arousal.

As he neared the stairs, he heard his name wafting above the music and he slowed to an impatient halt. Dressed in a fine silk tunic trimmed in gold embroider, Brian approached his son, his dark face creased with surprise.

"What's this?" he demanded, gesturing to Peyton. "Where have you been? Lady Caroline has been asking for you. Her father is...."

Alec cut him off, mounting the first step. "I have no time to stand and chat. I must get Lady Peyton to her room."

Brian frowned at his son's rudeness and was prepared to rebuke him when the meaning of Alec's words abruptly settled. "Lady Peyton? What do you mean?"

Alec did not answer his father until he reached the second floor corridor. Brian tailed after him like an eager dog. "Lady Peyton has injured herself," he said. "I have sent for Pauly."

Brian had a shortage of patience and stopped his son as he attempted to enter the assigned de Fluornoy rooms. "Lady Peyton? Alec, I thought we agreed that Lady Peyton was to return home. If she is injured, then...."

Alec pushed past his father and into the room. Carefully, he laid Peyton's limp body on the soft mattress and stood back, gazing down at her unbelievable beauty. Beside him, he heard his father gasp.

"This is Lady Peyton?" he echoed in disbelief. "Well.... damnation, I do not understand. If this is Lady Peyton, then who was that creature in the bailey today?"

"'Twas she," Alec said, still gazing at her. Then he turned humored eyes to his father. "It would seem that she and her sister were intent on discouraging you from selecting husbands for them. They believed that the more unattractive they appeared, the less likely you would force them into betrothals."

Brian looked aghast. Open mouthed, he looked to Peyton once more. "The vixen!" he peered closely at her, leaning over the bed and studying her carefully. "By God, Alec, she is a fine piece of work," he leaned closer, observing the color of her hair in the firelight. Then he snorted. "Fine, indeed. I had no idea Albert's daughter was so fair. I cannot remember ever witnessing such beauty."

Alec watched his father inspect Peyton as he would have inspected a prize mare, scrutinizing every feature. Alec would have been inspecting her too had he not been so concerned for her health. The knot on her head was the size of an egg and her lack of lucidity was not a good sign.

"What about the other sister? Is she fair as well?" Brian asked, still hunched over Peyton.

"Fair enough," Alec answered, his gaze lingering on Peyton's sweet face. "Not the beauty her sister is, but pretty nonetheless."

"Excellent," Brian said. "I am pleased to hear…."

Before he could finish his sentence, a balled fist suddenly came up and caught him on the lip. Brian stumbled back as Peyton came to life, struggling to scramble off the bed as Alec moved to intercept her. Her feet were nearly to the floor when Alec was upon her, pushing her back onto the mattress.

Frightened and disoriented, Peyton shrieked and struggled towards the other side of the bed, but Brian was positioned to stop her. Effectively boxed in, she froze in the center of the wide bed with the expression of a hunted deer.

"It's all right, my lady," Brian insisted gently. "You are at Blackstone. All is well."

Peyton did not quite comprehend him and moved to escape once more. Alec leapt in front of her and she visibly recoiled; then, slowly, her agitation lessened as realization dawned. A shaking hand moved to her face as she backed away from Brian, away from Alec, and pressed herself against the head of the bed. Her sapphire blue eyes were wide with disorientation as she gazed at the two men.

"What….why am I..?" she suddenly turned accusing eyes to Alec. "You abducted me! You tried to..!"

"I was returning you to the party when you fell and hit your head," Alec said calmly.

"Fell and hit my head?" Peyton repeated with disbelief, wincing when her own loud voice tweaked her pained head. "You threw me over your shoulder like…. like an animal and I was forced to fight for my very life. I hit my head when I fell from your horse."

Brian shot his son a suspicious look. "For whatever the circumstances, my lady, you are here now and I wish you to remain," he refocused on Peyton. "How does your head feel?"

She blinked slowly, feeling an ache in her head the likes of which she had never experienced. To compound the problem, her stomach was rolling like waves on the sea. "Appalling, my lord. In fact, there is not one part of my body that is not revolting at this moment."

Brian grinned faintly. "I do apologize. Alec has sent for the surgeon and he should be able to ease your aches."

Peyton nodded, averting her gaze. She wished the two of them would simply go away and leave her alone with her illness, but they seemed intent to linger and stare. She remained huddled at the head of the bed, fearful to move and unwilling to look at either of them. She wondered where Ivy and Jubil were but did not dare ask.

When they were sure she wasn't going to bolt from the bed again, Brian and Alec moved toward the chamber door.

"I have a hall full of guests to attend to," Brian said quietly, glancing at Peyton's red head. "I shall send your mother up when I find her."

"Pauly should be here momentarily. Until then, I shall stay with the lady."

Brian raised an eyebrow. "Only until your mother arrives. I shall expect you down in the hall thereafter to help me entertain the throng," he thrust a finger at his son. "No lingering. You have neglected your duties all afternoon and I shall not be left to amuse the horde alone."

When his father was gone, Alec closed the door and moved for the bed, cautiously eyeing Peyton. She looked pathetic and weary, curled up in a protective ball, and he felt a twinge of remorse for what had happened.

"A pity you will not be able to attend the party. My mother put a great deal of effort into the food and entertainment."

She ignored him and he meandered closer to the bed, standing at the foot of the mattress as he gazed at her pale face. "Did the fall rob you of your manners as well?"

Her answer was to shoot him a cold glare before turning away.

Undaunted by her rudeness, he perched himself on the edge of the bed and was amused when she stiffened. "I threatened to pry the truth from your lips once before. Do I need to pry an entire conversation forth in the same manner?"

Her head snapped to him. "If you had any manners at all, you would realize that I do not wish to speak with you. If you would go away, I would be most grateful."

He raised his eyebrows slightly. "Are you always so disagreeable?"

"Are you always so annoying?"

"I asked you first."

Peyton scowled and turned away. "Leave me alone."

Alec fought off a grin and stood from the bed. "Never let it be said that I do not obey a lady's wish," he moved for the door. "I am sorry you are feeling so poorly, my lady. I shall leave you alone to enjoy your evening."

She eyed him as he unlatched the door. "I shall enjoy it a good deal more when you have gone."

He gave her a wry smile. "That is your choice. Good eve to you."

He closed the door softly and was gone, affording Peyton the opportunity to stretch out of her huddle. Alec frightened her terribly, although she would never let on, simply because of his sheer size. He was far too large and quite frankly intimidated her. James had been the perfect size in her opinion, average of height with a lean, muscular build. He was the consummate compliment to her petite stature. Alec was easily two of James, uncouth baboon that he was.

She'd barely known the man three hours and already she knew that she hated him. Not that it mattered in the grand scheme of things; her greatest concern now was that Lord Summerlin had undoubtedly discovered her secret and she was desperate to know his plans for her future. Angered that her perfect plan had been foiled by none other than Alec the Giant, it gave her yet another reason to hate him.

She was gingerly stretching out on the bed when the oak panel opened again. She jumped, immediately seeing that Alec had opened the door. But her hostility fled when Ivy and Jubil entered.

A young knight had hold of Jubil's arm, for the woman was flying high with her divining potion and barely able to function. The knight sat her in a chair, eyeing the woman as if she were one of the great mysteries of the world. Behind them, several servants brought in the baggage and quickly retreated from the chamber.

Peyton remained on the bed, watching the activity and feeling nauseous. As the servants quit the room, Ivy went to her sister.

"Are you feeling well?" she demanded. "You were unconscious ever so long."

"I was?" Peyton carefully touched the large bump and winced. "How long?"

"Over an hour," Alec still stood in the doorway, watching her intently. He tore his eyes away from her long enough to snap at the young knight. "Enough gawking, Toby. Leave the ladies."

Toby passed a lingering glance at Jubil as if he were waiting for her to burp snakes, but did as he was ordered. Ivy glowered at him, daring him to meet her eye but meeting Alec's cool gaze instead. Without a word, he closed the door once more.

Ivy let out a hiss. "Damnable Summerlins. They are going to keep us prisoner as punishment for our disobedience!"

"Quiet, Ivy," Peyton waved at her. "I am in no mood for your ranting. My head is killing me and my stomach is lurching."

From her seat in the corner, Jubil stirred. "You will be married before you leave here, sweetlings."

Peyton and Ivy turned to their aunt. The woman was staring at the wall, her blue eyes distant. They gazed at her a moment without responding; they'd ceased responding to Jubil's ravings long ago, but there was something in her tone that caused them to reconsider. Mayhap it was their own paranoia insisting they listen to the crazy woman; for whatever the reason, they were curious to know what she had to say.

"What do you see, Jubil?" Ivy asked finally.

Jubil continued to stare, glassy eyed. "I see you with a dark-haired babe, a beautiful son with onyx hair and blue eyes. And I see Peyton carrying on the Summerlin line."

"Ridiculous!" Peyton immediately scoffed. "Jubil, you are mad. Keep your visions to yourself."

The young women turned away from their aunt, unnerved by the predictions and trying their best to ignore the ramblings of a mad woman.

Pauly, the castle surgeon, arrived shortly thereafter and inspected the lump on the side of her head. Thinking that mayhap she had cracked her skull, he demanded that she not sleep for the rest of the night for fear that she might not awaken and proceeded to give her a bitter-tasting willow brew for her aching head. When the surgeon left, Peyton rose unsteadily from the bed to stretch her cramped body.

"Well, chicks, it looks as if I am in for a long night," she said, not particularly grieved. In spite of the headache, her fatigue was minimal. "How should I occupy myself?"

"The party will be going on all night," Ivy shrugged. "Why not enjoy it?"

"I am not exactly in a party mood," she passed a glance at her sister. "Why do you not go?"

Ivy shrugged, inspecting a fine rug at the foot of the bed. "The Summerlins are wealthy, are they not? I have seen rugs like this at the faire in Northampton, from the Holy Land they say."

Peyton glanced at the rug disinterestedly. "I think I would like to wash my hair of the blood and dirt," she turned to their trunks. "Help me find the soap and linens."

Trunks flew open and the women began rummaging through, laying out gowns and removing possessions. Their moods lightened as they worked and Peyton's aching head lessened somewhat, calming her stomach. By the time her hair was washed and drying, she was feeling better and even considered joining the festivities in the gallery. But Ivy was staunch in her refusal to attend.

They could hear the music and voices drifting upon the warm July air, tempting invitations for a night of gaiety. Dogs barked in the bailey as soldiers made their rounds on the battlements, illuminating the evening with their glowing torches as they maintained vigilance for the celebration inside. Ivy parked herself by one of the lancet windows, watching the activity in the bailey below and listening to the sounds of revelry. Beside her, Jubil continued to sit and stare as if she were in a world of her own. In truth, she was.

Peyton sat by the small fire, brushing out her drying tresses and trying to not think of Lord Summerlin's inevitable wrath. She could not anticipate how he was going to react to their performance earlier in the day and she hoped he was not easily angered. Their father, Albert, had been simple to manipulate and the two sisters never worried about punishment no matter what the crime. But Peyton knew, somehow, that Lord Summerlin would be different.

"There was a dark man in the bailey when we rode in tonight," Ivy remarked, still gazing over the scene below. "His skin was as black as coal. I have never seen anything like it."

Peyton looked at her strangely. "A black man? Are you sure?"

Ivy nodded, moving away from the window. "As black as night. I remember father saying that Lord Summerlin spent a great deal of time in the Holy Land. Do you think he brought the black man back with him as a prisoner?"

"'Tis possible. Could the black man speak? Are you sure he wasn't an animal of sorts?"

"He spoke very well, but his accent was peculiar. I wonder who he is?"

Peyton shook her head. "Sounds most curious. Mayhap we should attend the party simply to see if we can catch a glimpse of him."

Ivy opened her mouth to reply but there was a soft rap at the door. Before Peyton could bid the caller enter, the door opened and an extremely well-dressed woman let herself in. Peyton and Ivy studied her openly; tall and slender, she possessed a beautiful face with sky-blue eyes. Her blond hair was pulled back severely and hidden beneath her bejeweled wimple, and she smiled pleasantly at the three women.

"I am Lady Summerlin," she said. "Who is Lady Peyton?"

"I am, my lady," Peyton rose and bobbed a curtsy.

Lady Summerlin focused on her and Peyton could immediately see Alec's resemblance to his fair mother. "I understand you were injured, dear. How is your head?"

"Much better, thank you," Peyton replied. "Your surgeon gave me a remarkable medicine and the ache is nearly gone."

"Excellent," Lady Summerlin replied. "How misfortunate that you fell and struck your head. Are you always so clumsy, dear?"

Peyton raised an eyebrow, hearing Alec's version of the story in his mother's words. "I…. nay, my lady, not usually."

Lady Summerlin nodded faintly, her eyes roving over Peyton as she inspected her closely. Peyton was self-conscious with the scrutiny and lowered her gaze, wondering what else Alec had told his mother.

Inspection complete, Lady Summerlin took a deep breath and put her bejeweled hands on her hips. "I can see that you do not require any further attention from me. My husband requested that I assist you, but you seem to be well enough," she gazed at the gowns strewn across the bed. "I shall expect you ladies downstairs, then. Alec and Ali will be up shortly to escort you."

Peyton and Ivy glanced at each other. "We are not planning on attending the party, Lady Summerlin," Peyton said. "I…. I still do not feel well and my sister is..," she looked to Ivy, "fatigued."

"Nonsense," Lady Summerlin snapped gently. "I demand you show yourselves for a few moments. Surely a bit of fine wine and music will not tax you overly."

Peyton grappled for words; she did not want to offend Lady Summerlin, but she had no desire to attend her gala. She looked to Ivy for help, but Ivy was at a loss for words too. They both watched impotently as Lady Summerlin shuffled through the gowns on the bed, pausing a moment to hold up a brilliant red silk. She turned to Ivy.

"This would be perfect on you, dear," she said firmly. "Put it on now or I shall do it for you."

Mouth agape, Ivy kept silent for once and did as she was told. And as her sister had little choice against Lady Summerlin's directives, the same went double for Peyton.

Alec's mother quit the chamber to seek escorts for her young guests. The two sisters gazed at each other with great hesitation, primped and dressed and glittering with accessories. One moment, they were preparing for a quiet evening in their chamber; in the very next, a beautiful bully of a woman practically shoved them into their finest garments. Peyton was willing to attend the party for fear of Lady Summerlin's wrath. Certainly, she did not want to pique the woman's anger as she had done so well with the husband. She knew that Lady Summerlin's fury would be far worse than Lord Brian's.

But the inherent stubbornness still lingered. Once Lady Summerlin was gone, Peyton stared at her sister a long while before speaking.

"Are you a brave girl, Ivy?"

Ivy met her sister's sapphire blue eyes, the familiar words ringing in her ears. "I knew you would not disappoint, Peyton. What do you have in mind this time?"

A defiant smile creased the peach-ripe lips.

☙

ALEC WAS ENJOYING his fourth glass of wine when his mother brushed alongside him, her blue eyes drifting appreciatively over her gay party.

"Go upstairs and escort Lady Peyton to the party," she ordered quietly. "And find Ali. Her sister will need an escort as well."

Alec swirled the wine in his chalice. "I am sure Lady Peyton would rather be escorted by someone else, and there is no love between Lady Ivy and Ali. They were fighting like rabid dogs earlier today."

"That is not my concern," Lady Celine replied steadily. "You will do as you are told. Go and retrieve them."

Alec looked at his mother, careful to remain expressionless. His mother was not beyond pinching him or taking him by the ear in public. "I would rather not, Mother. Besides, I promised Lady Caroline I would dance with her."

Celine passed a glance at Lady Caroline Morford. "Lady Caroline has no shortage of suitors. And no shortage of bed partners either, I am told. I am sure she shall find another to keep her company while you are occupied."

Alec's mouth twisted wryly for a split-second as he prepared another refusal, but his father's rapid approach saved him from his mother's wrath.

"Did you see to Lady Peyton?" he asked his wife. "How does she fare?"

"Well enough," Celine replied, eyeing her stubborn son. "A beautiful girl, truly. I had the privilege of helping her dress for the party and found her to be delightful. A most attractive figure. I do not believe I have ever seen a woman more perfectly formed than she."

"I am glad to hear she is not seriously injured," Brian answered, seeing that Celine was attempting to interest Alec. His son remained as impassive as always, his blue eyes focused on the activities of the room. Stubborn man that he was, he would need more than simple words to interest him. He needed a kick in the arse. "Well, Alec? Are you going to retrieve your betrothed and introduce her to our guests?"

Alec did not react for a moment. Then, slowly, he turned to his parents. "My betrothed?"

Brian met his gaze firmly. "I suggest you do it soon before everyone drinks themselves into oblivion. We want them to remember the proclamation."

Alec's eyes were like ice. "We have had this discussion, Da. The purpose of this celebration was for me to inspect Lady Peyton. I have yet to approve the betrothal."

"There is nothing to approve or disapprove, Alec. I have made up my mind and you will marry Lady Peyton."

Alec's jaw tightened; both of his parents saw the muscles contract and they were mildly surprised. Alec was always controlled and emotionless, and the faint gesture was disturbing. Celine could see a grand argument coming on and she put herself between her husband and son.

"Alec, is there some reason why you do not wish to marry Lady Peyton? Is she somehow unacceptable?"

Alec looked at his mother. "I am not interested in marriage, mother. I have nothing against Lady Peyton personally."

"But you must marry! You must carry on the Summerlin legacy and perpetuate the family. Lady Peyton is certainly lovely and charming enough for the duty as your wife."

Alec could see that his mother was very eager for him to accept Lady Peyton and he felt himself losing the battle already. With his mother and father against him, there was naught he could do but concede defeat. Yet Alec did not give in to defeat so easily.

"No," he turned back to the party. "I do not wish to marry and I will not be forced."

Celine began to bristle, but Brian quieted her. "Would you be so kind as to bring me a goblet of wine, love? I would speak to Alec alone."

Celine, glaring at her son, then did as she was asked. When she moved out of earshot, Brian took a step closer to Alec and lowered his voice. His tone was quiet and pleasant, but there was no mistaking the seriousness. "Alec, you will listen to me and listen well. You will indeed marry Lady Peyton and administrate St. Cloven, or I shall disown you. No more money, no more advantages. Nothing. You will be on your own without a mark to your name. This I vow."

Alec remained stoic. "I am your only son left. You would do this over a mere betrothal?"

"I still have Paul. He is my heir and I do not need you. You will do as I say for once, without questions. Your stolid stubbornness grows tiresome and I have had enough. I am your father, Alec. I brought you into this world and you will obey my wishes."

The conversation was no longer pleasant. It had grown deadly serious and Alec was surprised; his father was an amiable man and he had never known him to use threats. But there was also another Summerlin characteristic that Brian possessed; he was true to his word. Alec knew without a doubt that his father meant what he said.

Slowly, he turned to his father. "She has no desire to marry, either. Do you realize you are condemning both of us to a hellish existence? We will only grow to hate and resent one another and that is no way live."

"It will be what you make of it," Brian responded quietly. "She is a beautiful woman, Alec. Surely on that basis you can make an attempt at a workable marriage."

"It's not that easy, as you well know," Alec hissed. "Would that have been enough to sustain your marriage to mother? There must be more than physical appearance and I for one refuse to spend the rest of my life with a woman who wants nothing to do with me."

Brian did not waver. "The decision has been made. Go and retrieve your betrothed and be quick about it."

Alec clenched his teeth but possessed enough sense not to respond. Anger flooded him, bitterness that his father was so unbending. Why was it so damn important that he marry Lady Peyton? Alec simply wasn't ready for a wife; at thirty-two years of age, he was too young. He wasn't prepared for the restrictive life of a husband.

A deep resentment settled as he thought on his father's words. He would not be penniless should Brian choose to disown him; he had a small fortune of his own, certainly enough to establish himself far from Blackstone. With his knowledge of horses and sheep rearing, he could easily amass enough wealth to sustain him comfortably. He did not need the damn Summerlin fortune.

Alec gazed at his father, angrier than he had been in a long while. Mayhap he should simply leave to establish to his father that he could not be manipulated, and prove moreover that he was completely independent of the Summerlin wealth. He did not need it, he did not want it, and he certainly did not welcome a wife.

If his father wanted to be difficult and disown him, that was his choice. But Alec could not be threatened or coerced into doing something against his will.

Without another word, he spun on his heel and marched from the hall.

Cℬ

DAWN WAS AN hour off as Peyton and Ivy trudged down the road toward St. Cloven. They had been walking most of the night, ducking into trees at any fleeting snap or rustle, giggling at their own nervousness but continuing on. Peyton's head had started to ache again and she was a bit unsteady on her feet, but she strove onward to reach the welcoming halls of St. Cloven.

On foot, they were perhaps another hour or two from home as the horizon pinkened, and Peyton was ready to rest. She deposited herself on a rotten stump as Ivy planted herself on the edge of the road, ears and eyes alert for any threats.

"Another hour or so," Peyton remarked wearily.

"Aye," Ivy gazed up at two chattering bluebirds greeting the day. "Honestly, I shall be glad to get back. I feel as if we are criminals, sneaking away as we did. Do you suppose Lord Summerlin has discovered we are gone?"

"Undoubtedly. We were supposed to attend the festivities, remember?"

Ivy nodded in recollection, scanning the countryside nervously. "They'll come looking for us. They're probably already on their way."

That thought prompted Peyton to stand up and glance down the road. After a moment, she turned for the heavy brush that flanked the thoroughfare. "Then we had better continue. We will stay to the trees."

Ivy followed her sister into the bramble. "You realize that this was foolhardy. It's not as if we can truly escape Lord Summerlin."

"We can try," Peyton said stubbornly. "Mayhap if he realizes how firm our resistance is, he shall not be so demanding that we marry immediately. Mayhap he shall give us more time."

"More time for what?"

Peyton did not have an answer, aware that Ivy's reasoning was sound. Skipping, hopping, and walking quickly, the two sisters progressed down the road as the sky grew lighter. The day was coming alive and there were a few villeins along the path, passing startling glances at the well-dressed women as they dashed by. Peyton was aware that the villeins would identify them to the searching Summerlin soldiers, but she was not familiar enough with this portion of the province to risk moving off the established road. 'Twould not do to become lost before they were able to reach their destination.

The second attempt to escape had been foolish. She realized that but there was something deep inside her that refused to give in so easily. Mayhap it was the spirit of James, demanding that she resist another husband. For whatever the case, she was adamant in her refusal to be wed.

They were moving through a clearing when the unmistakable rumble of hooves sounded in the distance, carrying loudly on the damp dawn air. Peyton and Ivy stared at each other, startled.

"Here they come," Ivy strained to see their pursuers. "What now?"

Peyton glanced about nervously. To the northwest was a large bank of forest. To the south, across the road, was another block of trees that stretched as far as the eye could see. She thought quickly.

"We part company. You go south and stay to the trees. I shall go north and lose myself in the forest. I shall meet you at home."

"That's madness! We will become lost and…!"

"Would you rather return to Blackstone? I, for one, would rather face the dark forest than Lord Summerlin's wrath."

Ivy gave her sister a reluctant look, turning once again to the sound of approaching chargers. "Very well. I shall meet you in the ale storehouse."

"Good. Hurry, now; there is no time to lose."

Ivy darted off across the road and loped down the embankment.

Peyton watched as the dark blue cloak faded into a grove of trees before she turned for the northern route. Just as she entered the canopy, the posse passed by and she cringed as the sounds of destriers filled her ears.

The hooves faded and Peyton was finally alone again. Glancing about to catch her bearings, she continued northeast.

Unfortunately, the line of the trees did not follow the road and as the sun rose, Peyton found herself lost. She tried to ignore the growing apprehension and steer herself in the proper direction, but it was growing increasingly apparent that she was only succeeding in confusing herself further. Tired, head aching, she found a stump and planted herself.

Above, the sky was brilliant and the birds were singing loudly. Discouraged and frightened, Peyton verged on tears as she pondered what to do. Knowing the sun moved from east to west, she decided to wait and watch the direction of the sun. Then, mayhap, she could regain her bearings. A few feet away, a red-breasted bird landed on the grass and watched her with beady black eyes. It screeched at her and she frowned.

"Be quiet, you. I do not need your grief." The bird twittered again and Peyton threw a stick at it, but the bird did not move. "I know I should not have come into the woods, but I had no choice." The bird screamed and she shrugged. "Instead of scolding me, you could help me find my way out."

"I do not think the bird can help you," came a deep voice.

Peyton jumped off the stump, tripping over her own feet and crashing to her bottom. As her initial terror subsided, her mouth went agape with surprise. Alec gazed down at her, sitting on her rump, and lifted an eyebrow.

"I will not ask what you are doing out here in the middle of the woods, for I have a rough idea. Where is your sister?"

Peyton struggled to her feet, brushing off her gown. "I am not going back. I.... I shall kill myself first!"

He continued to gaze at her and Peyton noticed he was not wearing armor, or a sword, and there weren't any soldiers with him. His destrier, several yards away, was loaded with satchels and other equipment. Alec wore thick breeches and boots that ended just above the knee, a thick tunic and leather overtunic made from strips of fine hide sewn together. His monstrous hands were covered by heavy leather gloves and she was suddenly puzzled. He appeared to be dressed for travel.

"Killing yourself seems rather severe to me," he said.

She took a step back, trying to maintain her courage in the face of his massive presence. "It is not when one considers the alternative."

"You would kill yourself rather than marry? 'Tis not only severe, but foolish. Why do you have such an adverse opinion of marriage?"

She eyed him. If he was going to return her, then why hadn't he moved against her? He stood talking as if they had all the time in the world. Her eyes roved to the destrier and its burden.

"Are you going somewhere?"

He passed a glance at his charger and cleared his throat, his commanding manner faltering slightly. "We were speaking of you. You have yet to tell me why you are so opposed to marriage."

"Where are you going?" Intuitively, Peyton could sense his evasiveness and her anxiety faded somewhat. He, on the other hand, appeared somewhat unnerved.

"Stop evading my question."

"I shall answer yours if you answer mine."

"I did answer your question."

"Nay, you did not," she moved toward him, gesturing to his destrier. "You are loaded for travel, Sir Alec. Are you going on a journey?"

He sighed heavily and moved for the stump Peyton had occupied. Gracefully, he lowered his huge frame upon it. Peyton was a mere foot or so in front of him, a curious twinkle in her eye. He met her gaze, thinking her to be an incredibly lovely creature.

"Aye, I was traveling. A short respite. Now...."

"Where were you going?"

His brow furrowed. "Are you always so prying?"

"Always. Tell me or I shall haunt you forever."

He made a wry face. "God help me, I believe you. Very well, then. I was traveling north to visit relatives."

"Is that so?" she looked interested. "Where north?"

He shook his head at her nosy nature. "North. North of Durham, to a keep called Northwood. 'Tis where I fostered. Now answer my question or I shall take you over my knee."

To his surprise, she smiled. He was absolutely enchanted; straight white teeth, slightly prominent canines, set in a bow-shaped mouth. Aye, she was utterly beautiful when she smiled and he felt a strange warmth settle in his limbs.

"Did not your father send you and the soldiers to find me?"

"And I thought those soldiers were looking for me," he muttered to himself, and then turned to Peyton with a raised brow. "'Twas unwise to run away, my lady. You only delay the inevitable and risk provoking my father's wrath."

"Who says I ran?" she said innocently. "Who is to say that I wasn't simply out walking, enjoying the morning, and got lost?"

"You are nearly to St. Cloven. A most exhausting morning constitutional."

"I like to walk," she insisted, averting her gaze coyly. "I could walk all the way to London if I so choose."

He absorbed the flirtatious lowering of lashes, smiling faintly in spite of himself. "That may be. But you put me in a most awkward position. I was not planning on returning to Blackstone, yet I cannot leave you out here on your own."

"Surely you can, my lord," she insisted. "Simply point me out of these hellish woods and I shall be on my way."

"I think not," he reached out and grabbed her arm, whipping her into a most intimate position between his thick legs. Standing her full height, she was exactly level with him where he sat. Their eyes, sapphire blue flame to smoldering white-blue, riveted to each other as if somehow physically attached.

Peyton knew she should pull away from him but she couldn't seem to manage the effort. His huge hands gripped her arms and scalded her tender skin. His touch was vibrant, his gaze consuming, and a strange liquid heat flooded her limbs. She could feel his hot breath on her face.

"Tell me why you hate marriage so and I will take it into consideration when I decide what to do with you," his voice was oddly hoarse.

She swallowed, feeling as if his eyes were somehow molesting her. "What to *do* with me? What do you..?

He shook her gently, stopping her words. "Tell me."

"But...."

"Tell me!"

She had no choice and found herself choking on her answer. "I do not hate marriage. I just.... that is to say, I simply do not wish to be married yet. I have no desire for a husband at the moment."

She felt his grip relax. "So you do not hate marriage in general, but you feel that you are not ready for a husband. Is that correct?"

She shrugged uncertainly. "Aye, sort of.... and not knowing who your father has in mind as my prospective husband, I am intent on discouraging him as long as I can."

Alec's grip relaxed further but he did not let her go. He rather liked the feel of her. "And you are frightened?"

She let out a long, harsh sigh. How could she explain it to him? It wasn't any of his affair yet she felt herself confessing nonetheless. "The only man I wish to marry is dead and I do not want anyone else. Aye, I am frightened. I am frightened of spending the rest of my life with someone I do not know."

Alec studied her fine features, seeing her sorrow. This woman knew the pain of death as he did and he somehow felt kindred with her in that respect. "Were you betrothed to this man?"

"I was until he was killed on the tournament circuit," her voice grew soft with grief. "There is no one else for me."

Alec understood a great deal in that brief explanation. She had lived through the death of a man she obviously cared for and her wounds ran deep. Her prank, her desire to flee, made sense and he could see that she wasn't running from marriage as an institution, merely from the pain it provoked. He suddenly found himself wondering if he could heal her pain.

He had no idea why he was even considering approving the betrothal. He did not want to be married, either, but as he gazed at the glorious red hair and creamy skin, marriage did not look so terrible. With this exquisite creature on his arm, bearing his children, he could redeem a measure of his lost pride. Pride dashed when he lay down his arms and retreated to Blackstone like a coward.

Her pain touched his own. He was intrigued and confused at the same time. The hands that gripped her arms began to caress her of their own accord.

"You certainly do not want to be alone for the rest of your life, do you?" he asked. "'Tis a terrible thing to grow old alone."

"I would not be alone, I would have Ivy," she insisted, his caresses causing her mind to scatter, her thoughts to evaporate. The urge to pull away was greater than before; so was the urge to stay.

"But what if Ivy marries and leaves you? You would indeed be alone, all by yourself at St. Cloven."

She shrugged, attempting to shirk the friction his caresses seemed to create. "I never said that I would never be married. I simply do not wish to be married right now."

"Now, or in five years. What difference does it make?"

She pulled herself free at that moment, her manner laced with irritation. "It does, that's all. Why must I explain this to you?"

He looked at her as she backed away, scrutinizing the beautiful face. Far too beautiful to be alone. He almost laughed at himself for being swayed by a pretty face; he thought himself quite immune.

"Because I am the man you are to marry."

Her eyes widened. "*You?*" she gasped. "You.... why did not you tell me that before I made a fool of myself and told you all of those.... Oh!"

she suddenly slapped at him, catching his arm. "How dare you not tell me that you were my intended from the very beginning. You let me go on like an idiot and…!" she slapped him again and again, angrily batting his arms and he fought off a laugh as he snatched her hands.

"Do not hit me. I do not like it," he growled.

She struggled ferociously against his iron grasp. "If I had a dagger, I would do more than hit you! I would slit your throat!"

"Temper, lady. No future wife of mine will speak of slitting throats."

"Future wi….! I do not want to marry you! Did you not understand one word I said? I do not want you!"

"And I do not particularly want you, but my father is insistent that I marry. So it would seem that we are stuck with one another."

"Never!" she roared. "I refuse to marry you, Alec Summerlin. I hate you!"

"You do? How unfortunate for you. I am rather fond of myself."

Her wrestling stopped and she scowled. "You self-centered, pompous boor! Marry yourself, then. I shall not be your wife, not ever!"

He still held her by the wrists, amused at her display of temper. The more she raged, the cooler he became and he could see that his calm infuriated her further. "Never is a long time, my lady. You said yourself you were fearful of being forced to wed someone you did not know. At least you know me."

"And I hate you!"

"Why?"

She paused in her rage, focusing her sapphire blue eyes on him. "Because…. because you threatened me, treated me with disrespect and humiliated me in front of my sister. And because you completely disregarded my safety by allowing me to fall and strike my head, and…. shall I go on?"

"Please."

She puckered her lips in an angry pout. Why else *did* she hate him? Oh, yes. "And because you are far too large. I do not like large men."

He raised his brows as if he hadn't heard correctly. "I am too *large*?

Christ, what does that have to do with anything? Why should my size cause you this hatred? Moreover, if we are going to sling personal insults, then you are too skinny. And I do not like red hair."

Her eyes widened at the insult and she succeeded in yanking her hands free of his grip. "And I hate blonds. Why is it that you keep your hair so short? You look like a thistle."

He folded his massive arms across his chest. "At least my hair is kept and not looking like the tail of a horse."

He almost laughed at the look of extreme outrage on her face. Her pretty cheeks were flushing bright with anger and he was expecting another barrage of slaps any moment. "You are a giant, a misshapen beast. And you have the disposition of a swine."

"And you have the disposition of an obnoxious chicken. In fact, you look like one, too. A slovenly little bird with wild red plumage."

Her face was contorted with rage. "Is that so?"

"Cluck, cluck, cluck."

Peyton's eyes widened and he was quite positive that if the red mottling her cheeks further deepened, she would explode. She opened her mouth to forcefully return the insult, but suddenly turned away from him and choked out a sob instead. "You are a hateful monster, Alec Summerlin!"

He was immediately contrite. He hadn't meant a word of what he said, dealing insult for insult. He'd only said those things to put her in her place.

"I am sorry, Patton. I did not mean it."

"Peyton!" she yelled. "Are you dense as well as malformed? My name is Peyton! Pay-*tin*!"

"Peyton, Peyton," he repeated quickly, softly. "I did not mean what I said, sweetheart. Truly."

"Do not call me 'sweetheart'," she sobbed, wiping furiously at her eyes as she faced him. "I have been up all night traipsing along these dirty roads and I haven't eaten since yesterday at noon, and my head aches and I do not need your overbearing presence. Go away!"

He sighed. The situation was certainly going from bad to worse and he did not like to see her cry. Soundlessly, he rose from the tree stump and made his way through the bramble back to his charger. Unloading a few items, he returned to the stump and arranged them orderly.

As Peyton sobbed, he built a fire from dry wood and manure and set a pot on it. Into the pot he put a chunk of dried beef stock and filled it half-full with water. When the water began to steam and the stock began to dissolve, he turned to Peyton.

"Come here."

"No!" she snapped, gaining control of her tears. Pulling her cloak tightly about her body, she gazed up at the sun and then to the woods before her. "I am going home now."

"Nay, lady, you are not," Alec rose from his crouch by the fire. "You are going to stay here with me."

Sapphire eyes flashed at him. "No. I think we have said quite enough to one another."

He looked truly remorseful. "I did not mean what I said, my lady. You are not too skinny, you do not resemble a chicken, and I think you have the most beautiful hair I have ever seen. The color of liquid fire."

She sniffed, lowering her gaze uncertainly in the face of his compliment. She did not know what to say for a moment. "And how do you know what liquid fire looks like?"

Huge boots met with the damp ground as he walked towards her. Peyton swore she could feel the heat from his body as he closed in, stopping a mere foot or so away. She refused to meet his gaze, still wiping at her eyes and nose, when an enormous hand reached out to tenderly grasp a portion of her hair, fingering the silken strands.

"It looks like this," he whispered. "Red and golden and full of brilliance."

She allowed him to touch her hair as the very air about them ceased to move. She was only aware of his huge body before her and his fingers in her hair. She watched, transfixed, as the hand fondling the strands moved to her head and she felt gentle fingers caress her scalp. His other hand came up and Peyton's entire head was suddenly encompassed in his great grasp, a grip of such warmth and tenderness that she felt weak with the painful tingling it evoked.

Her eyes lifted, focusing on his intense blue orbs. She couldn't have looked away if she tried. She did not want to try.

Alec was going to kiss her. He'd decided that some time back and this was the perfect opportunity. Her peach-ripe lips beckoned him like the finest wine and he was determined to taste her. Her hair and skin was silk underneath his inquisitive fingers and he could smell the faint whisper of freesia emitting from her entire body. It lured him until he was mindless.

He lowered his head, inch by inch, surprised when she did not yank away from him. The distance closed with painful anticipation and when his lips slanted over hers timidly, he was aware that he had never tasted anything so sweet in all his life. The gentle kiss turned hungry.

Peyton couldn't move. Rooted to the spot, her whole world revolved around the heated kiss Alec was delivering. James had kissed her, always sweetly and occasionally lustily, but it had been nothing compared to this. Alec's kiss was demanding, passionate, searing…. she was barely aware when her arms came up, timidly grasping the wrists that held her head. When his tongue pried her lips open, she instinctively opened wide to him and her nails dug crescent-shaped wounds into his flesh.

She mimicked his actions, licking his mouth as he licked hers, tasting his male musk for the first time and finding that it drove her wild. He dropped his hands from her head long enough to wrap her torso in an iron embrace and Peyton wound her arms about his neck as their mouths fused in a wonderful clash of awakening desire.

She couldn't breathe. She did not want to. All she wanted was for Alec to continue kissing her until the end of time. He suckled and licked until her lips were raw and swollen, tasting all she had to offer and then some. His mind was inflamed with the feel of her, the smell of her. She gasped as his mouth left her distended lips, suckling the delicate line of her jaw and moving to the white flesh of her neck. Peyton clung to him, incoherent, weak with the newly discovered heat of desire.

He tore away the cloak, revealing the soft swell of her white bosom. He immediately plunged his face into the creamy flesh and Peyton moaned, nearly swooning with the sensation. He ran his tongue along the valley between her breasts, suckling the silky soft curves. His close cropped hair acted like an erotic brush, stroking her neck and chin seductively as his mouth worked eagerly towards the tender fruit of her breasts.

But the bodice of her dress was too snug and the material would not give, and all he could think of was removing her from her gown. He tore his mouth away from her breast and fastened them to her lips hungrily as his hands moved to the stays of her gown.

Peyton felt his hands, knowing he intended to disrobe her but not particularly caring. The man inflamed such passion in her that she found she would forget her modesty and innocence all together if he would only continue to make her feel as if there was nothing else on this earth as wonderful as his skilled touch. The virginity she had kept so carefully guarded against James was dangerously close to being plucked.

As his lips nibbled her earlobe, Peyton's last thought stuck with her and she felt herself descending slightly from the lofty heights of desire. Fear suddenly clasped her and she pulled away from him, her eyes wide. The gleam in his sky-blue orbs nearly drove her to her knees, smoky and glazed with lust.

"No, Alec," she whispered. "I cannot…."

His fingers stopped their advance, but he continued to hold her tightly against him. "You can and you will. Agree to the betrothal, Peyton."

She shook her head and his mouth clamped down on her lips, draining her control. "Say you will marry me," he demanded huskily.

"I…." she began and he cut her off with another brutal kiss until she was gasping for air.

"Say it!" he ordered.

"Alec….!" she tried to pull away from his consuming mouth but he would not allow her to.

"I shall have your agreement if I have to kiss it out of you," he rasped, his tongue licking her mouth indecently.

She moaned and responded to his onslaught, but only momentarily before she returned to her slimly-held senses. "I do not want to."

"But you will," he suckled her lower lip furiously and her breathing came out in sharp little pants. "Say it."

She gasped and his mouth closed over her lips violently. She was only aware of Alec and his passion, of their tongues tangling, of the feel of him against her. She could barely comprehend her thoughts, but she knew clearly that she wanted more of him. For the first time in her life, she gave into the wicked world of desire.

"I shall…. I shall agree!" she breathed as his mouth released her.

He grinned, his eyes half-lidded with lust. "Promise?"

She could barely nod and her eyes opened slowly; she was positively dazed. He continued to smile at her and brushed her lips with his own, gently this time.

"Truly?" he murmured. "No regrets?"

She blinked and swallowed hard, her lucidity returning. "I said I would. What choice did you give me?"

"None at all," he said honestly, kissing her deeply once more. "I may not be ready for marriage, and mayhap you aren't either. But I shall be damned if another man will have you. I would regret it sorely if my father married you to another."

She sighed raggedly, gazing into his sky-blue eyes. "Why?"

His grin turned wolfish. "Because you are a tasty morsel and I intend to have you all to myself. Besides, you are so beautiful that I shall find you very pleasant to look at in years to come."

She stared at him, regaining her senses bit by bit until she realized he was holding her aloft without any trouble whatsoever. Her booted feet dangled a dozen inches off the ground and she attempted to release him, but his grip held her fast.

"Put me down, Alec," she said quietly. The severity of her wanton behavior was bearing down on her and she was suddenly ashamed and confused. Moreover, she had just agreed to marry him and she wasn't at all sure how to feel about it.

"As you wish, my lady," he complied, but not before kissing her again. Good lord, he could melt her to the core with his sweet kisses.

He took her hand and led her over to the fire where the pot was boiling furiously. Still dazed, Peyton sat on the stump stupidly as he fussed with the contents of his satchel.

"We will break the night's fast with broth and bread and then I shall take you back to Blackstone," he said.

Peyton stared at him, taking another look at his profile. She'd noticed that he was handsome before, but she did not stop to realize precisely how handsome. His features were sculpted and perfect, lending credit to his aura of pure strength. In spite of his size, he moved with awesome grace and agility. It was an extremely pleasing combination.

This man is to be my husband, she thought as if the full impact of the idea had just occurred to her. She felt defeated and giddy at the same time.

"Which way did Ivy go?" he asked, putting the broth into a tin cup.

"South, to the woods," she replied dully, still caught up in her own thoughts.

"We will go and search for her, then," he handed her the broth and a hunk of brown bread. "'Tis not safe for her to be traveling the woods alone, although from what I have seen she can take care of herself."

Peyton sipped the broth and devoured the bread; she was starving. Alec stood several feet away, chewing on a large piece of bread and looking thoughtful. "Are your sister's ideas on marriage the same as yours?"

"Very much so," Peyton said firmly. "She doesn't like men."

Alec snorted, chewing. "My sister's ideas are much the same."

"I did not know you had a sister."

Alec finished the bread and brushed the crumbs off his hands. "I have a younger sister and an older brother."

Peyton drank the last of the broth, feeling warm and satisfied by the food. Alec cleaned up the remnants of the meal and stashed them away in his satchel.

Dousing the fire, he emitted a piercing whistle from between his teeth and the charger bolted from its grazing spot in the bramble, trotting towards his master. Peyton watched, impressed, as the massive horse came to a halt and Alec strapped the bag onto the saddle. When he was finished, he turned to Peyton expectantly.

"Shall we go, lady? My father will be most anxious to see you."

Begrudgingly, Peyton rose. "Most anxious to take a tassel whip to my backside, I shall wager."

Alec grinned as he held out his hand. "If he is going to lash anyone, 'twill be me. And I shall take your lashes for you, have no fear."

"Why do you say that?" she put her hand in his, feeling the heated energy flow between them. How on earth a touch could affect her so powerfully was baffling.

Alec lifted her onto the destrier, avoiding her gaze. "Because I.... well, it's not important. He shall be ecstatic to hear that you have agreed to our betrothal."

He was evading her question and she reached out her hand, pulling his great head up to face her. Timid fingers absently touched his stubbled jaw. "Because why? If we are to be married, my lord, I will demand one thing from my husband. That you always be truthful with me. I do not like secrets or lies."

He met her gaze, feeling himself being devoured by her great sapphire eyes. She was so very fragile and delicate in appearance, like a beautiful blossom. But her words were sound and firm, and he was compelled to agree with the philosophy; honesty was an important trait in a marriage. He cleared his throat, forcing reluctant words to his lips.

"Because I was running away. I was fleeing north because my father and I had an argument."

Peyton looked at him closely, seeing his sheepish expression. A faint smile creased her lips. "Because of me?"

He nodded hesitantly. "I did not want to marry you and he was insistent that I accept the betrothal. Hell, I took to the woods because I thought the soldiers on the road had come after me. 'Twas only by chance that I came across you."

Her smile broadened. "Then it would seem that your father will be glad to see the both of us."

He returned her smile sheepishly, embarrassed at his admission.

"I still do not want to marry you," she said after a moment.

"And I do not want to marry you."

"Then why are we agreeing to this betrothal?"

He looked thoughtful a moment. "I do not know. I suppose because I must marry eventually, and so must you. We might as well marry each other and breed an entire keep full of Summerlin heirs."

"We will be living at St. Cloven. It is not that big."

"It will be after I have expanded the base. I have got big plans for my keep, my lady."

"It's my keep, my lord."

He lifted an eyebrow at her, moving to mount the charger. "Not for long."

He mounted behind her, settling himself in the saddle and then pulling her soft bottom onto his thighs. She squirmed innocently to find a comfortable position, but Alec was quickly succumbing to misery; feeling her supple backside against his thighs and groin was torture at the very least. He waited with thin patience, biting off a groan as she fussed.

"Are you finished?" he demanded weakly.

"Aye," she replied, but she shifted one last time and brushed against his semi-arousal and he grunted. "What's wrong?"

"Nothing," he growled. "Cease your fidgets so that we might be home before sundown."

"But your thighs are like rocks," she sniffed. "'Tis as if I am sitting on the stone floor."

His thick arm snatched her against his hard chest, stilling any further movement. "Enough."

He was preparing to rein the horse from the small clearing when there was suddenly movement through the trees ahead of them. Alec stiffened, moving to unstrap his crossbow, when a familiar warrior burst through the trees and headed straight for him.

"Alec!" Ali bellowed. "Where in the hell have you been? Your father is distraught!"

Alec watched impassively as his friend approached. "I was.... out looking for Lady Peyton and her sister. I have only just come across her. How did you find me?"

Peyton's eyebrows rose slightly at the lie, but the knight simply nodded his helmed head as he reined his snorting charger next to them.

"I heard you whistle for Midas, of course. Greetings, demoiselle," Ali dipped his head to Peyton. "Lord Summerlin will be glad to see that you have survived your adventure whole."

"Her sister took to the south, through the woods. Make yourself useful and go find her. I shall return Lady Peyton to Blackstone."

Ali shook his head, resting a massive gloved hand on his thigh. "I am afraid of her, Alec. Can I not take Lady Peyton while you search for the sister?"

"Whelp," Alec grumbled. "What is it about Lady Ivy that frightens you? She is a lovely girl."

"She is indeed, but she can best me in a fight, I know it. And she will most certainly not come peacefully, which could only result in my severe injury or worse."

Peyton could sense the humor between them and was therefore not offended by the insult dealt to her sister. In fact, it was the truth.

"I will tell you a secret about my sister, my lord," she said to Ali. "She has a weakness on her left side. She focuses on the right."

Underneath his visor, Ali grinned. "Thank you, demoiselle. I shall remember to blindside her. We have not yet been introduced, but I am Ali Boratu."

"Sir Ali," she greeted. "I remember you from last night."

"It is not 'Sir' Ali, but simply Ali," he corrected her.

Peyton looked puzzled. "I.... I apologize for the mistake, but I assumed you were.... you are not a knight?"

"Nay," he said flatly, turning his attention to Alec. "Your mother is raging, Alec. Mayhap you should return immediately and soothe her. You left without a word last night and she is in a foul mood, and the ladies' disappearance has exacerbated her terribly."

Alec grunted. "Mother is always aggravated."

Ali suddenly flipped up his visor, wiping his damp forehead and Peyton's mouth went agape with surprise.

"You are the black man!" she blurted.

Ali looked at her as if she had just accused him of being a leper. His onyx eyes bulging, he ripped off his gauntlet and let out a high-pitched scream at the sight of his naked hand. "My God! I am!"

Alec grinned as Ali played off Peyton's shock. Peyton, however, was too consumed with the dark vision before her to lend credence to the humor of Ali's jest. Instead, her jaw hung slack and she continued to gaze at him as if beholding Lucifer's demon. She'd never seen anything like him in her entire life and was understandably astonished. It was a moment before she found her tongue.

"Where.... where are you from?"

Ali was smiling in response to Alec's humorous reaction, glancing at his friend over Peyton's head. "My family is from a land very far away, demoiselle."

She closed her hanging mouth, but her expression was decidedly wary. She could only see his eyes and a portion of his face through the raised visor and wondered if the complete picture of him was more animalistic than human. The prospect was terrifying and fascinating at the same time.

"How did you come to England?"

Ali's smile faded; he could tell from her furrowed brow that she was preparing to view him as every other woman did. Like a beast. She did not have to utter a word regarding her thoughts; he could read them easily. Mind-reading had become a practiced talent for him.

His inbred bitterness made an instant, familiar appearance. "Not by cage or animal caravan, I assure you. I was born in England. England is my home."

Her shock subsided somewhat with his biting response and she sought to ease his displeasure. Even if he was a peculiarity, she had no desire to offend him. "As England is my home as well. I apologize if I offended you by asking. It's just that I have never seen a black.... man before."

Alec's own smile had long since faded as he watched Ali react to Peyton's inquiry. As was usual, he refrained from intervening simply because Ali was better adept at handling discrimination than he was. But listening to Peyton's even reply to Ali's biting statement, he found himself praying that the woman seated before him would somehow be different than the rest.

God only knew he was used to the way women treated Ali; it had never varied much from woman to woman; if they weren't outright denouncing him as an ape, they were showering him with a peculiar blend of pity reserved for cripples and orphaned children. Both reactions usually spurred a deep anger within Alec, a fierce protectiveness to defend his friend from the cruelty of the fairer sex.

He did not want Peyton to follow the familiar path. He found that he wanted her to accept Ali for what he was; no reservations, no questions, no hesitation. He did so want his future wife and his best friend to be companionable, and he realized with dismay that it was because he couldn't bring himself to hate her. Bad temper, bitterness and all, he did not want to hate her.

Ali, too, was studying Peyton guardedly. Her answer to his harsh reply had been honest and calm, a combination rarely seen where it pertained to him. His natural reaction was to protect himself, to remain aloof and to prove to the woman that nothing she could say could harm him. But, somehow, the sapphire blue eyes weren't immediately intent on harming him, and that in itself was very puzzling.

Still, it was difficult to let his guard down, as she truthfully hadn't given him any reason to. "You did not offend me, demoiselle. There is nothing you could possibly say that would offend me. And as for the fact that you have never seen a black man before, I would wager to say that you never will again, either. I am something of a deviation."

The tone was still sharp but Peyton did not flinch. Instead, her apprehensive expression had become most curious. After several moments, she cocked her head thoughtfully. "Are you black all over? Or just your face?"

Ali nearly choked with surprise, fighting the sudden urge to laugh loudly at the question. Alec cleared his throat, determining that it was time he enter the conversation.

"Ali must go and find your sister before the day progresses any further," he said firmly. "Ali, we will meet you back at the keep."

"Wait, my lord," she stopped him, still eyeing Ali. "Ivy is likely to run from him. Mayhap we should accompany him in the search."

He cast a long glance at Ali, knowing Peyton's words to be the truth. "Very well, then." He reined his destrier into the trees as Ali ordered the soldiers that had accompanied him to return homeward.

"Which direction did she take?" Alec asked as the canopy of trees swallowed them up.

Peyton pointed south. "That way. I saw her go into the forest. Is it possible that she has made it home already?"

The corner of Alec's lips twitched. "If she is anything like you, I doubt it. She is probably sitting on a stump somewhere, arguing with a bird."

She made a face at him as he drove his destrier into the trees in search of Ivy.

Ali caught up to them after sending the soldiers back to Blackstone, maintaining his raised visor and continuing to eye Peyton as if her mild reaction to his color confused him. As they rode in search of Ivy, he caught an occasional glance now and again, but the lady would quickly look away when their eyes met. Her expression wasn't hostile in the least, or condescending in any way. But she was definitely bewildered.

Ali could deal with bewilderment; a moderate enough emotion that usually did not precede screaming or taunts. He began to wonder if her sister would react in the same mild fashion. It was the very first time in a long while he could remember feeling the least bit of encouragement. Hope for the wild dream of acceptance he never truly hoped to attain, and couldn't dare to believe.

CHAPTER FOUR

PEYTON, ALEC AND Ali were at St. Cloven by noon. As they entered the fortified manse, Alec greedily drank in the sight of what was to become his. In front of him, Peyton was already squirming from his grasp and he lowered her to the ground. Anxious for her sister's safety, Peyton gathered her skirts and immediately made haste to the storehouse. Alec and Ali dismounted and followed.

The ale storehouse was a huge barn, the hard-packed floor covered with straw and stocked with barrels of ale maturing in sectioned lots. The servants who tended the ripening liquor were nowhere to be found as Peyton pushed open the great door and went inside.

"Ivy?" she called loudly. "Are you here?"

Immediately, there was a loud thump. "Peyton!" Ivy jumped from her hiding place up on a small loft and rounded a pyramid of ale barrels. But her gleeful expression was immediately cut short by the sight of Alec and Ali. "Peyton! They caught you!"

"Nay," Peyton assured her quickly, but Ivy was already moving for a weapon. An iron implement used to open the barrels was within her grasp and she wielded it threatening.

"Let her go," Ivy snarled.

"Cease, Ivy," Peyton advanced on her sister. "Put that down. They've not captured me."

Ivy refused to do as she was told. When Peyton came within arm's length, she reached out and attempted to disarm her sister. Ivy, however, was not at all convinced of her sister's sincerity and instantly the two of them were struggling for the weapon.

Alec and Ali looked at each other, wondering if they should intervene in the physical confrontation. They listened to Peyton plead, coax, and finally scold her sister harshly for her foolishness. Frustrated and angry, Peyton had been dealt enough of Ivy's refusals and gave the iron length a sharp twist, breaking her sister's grip. Tossing it away, she slapped Ivy on the side of the head.

"Stupid cow! Why do you not listen to me?"

Ivy slapped her back. "Do not hit me!"

Peyton advanced but Alec cleared his throat loudly and closed the gap between them. "Enough, ladies. This will not deteriorate further. Lady Ivy, your sister has not been captured. She is a willing party in this matter."

Ivy glared at him. "Matter? What matter?"

"Returning to Blackstone, of course," Alec replied. "You will accompany us as well."

Ivy looked at her sister, trying to determine the situation for what it was. Was Peyton being forced? Ivy wasn't completely convinced that her sister was willing to return to Blackstone in light of the events of the past day, and Peyton could read her doubt.

"Might I have a word with my sister alone, my lord?" she asked Alec.

"By all means," Alec waved her off, his eyes roving the contents of the storehouse. "Take your time. 'Twill give me a chance to inspect my acquisition."

Peyton winced as Ivy's eyes opened wide. "What is he talking about?"

Peyton hastened to control the damage. "Calm yourself. Give me a moment and I shall tell you."

"Peyton, what is he saying?" Ivy demanded loudly, ignoring her sister's advice to relax. "What have you done?"

A flash of anger bolted through Peyton. "I haven't done anything. Why must you always assume I have done something?"

So much for the private conversation. Ivy faced off against her sister angrily. "He called St. Cloven his acquisition. Did you sell it to him?"

Peyton was cornered, flushing with uncertainty. Her gaze flickered guiltily to Alec, who decided to take matters into his own hands.

"She did not sell St. Cloven, my lady," he said quietly, meeting Ivy's hostile gaze. "Your sister is my future wife; therefore, the keep will be mine."

Ivy visibly paled. "No!" she gasped.

Ali moved to stand beside Alec in support of his friend's claim. "Do not appear so shocked, demoiselle. Your sister is not the only de Fluornoy woman taking a husband."

Ivy went from chalk white to sickly gray. "Oh, Christ."

Peyton looked surprised, gazing at Ali's helmed head. "What are you talking about? Sir Alec did not allude to a husband for Ivy."

Alec and Ali looked at each other, silent words of approval passing between them. In Ali's short, concise statement, he had obviously accepted the contract and Alec returned his gaze to the two women. "Did not I mention it? My apologies. I cannot imagine that I have become so forgetful," he smiled humorlessly and gestured towards his armored friend with a gloved hand. "Ivy is to marry Ali."

"No!" Peyton and Ivy gasped in unison.

"Yes," Alec and Ali answered in equal synchronization.

Shock filled the storehouse as Peyton and Ivy stared at the two men as if they had suddenly lost their minds. "I am too young!" Ivy bemoaned. "I am only seventeen! I do not..!"

"God's Blood, You are seventeen? You are an old maid, wench," Ali turned to Alec. "I cannot marry her, Alec. She is far too old."

"I am not," Ivy retorted hotly in an abrupt turnabout. "I am only seventeen."

Ali shook his head regretfully. "You should have been married at twelve. How is it that you are so old and unmarried?"

Ivy frowned terribly and Ali smiled beneath his lowered visor. He had decided the moment he saw the Lady Ivy wrestling with her sister that he would marry her, for she would bear him strong sons. Moreover, she was a very pretty girl with hair of spun gold and the body of a ripe goddess. Aye, a most pleasing wench for his taste and he was eager to learn of her reaction to his heritage. Without hesitation, he raised his faceplate.

Ivy's scowl vanished with unnatural rapidity. Her blue eyes were riveted to him for several long moments, gazing at the smooth mahogany skin, the onyx eyes. Gone was her blatant defiance, her natural resistance. Her breathing began to come in labored drags as she stared at the man she was to marry with growing horror.

"No," she gasped after a moment. Then louder: "You cannot be serious. I shall not…. I cannot marry you."

Peyton eyed her sister distressfully. She wasn't entirely comfortable with Ali's dark appearance, either, and the fact that the man was to be Ivy's husband came as a shock. But for Ivy's sake, she struggled to maintain her composure.

"'Twill be all right, darling," she said softly. "Do not work yourself into a frenzy over…."

Ivy whirled to her sister, grabbing her by the arms as if to use her as a shield between her and Ali. "No, Peyton, I shall not marry him. He is not like us at all. He….he is dark, he is a….what is he?"

Peyton passed an uneasy glance between Ali and Alec; Alec's usually impassive face was unnaturally hard and he turned away, meandering aimlessly toward the barrels of aging ale. Peyton watched his stiff back, his massive hands clenching and unclenching. Obviously, he was displeased with Ivy's lack of acceptance in the matter. But she hardly blamed her sister.

"Sir Alec, mayhap you should reconsider my sister's betrothal," she said as politely as she could. "She is, after all, a lady of noble breeding and deserving of such consideration. Meaning no disrespect to your…. soldier, but is my sister not entitled to an English husband?"

"I am English," Ali's voice was low. "God's Blood, woman, I told you I was born and raised in England. I have fought for our king. What more proof do you require?"

Peyton's gaze moved from Alec to Ali. Her expression was open, protective, and mayhap the least bit remorseful. Although her nature was independent and, occasionally blunt, she had become aware earlier that the black man before her was vibrant with emotion and feeling. Even if she wasn't fully convinced that he was a true man in every sense of the word, she had no desire to injure his feelings with the realities of their obvious difference. His dark countenance aside, he was still a mere soldier. Not even a knight.

As she struggled for a tactful reply, Ivy moved from behind her.

"You are not English," she accused sharply. "I have never seen a black Englishman. Your skin is black like the feathers of a raven. Certainly it is not white like mine, or my sister's, or Sir Alec's. I refuse to marry a man with black skin with limited intelligence that has been taught to behave and speak like a well-trained dog!"

Alec whirled toward Ivy, the veins on his neck throbbing. He appeared sincerely intent on doing Ivy great harm and Peyton was terrified for her sister's safety. But one look from Ali was all that was required to steer Alec away from the blond woman, and he resumed his wandering toward the barrels of ale with reined agitation. Peyton could see his jaw ticking.

Ali, however, was quite calm. Far calmer than he had been when he and Peyton had first exchanged words in the forest. He focused on Ivy intently.

"What gives you the impression that the color of my skin is indicative of my intelligence?" he asked quietly. "I am far more intelligent that most of my white counterparts, Alec Summerlin included. He will vouch for this."

Alec could feel the stares of the two women on his back, waiting for confirmation. Fighting to calm his natural anger for the insults dealt to his friend, he glanced over his shoulder.

"Ali was the best student amongst the pages while we were fostering," his voice was strangely tight. "He can figure the most difficult mathematics in his head, he can decipher Greek, French, Latin and Arabic without any effort whatsoever. My strengths lie in finances and other areas, but his skills and knowledge in the aforementioned subjects can put the most learned scholars to shame. He is anything but simple."

Peyton looked to Ali, struggling against the disbelief that threatened. Ivy, however, was not so discreet. She was still focused on Alec. "There are horses and pigs that harbor intelligence, too. We could spend all day comparing one animal to the next."

Alec's thinly-held control slipped and he moved toward Ivy, his ears mottled with flush. "Ali is a man, my lady, not an animal. If I hear you refer to him in that manner again, I shall…."

"Alec," Ali grabbed his friend by the arm, cutting off his advance. He shook the massive man, forcing his focus away from the object of his fury. "I shall deal with my future wife, if you please. There is no need for your intervention."

Alec's jaw ticked as he struggled to rein his anger. "Christ, Ali, I should have known…."

Ali cut him off with a faint smile, a hard squeeze to the arm. "Be quiet, my friend. What occurs between Lady Ivy and myself is none of your concern."

Alec stared at him, a degree of helplessness crossing his features. "Do not do this to yourself," his voice came out a pleading whisper. "There will be other…."

Ali squeezed his arm again, one last time to effectively shut him down. "No more, Alec. I can handle my own affairs." Calmly, he turned to Ivy. "Will you accompany me on a walk, demoiselle? 'Twould seem there are a great many things to discuss."

Ivy shook her head firmly. "I shall not be seen with you. I do not want to have anything to do with you, you…. black beast!"

Peyton averted her gaze from Ali as her sister blatantly insulted him. Although her reaction to her betrothal to Alec had not been much different from Ivy's reaction to Ali, there was a deeper element involved now than mere refusal. Ivy was cutting close to the soul with her sharp tongue, accusing the dark soldier of being an animal, or worse. But Peyton was wise enough to take her cue from Alec; she would not intervene. Whatever happened would have to take place between Ali and Ivy alone.

"You will walk with me, demoiselle," Ali said steadily. "I have a need to speak with you."

Ivy's shock and fear were wearing thin, replaced by a burning contempt. She fixed her heady blue gaze on him, her round body tense with fury. "I will not speak with you, as I have said. There is nothing to discuss."

Ali's black eyes were blazing embers as he took a step toward her, slowly and deliberately. He would not accept her rejection. In fact, contrary to his usual habit, he would do everything in his power to show her how wrong she was.

"You do not consider me man enough to be your husband," it was a statement. "I will prove to you that you are mistaken."

"What?" Ivy and Peyton responded in unison, horrified at the suggestion. Even as Peyton moved toward her sister as if to shield her from the black soldier, Alec reached out and grabbed her arm.

"Leave them alone, my lady," his voice was soft, but his expression was taut. "Ali will do what needs to be done."

Peyton opened her mouth to protest vigorously as Ali moved to Ivy, enclosing her elbow in a massive gauntlet. "Come along, demoiselle," he said encouragingly.

Peyton was seized with apprehension, but Alec held her firm, preventing her from moving to protect her sister. When she sputtered a helpless cry, he leaned down and whispered in her ear. "Have faith, Lady Peyton. Your sister shall not be harmed in any way. I swear it."

His hot breath sent rivers of heat down her spine and she found herself melting against him, fighting the liquid fire that threatened. Swallowing hard, she could only gaze impotently as her sister struggled against the dark warrior. Whether or not she wanted to, she believed Alec. She trusted him.

"But…." she licked her dry lips, highly aware of Alec's searing body against her. "'Tis…. improper for them to be alone together, unescorted. I would prefer…."

Alec had not the chance to respond as Ivy brought up a balled fist and tried to wreak havoc on Ali's face. The warrior, however, was quick as lightning and effectively halted her assault. "Resistance is futile, demoiselle. Kindly walk with me or I shall take you over my shoulder."

Ivy's struggles increased. "You would not dare, you filthy barbarian!"

Without hesitation, Ali bent at the waist and tossed the woman over his shoulder. As Ivy kicked and twisted, Ali carted her quite effortlessly from the storehouse.

Peyton was left staring at the open door, her eyes wide and her mouth agape. In her shock, she had nearly forgotten about Alec's presence until he shifted behind her, brushing against her back. Swallowing hard, she turned to him. With one last valiant effort, she attempted to protest Ivy's betrothal.

"Why…. why did not you tell me my sister was intended for him?"

His gaze was even, although she could detect an underlying hint of disturbance. "Does it matter? Her fate was decided along with yours, and there is nothing either of you can do about it."

Her eyes clouded with uncertainty, distress. "But he is not like us, Sir Alec. He is obviously different. How could you allow….?"

Alec knew what she was going to say before the words spilled forth from her delicious lips. Aye, he knew what she was going to say and he would not hear it. He would not allow her to voice what she was thinking, rekindling the blaze of anger that had so recently abated against Ivy. Once the blaze escalated, it was extremely difficult to douse and could quickly grow out of control. Sharply, he held up a warning finger to prevent any further slander from being cast.

"Not a word, my lady," his voice was low. "It is no longer your concern and I shall not hear another word. Do you understand me?"

Peyton read the fluctuating emotions in his eyes and a spark of fear ignited deep within her heart. It was obvious that Alec was deeply protective of the black man and she resisted the urge to defy him, to speak her mind. Instead, she lowered her gaze and nodded faintly. Head-strong and vocal though she might be, she was not daft.

"Excellent," he whispered, his tone laced with sincerity. He was glad to see that she was obedient when it was truly required of her. After a moment, he sighed. "As they are becoming better acquainted, so shall you and I. You will show me my new keep."

His keep. It had an alien ring to it. Resignation in her expression, Peyton forced herself into compliance. "What do you wish to see first, my lord?"

His gaze lingered on her red head. Thank God she hadn't given him a reason to despise her. He was so coming to enjoy her spirit, her fire, her unearthly beauty. He was coming to enjoy her, more than he realized.

"We will start with the manse."

ଓ

ALI HAD NO idea where he was going. Ivy was an armful in every sense of the term, kicking and hollering over his shoulder as if he was causing her great torment. But he ignored her shouts, her demands and rude comments as he continued to march purposefully toward the manse. As the wide door of the massive structure beckoned him wordlessly into the cavernous rooms beyond, he found himself strolling into the foyer.

He glanced about the elaborate entry as Ivy attempted to dislodge herself. Slapping her sharply on the buttocks, he grinned when she cursed him soundly for his brutal manners and sought to locate a more private chamber where he and the lady would be uninterrupted. What he intended to accomplish with his future wife would take time, patience and privacy. Although he could not vouch for the first two requirements, he intended to have the third.

Truthfully, he did not understand his own motives. He could not comprehend why it was so important that he force this woman to understand that he was not a beast or an animal, but that he possessed the finer qualities sought in a husband. He did not understand why he was so determined to waste his time; only that he had to try. He had to make her understand.

There was a dim corridor under the winding stairs. Thinking it to be a rather logical place to start, he entered the hall with Ivy still squirming against him. He passed a curious glance at the first two rooms he came to, unsatisfied until he came to a third such chamber. Moving into the lightly furnished room, he closed the door and bolted it before setting Ivy to her feet.

Ivy's face was flushed with anger and apprehension as she faced off against the tall ebony warrior. Although her first instinct was to charge at him and push her fist into his eye, she resisted the urge and, instead, took several steps away from him.

"How dare you handle me like a common wench," she snarled.

He crossed his thick arms. "Your actions dictate mine, demoiselle. If you had not acted like a common wench, I would not have treated you as one."

She was shaking with emotion, more fury and confusion than she could grasp. "Let me out of here. I told you once that I have nothing to say to you."

He raised an eyebrow. "But I have a great deal to say to you." When she clenched her jaw and looked away, he pondered her lovely profile a moment before moving to dislodge his gauntlets. The mood between them settled into one of brittle tension. After a moment, he spoke. "Do you truly find my black color appalling?"

Her gaze averted, Ivy rolled her eyes with frustration and bewilderment. "You are not English."

He peered at her curiously, loosening a glove. "Define this statement to me."

Her brows drew together and she cast him a sidelong glance. "What is to define? You are not from England."

"I was born in England. Does that not make me English?"

She exhaled sharply in exasperation. "But you are black."

"And you are white. Does the color of my skin make me less of an Englishman than yourself? In truth, I was born in England before you; therefore, I was English before you were. Would this not make me more of an Englishman than you?"

She frowned, contemplating his statement with the growing realization that, indeed, he appeared to have a point. Her hostility, her anger, cooled as a dark confusion swept her; why was she even listening to the beast? He was attempting to cloud the issue, to confuse her. Fervently, she attempted to find a crack in his logic that she could latch on to, but there were no such footholds in his solid argument.

For whatever his appearance, she was forced to concede that his reasoning was sound.

She lowered her gaze, staring at the cracks in the wall. "My family has been in England for two hundred years. This makes me more of an Englishman than you."

"But your roots are not indigenous to England. Nor are mine. Two hundred years or twenty years, there is no difference. Who is less of an Englishman between you and I?"

She stared at the wall a moment, mulling over his argument. Through her bafflement and anger, the strength of his wisdom rang true and she was further weakened, further crushed. But a strong portion of her still demanded to resist, to defeat him, to dash his words and his dignity.

"You are, I suppose. You are not white like the English, but different. You are as black as sin."

Ali gazed at her a moment, feeling her words like hammer blows in spite of his feigned indifference. He sighed imperceptibly, unlatching his helm. Removing it cleanly, he set it and the gauntlets to a small scrubbed table.

"I am indeed black, demoiselle, but sin has nothing to do with it."

He turned to her fully, crossing his arms once again as if to show her that she could not harm him with her slander. He began to wonder if forcing her to understand his nature had been such a wise concept; the further she resisted, the further his confidence and patience was weakened.

"Look at me, Ivy."

Hearing him speak her name sent a bolt of fire through her, shocking her, although she knew not why. Mayhap it was the fact that he had disregarded her respectful title. Or mayhap it was the fact that his voice, as rich and deep as the finest wine, caressed her name with unimagined beauty.

The latter thought never occurred to her, as truthful as it might be. She was only aware of her pounding heart, her swirling thoughts as she resisted with every fiber of her being not to obey his command. Opposition or not, she suddenly found herself looking at the exposed head of the black soldier.

She had only caught a glimpse of his face from beneath his raised visor, a small taste that did nothing to display his true features. His skin was smooth and glowing, like the most exquisite polished wood, and his eyes were as black as a moonless night. Although the shape of his features differed from those of a white male, they were nonetheless extremely well-formed.

Ivy found herself studying him, her gaze roving over his features, coming to rest on the kinky nest of black hair that carpeted his skull. Ali watched her closely, his entire body taut with anticipation. Would she turn away in disgust after a thorough inspection? Would it merely serve to reaffirm her opinion that he was nothing short of a marginally intelligent ape? Had he, in fact, created further damage by revealing himself to her far too soon? Judging from her nondescript reaction, it was difficult to tell.

In faith, Ivy did not know how to respond. Certainly, he wasn't the horrible, hairy beast she had imagined underneath the polished armor. Deep confusion consumed her as she found herself moving from his hair to his face once again, pondering the sculpted ebony features. His skin was so unbelievable smooth and glossy that she repressed the urge to stroke his face purely for curiosity's sake. She simply had never seen anything quite so perfect and she could feel the harsh resistance fading.

Ali continued to watch her face, fighting the powerful apprehension simmering in his chest. 'Twas difficult to combat the silence he was facing, even more difficult to bear than a blatant rejection or sneer. He could meet open disapproval far more easily than stony silence.

After an eternity of uneasy hush, he could stand it no longer. Averting his gaze, he took slow steps towards the lancet window facing onto the bailey. Ivy's eyes followed him closely, growing more uncomfortable with the rising bewilderment she was feeling. She should have been disgusted by his appearance, but she simply couldn't find it within herself to disapprove of the picture presented before her. There was nothing distasteful about it in the least.

Underneath the window was a carved chair built for two, decorated with tapestry pillows, and Ali lowered himself carefully onto the bench.

His black eyes came up to her. "Would you sit, demoiselle?"

Her first reaction was to refuse. But something made her pause, reconsider, and she realized that she was actually contemplating his request. More than that, her legs seemed to already be moving toward him. Without knowing how or why, Ivy found herself sitting next to the black warrior.

Ali's expression was gentle as he gazed into her blue eyes. "You are curious about me. 'Tis perfectly understandable."

Ivy was mesmerized by the black orbs and she swallowed hard, attempting to regain the composure that was so rapidly slipping away. "I.... I have never seen a black man before."

He smiled, revealing an even row of brilliant ivory. "You already said that."

Ivy couldn't help but stare at his open smile, facing the most perfect set of teeth she had ever seen.

"'Tis the truth," she stammered. "I have never heard of your presence at Blackstone, either. How long have you lived there?"

"All of my life," he replied, his gaze never leaving her pretty face. "I am surprised you have not heard of me. Nearly everyone in the barony is aware of my family and I."

Ivy's brow furrowed slightly. "I saw another black man yesterday, in the bailey at Blackstone. Was that your brother?"

"My father," he corrected. "And my mother resides at Blackstone, as well. There are three of us."

Ivy watched his mouth as he spoke, his delightfully smooth brown lips. "How odd that there are three black people at Blackstone and I have never heard the tale. You say that the entire barony is aware of your existence?"

"Indeed. Most tolerate us, but there are a few who have extended what they consider to be friendship. For the most part, they tend to ignore our presence like one would ignore a senile relative. 'Tis better to pretend that we do not exist, I suppose."

Ivy listened to his faintly bitter statement. "How did you come to live with Lord Brian?"

Ali reclined against the arm of the chair. "My father met Lord Brian while he was studying in the lands of the east. He and my mother accompanied Baron Rothwell back to England as sort of a mutual exchange of culture; my father, too, is a brilliant scholar and was eager to learn of the white man's world. It held such fascination for him that he never left."

Ivy listened to his voice, rich and warm, as his gentle manner eased her. Far calmer than she had been when he had first carted her into the room, she was better able to deal with him on a rational level. In fact, the rational tone of their conversation was quickly turning pleasant.

Ali watched her pretty features, reading the emotions as they rippled across her brow. He prayed fervently that she was considering his words, coming to realize that he was exactly as he described himself; a man with dark skin, born and raised in the same country that had also bred her.

She kept staring at his hair. Noting her fascination, he gently reached out and took her hand. Ivy stiffened and attempted to dislodge her fingers, but his grasp tightened.

"I shall not harm you, demoiselle, I promise," his voice was soft. Grinning into her astonished face, he brought her rigid palm to bear on his scalp.

Ivy's eyes widened as he vigorously brushed her hand over his coarse hair. Ali laughed softly, a deep throaty laugh that sent chills racing down her spine. After a moment, he released her hand and was amazed when she continued to finger his hair. Ivy was content to experience the black hair tickle her palm until she abruptly realized that he was no longer controlling her actions; she was. Sharply, she retracted her hand and lowered her gaze, praying desperately that he did not notice her flushed cheeks.

Ali not only noticed, he was enchanted. "Why do you look away from me? You are most beautiful when your cheeks are kissed red."

Ivy lowered her head even further, an unconscious hand flying to her cheek. "I…. is there anything else you wished to speak with me about or is our conversation concluded?"

His smile faded, although it remained warm. "If you wish, it is concluded. I have said what I intended to say."

Sheepishly, she slanted him a gaze, her hand still to her blazing cheek. Over the past several minutes, she had come to realize that Ali the soldier was not the well-trained dog she had accused him of being, nor a barbarian, nor any of the other slanderous insults she had flung at him. On the contrary; he was well-spoken, polite and gentle. Everything a chivalrous knight should be.

Although she was still wary of his presence, her understanding of his odd appearance was beginning to grow and she was suddenly remorseful for being so cruel. He did not deserve the jeers she had been so liberal in dispensing.

But it was difficult to admit her fault and she swallowed hard before she was able to bring the words to her lips. Apologizing had never come easy for her.

"I am sorry I called you a black barbarian," she said quietly. "You had succeeded in piquing my anger, and I say a great many things when I am angry."

His smile abruptly subsided and she could read the shock in his eyes. Puzzled with his reaction, her eyebrows drew together. "Why do you look like that?" she demanded. "I just told you that I am sorry for insulting you."

He swallowed, a most amazed expression igniting a fire in his onyx eyes. After a moment, he simply shook his head. "I have simply never known a woman to apologize for insulting me," his voice was strangely tight.

Ivy's demeanor began to return as Ali's seemed to slip. She cocked a blond eyebrow. "Do you go around provoking insults from other women, as well? I see that I am not an isolated case. What did you do to warrant such an attack? Abduct them as you abducted me? Or, mayhap, tie them to a tree and use them for sword practice?"

His gaze was steady, but his eyes had lost none of their magical spark. "Their insults were not borne from provocation. They were delivered from ignorance."

Ivy's expression evened, the seed of humor so recently sewn cooling into a new depth of realization. She could read pain in his eyes that nearly made her cringe. Black or not, he was a man with emotions and feelings, of pain and longing, and her clouded perception of the dark warrior began to lift just the slightest. He was not a beast. He was a man.

She shifted her bottom in the carved oak bench; suddenly, they were seated thigh-to-thigh, arm-to-arm. Her gaze grew steady, curious even, and he met her inquisitive stare as impassively as he could. Inside, however, he was quivering like a young knave; the quaking anticipation of the next step in their conversation. Was she attempting to throw him off his guard in preparation for damning him, like all the rest?

But her reply dashed his anxieties. "My insults were borne from ignorance, too," she said quietly. "The next insult I slap you with will be the result of pure irritation and nothing more."

He simply could not believe what he was hearing. He did not care if she insulted him a thousand times a day, so long as the taunts weren't rooted in disgust for his color. But as much as he wanted to have faith in her declaration, it came difficultly. There had been too much hatred and stupidity that he had been forced to assume to easily believe that she could disregard his differences with so little struggle. Even with all of the harsh words and physical tussling, compared to the majority of women he had encountered, he considered Ivy's resistance minor. He wanted to believe her, but only time would tell.

He smiled weakly. "Then I shall endeavor not to irritate you."

The conversation was concluded.

☙

MEANWHILE, PEYTON'S TOUR of St. Cloven had not been an extensive one. She stuck to the main points of interest, the great hall, the small solar, and the kitchens. Alec paused in the kitchens to speak with the cook and inspect the entire stock, much to his future wife's annoyance.

He criticized the method in which the grains were stored and vowed to make immediate improvements. The salted meats were stored adequately, but he did not feel that the buttery was cool enough for the dairy products and promised he would seek advice for its betterment. Peyton chewed her lip irritably as Alec and the cook reviewed kitchen procedures.

After a lengthy discussion with the wrinkled woman who had cooked for two generations of de Fluornoy's, Peyton took Alec to the second floor where he proceeded to inspect each room carefully, making note of the furnishings and state of repair. He was pleased to discover that the interior was well kept and clean; with two young women living alone, he wasn't sure what he would find.

But his fears had been for naught, as he was rapidly discovering. As they moved down the corridor, all of the doors were open for Alec's scrutiny save one. Peyton led him past the closed cedar panel en route to the master chamber, but he stopped curiously and put his hand on the latch.

"What is this room?"

Peyton gazed at the closed door as if she were considering that very question. "A chamber like all the others. The master chamber is this way."

He did not reply, nor did he follow her. Instead, he opened the chamber door and stepped through the archway.

Color greeted him. Rainbows of vibrant hues were all over the room. Several easels were placed in various spots, vellum nailed to frames hung upon them. Pictures of brilliance and talent kissed the parchment; flowers, birds, landscape scenes. Other pieces of vellum were strewn across the room in various stages of completion. Paints, neatly grouped, graced a large cherrywood table as well as several brushes of different shapes and sizes.

The entire room cried of spirit, of life, of happiness. As if a whole magical world had opened up before him, Alec was enchanted.

He peered curiously at the painting closest to him, a scene depicting wildflowers. Illustrated from watercolor on parchment, they were realistic and he shook his head in wonder.

"These are magnificent," he exclaimed softly. "Who painted these?"

Peyton stood at the door, her gaze combing the room. "I did."

His eyes snapped to her. "You? Peyton, they're remarkable. I have never seen such talent."

She shrugged, not answering. This room reminded her too much of James; her painting and her ale had been the only diversions to keep her going after his death. The room brought solace, but it brought memories as well. This was her private haven and she was unhappy with Alec's invasion.

But he was oblivious to her discomfort. He moved from easel to easel, inspecting each painting thoroughly. Peyton folded her arms protectively across her chest as he scrutinized her most personal works, feeling open and vulnerable. He paused by a group of paintings near the window and crouched down, observing them closely.

"When did you paint these?" he asked.

She glanced over at him, noticing the cluster of paintings he was regarding. A chill of sorrow ran through her. "Last year."

He examined the vellum panels portraying dark scenes; a knight entirely in black standing on what looked to be a background of blood. The depths and shading that composed the figure of the knight were extraordinary and it appeared that at any moment he would stroll from the confines of the parchment. But for all the realism, Alec saw a good deal of hopelessness to the paintings. He remembered her mentioning that she had been betrothed once before and he suspected these paintings had something to do with her grief. As his eyes trailed up to a painting on the window sill, a splash of bright color caught his eye.

A joust pole stood in the corner, broken in half. Its twelve foot length was bent, twisted and dirty. The faded yellow and white colors were still bright, still proud, and he felt a strange tug at his heart as he beheld the bent pole. It reminded him of the days when he was unbeatable on the tournament field, the days when he and Peter would fight side by side, encouraging and assisting one another. Between the dark pictures and the broken pole, his mood rapidly dampened.

On the floor next to the pole was a scabbard. It was plain but well-kept, not nearly as ornate as some of the scabbards he has seen. It looked lonely and stark with the broken pole and Alec found himself rising to his feet, pacing toward the forlorn tokens.

"Who did these belong to?" he asked softly.

Peyton stared at the two items, her face pale and drawn. "They belonged to James, my betrothed."

Alec continued to look at the reminders, feeling her grief as it mingled with grief of his own. He couldn't help himself from asking. "How did he die?"

Peyton closed her eyes and turned away. "He was speared last year at a tournament in Norwich."

"And you were there?"

"Aye."

Her voice was barely audible. She had tried so desperately to forget that terrible day, but his questions brought the memories back like a stab to her heart. The words came spilling out before she could stop them.

"It was the first tournament I had ever attended," she went on, softly. "James had been competing for years and had amassed an excellent reputation and a good deal of wealth. He promised me it would be his last competition before we were married and my father allowed me to attend. It was exciting until the very last, when he was gored by a spear-tipped joust pole. I am told that spear-tipped poles had not been used since the days of the Lion Heart, but the knight that competed against James had broken his crows-foot pole earlier in the day and was forced to use his spare. He did not mean to do it; it was an accident." She drifted over to a bright painting of roses and touched it absently, tears spilling onto her cheeks. "I held him while he died. The pole you see leaning against the wall was the pole he was using that day. It broke when he fell."

Alec stared at the mementos a moment longer and turned away. Hearing her story and seeing the bleak reminders brought back his own pain of losing a brother and he refused to be swept up by the black grief. The coldness of self-preservation consumed him, turning his demeanor to ice.

"The paintings are beautiful," he muttered. "Show me the master chamber now."

He quit the room hastily, nearly bumping Peyton in his urgency. Immediately, she sensed his change in mood and it did nothing to ease her anguish. Wiping her tears away with a shaking hand, her sorrow became something deeper, darker, and far more disruptive. It was an emotion she was coming to readily associate with Alec.

Obviously, her future husband was insensitive and uncaring and she felt the powerful return of her self-protection. Embarrassment filled her. What had she expected from him as she spilled her innermost feelings? Compassion, sympathy at the very least? Mayhap an apology for her sorrows? Instead, he had brushed past her without a word, and she was deeply hurt.

But the hurt ignited an unsettling loathing and she vowed that her confession in the chamber would be her very last. Never again would she give him the opportunity to rebuff her feelings.

She showed him the master chamber coldly, watching him inspect the bed and wardrobe. Her father's clothes were still in the cabinet and he gestured to them.

"These will be removed immediately to make way for my possessions," he said. "We will have to move another wardrobe in here for you. There is not enough room in this one for both of us."

She looked at him. "My things are in my room. We will not share a wardrobe."

"Nay, we will not, but we will be sharing this chamber and it will prove bothersome for you to constantly be moving from one room to the other to retrieve your belongings."

She gazed at him as if the thought of sharing a chamber with him had never occurred to her. "I do not intend to share this chamber with you. You may have it to yourself."

He slanted her a glance. "You will be my wife and you will share my chamber. This will be our chamber."

"I do not want to share your chamber," she repeated, her jaw ticking stubbornly. Marrying him was one thing, but sharing his chamber was entirely another. "I will demand my privacy, my lord. Husband or no."

"And I will demand my wife, whenever I please. We will not discuss this, my lady. I have made my wishes known."

"As have I," she backed away from him, her hatred blooming. "I do not wish to share your chamber. I will not."

"Aye, you will."

She turned on her heel and marched from the room. Quick as a flash, Alec bolted after her, throwing her up over his shoulder and hauling her back into the bedchamber. Tossing the kicking, shouting bundle onto the mattress of the oversized bed, he threw himself atop her.

Peyton fought and twisted and beat at him, but it was like striking iron. His hands captured her wrists as his body pinned her firmly to the bed and he waited patiently for the tirade to die down. Movements lessened as Peyton exhausted herself, although Alec was surprised to realize how strong she was. As petite and fragile as she appeared, her strength was amazing.

When her movements diminished to hard panting and angry grunts, he cocked a reproving eyebrow.

"That will be enough of that," he rumbled. "The future is dictated to you and all of the protesting in the world will not change what is to be. The sooner you accept it, the better."

She refused to meet his eye. She could feel his hot breath on her cheek as he spoke, his voice low and quiet. But the power behind the tone was unmistakable and she was frightened and infuriated further.

His reaction to her confession in the painting room stayed with her, his cold response. She tried to tell herself that it did not matter, that she was merely marrying him because she was being forced to and that the chances for emotional attachment were impossible. Yet there was a small part of her that wanted to hear a word of sympathy, to let her know that he understood her loss just the slightest. The idea of spending the rest of her life with a man as cold as the Welsh snows was depressing.

"Are you rational enough that I might let you up?" he asked quietly, breaking into her tumultuous thoughts.

She nodded once. Promptly, he pushed himself up and Peyton bolted from the bed, straightening her gown as Alec resumed his position before the wardrobe. "Now, as I was saying. Before we leave here today, I will set the servants to clean out this wardrobe and…."

"I hate you," she whispered, interrupting him.

He paused to look at her. "What did you say?"

Peyton turned her gaze to him then, the sapphire blue eyes blazing. "You heard me. I said I hate you. I shall always hate you. I hope the reward of St. Cloven is enough to balance the animosity of your wife."

He stared at her, reading her anger and a great deal of pain, although he wasn't sure where the pain was rooted. Was it because he had asked about her betrothed? Because he had forced her to speak of a tragedy she was still coming to grips with? He wished he could tell her of his own brush with sorrow, but he simply wasn't ready to. Not yet.

Strangely, he felt a genuine twinge of remorse at her negative declaration. He did not want her to hate him, just as he did not want to hate her.

"Time will tell, my lady," he replied softly.

She left the room and he let her go.

☙

THE RIDE TO Blackstone was silent. Ivy sat before Ali, quiet and befuddled while Peyton and Alec all but ignored one another. The birds in the trees twittered noisily and an occasional rabbit scuttled through the underbrush, but astride the massive chargers, the four riders were as still as stone as each one was lost to their own thoughts.

Peyton wasn't particularly concerned with Alec's thoughts at the moment, merely her own. The whole world was unbalanced; she was to marry a cold, unfeeling man whom she loathed. Ivy had not spoken since Ali had carted her from the ale storehouse, adding more troubles to her confusion. Fretting over what had happened between her sister and the black soldier set her head aching again and she was eager to be alone with Ivy if only so they could commiserate their miserable futures.

She found herself damning the satchel of valuables that had been left behind on their hasty retreat from Blackstone. Had they been careful enough to count their baggage, the mistake would not have been made. Alec Summerlin would not have been forced to return their parcel, and their grand scheme to disillusion Baron Rothwell would have succeeded.

The uncomfortable silence stretched into endless miles. Then, somewhere in the midst of the silence Ivy's voice could be heard. Much to Peyton's surprise, she realized that her sister was making an attempt at conversation with Ali. She cast her sister a curious glance and was shocked to note a smile on Ivy's lips as she spoke.

Ivy wasn't merely chatting; she was actually pleasant. As Peyton watched with growing astonishment, she suddenly realized that Ivy was intent on pulling her into the conversation. She tried to ignore them, to avert her eyes and ears, but her path had already been chosen. Ivy sucked her sister into the dialogue.

"Peyton paints beautifully, too," she told Ali. "You should see her work. Father wanted to sell a few of her portraits at the faire in Petersborough last year, but James would not allow it. Isn't that right, Peyton?"

Peyton managed a disinterested shrug, maintaining her averted gaze. Ivy was suddenly contrite. "I am sorry, darling. I did not mean to bring up James."

"Who is James?" Ali asked.

Peyton decided she would answer him, if only for Alec's benefit. She was eager to reiterate her hatred of him. "The man I love. He was to be my husband, but he was killed. How unfortunate for me."

Ivy sighed, regretful that she had mentioned the man. She glanced to Alec, noting his even expression as he gazed at the road ahead and she found herself wondering if Peyton had informed him of her previous betrothal. Obviously, Alec wasn't surprised or concerned with the topic.

"He sounds to have been a wise man. I would not allow my future wife to sell her wares like a common merchant, either," Alec replied after a moment.

"But they're beautiful," Ivy insisted. "Have you not seen them?"

"I have. They will look marvelous displayed throughout St. Cloven and Blackstone."

"I do not want them displayed," Peyton muttered softly. "I want them to remain where they are. I shall not have people criticizing my work."

"They will not criticize it, I assure you," Alec said evenly. "They will be as enchanted with it as I am. 'Twould make me proud to exhibit my wife's talent."

"I am not your wife yet," she grumbled, but he heard her and leaned close to her ear.

"Tomorrow at the latest we will see that situation remedied," his breath was hot on her ear, sending involuntary shivers up her spine.

She did not reply, too angry and confused to form a response. Not only was she adamant in her desire not marry the massive man seated against her, but she was aware that Ivy was acting most peculiar toward the black soldier. 'Twas almost as if she was growing comfortable with him.

If the world was upended before, it was most definitely spinning wildly out of control with the recent addition of Ivy's behavior. Peyton was having difficulty comprehending all of it.

The group again rode silently for several minutes until Ivy struck up another conversation, hoping to alleviate the somber mood that had been pervasive since they had left St. Cloven. She had no idea that she could not have selected a worse subject.

"Why is it that you do not wear armor, Sir Alec?" she asked the massive blond man. "You are a knight, are you not? And you are unarmed, too. Why?"

Alec passed a glance at her. "It is true that I am a knight, but I gave up warring long ago. I prefer less-violent pursuits."

"Weren't you any good?" Ivy asked, remembering what Jubil had said about him but wanting to hear an explanation from his own lips.

Ali laughed softly at the question. "There was none better than Alec. No better knight in the realm, I assure you."

"But you gave it up?" Ivy was still focused on Alec.

Alec did not reply and Ali sought to change the subject. "I find this portion of the country lovely, much nicer than London. Have you ever been to London, Lady Ivy?"

The conversation took an immediate turn and Alec was grateful. He had already alienated one lady this day and was close to distancing another had Ali not taken the helm. With Ivy distracted, he was better able to focus on the events of the day that had led to this point in time. What had started out as a most pleasant and promising day had decayed into a sullen, uncomfortable experience and he was aware that the change had taken place the moment he entered Peyton's painting room.

He was puzzled but tried not to let Peyton's attitude overly concern him. It would blow over like a storm, he told himself. Tomorrow she would forget all about whatever unpleasantries he managed to unearth. Her hostilities stemmed from her painful memories, he was sure. Mayhap in some way she blamed him, although he could not imagine why. But the more he tried to pretend her animosity did not matter, the more he realized that it did.

She was so stiff and unmoving in his arms, not at all like the sweet, heated bit of flesh he had kissed that morn. Every time he thought about the encounter his lips ached to kiss her again and his arms yearned to hold her, seeking the fire that she kindled within his soul. She seemed to fit against him with odd familiarity and he wondered if the reaction would be the same when next he took her in his arms.

Distracted and silent, he found himself pondering that very question. He did not like the coldness between them.

Blackstone loomed into view not long thereafter, distracting the party from their moody thoughts. Black, haunting, strong, the edifice emerged in the distance like a great preying beast.

Ivy's confusing behavior and her own resentment aside, Peyton found herself focusing on the massive black bastion with a good deal of apprehension. With all of her other concerns, the impending wrath of Alec's father did nothing to offset her turmoil. She realized there was naught else to do but plead for the man's mercy and pray his grace was infinite. She was so consumed with her turbulent thoughts that she was startled when hot breath delicately caressed her ear.

"I shall handle my father," Alec said softly. "Simply agree with everything I say."

"What are you going to say?" she asked, feeling her cheeks flush as he purred against her ear.

"Trust me, my lady. I shall not say anything incriminating in the least. Besides, I suspect his anger will be immediately doused when he discovers we have come to our senses and agreed to a betrothal."

For the first time during the entire journey, she turned to look at him. "That, my lord, is a matter of opinion."

He cocked an eyebrow. "I was under the impression that our decision was mutual."

Her cheeks mottled a deeper red, remembering how, exactly, they came about that decision. Noting the pink color to her porcelain cheeks, Alec smiled a brilliant, broad display. He couldn't help but laugh softly at her embarrassment, her bewilderment for a decision that was literally wrung out of her. Even with the animosity, the anger, the reaction to Ali, he wasn't sorry he had practically forced her into submission. After pondering his thoughts the majority of the afternoon, he realized in spite of everything that he was quite pleased with the fire of the Lady Peyton de Fluornoy.

"There is no need for humiliation," his voice was low, rumbling and warm. "I quite enjoyed our encounter in the forest."

Peyton looked away from him, horrified with her scarlet cheeks. Odd chills raced through her at his tone, her anger with him dampening somewhat. Why was he so confusing? Cold and hard one moment, soothing and warm the next. She couldn't hate him when his mood was calm and his manner soft, and her heart swelled strangely when she remembered their brief rendezvous under the canopy of trees.

The strange swell against her ribs almost made her smile, but she fought it. She had no idea what she was possibly feeling, or why. She was so confused she was barely aware of anything anymore.

CHAPTER FIVE

THE GATES OF Blackstone were already open as Alec and Ali guided their dancing steeds into the dusty bailey. Sharp sentries on the wall had spotted the distinctive silver charger from a distance and the announcement of the impending return had prompted Olphampa to urgently seek his liege. Just as Alec reined his horse to a halt in the immaculate yard, Brian came marching from the innards of the castle.

"Alec!" he roared. "Where in God's name have you been?"

Alec dismounted calmly and pulled Peyton off with him. She was glad when he kept his arm on her as Lord Brian approached angrily.

"I am waiting, Alec."

"'Tis a long story, Da. We will retreat inside and…."

"Nay!" Brian boomed. "Here and now. Where have you been? Where have you all been?"

Peyton shrank from the furious, loud voice, but Alec's grip on her was firm and comforting.

"Very well, then, if you will stop shouting," he said to his father. "You are upsetting the ladies. The story is simple, really; mother sent me to Lady Peyton's rooms last night to escort her to the party, but the lady was feeling so poorly that I suggested we take a ride to clear her head. We lost track of time and paused to rest until dawn."

"It is well past dawn," Brian pointed out, arms crossed impatiently.

"Aye, it is. I did not say we set out at dawn to return, did I? I simply said we rested until dawn. The remainder of the time was spent hunting for Lady Ivy."

"Lady Ivy?"

"She thought her sister had run away, afraid of the impending betrothal, and hastened to retrieve her. However, she became lost and when you sent Ali in search of our missing guests, we met up with him upon our return. I insisted on helping him hunt for the lady."

"How did you know Lady Ivy was missing? After all, if you and Lady Peyton left before her sister's departure, then how..?"

"Ali told us, of course. We found Lady Ivy at St. Cloven."

Some of his bluster gone with the steady explanation, Brian looked to Peyton dubiously. It took every ounce of summoned courage for her to respond to him with a weak smile. He then took turns glaring at Ali and Ivy as if he did not believe his son's excuse in the least, but he was wiser than to dispute Alec in public.

"As you say," he motioned to his son, still doubtful of the story presented. "Bring them inside. Your mother has been frantic with worry."

Gripping Peyton's arm gently, Alec cast her a bold wink and escorted her toward the castle while Ali and Ivy remained behind in anticipation of the private family conversation that would undoubtedly take place now that Alec was returned. Ali knew that Lady Celine would vent her rage on her delinquent son and he had no desire to be caught in the crossfire. Instead, he took Ivy gently by the arm.

"I would be honored if you would allow me to introduce you to my parents, demoiselle," he said politely.

His voice was amazingly warm, caressing even, and Ivy found herself gazing into his onyx eyes. The confusion she had tried to alleviate with aimless chatter earlier in the day had not abated; it was as persistent as a rash, though lessening somewhat. As time passed it was becoming easier to come to terms with the tolerance she was feeling for the dark soldier, but still, a faint puzzlement lingered.

Yet she met Ali's inquisitive gaze. "I would like to meet your parents, as well." She realized she meant it.

He smiled faintly, waging his own peculiar battle against her apparent tolerance. It was a difficult battle for self-protection that he, too, forced down as he gazed into her blue eyes. "My mother might even make a warm milk brew for your approval. She only prepares it on special occasions."

Ivy looked at him curiously. "And what is the special occasion?"

His eyes twinkled. "Why, making your acquaintance, of course."

She was thoroughly puzzled. "Making my acquaintance is a special occasion?"

His smile faded as he thought on the question. She truly had no idea the extent of it.

"Aye, demoiselle, it is."

☙

LADY CELINE WAS in Brian's solar. When her son entered the room, she flew into a rage and rebuked him for his irresponsible actions. The more Brian attempted to explain the circumstances, the more upset she became and Peyton stood by, stunned, as the woman admonished Alec as if he were a naughty child.

Alec remained quite calm in the face of his mother's rage and Peyton was positive she saw the corners of his mouth twitch with humor. Lady Celine's fury continued for several long, agonizing minutes, but as her tirade began to die somewhat, she turned her attention to Peyton. Startled to find herself the focus of blazing sky-blue eyes, she was expecting to be dealt a measure of Alec's treatment and braced herself for the reprimand. Instead, Lady Celine surprised both her son and his future bride by pulling Peyton into a protective embrace.

"Furthermore, Alec, you should know better than to force a delicate lady into the wilderness where God only knows what sort of horrible catastrophe could befall her. Wild animals, bandits.... and you do not carry a sword, dear, and it would be difficult to protect her. Did you not think of her safety when you suggested taking her from the protective innards of the keep?"

Alec looked at Peyton and she was shocked to see his gaze soften. "The lady can take care of herself, mother."

"Ridiculous!" Lady Celine snapped. "I will hear no more of your nonsense, Alec. Get out of my sight; I am too angry to deal with you at the moment."

Alec raised an eyebrow faintly and did as he was told. "Take good care of my wife, mother," he said softly as he strolled past Celine.

Celine's eyes widened with surprise as her gaze found her husband. Brian, sputtering with shock, stopped his son just as he cleared the doorway. "Alec? What's this you say?"

Alec paused, turning to his stunned parents with faint amusement. "Why so surprised? Are you not pleased that I am doing as ordered?"

"Yes, of course, but…." Brian turned to Peyton, amazed to see that she was completely calm. "He…. informed you, my lady?"

Peyton nodded. "He did, my lord. And I have agreed."

Brian's amazement increased. "You have? Well…. of course you have!" he suddenly laughed loudly, from relief and joy. "A wise decision, both of you. What a pleasure it will be to have relations to the de Fluornoys. By this time next year, I shall have a grandson!"

Peyton blushed furiously as Alec grinned. "One step at a time, Da. We have not been married yet."

"Soon!" Brian exclaimed, suddenly taking Peyton into his arms and kissing her loudly on the cheek. "Soon! And…. oh, my, you do taste nice. Alec, I cannot tell you how very pleased I am."

They were laughing at his enthusiasm as well as his comment regarding Peyton's flavor. Lady Celine wrapped her arms about her new daughter and hugged her gently as Alec came back into the room. Peyton, rosy with the compliments and excitement, met his gaze shyly and he smiled at her.

"As am I," he responded softly. "I appreciate your insistence in the matter."

"I am glad you think so," Brian put his hand on his son's shoulder and pushed him to the door. "We have many plans to make, Alec. I should like to see you married before the end of the week," he suddenly paused. "But what of the other sister? Did..?"

"Ask Ali," Alec stopped him. "He shall not dispute you in the matter."

Brian smiled again, broadly. "I am pleased to see that you two are not intent on fighting me anymore on this matter. 'Tis time you both realize that I know what is best for your respective futures."

Alec's gaze never wavered from Peyton. Clasped against his mother's breast she looked uncomfortable and uncertain, yet there was an excited flush to her cheeks. He was pleased that she was not intent on ruining his parents' delight with declarations of her hatred for her future husband.

As he gazed into her lovely face, he reiterated his earlier thoughts; he did not want her to hate him. Strange that for a man who never wanted a wife, he was willing to accept this particular woman with a good deal of ease. He hoped that whatever animosity had occurred between them earlier would somehow slip away into forgetful oblivion. He was more than willing to forget their bitter words.

"I must send for Ali and Lady Ivy," Brian muttered with excitement, distracting Alec from his thoughts as a servant dashed off. "We must celebrate. And, God's Blood, I have forgotten Olphampa and Sula. I must....!"

"I shall send for them, dear," Celine smiled at her husband. "You will sit and calm yourself before your chest begins to ache."

Celine exited the room, but not before swatting her six-and-a-half foot son on the behind as if he were a wayward child. Peyton hid her grin as her future husband did not so much as move a muscle in response to his mother's spank. Apparently, he was accustomed to Lady Celine's gestures.

"Wine!" Brian suddenly boomed as if he had just remembered the secret to life. "Only the finest reserve will do. I must retrieve it this instant!"

He darted from the room, mumbling to himself and snickering at Alec as he moved past his son. The room was silent but for the sounds in the bailey as Alec meandered toward his father's massive oak desk, cluttered with vellum and broken quills.

"My father is not usually so excitable," he remarked.

Peyton perched herself on a silken chair. "Is your mother always so abusive?"

Alec lifted a blond eyebrow. "Aye. She used to beat my brothers and I daily when we were young. She was a firm believer in discipline."

Peyton looked at him curiously. "Brothers? But I thought you had only one brother."

Any warmth that might have graced Alec's features vanished. His expression was calm, but his eyes were like ice and Peyton immediately sensed his change of mood. Just as his manner had changed at St. Cloven when she told him of James.

"I had two brothers. One died several years ago."

"I am sorry for your loss," she said, wondering if she should simply keep silent. Having no idea why he had suddenly grown hard, she was unsure if further words would provoke him. Surely extending sympathies would not anger him, she reasoned.

His jaw ticked and he moved to the narrow lancet window overlooking the bailey. He unlatched the pretty lattice shutter and opened it, breathing in the late July air. Sensing there was nothing more to say on the matter, Peyton looked at her hands and remained silent.

Alec's gaze roved the bailey and he caught sight of Olphampa crossing towards the main house. But his mind wandered, moving from Peter to the events of the past several hours; it was difficult not to ponder the eventful day. Beyond the hostilities and the harsh words had been a most impacting occurrence; the kiss he and Peyton had shared permeated his senses and the heat of their contact left him breathless. Never had he felt such passion as if their being together was completely right and natural.

A young woman entered the solar at that moment. Peyton looked up to find herself gazing at another Summerlin. The family resemblance was uncanny, but unfortunately, the strong features that made Alec so terribly handsome looked thick and harsh on a woman's face. She gazed intently at Peyton.

"Greetings, Moppet," Alec said, breaking from his deeper thoughts. "By your expression, I would assume you have been speaking to mother."

"To father," the girl corrected, her intense stare almost hostile. "Is this your future wife?"

Peyton stood up politely as Alec replied. "This is the Lady Peyton de Fluornoy. My lady, this is my sister, the Lady Thia Summerlin."

Peyton bobbed a curtsy. "My lady, 'tis a pleasure to meet you."

Thia put her hands on her hips; broad, beefy hips. She was nearly Peyton's height but a good deal heavier. She had small blue eyes and the aforementioned thick features, but to her credit she possessed a glorious head of wavy hair, the color of dark honey. In reaction to Peyton's greeting, she simply sized up her future sister-in-law from head to toe before turning to her brother.

"I had no idea you were to be betrothed. When did this come about?"

Peyton felt the sting of Thia's rebuff and regained her seat. Her mood darkened as she watched Alec warm to his sister, feeling distinctly belittled as he responded.

"A few days ago," Alec said. "Where have you been, love? You usually greet me in the bailey when I arrive."

Love, Peyton thought with contempt. *He calls her love! What is there to love about horsey, bad-mannered Thia?* Amidst her dark thoughts, it never occurred to her that she was actually jealous of the affection Alec held for his sister.

Yet it was far more than simple envy; every time she and Alec seemed to be getting comfortable with each other, something would occur and the chasm between them would widen. The more she watched Thia interact with Alec, the wider the chasm yawned. Peyton wasn't feeling hatred so much anymore as she was simply feeling despondent and uncertain. Her entire world was out of sync.

"Helping the cook with the lambs," Thia replied to her brother's question. "Sometimes she isn't strong enough to snap the necks and requires my help."

"There are plenty of male servants to accomplish that task," Alec said reprovingly. "Hardly a duty for a well-bred young woman. I believe we have had this discussion before."

"We have, but I choose to ignore you," Thia said stubbornly. "I like to work."

Considering she looks like an ox, I am not surprised, Peyton smirked inwardly. Past the point of remaining on her best behavior in the face of Alec and Thia's rejection, she crossed her arms and looked away, pondering her own thoughts. If they were going to be rude, then so would she.

The more Alec and his sister conversed, the angrier Peyton became. It would have been polite to have included her in the conversation and she was incensed that they did not consider her worthy of their attentions. She listened to every word between them and prepared to give her own rebuff when the conversation turned toward St. Cloven. She would give them a taste of their own medicine.

"Lady Peyton is a marvelous artist," Alec said, finally turning his attention to Peyton. "How long have you been painting?"

Peyton ignored him; she was looking away, pretending to study the tapestry on the wall and Alec moved toward her.

"My lady? I asked you how long you have been painting?"

Slowly, and with great contempt, Peyton focused on the two of them. There was no mistaking the hostility. "Are you addressing me, my lord? Forgive me for ignoring you, but I thought you were speaking to your sister. Still."

He gazed at her, seeing that battle lines were drawn again and having no idea why. "I was speaking to you."

Peyton cocked an eyebrow, shooting Thia a most baleful glance before responding to Alec. "Then I shall answer you. I have been painting since I was old enough to hold a brush."

Thia bristled at the open animosity. "Are you going to allow her to speak to you in such a manner?"

Alec would not be pulled into a confrontation and his expression remained calm as he turned to his sister. "What manner? She simply answered my question."

Thia's mouth opened in outrage. "Surely you are not that blind, Alec. 'Twould seem that your betrothed is somewhat of a disrespectful shrew. And you say you agreed to this arrangement?"

Peyton refused to be intimidated or insulted by Alec's sister. She fixed her with a pointed look. "I would rather be a shrew than an ox. And furthermore, at least your brother has found a mate. I doubt the same can be said for you unless, of course, your father intends to raid the barnyards for a suitable consort."

Alec's eyes widened at the insult and he choked off a loud guffaw, coming out as a harsh series of coughs. Instead of being angry, he found he was actually proud of Peyton for refusing to allow Thia to belittle her. His sister could be a sweet woman with a heart of gold, but she had a sharp tongue and a bullying manner. He was immensely pleased to see that Peyton would not allow his sister to demean her and he stepped back, carefully observing the unfolding battle.

Thia's eyes narrowed, surprised that the petite, fragile-looking lady was bold enough to return the insult. But Lady Peyton's moxy only served to fuel her anger.

"You are an ill-bred little wench. How unfortunate that the Summerlins are to be saddled with your sickening presence," she shook her head at Alec regretfully. "My sympathies, Alec. I sincerely hope St. Cloven is worth the asking price."

Peyton stood up; she did not want Alec forced into taking sides, for he would undoubted ally with his sister and she did not need any more reason to loathe him. Instead of losing her control and raging at Thia as she did with Ivy, she smiled thinly.

"At least I have something attractive to offer a prospective husband, my lady," she said. "I doubt the crown jewels would serve as enough bribery in your case. But try not to let your bitterness show; mayhap a blind man shall happen across your path someday who will be impervious to your appearance. One can always hope."

Thia glared at her, seeing that Lady Peyton was able to match her insult for insult. Acid-tongued chit. Since her own venomous mouth was unsuccessful in humiliating Lady Peyton, she resorted to the next weapon in her arsenal. Her size.

"Do not make light of my appearance, my lady. What I lack in physical beauty I make up for in power. Any man at Blackstone can tell you that my strength in nearly equal their own. I would wager to say you would not last long in a challenge."

Peyton couldn't help it; she started to laugh. Loud, bright laughter pealed from her lips and Alec smiled simply because she was so beautiful when she laughed. And he was enjoying himself, too, oddly enough.

"A challenge?" Peyton repeated incredulously. "Surely you jest, Lady Thia. Only men issue challenges and only men fight them. But…. in that case, I suppose it is perfectly natural for you to propose a duel then, isn't it?"

"'Twas no challenge I issued. Call it a promise."

Peyton raised a well-arched brow, not the least bit intimidated. "And I promise you will regret it for, you see, I have a sister a sight larger than you. Were you to do me any harm, she would see to it that it would be your very last transgression. Call *that* a promise."

Thia shrugged. "As you wish."

Peyton regained her seat, still shaking her head with mirth. "I am weary of this conversation. Do you not have lambs to slaughter or peasants to terrorize?"

Alec could see that the next step in their argument would most likely entail a physical brawl. Choosing to intervene, he stepped forward and put his hand on Thia's shoulder. "I am afraid you cannot bully my future wife as you do every other woman. Call a truce and I will hear no more hostile words between the two of you. Understood?"

Thia's small blue eyes gazed at Peyton a moment longer. "Only for you, Alec. But I cannot guarantee future peace."

"I realize that," he said quietly. "Just as there are mere civilities between you and Rachel. It would seem, Moppet, that you are not destined to be chummy with either of your brother's wives."

Thia snorted and looked away. "Rachel is a stupid bitch. And it would seem that at least one of those terms describes Lady Peyton as well."

Peyton had moved past anger and found a strange sense of satisfaction clashing with Thia. Mayhap in some way she was taking out her anger on the woman's brother. But the fact that Alec had not taken sides made Thia's attitude far easier to deal with, and she was furthermore pleased to demonstrate that she could not be harassed. She smiled genuinely at Thia.

"I will not dispute your opinion. But I would rather be a bitch than a bitter, empty spinster with only brothers for male companionship."

Thia's jaw twitched and Alec stepped in between the two to remind them that he had ordered their insults ended.

"Enough, both of you. If this is to be the extent of conversation between you, then I would prefer that you did not speak to one another at all. I shall not spend the rest of my life pulling my sister and wife apart."

Brian returned to the room then, bearing two dark bottles of wine. His face was flushed with pleasure as he breezed across the room to where several pewter goblets were shelved. "Burgundy!" he announced, handing Alec a bottle to open. "The very finest! I have had it in storage for years simply waiting for the right opportunity to consume it."

Alec drew out the cork and returned the bottle to Brian. As Thia moved to assist her father, Alec moved to Peyton and stood next to her chair. She sat stiffly, as if waiting for the next hostile barrage from the Summerlin sibling. He found himself gazing down at her, studying the myriad of colors in the magnificent red hair and amazed with the perfect beauty of his betrothed. It would seem that every moment, every hour brought about a new discovery, and he was intrigued.

Shortly, the room was filled with people. Olphampa and Sula, Ali and Ivy and Celine arrived in a cozy group and Peyton was amazed to find not one, but three black-skinned people living at Blackstone. Olphampa, a stocky little man nearly half the size of his massive son, seemed to be charming and his slight wife appeared very pleasant. And the two were warmly receptive to Ivy, who seemed to be warming to them in return.

In fact, Ivy seemed far more at ease than Peyton herself and Peyton was envious and baffled with her sister's relaxed mannerisms. She found herself again wondering what Ali had said to Ivy to cause such alleviation, such approval within a woman who not hours earlier had been intent on accusing him of being a beast. The frustration, the pure puzzlement as she watched her only sibling converse with coal-hued people left her virtually speechless.

As Brian was pouring the wine, another pair entered the hall and Peyton turned to them curiously. The man was slight of stature and build, with dark hair and brown eyes. He would have been handsome were it not for the strange expression on his face and his slightly disheveled appearance. The pregnant woman beside him was slight as well, with a plain face and unremarkable brown hair. But she smiled politely at Peyton as Alec introduced the couple as his older brother, Paul, and his wife, Lady Rachel.

Paul moved directly to a corner and stood as if he were being punished. His eyes darted about nervously as his wife retrieved a goblet of wine for him, and he drank deeply before anyone else had even been served. He slurped the drink and wiped his mouth on his sleeve, looking uncertain and tense.

Peyton tore her eyes away from him after a moment. Obviously, there was something terribly wrong with him. Either that, or he was a horribly ill-mannered lout just like his sister. His petite wife stood next to him vigilantly, admonishing him softly as a mother would a child. Puzzled, Peyton tried not to let her confusion show.

The congratulatory toasts went well into the evening. Brian and Alec imbibed a good deal of wine, whereas Olphampa declined all offers and drank fruit juices instead. Paul drank heavily, too, but remained in the corner away from the rest of the group. Ivy and Ali stood with Sula and Celine and chatted amiably, leaving Peyton seated alone.

Yet it was by her own choice; the verbal confrontation with Thia had left her drained and it was all she could do to reply politely when spoken to much less keep up a gay conversation. Thia, still next to the thin windows, drank her wine in moody silence.

Peyton would glance at Alec occasionally, angered that he was not making an attempt to converse with her, yet convincing herself that she was glad he wasn't attempting the venture. She had no desire to speak with him at the moment, but in the recesses of her mind she wanted him to talk to her so that she could show him that she had no interest in addressing him. It was pointless to ignore someone if they weren't striving to capture your attention in the first place.

It was the most peculiar craziness and she knew it, but it did not occur to her that she was wallowing in self-pity because her betrothed, whom she admitted to loathe, was neglecting her.

I am going mad, she told herself calmly. *Alec is driving me insane with his feverish kisses and icy, callous demeanor.* She certainly did not want a cold, bitter man paying attention to her.

…. *did* she?

"You are beautiful," came a soft male voice.

Peyton was jolted from her train of thought and glanced up to see Paul staring down at her. He was perspiring heavily and she instinctively drew back from him.

"I…. thank you, my lord," she replied warily.

He continued to stare at her until she felt terribly uncomfortable. She found herself wishing someone would rush to her aid, for she had no idea how to deal with the man. Peyton rose from her chair to put a safe distance between them, frantically wondering where his watchdog wife had gone to.

"Your hair is so bright," he said gently, reaching out and grasping a strand. "It looks like molten metal. Have you ever seen molten metal when the smiths fire broadswords?"

She was trying to remain calm as he fingered her hair in front of a room full of people who were not paying any attention. The urge to jerk away from him was overpowering.

"I have never seen molten metal," she replied steadily. "Do you like to watch the smith?"

He did not answer, his eyes raking over her body in a most unnerving manner, and Peyton was growing quite apprehensive. There was something about the man that was just not right, something odd, and she took another step back.

Before Paul could reply, Alec was beside Peyton and firmly dislodging her hair from his brother's grasp. When Peyton felt a protective arm go about her waist, she nearly collapsed against him from sheer relief. She hadn't realized how frightened she had been until that very moment.

"You know better than to touch her, Paul," Alec's voice was quiet.

Paul's eyes widened outrageously at the sight of his brother and he suddenly looked ashamed and uncertain. Peyton almost felt sorry for him and winced at Alec's firm, unkind tone.

"Do you understand me?" he asked his brother. "You will never touch Lady Peyton again."

Paul's twitching eyes looked away, anywhere that was safe from his brother's piercing gaze. His nervous hands worked and flitted about the chair, his tunic.

"I.... she is so lovely, Alec," he said softly.

"I know. But she is mine. I forbid you to touch her."

"I.... I apologize," Paul whispered. "I only wanted to touch her hair. Like molten metal, Alec, from the smith's forge. Did you notice?"

"I noticed," Alec replied, his tone less unkind. "Go to Rachel now. 'Tis nearly time for you to retire."

Paul's guarded eyes shifted to Peyton once more before he turned away like a scolded child. Peyton watched him return to his wide-eyed wife, as did everyone else in the room. But they quickly turned back to their conversations, pretending not to have witnessed the exchange.

Alec still clutched Peyton and she was unaware that she was pressed into the curve of his torso comfortably. It was such a completely natural position that she still did not notice their close proximity, even when he gazed down into her sapphire blue eyes.

The blue of the sky bore into her and suddenly, she was only cognizant of his soft expression, his virile masculinity, his presence. To hell with everyone else in the room and her own feelings of hostility; she suddenly found herself wishing he would kiss her again. She wanted it so badly she was nearly quivering.

"He is harmless," he said softly. "But I must establish at the very onset that you are not to be molested."

"Molested?" she repeated with concern. "But you said he is harmless."

"He is, truly. His extent of molesting would probably entail touching your hair or trying to kiss your hand. Anything else is beyond his scope of comprehension."

She gazed back at him a moment. "What's wrong with him? Did he suffer an accident or mishap?"

Alec shook his head. "He was born dull-witted, sweetheart. His mental intelligence is that of a young boy."

"And he is your father's heir? How...," she suddenly stopped, peering at him. "What did you call me?"

"Call you?" he lifted an eyebrow thoughtfully. "Nothing.... oh, do you mean 'sweetheart'? Forgive me, my lady, I forgot myself. You did, after all, ask me not to address you by that name."

She was preparing to sharply agree, but her firm stance suddenly softened and she lowered her gaze. "Aye, I did."

He shifted his grip on her, moving to wrap his other arm about her waist without even realizing it. In front of a room full of people, they were in a closely intimate position. A natural state. "Pray forgive me, my lady. I simply could not help myself," he grinned.

She tried to maintain her unbending manner. She had asked him not to call her sweetheart for good reason; James had called her by the term. To hear it brought a myriad of aching memories; yet, somehow, hearing it from Alec's lips seemed the most natural of things. She realized she wanted him to use the expression often.

She smiled weakly at his warm expression. "I suppose using my proper name all the time does seem rather formal."

He smile broadened. "May I then call you sweetheart? Or any other term of endearment that comes to mind? Or, should the situation dictate, mayhap an expression of insult in self-defense?"

She tried not to smile at his gentle taunts, but it was difficult. Instead, she lifted her eyebrows haughtily. "I shall consider your requests, both of them. But until I can make my decision, I will expect to be addressed as Lady Summerlin."

"I am to address my own wife as Lady Summerlin?" he repeated with a mock frown. "Very well. You must call me Sir Alec. Or My Lord Darling. Or My Most Auspicious Sweetling."

The tone of the conversation had become light and enjoyable and Peyton completely forgot about the events during the day that had brought her to the unalterable conclusion that she hated him. When he gazed upon her as he was now, she was oblivious to everything but the heat on her cheeks and the expression on his face.

"As you say," she shrugged. "At least you have not demanded that I prostrate myself in your presence."

"Ah, but I shall," he raised an arrogant eyebrow.

She matched his arrogance with a smile. "And I shall refuse, my lord."

His grip on her waist tightened as he frowned disapprovingly. "You are an entirely disagreeable wench."

She opened her mouth to reply when Brian suddenly intervened. Peyton realized Alec had been holding her tightly only when his massive arms were removed. She missed him already.

"Not here," Brian admonished laughingly. "Can you not wait until the nuptials? I may have a grandson sooner than I hoped if your attentions toward each other are any indication of marital appetites."

Peyton flushed furiously and lowered her gaze, embarrassed at Brian's words and her own actions. Being enveloped in Alec's arms was so natural that she hadn't given it a thought. As Alec and his father chuckled over something Peyton did not quite hear, Ivy appeared at her sister's side to divert her attention.

"Ali is taking me for a walk about the compound," she said. "Why don't you and Alec join us?"

"A walk?" Peyton repeated, embarrassment forgotten as she focused on her sister. Passing a glance at Brian and Alec as they huddled in private conversation, she grasped Ivy by the arm and escorted her into their own secluded huddle. Her manner was harsh as her chaotic thoughts demanded to be voiced; thoughts that had simmered in her mind for the length of the day. Now was the time to be heard.

"Good Lord, Ivy, you were ready to kill him earlier this day, and now you are allowing him to escort you on a walk without so much as a protest?"

Ivy's cheeks mottled a faint red. How could she explain her feelings to Peyton when she herself did not fully understand? After a moment, she looked away uncomfortably. "We had a long conversation and I came to understand him somewhat. He.... He is very kind, Peyton, intelligent and considerate."

"But he is black, for God's sake!" Peyton hissed, making a valiant attempt to keep from being heard. "He is not like us. What did he say to convince you to accept him as easily as you have?"

The red in Ivy's cheeks deepened. "I never said that I have accepted him. I have simply come to see things a bit more clearly, that's all. I am coming to tolerate his company."

Peyton shook her head in frustration. "You are acting like a fool. He is a lesser being, entitled to no more consideration or acceptance than those whom God has seen fit to create less fortunate than ourselves. He is not the equal you are suggesting."

Ivy's jaw quivered faintly. "He is a wise, chivalrous man and I shall not allow you to say such terrible things against him."

Peyton stared at her sister, sensing the hostility and the confusion, but quite consumed with her own feelings of resentment and bafflement. She simply couldn't deal rationally with Ivy at the moment and her demeanor hardened. "You are not going for a walk with him. After politely excusing ourselves, we will be retreating to our bedchamber. Alone."

Ivy's jaw ticked stubbornly. "I am going for a walk first. With Ali."

Peyton gazed at her sister as if the woman had lost her mind. "You have indeed accepted him, then. Listen to yourself, Ivy. You might not have admitted your approval in words, but undoubtedly in action. How could you do this? He is not like us, darling, not at all. He…. he is a beast."

Ivy's face went from a dull red to a sickly white. "If you refer to him in that term again, I shall kill you. I swear it, Peyton, with every breath in my body. He is nothing of the kind."

Peyton was struck by Ivy's defense of the man. She'd never seen her sister look so absolutely serious. Ivy's sincerity unearthed a chord of remorse for referring to Ali in a derogatory term. When Ivy had referred to him in the same manner, Peyton had been deeply embarrassed. Now, out of frustration and fear, she had done the very same thing and she was appalled at her hypocrisy.

But her stubborn nature prevented her from apologizing. She sighed heavily, unable to match her sister's intense gaze. "Mayhap I simply do not know you as I thought I did, Ivy."

Ivy mulled over the muttered words, sensing the confusion within them. Since her private conversation with Ali and the journey to Blackstone, her confusion towards the dark soldier was fading and she wished she could tell her sister the fear, the excitement, the wonder she was experiencing. But gazing into Peyton's sapphire orbs, she could see that now was not the time.

When Ivy spoke, it was in a hushed whisper. "Nay, darling, I do not suppose you do."

Stung and disoriented, Peyton turned away and moved to the windows at the opposite end of the room. The pleasant July evening filled the air, the scents of blossoms and the smell of hay wafting on the breeze as she tried to orient herself after a shocking conversation. A situation that had been unpleasant from the onset had suddenly become worse, and she had no concept of where it would end. Her future, her life, was careening out of control and there was no way to stop it.

She did not realize she was wiping at her eyes as she stood by the window deep in thought. She wanted to return home, tired of the disorientation she was feeling. But she was resigned to remaining at Blackstone, in a keep full of strangers, including her sister.

"Are you feeling poorly, dear?" Lady Celine was beside her, her lovely face concerned. "It has been a trying day. Mayhap you should retire early."

She straightened respectfully as Alec's mother addressed her. Thinking on the woman's perceptive statement, she realized her head was aching and her stomach hurt terribly. The thought of a soft, cool bed sounded wonderful.

"I haven't slept since yesterday, my lady," she replied softly. In spite of Lady Celine's somewhat harsh personality, Peyton could honestly admit that she found the woman comforting. Having never truly known a mother's love, she found it very easy to succumb to Celine's motherly attentions.

"Poor dear," Celine's arm went about her shoulders and she turned to her husband. "My lord, Lady Peyton is most fatigued. She shall retire for the evening, with your permission."

Brian and Alec, standing together in conversation, looked at Peyton closely and Brian nodded firmly. "Absolutely," he said. "Good eve to you, my lady. And welcome to our family."

"Thank you, my lord," she said softly, feeling her exhaustion a good deal more with Lady Celine's consoling manner. The more the woman hugged and patted, the more Peyton's strength waned. Eyeing Ivy across the room, she knew that Lady Celine was her only friend in the world. Selfish pity bloomed.

"I shall take her, mother," Alec said quietly, setting his chalice to the table.

"You will not," Lady Celine rejected her son's offer. "I am quite capable of caring for your betrothed. You may stay and enjoy your wine."

Peyton could see by Alec's expression that he was reluctant to do as he was told, but he obediently offered his future wife a good night and lifted her white hand to his lips for a chaste kiss. Peyton felt the kiss like a scalding iron, matching the look in his eyes. Her cheeks flushing a dull red, she lowered her gaze and allowed Lady Celine to lead her from the room.

☙

AFTER PEYTON HAD retired for the evening, Ali excused he and Ivy from Brian's gathering. He had promised the lady a leisurely stroll about the grounds, and stroll they would. As they were becoming increasingly comfortable with one another, he was desperate to know her further.

Ivy was silent and distracted as he led her out into the moonlit July eve, gazing up at the brilliant display in the heavens. He was acutely aware of Ivy's soft footfalls beside him, crunching softly against the hard-packed earth of the bailey.

"I cannot remember such a beautiful night," Ali said softly, making idle conversation as he glanced at her lowered head.

Ivy's blue eyes turned upward, staring at the diamond sky above. "One can see the North Star most clearly."

He nodded, still studying the sky. After a moment, he sighed. "I find it fascinating to imagine that the great masters, Socrates, Homer, Euclid and the like, have seen the same stars as I have. They have gazed upon the same moon, or been burnt by the same sun. An engrossing concept, really."

He cast Ivy another sidelong glance and was surprised to find her focused on him. He smiled faintly, moving beyond the trivial discourse he was attempting. "What is it, demoiselle? You seem distant."

She held his gaze a moment. Then she looked away. "'Tis nothing," she said softly.

He stopped; so did she. Raising a black eyebrow, he clasped his hands behind his back. "Nothing indeed. You have been unusually quiet. Is there something the matter?"

"No, truly," she repeated, but there was uncertainty in her eyes. She was confused and he knew it.

"You are looking at me strangely," he said.

"Was I? I did not mean to."

He took a step closer, towering over her. "Aye, lady, you did. You are still uncertain of me, are you not?"

Her smile faded, her cheeks flushing as she gazed up at him; smooth, brown, beautiful. "I…. I never said that," she stammered.

"You did not have to. I can read it in your eyes."

"I am thinking nothing of the sort," she said quickly, hoarsely. "I was merely…. thinking."

"About what?"

She paused a moment. As with her other bold qualities, she had never been lacking in the trait of honesty. Gazing into his eyes, she felt compelled to answer his question. "You."

His eyebrows flickered slightly, a faint smile creasing his lips. "I would have never guessed. What, may I ask, are you thinking?"

She cocked her head thoughtfully, her gaze trailing down his armor. "I am thinking that you confuse me."

"And you confuse me."

Her eyebrows rose with surprise. "I do? How?"

He did not say anything for a moment. Then, slowly, a mailed hand came up to gently grasp a blond tendril. Ivy froze, feeling the heat from his flesh through the steel gauntlet as if it were searing her tender skin.

"Because you are the only woman I have met that seems to be willing to make an attempt to know me before passing judgment," his onyx eyes were soft. "Have you decided whether or not to damn me?"

She cocked an eyebrow, slowly. She had been pondering that very dilemma since their introduction. "And if I do not?"

The corner of his mouth twitched as he continued to rub the silken strands of hair between his fingers. "Then you would be the first. And I find that confusing."

"Why?"

He chuckled softly. "Because I have grown accustomed to rejection, I suppose. I would not have the first idea how to handle feminine acceptance."

Ivy gazed at him, uncertainty in her eyes. "No woman has ever accepted you as you are? Not one?"

He shook his head, the brilliant stars reflecting in his raven-colored eyes. "Look into your heart and answer you own question, demoiselle. Not even you have accepted me as such, and your reaction to my color has been considerably mild in comparison to some."

Ivy swallowed, feeling ashamed as well as confused. "I.... I believe I must grow accustomed to your color before I can truly accept you as my betrothed," she met his gaze again, her brow furrowing in thought. "Truthfully, how can you resent women for being shocked with your appearance? Certainly, there are very few English women who have seen a man of color before."

His smile faded. "I resent those who overlook the soul of a man simply because he is different."

She did not say anything for a moment, pondering his words. "Your bitterness is causing you prejudice against the entire English race as the result of a few who have judged you on the basis of your skin."

He stared at her a moment, seeing a seed of truth in her words.

Sound, intelligent words from woman who was beginning to understand him just the slightest. "Mayhap I do indeed harbor more than my share of bitterness. But more than a few have judged me by my color," his voice was faint. "I am only human, demoiselle. Bitterness is a negative quality of the human character."

She continued to gaze at him, a lengthy, thoughtful pause. "So is stupefaction."

He cocked an eyebrow. "And you refer to me?"

Looking deep into his black eyes, she could feel all doubt, all reserve fading. Never had she met with such honesty, such aching desperation for acceptance. Before her was a man of uncommon patience and grace, of uncanny emotion and wisdom. In the short time she had come to know him, it was the most obvious of his qualities. More obvious than his dark skin. The fog was lifting in Ivy's mind and the truth was as bright as the sun.

"Nay," she whispered. "I was referring to me."

She stopped fighting herself, giving in to the acceptance, the approval that had been struggling to break forth. For once in her life, her stubborn nature was conquered by her inner convictions. Ivy de Fluornoy was finally growing up.

His brown lips, smooth and glossy, drew her open stare. She found herself wondering what they would feel like, mingled with her own pink. As quaking heat flooded her limbs, she was unaware when the odd weakness caused her to sway in his direction.

Ali was aware indeed; had he not reached out to grasp her, she would have pitched forward. His mailed gloves bit into her arms, holding her steady, noting the heated expression with disbelief. Had he not known better, he would have thought she was intending to seduce him.

"You truly do not know how to handle feminine acceptance?" Ivy heard her own breathy voice, aware she wanted him to kiss her in the very worst way.

Ali's breathing tightened, a peculiar tingling sensation filling his big body. The hands that steadied her suddenly came alive, caressing her arms tenderly before pulling her into a crushing embrace. Enveloped by the shadows of the massive fortress, they were shielded from the sentries on the battlements and quite alone.

Onyx orbs locked with those of pure blue. Ivy gazed up into his magnificent face, so consumed with his alien beauty that she was nearly possessed by it. All that seemed to matter was that he was more man than she would ever need.

"Demoiselle," his voice was raspy, tight. "Would you allow me to kiss you?"

She swallowed, licking her lips to alleviate the odd dryness that plagued them. "You would kiss a woman who confuses you?"

He watched her pink tongue moisten her soft, sensuous lips and he resisted the urge to sink his teeth into the fleshy morsel. Every moment that he held her, every second that he delayed, his control slipped further. He did not want to frighten her with an aggressive move, not when he was so desperate to gain her trust. But when a faint smile danced across her quivering lips, his composure crumbled into dust.

"Aye, demoiselle, I would."

CHAPTER SIX

PEYTON AWOKE TO a dark room and an empty bed. Groggily, she rolled about in search of Ivy, but her sister was nowhere to be found. Puzzled and concerned, she crawled from the great bed and moved to the window, gazing sleepily over the bailey.

The courtyard was completely silent. A handful of soldiers stood watch on the battlements and the moon was gone from the sky, indicative of the late hour. Scratching her head, Peyton turned away from the window and focused on her aunt. Wide-eyed and hypnotized, Jubil never slept while entranced.

She hadn't seen her aunt in nearly two days and was not surprised to realize that the woman probably hadn't moved a muscle during that time. Jubil sat where they had left her, beside the lancet windows in a mindless fog. She and Ivy had briefly entertained the idea of taking Jubil with them when they had fled the previous evening, but their aunt was in no condition to make an escape. Leaving the older woman to the graciousness of their liege had been a difficult decision, but a necessary one in their opinion.

"Where's Ivy?" she asked as if Jubil could gaze into the mystic vapors and locate her errant sister.

Jubil did not reply and Peyton ran her fingers through her mussed hair irritably. The potions Jubil ingested usually wore off in two or three days, but her aunt was still exhibiting signs of full entrancement.

Different potions caused her to display various characteristics, like continuous laughter or catatonic states. Jubil was still flying high with this most recent concoction and Peyton was losing her patience.

"Jubil, what did you take this time?" she leaned down and shook her aunt gently. "Jubil, do you comprehend me?"

"Thorn apples," came a faint whisper.

Peyton studied her aunt a moment with grim resignation. Jubil was highly sensitive to thorn apples and she believed them to be the most powerful of her potions, allowing her days of visions and flight. Peyton reconciled herself to the fact that Jubil would maintain her irrational state for several more days at the very least.

Unable to enlist her aunt's help in locating Ivy, Peyton retrieved her brocade robe from the large oak wardrobe and wrapped it tightly about her slim body. As she was moving for the door, Jubil suddenly called out to her.

"You do not like him, do you?" she said.

Peyton gazed at her aunt a moment, suspecting to whom she was referring but unwilling to play the game. "Who, Jubil? I have no time for your gibberish."

"Alec, sweetheart," Jubil said in a weak voice. "He is not your James and you do not like him."

Peyton felt herself being teetered off balance by Jubil's perception, but she still refused to play the game. She had no desire to discuss her emotions with a madwoman.

"Go back to sleep. I shall return when I have found Ivy."

"The sorcerer's violet shall help your indecision, sweetheart. Have no fear that soon you shall love Alec more than you ever loved James."

"I do not want to love him!" Peyton suddenly exploded, rushing to her aunt and turning her violently, face to face. Jubil's eyes were glazed and fearful as she looked into Peyton's angry features. "Do you hear me, Jubil? No love potions or spells. No sorcerer's violet brews, or poppy love potions, or distilled rose elixirs. I do not want your help with Alec!"

"He is a great man, Peyton," Jubil stuttered. "I have seen him with his sword in hand. I have seen Lancelot and Galahad and Cuchulain bow at his feet and beg to kiss the soles of his shoes. Queen Maeve begs for his seed to bear a son worthy to protect the throne of Ireland."

Peyton reeled away from the woman, disgusted and furious. "Queen Maeve is a Celt legend, Jubil. If she existed at all it was centuries ago, as did the rest of your dream warriors. Alec is a man, like any other, and I am tired of your prattle about his greatness. I will hear no more!"

Jubil, limp in her chair after Peyton's rough shake, averted her gaze and focused on the wall once again. "You underestimate him, sweetheart. He is the greatest swordsman England has ever seen and you have been given a great mission in life. No woman can ask for more than to be the wife of a magnificent warrior and perpetuate his blood."

Peyton stared at her aunt, wondering how in the world Jubil knew that she and Alec were to marry. Someone must have told her, of course, but she couldn't help the creeping uneasiness at Jubil's words.

"No more," she said hoarsely, stumbling toward the door. "Another word and I shall cut your tongue out."

But Jubil did not heed her words; she simply stared at her niece with a blank expression. Peyton was almost through the door when she heard her aunt's voice again, soft and hoarse. "You have met the woman with a taste for female flesh, have you not?"

Peyton almost ignored her. Shaken and angry, she found herself pausing at the bizarre, unrelated statement. "Of whom do you speak? Your potion is making you insane, Jubil."

Jubil merely blinked, her blue eyes gazing at Peyton but not truly seeing her. "The unhappy one. She is afraid of you."

Peyton stared at her aunt a moment longer before letting out a hiss of exasperation; she had no time for such nonsense and moved to shut the door. As the door was nearly closed, she heard Jubil's final utterance.

"Alec's sister, sweetheart. She is afraid of you."

The door shut softly and still Jubil sat, staring at the wall. Her eyes were dull and unfocused, but her mind was soaring above the clouds, unaware that her niece had vacated the room. Unaware that Peyton had indeed heard the hushed whispers of a madwoman.

UNNERVED BY JUBIL'S muttering, Peyton fought to control her jitters and her anger as she went in search of her sister. She had no idea where to begin, truthfully, but it seemed most logical to begin in the solar where she had last seen her. The corridor and the stairs were void of servants as she made her way to Brian's well-appointed room.

It was empty, as she knew it would be, but she felt a distinct sense of despair nonetheless. With a weary sigh, she moved to the great desk that contained Brian's belongings and gazed absently at the papers and signet stamps. Her mind was exhausted and her head was still aching and, somberly, she deposited herself onto Baron Rothwell's great hide-covered chair.

Ivy was with Ali, she had no doubt. It did not matter that Ivy had been defiant upon initially meeting her intended, fighting and cursing him every step of the way. That brief show of opposition had been the only sign of rejection Ivy would offer in her own defense; since the moment Ali had taken her away to converse in private, it was as if Ivy had been transformed.

Ivy had told her that she had not yet come to accept him as a true man, or as her betrothed, merely acknowledging that she was coming to tolerate his company. To Peyton, it appeared to be a far sight more than mere tolerance. It seemed to be infatuation.

Unfortunately, Peyton was still too wrapped up in her own confusion and depression to be able to spare her sister some much needed understanding. What she truly needed was her sister's calm wisdom telling her that she was doing the right thing by marrying Alec Summerlin, but it was apparent Ivy cared for no one but herself.

Peyton thought about Ali for a moment, coming to the realization that her frustration wasn't based on the fact that she found Ali repulsive or bestial; on the contrary, she was becoming rather curious about him in an odd sort of way. It occurred to her that she resented the fact that Ali seemed to be diverting Ivy's attention when Peyton was in need of her. That, she discovered, was the foundation of her resistance. He was taking Ivy away from her.

Ivy was all she had in the world. With their father gone, there was no one left to console and support her, and hot, tired tears welled in Peyton's sapphire eyes. She let them fall, feeling them bathe her cheeks in comforting warmth. It felt good to cry, to cleanse her puzzled soul, and the tears fell freely onto the tempting swell of her breasts. She was completely miserable.

Alec was strolling past the solar at that moment when he caught a snippet of a sob. On his way to bed after a long conversation with his father, he ignored the noise and continued onward until something inexplicably made him stop.

He had no idea why he should concern himself over a sniffle, but a peculiar hunch forced him to turn around and peer into the solar. His sky blue eyes passed over the empty room and he nearly turned away until his sights came to rest on the top of a red head of unkempt curls. Half-shielded by the high back of the chair, he heard Peyton sob again.

"Peyton?" he asked softly, stepping into the room. "What's wrong, sweetheart?"

Startled, she wiped hastily at her cheeks as he approached. His concerned gaze left her stammering for a convincing answer. "N-nothing, my lord," she hiccupped. "My head hurts s-still and I was walking a-and the ache has not gone away."

He did not believe her for a moment. The woman who met him in a physical confrontation and matched verbal daggers with his sister suddenly looked extremely fragile seated in his father's great chair. Her cheeks were damp and there were even tears on the luscious white rise of her beautiful breasts.

He stood over her, hands on his hips. "Pauly can give you something for the ache. It must hurt terribly if you are crying so."

She nodded, afraid to answer because her lower lip was quivering; once she started crying, she could easily slide into a jag and carry on for hours. She was fearful that she would turn into a blathering fool if she tried to speak and hoped he would simply leave after receiving a satisfactory answer. Instead, he knelt before her and put his great hands on the arms of the chair, trapping her.

"Is that the true reason why you are crying? Or has something else upset you? Must I run a knave through for distressing you this night?"

She shook her head, wiping at the tears that refused to stop falling. It occurred to her that they might be here all night if she refused to answer him, and it furthermore occurred to her that he might know where Ivy had gone. There was one way to find out.

"D-do you know where Ivy is?" she sniffled.

He smiled faintly, the soft glow from the hearth caressing his masculine features. "Of course. She is with Ali and his parents. Is that what has you terribly upset? Then put your mind to rest and know that she is properly escorted and in no danger whatsoever."

She took a ragged, deep breath and met his gaze for the first time. Another tear fell and before she could dash it, Alec reached out a thick finger and flicked it away. His gaze was terribly tender on her, his smile gentle, and she felt herself being drawn into his trap.

He was cold and insensitive, she reminded herself quickly. Remember his rebuff, his stinging indifference. Remember before you forget everything and allow yourself to believe him to be tender! And for God's sake, remember James!

"Th-thank you," she struggled to regain her composure as she tore her eyes away. "I-I can return to bed now, knowing she is safe."

But he wasn't moving and she was still trapped on the chair. When she dared to look at his face again, his expression was still soft.

"May I tell you something?" he asked.

Since he wasn't moving, she made sure she was pressed flush against the back of the chair, far away from him. She hoped it was far enough. "What?"

He opened his mouth to speak, but suddenly closed it again. With an embarrassed little chuckle, he averted his gaze and stood up. "I was going to say that…. well, 'tis not important. Would you allow me to escort you back to your room, my lady?"

She should not have wondered, but she was curious with his sheepish manner. He almost seemed ashamed of what he was about to say and caught himself before he could humiliate himself further. The focus of the conversation shifted as Peyton dried her tears.

"I told you this morning that I would demand one thing from you in this marriage, Alec. Honesty," her voice was steady now. "What is it that you were going to say?"

He looked down at her, finally snatching a stool by the hearth and seating himself next to her chair. His pure blue eyes watched the dying embers thoughtfully. After a moment, he sighed.

"I was going to say that I was proud of the way you handled my sister," he said softly. "To see you at this moment appearing so vulnerable and delicate, I have difficulty believing you and the woman who matched vicious barbs with Thia are one in the same."

She was genuinely surprised. "You are proud of me?"

He nodded, his gaze finding her. "There is a fire to your spirit. I think I shall enjoy our marriage, my lady. At least I hope so."

She could see that he was absolutely sincere and she believed him. Her chest tightened strangely and her limbs began to tingle as he continued to gaze at her with his magnificent blue eyes. It was the same quivering feeling she'd experienced earlier when he had kissed her and she suddenly found herself wishing he would kiss her again.

The defenses that she tried so desperate to instill in herself were crumbling like rotted wood; she wasn't nearly as strong as she hoped. But in one last attempt to prove her strength, she forced herself to divert the subject. Any more talk of marriage would have them doing things that were morally allowed only within the bounds of matrimony. She could see it in his eyes and she would be powerless to stop him.

"Will…. will Ali and Ivy live with us at St. Cloven?" she managed to choke out.

"Of course," Alec replied softly. "Ali has some fine ideas as to additions and improvements. I think we will build him and Ivy their own wing for their family," he gaze lingered, studying her face. "You seem to have accepted his betrothal to your sister easily enough."

She shrugged, attempting to distract herself from the heat his gaze provoked. "'Twas never my decision to accept or reject. I am simply resigned to deal with the situation, as my sister is."

He was silent a moment. "'Twas a wise choice on her part. Does this upset you that she seems to have approved Ali?"

"Nay," she said quickly; too quickly. She could sense his questioning gaze and her head throbbed harder. She did not want to talk any more on a subject that was causing her a great deal of frustration. "My head is aching terribly. I would retire now."

He did not answer and she raised her eyes to look at him. Suddenly, he was much closer than she remembered and moving closer. She opened her mouth to protest, but his big body was abruptly upon her and she heard the stool topple.

Her protests died in her throat; his arms were wrapping about her torso and her own arms were winding about his neck as the same giddy feelings she had experienced with their first encounter returned tenfold. The kiss was hot, sultry and erotic; their tongues danced the sensual rhythm of discovering passion and Peyton heard Alec's low moan of desire. It sent a bolt of excitement through her and she tightened her grip on his neck, soft whimpers coming from her own throat.

He left her mouth quickly and trailed to her neck, moving much faster than he had earlier in the day. It was as if he intended to resume where they had left off, when he was about to tread virgin territory and touch her where no man, not even James, had ventured. Peyton knew she should stop him, but she couldn't seem to find the strength. She wanted him to touch her, to explore her sensual curves.

"My God, Alec," she breathed into the top of his cropped blond hair, her hands gripping his head.

He responded by yanking the edges of her robe apart, revealing the web-thin shift. Peyton thought the garment might slow his pursuit, but she was wrong. His massive hands gripped the material and ripped it in half in one clean motion.

She was wide open, her most private areas revealed to a man who confused her desperately. Alec's breath came in ragged gasps as he ran a finger along the crests of her breasts, observing their flawlessness as his gaze locked onto the triangle of golden-red curls between her legs. Peyton shuddered violently against his touch.

"Christ, Peyton," he whispered raggedly. "You are so perfect. So…. beautiful."

He dipped his head and began to kiss the swell of her round, firm breasts as she bit off a rattling moan. His huge hands gently traced underneath the swell of the globes, moving to grasp her slim waist and completely encircling her torso as his mouth worked lower and lower, feasting.

Peyton was nearly incoherent, knowing he was moving for the brazenly taunting nipples and not wanting to wait any longer to experience the pleasure. He was torturing her with his leisurely pace and she refused to endure the anguish; turning her body slightly, a tender morsel of nipple slipped easily into the glove of his mouth.

Alec clamped down and she let out a loud gasp of ecstasy. It was better than she imagined, more wonderful than she could have hoped for. His hot mouth suckled hard and Peyton bit her lip to keep from screaming. Her whole body was a quivering, hot mass and she felt as if every bone had left her. Her hands cradled his great head firmly, forcing him against her nipple as if she were nursing a starving child. Alec suckled her until she was raw with ache, but still she gasped for more.

She was unaware of the tears of pleasure that were filling her eyes, dampening her cheeks as he moved from one breast to the other with great desire. His huge hands were clutching her torso, his fingers digging into the soft white of her flesh as his mouth ravished her thoroughly. His lust was running rampant and his hands left her waist, fondling the creamy globes with tender power as his lips left her nipples and forged a hot trail down the division between her ribs.

She groaned softly as he reached her soft abdomen and he felt a violent surge of passion surge though his body; he suddenly bit down and suckled her sweet skin so forcefully that a purple love bite appeared immediately. Peyton's only response to the erotic mark was a low growl.

Alec was possessed; he'd never lost control in his life and he was shocked to realize that he had done precisely that. He hadn't meant for their encounter to go this far, having truly only intended to taste her again as he had this morning, but the moment his tongue met with her honeyed flesh he was spiraling out of control and he did not care. Not only was he experiencing the fire again, he was a roaring inferno. He'd never had a woman who inflamed him as Peyton did.

In fact, he'd never had a woman before. Period.

Aye, he'd tasted the exotic flesh of the Holy Land just as he had sampled the wares of his native England. But he'd never lain with a woman simply because he had never possessed the complete desire to bed any one particular woman and, mostly, he'd submitted to their hot mouths purely to satisfy his own selfish lust.

Completely self-centered, he had demanded the women service him. And they had, willingly; the result being that Alec had probably lived through more sexual experiences than any man alive; technically, however, he'd never experienced intercourse. His pleasure had come upon the bed of the female tongue.

But he realized as he feasted on Peyton's flesh the most prevalent reason he had never lain with a woman was because he had never found one that tempted him beyond reason. Until now. He did not want Peyton to service him; he wanted to service her and gorge himself doing so. For the first time in his life, he wasn't concerned with his own relief.

He had found the woman he would marry, the only woman worthy of his bed, and he would have her. His massive, heavy organ was straining against his hose uncomfortably and to make matters worse, Peyton had unknowing wrapped her legs about his body as he ravished her in the chair. Her body was responding to him wildly, without reserve, and he suddenly lifted her out of the chair and laid her on the Saracen rug in front of his father's desk.

"Alec!" she gasped, attempting to regain her senses from the throes of passion. "What are you doing?"

He grinned seductively. "What does it appear, my lady? The chair is most restrictive for our needs."

Peyton did not wish to forfeit her virginity on the scratchy bed of a woolen rug and remembered well the time when James had tried to do just that. But if Alec tried to kiss her again, she was lost. The man had power over her that James never had; it had always been exceedingly easy to control James, to manipulate him, and she had taken great pleasure with the control she exerted over him. With Alec, it seemed as if the tables were turned and she was mindless, willing to do anything he asked. But with James….

James.

Guilt swept her. How could she allow herself to respond to Alec so freely, so wantonly, when she still loved James? She was betraying their love in the deepest sense by reacting to the passions of another man. Alec knew too well that he could incite her into a frenzy with his passionate touch and blazing mouth, and she was suddenly angry with him. How dare he force her to submit, to forget her loyalties!

But she knew as she gazed at him that he was to be her legal husband. James was gone, dead for nearly a year, and there was nothing she could do to alter the course her future had decided to take. Yet, a fighting spirit deep inside her could not give in. Not yet.

"You will not have me on the floor, Alec," she said firmly, rolling away from him and rising to her knees.

He was lying on his side, gazing up at her. "I…. I apologize, then. My bedchamber is at the top of the stairs."

She shook her head, her red hair wild and untamed and completely charming. Primly, she closed her robe from his scalding eyes. "I think it best if I return to my bedchamber, alone."

He reached out and gently grasped her arm. "What have I done? If I have done something, then…."

"You haven't done anything," she assured him, rising to stand. "'Tis just that my head aches terribly and I want to sleep."

"I see," he said softly, but she could hear the disappointment in his tone. "I am sorry to have forced myself upon you when you are not feeling well. Would you allow me to escort you to your room, then?"

She almost refused, but his beautiful blue eyes were looking at her earnestly and she felt herself relenting. "Aye."

He rose swiftly, entirely too swiftly for a man his size. He startled her with his rapid movements and she took a step back from the huge body that was suddenly standing in front of her. He smiled down at her and protectively pulled the top of her robe together, covering her white chest completely.

"I am sorry I tore your shift," he said softly. "I…. well, I sort of lost myself…."

She put up a hand to silence him. "I let you. I should not have, but I did, so there is no one to blame. Jubil will fix it."

"Jubil?" he looked puzzled. "Of course, your aunt. I understand she has been in some sort of fit since her arrival."

Peyton gave him an embarrassed look and was about to provide him with an evasive reply, but she reconsidered her strategy. He was, after all, the next lord of St. Cloven and would find out about Jubil's peculiarities soon enough. Better to forewarn him.

"She has not been in a fit. She has been…. having visions."

"Visions? What sort of visions?"

Peyton sighed sheepishly. "Jubil believes herself to be a witch. She divines fortunes and foretells the future. Sometimes, anyway, depending on what potion she ingests. More often than not, however, the concoctions simply make her crazy."

He grinned faintly. "A crazy witch, did you say? What an interesting family I am marrying into."

She raised a droll eyebrow. "As if your family is any less peculiar. A belligerent sister you call Moppet, an older brother who is most strange, and a father who thinks I taste nice. Really, Alec, how can you accuse my family of being odd?"

"I never said odd, I said interesting," he corrected her, taking her arm as they moved from the room. "And my father isn't the only one who thinks you taste nice."

She blushed to the roots of her hair and he laughed a soft, throaty rumble. "Your innocence is charming, for such a firebrand."

She gasped in outrage, slapping his arm feebly. "Not another word, Alec."

He snickered, enjoying her embarrassment. "Why not? Your response pleases me more than you can know. We will do well together, you and I."

She did not want them to do well together. She wanted to continue to keep him at a distance, his wife in name only and in body only. She did not want him to become a part of her mind, as well. James had become an integral part of her soul and his death had caused her nothing but torture.

He sensed her brooding silence as he led her to the stairs. "Now why so quiet? You do not want us to do well together?"

"Nay," she said before she could stop herself. "What I mean is…."

Alec froze at the base of the stairs, the warmth gone from his expression. "Do you truly intend to hate me for the duration of our married life, Peyton? I do not want you to hate me."

Her eyes were laced with uncertainty. She did not want to hate him either, but he was cold and…. certainly, he was not cold now, but it was all a grand performance to force her to relax her guard.

…. wasn't it?

Gently, she pulled her hand from the crook of his arm and felt the sting of puzzled tears tweaking her eyes. "I cannot love you, if that is what you want."

"I do not care if you love me or not. I simply do not want to spend the rest of my life with a woman who loathes me."

Peyton gazed at him a moment, swallowing the tears, the confusion. She had been very clear that honesty was to be the cornerstone of their marriage and she suddenly felt the urge to tell him everything that had been making her insane with frustration. Gazing into his sky blue eyes, she knew that the time had come.

"I would be truthful with you, Alec," she said quietly. "The only time you are pleasant with me is when I yield to your passion. The rest of the time, we are usually arguing or fighting over something. Your cold demeanor confuses me greatly. If I told you I hated you, it was because you frustrated me terribly. I simply do not know what to think of you at times."

He was still expressionless, but the tone of his voice changed dramatically. It was soft, almost pleading. "You think me cold? What have I done to convey this to you?"

Peyton lowered her gaze. By his tone, she understood that he was truly perplexed with her assessment and she thought a moment on her reply. She had come this far in her admission and it was only logical that she follow through. She had to work through whatever she was feeling and deal with it.

"When I told you of James' death, you suddenly became cold and distant. I was opening myself up to you, Alec, and you stepped on my outstretched hand. When we speak of Ali, you become defensive and hard. When I questioned you about your dead brother, you became a rock," she lifted her gaze to him. "It would seem that when I attempt to know you personally, as you are to be my husband, you cut me off. It's as if you do not want me to know you at all, so all that I know of you is that you are an unfeeling, callous man merely concerned with your own wants and needs."

He looked at her a moment, suddenly seeing a great deal that he had been blind to all along. Of course she professed her hate for him; he had given her very little reason to like him.

"I am sorry if it seems that way. I assure you, my actions were never intentional," his voice was soft. "I simply do not express myself as well as some and if I convey harshness and insensitivity, it is unintentional. At least to you it is unintentional. I never meant to imply that I was cold and unfeeling."

Peyton was somewhat appeased by his apology, but he did not address her specific complaints. She had been completely honest and expected the same of him.

"Why were you so cold after I told you of James? Are you envious of his memory?"

"Of course not," he snapped softly. "Nothing of the kind. 'Tis just.... seeing the joust pole and the scabbard brought back unpleasant memories of my own, 'tis all. I apologize if I hurt your feelings, Peyton. You must believe I never meant to."

Her self-protection vanished. "What memories, Alec?" she whispered, winding her hand into his huge warm palm and feeling his strength touch her. "Won't you tell me?"

He gazed at her a moment, feeling her question to his soul. As much as he tried to ward off the memories, they refused to bank and he felt his chest tighten with the familiar ache. Looking into the soft sapphire blue of her eyes, he could read comfort in the depths if he would only relent. His knees suddenly weakened and he deposited himself on the stairs, pulling her down with him.

Instead of sitting next to him, she sat between his legs, still holding his hand. The anger, the hatred, the confusion was forgotten as she patiently waited for him to speak. His head was bowed, staring at the stone steps as his other hand came up to clasp her single hand tightly in a two-fisted grip. It occurred to Peyton that the man Alec was today, the unfeeling human with moments of brightness, shielded something much deeper. She never realized that his demeanor was an act of self-protection, just as hers was.

"Tell me, Alec," she whispered, squeezing his hand. "I shall not bite you."

He smiled, a thin humorless gesture. "I know your pain," he finally said, quiet and faint. "The pain of losing a loved one. 'Tis a deep ache and I am too familiar with it," his great head came up, the blue eyes soft. "I.... I cannot speak of it, however. Since it happened I have not been able to speak of it. But it is not because I do not trust you, nor is it because I have anything to hide. I simply cannot speak on the subject."

She looked puzzled, her fingers tenderly caressing his hands as big as trenchers. "What subject?"

She saw him swallow hard. "My dead brother."

His pain was obvious. Without knowing any details, her eyes stung with tears, for she only knew how miserable she would be if a mishap ever befell Ivy. "Did this brother have a name?"

"Peter," he whispered and she barely heard him.

She paused a moment to ponder the name, the mysterious dead brother. Then, she touched his head gently. "We will not speak of him again. I will never mention his name in your presence."

He continued to hold her hand tightly and she continued to stroke his head like a child, feeling a good deal of pity for the huge man. To her surprise, he suddenly chuckled and focused on her. "He was a good deal like you, actually. Reddish-gold hair and a temper to match. He used to drive me daft at times."

She lifted an eyebrow at him. "Are you saying that I am your brother's revenge, sent to curse you for the rest of your life?"

Alec smiled broadly, a beautiful smile she found wonderful. He had the whitest teeth she had ever seen. "He would be so cruel, yes. Your aunt hasn't had any visions of him, demanding satisfaction on my mortal body?"

Peyton laughed. "Not that I am aware of. And do not believe for one moment that he has possessed me."

His smile softened, his expressionless face suddenly tender. "I would never think that."

He was vulnerable and Peyton's heart ached for him. He needed comfort from her as badly as she needed his understanding, and she cursed herself for being so stubborn towards him. Of course she did not hate him; she probably never would, no matter what he said or did. Suddenly Alec Summerlin wasn't as terrible as she had liked to imagine.

She couldn't help herself; she leaned forward and kissed his smooth lips tenderly in a show of sympathy. Yet the small kiss immediately turned into something far more passionate and she gasped as Alec gathered her fiercely into his arms.

"No, Alec," she whispered, speaking against his hungry lips. "No more. We must wait until…."

"I do not want to wait," he growled. "Whether I take you tonight or on our wedding night, it makes no difference. I plan to take you every night for the rest of eternity."

With her last shred of sanity, Peyton pulled from his probing lips and turned away from him, trying to twist from his iron grip. But he refused to let go and she ended up facing away from him while his hot lips devoured the tender flesh at the nape of her neck.

"Oh, God, Alec..," she breathed, struggling fiercely to retain her senses. "Would you please stop? I cannot bear anymore of your attentions this night. My head is already spinning."

"I shall make you forget your head," he promised seductively. "I shall make you forget everything if you will allow me."

She attempted to pull away from him but he held her firm. "Nay, I shall not allow it. We are not married yet and I refuse to allow you to sample your wedding gift early."

He started to laugh against her neck and she could feel him shaking with mirth. A smile crept onto her lips as he held her tightly and continued to snicker. "Very well, then," he snorted. "But we must be married by tomorrow night or I shall surely go insane. Do you suppose you will be ready by tomorrow?"

She yawned and snuggled against him; he was warm and comforting. "Nay. You will simply have to suffer."

"Vixen," he growled. "Ready or not, we will wed tomorrow. Understood?"

"Aye, my lord," she grinned, then paused a moment in thought. The mention of one marriage made her think of a second prospective ceremony, and her smile faded as she was reminded of her harsh words with Ivy earlier. She suddenly felt a great need to apologize to her sister for their earlier argument. "When will Ali and Ivy be married? Will it be a double ceremony?"

Alec's mirth faded. "I am afraid not," he knew she would demand an explanation and he continued. "To the church, Ali is an anomalistic half-man and half-beast, which is why he is not a knight. The church considers him unworthy to bear the title, just as they consider him unworthy to be a member of their religion."

Peyton's brow furrowed, understanding why Ali had cut her off when she inquired about his knighthood. It only served to reinforce her suspicion that she and Ivy hadn't been the only English to react negatively to his dark color. But with Ivy's gradual acceptance of the man, Peyton found herself questioning her own reservations. She had trusted Ivy's opinion before, more times that she could remember. She would trust her now, too.

Her silent ponderings gave way to a softly-spoken question. "Who made the decision regarding Ali's knighthood?"

Alec's eyes grew distant in remembrance. "King Henry himself, almost thirteen years ago. Ali stood by and watched all of the young men he had fostered with become knights. But he never let his bitterness show. He stood by the altar, dressed in his finest armor as his peers were inducted into the knighthood. He went through the motions, the readings, the prayers, as if they were meant for him. Never once did I see defeat in his eyes, but I knew differently. That night, we both became quite drunk and it was the only time I have ever seen him cry."

Peyton's expression was soft with pity. "How terrible for him. After training all of his life to be a knight, how horrible to have been denied the final rite."

Alec nodded. "Even if by some miracle the church would allow him to marry within their law, I doubt he would do it. He holds a grudge against the white man's religion."

"Then who will perform the ceremony?"

"A barrister, most likely. They can be married within the boundaries of the laws of England, but the church will not recognize the union."

Peyton turned to look at him. "Does Ivy know this?"

"Undoubtedly she does by now," he replied, his lips a mere inch or so from her own and thinking heavily on kissing her again. "She has spent the entire evening with Ali and his parents and I am sure they have explained things."

Peyton was not happy with the situation and turned away before Alec could kiss her again. But she leaned her head back against his great shoulder and sighed. "'Twill be a common-law marriage. As if they were not married at all."

Alec was silent a moment. "'Twill be legal nonetheless, within the laws of England."

Peyton did not reply. So Ivy's marriage was to be common-law, unrecognizable by God. What of their children, their heirs and descendants? Would their father have allowed such a marriage to occur? Certainly not. Peyton wondered why Lord Brian was willing to allow a marginally acceptable marriage to take place, but she kept silent.

She suspected her protests would not be well met by Alec, especially in light of his defensive manner when it came to Ali. Alec would believe her protests were because of Ali's color, which was far from the case. She had resigned herself to the man's dark appearance. Her protests would have been the same for any suitor offering a common-law marriage.

Still, the trouble plagued her and she was hard pressed to remain silent on the matter.

Behind her, she heard Alec sigh softly, his breath hot against her neck. Her thoughts were diverted for the moment as delicious shivers danced down her spine, tingling her arms, heating her belly.

"You and Ivy did not want to be married, remember? I suspect a common-law marriage is better than none at all and considering the appearance you two put forth the day of your initial arrival, you are lucky to have any offer at all."

There was a certain amount of humor to the statement and Peyton grinned slyly, turning to look at him. "I doubt a blind man would have been smitten with the image we presented."

"With good reason," Alec agreed. "Hideous!"

She laughed softly, pleased that she and Ivy had been able to accomplish a small part of their grand scheme. However, she realized she was pleased that the overall attempt had failed.

In spite of every tumultuous feeling she had experienced, she was beginning to feel comfortable with Alec in a completely different sense than she had felt comfortable with James. It was difficult to describe the dissimilarities, but she knew one thing; she liked Alec's arms around her. She liked being enfolded in his huge, strong body, whereas James had been considerably smaller. His embraces had not been nearly so satisfying and she thought herself wicked for thinking poorly of him.

"How is your head?" Alec asked after a moment.

"Rebelling against me," she said softly. "Does Pauly truly have a potion to make the ache stop?"

"Pauly has a potion for everything," Alec said frankly. "After I put you to bed, I shall go and see him."

"Jubil has a potion for everything, too, only her concoctions seem to be limited to things like love potions and virility and childbirth elixirs. Not exactly the kinds of brews I find useful."

"You may have need of a childbirth elixir if we are so blessed in the future," Alec said thoughtfully. "Unless, of course, you would rather be quite manly about the whole thing and shun all forms of relief. Pain is terribly male."

She rolled her eyes at his awful sense of humor.

"Alec, you are a beast. Take me to my room immediately before this conversation goes any further."

He laughed softly and rose, pulling her up with him. "I know for a fact you are most courageous. Birthing a child should be nothing to a woman like you. You should be able to recite poetry, sew a bedrug and slug it out with Thia between labor pains."

She pulled herself from his embrace and mounted the stairs. "And get up immediately afterward and plant an entire crop of summer vegetables. How terribly rugged I am."

"Terribly. I think I am afraid of you."

"You should be," she mounted the last step into the corridor and Alec paused a moment. Suddenly, their last two sentences took on an entirely different meaning.

He truly was afraid of her and with good reason. It would be too easy to develop feelings for her beyond fondness and he absolutely refused to love a woman; any woman. Love was a weak emotion and he had no desire to become swept up in its fickle torrents.

In faith, the frightening thought had not occurred to him until just now.

CHAPTER SEVEN

PEYTON AWOKE TO Ivy's snores late the following morning. Her head felt fine and her body refreshed, full of vigor in spite of having been jolted awake by her sister's loud breathing. After a sound sleep, the world appeared a little brighter, a little clearer. Gazing at her sister's contented face, she couldn't seem to remember when Ivy had come to join her during the night. For all Peyton knew, Ivy had been out until dawn with the black soldier.

But none of that mattered any longer as Ivy snored softly. She was returned and she was whole. As Peyton stared at the sleeping face, she thought mayhap an apology for their bitter words was unnecessary; better to simply forget the incident. She was more than willing to forget their hostilities and hoped Ivy was, too.

With an evil, sleepy grin, she leaned over and blew softly in her sister's ear. Ivy fidgeted and slapped a hand over her head and Peyton proceeded to nibble at the back of her hand with sharp white teeth until Ivy twitched and rolled onto her back.

Peyton held back the giggles. "Lady Ivy," she said in a mockingly deep voice. "My sweet wanton, how luscious is your unclothed body."

Ivy peeped one eye open at her sister, who burst out in loud laughter. Regardless of the fact that she had just been annoyed out of a deep sleep, Ivy smiled. "And you, my delicious brown warrior, taste as good as you look. How delectable is your…."

"Stop!" Peyton cried, choking on her laughter. "Say no more. I do not want to know what you may have sampled."

Ivy closed her eyes tightly and began to thrash about. "No more, I cannot stand it! Your hands to my….!"

"Ivy!" Peyton pleaded.

"…. breasts as you….!"

"Ivy!"

"…. attempt to milk me like a cow!"

Peyton smacked her sister on the rump and rolled off the bed with disgust. "Ivy, you are an uncouth trollop. I will not hear what he has done to you, do you understand?"

Ivy propped herself up on Peyton's pillow. "I never said he did anything to me," she raised an eyebrow at the tattered edges of Peyton's shift spilling from beneath the silk robe. "But why, may I ask, is your shift torn?"

Peyton's cheeks flushed as she looked down at the mussed robe and snatches of torn shift. She and Ivy had always been open with each other and she was not about to hide from her sister. Ivy would never think poorly of her no matter what she had done, even if she herself was ashamed.

Slowly, she untied the sash to her robe to reveal the entire torn length of shift.

Ivy gasped and sat up on the bed, her eyes wide. "What happened, Peyton? Did he force himself on you? Did he..?"

Peyton shook her head, sheepishly. "He did not," she stammered for words. "We…. I still do not know how exactly it came about, but…. oh, Ivy, I am so confused I do not know what to think anymore."

Ivy swung her legs over the side of the bed. "He was here last night when I arrived. He was sitting by the hearth and you were sound asleep. He said he had brought a potion for your headache but had decided to let you sleep rather than wake you so that you could take it. He left with Ali the moment I arrived," she stood up and moved to her sister, gazing at the ripped garment. "He did not…. you two did not..?"

"Nay!" Peyton exclaimed. "Of that I am certain."

Ivy moved to touch the shift and the entire robe fell open, revealing her sister's naked body and the very purple love bite on her upper abdomen. Ivy's mouth fell open.

"What is this?" she cried.

Peyton looked down at her white belly, marred with a vibrant bruise, and ran a finger across the mark. "You would not believe me if I told you."

Ivy nodded vigorously. "Aye, I would, because I have one to match."

It was Peyton's turn to be shocked. "You do?"

Ivy reached up and pulled back the neckline of her shift. On the top of her plump breast was a purple and green mark. She and Peyton exchanged confused glances.

"What's the matter with us?" Peyton whispered urgently.

Ivy simply shook her head. "I do not know."

Peyton's gaze lingered on Ivy's brilliant bite. "You said you hadn't yet accepted him as your betrothed."

Ivy touched her sister's mark, ignoring Peyton's piercing inquiry for the moment. When their gazes locked, inquiry and confusion rippled in Peyton's sapphire depths and Ivy could no longer ignore her.

She sighed helplessly. "I cannot describe how I feel about him, Peyton. Only that he has made me understand more about myself, more about life, than I ever dreamt possible. He is unlike any man I have ever met."

Peyton could read the sincerity of discovery and was suddenly determined to know the man through Ivy's eyes. "His color doesn't bother you any longer?"

Ivy shook her head. "His skin is magnificent to behold, exquisite to touch. And he makes me feel more beautiful than any woman on earth. There is a wonderful man beneath the outer facade, Peyton. And I like him."

"Enough to allow him to..," she cocked an eyebrow at the vivid love mark, "do that?"

Ivy ran a finger over the blemish. "Aye."

Peyton touched her own mark hesitantly, a tremendous confusion sweeping her. "I do not…. Ivy, I do not even like Alec, certainly not the way you have come to accept Ali. But something happens when we look at each other and it is as if I have no control over myself. And, lord, when he kisses me…. what's wrong with me, Ivy?"

"Nothing," her sister said evenly. "He is a gorgeous man, Peyton. Can you not accept the fact that you find him attractive?"

"Nay! He is…. He is not attractive to me. What I mean is, he is handsome and he has beautiful eyes and a beautiful smile, but…. damnation, I love James! I do not love Alec Summerlin!"

"Who said anything about love, darling?" Ivy said with a faint smile. "Love means different things to different people."

Peyton looked thoughtful, trying desperately to analyze the situation and her own feelings. Her gaze returned to her sister's colorful bite. "How far…. how much did Ali touch you?"

Ivy lowered her gaze for the first time. "He touched me nearly everywhere until his parents interrupted. I think had we continued unhindered, we might have…. and do you want to know something? I think I wanted him to bed me. I think I wanted it nearly as badly as he did."

"You *did*?" Peyton asked, awed.

Ivy nodded and Peyton shook her head in wonderment. "Is Ali so extraordinary that you would turn yourself over to him without reserve?"

Ivy lifted an eyebrow. "Ask yourself that same question. If you discover the answers, then let me know. I have none to give."

Peyton looked down at her own mark, feeling more baffled by the moment. "Neither do I. And do you know what else? I hated you yesterday."

Ivy did not look overly surprised. "I hated you, too. You were very cruel and unreasonable."

Peyton's pretty mouth twisted with regret. "I know, darling, and I am sorry. 'Twas just that I was so confused about everything and when I saw how you were coming to terms with Ali, I was angry at you for surrendering so easily. And.... and I think I was jealous in a way."

"What way?" Ivy asked softly.

"Because you have found someone you can tolerate, and I am saddled with Alec the Giant."

Ivy shook her head. "Peyton, I simply cannot believe that you do not find Alec attractive. He is the most beautiful man I have ever seen. Even Jubil is smitten with him."

Peyton sat down on the bed, looking dazed, and shook her head. "Ivy, I love James. I cannot find another man attractive."

Ivy felt a stab of pity for her sister. "I know, darling," she said gently. "But he is gone and Alec is to be your husband. You must come to understand that, the sooner the better for you both. Do you not think you could grow to like him?"

Peyton shrugged, confused. "He is kind at times and humorous too. I.... I simply do not know."

Ivy sat down on the mattress next to her sister, feeling the familiar pain they had shared so often over the past year. Grief, as ugly as it was, was a binding emotion and Ivy understood Peyton's reluctance.

A soft rap came to the door and Ivy rose to answer. Lady Celine's bright face entered the room as she smiled at the two young women.

"I heard voices," she said. "'Tis nearly the nooning meal and I thought to help you dress."

Before Peyton could open her mouth to reply, Thia entered the room behind her mother and immediately the tension in the chamber thickened. If Lady Celine detected the hostility, she did not react. Instead, she sent a serving woman running for hot water.

Ivy, however, sensed her sister's distress and cast a long glance at the large Summerlin sibling. They'd barely been introduced the day before, certainly not more than two words spoken between them, and Ivy had not been told about the confrontation between Peyton and

Alec's sister. Now, however, she sensed loathing from her sister toward the robust young woman and responded with dislike of her own.

Tactfully oblivious to the animosity between the three young women, Lady Celine went directly to the wardrobe. "Lord Brian is completing the marital arrangements this morn and tonight after vespers, the marriages will take place," coming across an acceptable dress, she tossed it to Thia and eyed the two sisters still huddled on the bed. "Hurry, ladies! There is much to do!"

Several serving wenches brought hot water in large basins and Lady Celine ordered the girls to disrobe. Her manner was brisk and no-nonsense, indicative of a woman who had raised four children, and Peyton and Ivy looked to one another in horror. Were they to disrobe in front of Lady Celine, the unmistakable marks of passion would be displayed. But they also knew they had no choice but to obey; Lady Celine was far gone into the large wardrobe, clearly expecting naked women to dress momentarily.

Peyton's eyes were fixed on Ivy. They simply stared helplessly at each other while Lady Celine chattered continuously and Thia stood silently by the bed. Finally, Peyton lifted a resigned eyebrow and began to untie her sash. After all, she and Alec were to be married and the fact that they had briefly tasted one another before the ties of matrimony were secured should come as no great shock to Lady Celine. At least, she hoped not. Moreover, she was at a loss to think of a plausible stalling tactic.

The robe and shift came off. Ivy's followed shortly.

☙

ALEC AND ALI were waiting patiently at the base of the stairs when the ladies descended, appreciation in their expressions. Ali moved directly for Ivy but was foiled by Lady Celine, who grabbed him by the ear and pulled him into the small solar near the entry. Ivy looked stricken and Peyton turned to Alec.

"Do something," she whispered urgently, pointing to the solar.

"What do you mean?" he was planning to greet her fondly but his compliments died on his lips.

Peyton motioned for him to lean closer to her and he did gladly. In fact, he was preparing to kiss her but she frowned at him irritably.

"Your mother discovered a passion mark on my sister while helping us with our toilette this morn," she whispered hastily. "I fear Ali is in for a thrashing."

She watched with satisfaction as Alec passed a concerned glance in the direction of the solar. "I would assume, then, that she did not see my signature on your abdomen?"

Peyton shook her head. "I was able to conceal it somewhat."

He wriggled his eyebrows. "Clearly. Had it been discovered, I would undoubtedly be receiving a thorough reaming at this very moment," patting her gently on the arm, he turned toward the solar. "You will excuse me for a moment, my lady."

He moved into the small room determinedly and the ladies could hear him exchanging words with his mother. Lady Celine's voice was angered while the low baritone of Alec's rumble was maintained and calm. As his mother became animated and agitated, Alec remained quite cool and collected. Even when she pinched him.

After several minutes, Lady Celine exited the solar with her head held high and motioned to Thia, standing by the stairs, who followed her mother obediently. Without a glance at Peyton or Ivy, the two women disappeared into the grand hall. The sisters looked to each other in confusion as Alec and Ali emerged from the solar, wolfish grins on their faces.

"Ali, are you all right?" Ivy asked with concern.

Ali rubbed his ear and Peyton found herself gazing closely at him; it was the first time she had seen him out of his armor and she was not displeased with her observations; he was a big man, far leaner than Alec however, and he had the longest legs she had ever seen. His torso was short for his size, but he was muscular and beautifully built.

"Fine, sweetling, fine," he grinned. "So she saw my mark, did she?

Ah, well, next time I shall be smarter and mark you where only I may see it."

Peyton shook her head at the remark and Alec eyed her. "I was wise enough to mark her sister where it could be easily covered," he said.

Peyton flushed bright red and slapped his arm, much to the amusement of the two men. Ivy merely cast a knowing gaze on her sister. "Peyton's is much darker than mine."

"It is? I must see!" Ali demanded.

Alec put his thick arm between Ali and Peyton to ward off his intentions. "You will not see anything, whelp. Although I must say, I am rather proud of it. It will take weeks to heal properly."

Peyton shook her head with disgust. "You two are no better than dogs pissing on trees to mark their territory. My sister and I are not trees to be scented."

"Nay, sweetheart, you are property to be claimed," Alec put his big arms around her affectionately. "I would announce to all of England that you are to be my wife."

He tried to kiss her but she dodged him, struggling in his huge embrace. But it was not without humor. "Release me, you brute. I shall not be fondled for all to see, especially when your mother most likely believes ill of me."

"Why would you say that?"

Peyton cast him a knowing, intolerant glance. "My sister has a mark of desire in a rather intimate place. I am sure she wonders if I bear a similar mark, being that you cannot keep your hands to yourself."

He laughed a deep, throaty chuckle. "She would not think ill of you in that case, but she would undoubtedly think ill of me."

Ivy smiled at her sister, pleased to see that her resistance to Alec was lessening. Mayhap she would heal from the loss of James sooner than expected. "She defended Ali most admirably against your mother's rantings when my, er, mark was discovered," her eyes twinkled at her sister. "She was magnificent."

"She was?" he gazed fondly at the redhead clasped stiffly in his embrace. "How noble, my lady, and we thank you."

"Do not bother. I was merely defending my sister's virtue," Peyton managed to wrest herself free of Alec's massive arms and straighten her gown irritably. "Now, my lord, will you be so kind as to inform my sister and I of our immediate future? Your mother mentioned that your father was making wedding plans."

"Indeed," Alec nodded, still smiling at her. "He has been doing little else but make arrangements for our vows come this eve after vespers. Coincidentally, since a few guests still remain within Blackstone after the party two nights ago, it looks as if we are in for another lavish celebration come tonight. Moreover, father has sent invitations to a few other valuable allies. It should prove to be quite an occasion."

Peyton raised her eyebrows at all of the planning that had taken place in the past day. "He has indeed been busy. What of Ivy and Ali's wedding?"

Alec took her arm and led her toward the grand hall. Ali and Ivy followed several paces back, whispering between themselves, and Peyton could almost hear them more prevalently over Alec's beautiful voice. The familiar jealousy she had felt yesterday threatened to return, but she firmly forced it away. She wanted Ivy to be happy, in spite of the fact that she knew she herself could not be. But even as she thought on her dismal future, she found herself riddled with doubt. Mayhap, in time, she could be happy.

Alec broke into her thoughts. "Father knows of a lawyer in Northampton who will be willing to perform a civil ceremony for a fee."

Peyton passed a glance at her sister, laughing softly with her husband-to-be. She sighed. "I suppose we must be satisfied with that. But I...." she lowered her voice. The same thoughts from the night before returned, stronger than before, and she felt the need to voice her concerns. They were legitimate worries, she felt, and could only pray that he would not become offended by her words. "I am distressed that the church will not recognize this marriage, Alec. If the church does not recognize it, then it does not exist and, technically, their children will be bastards. Am I not right in this assumption?"

Alec paused, watching as Ali and Ivy entered the grand hall. Peyton observed her sister with a guarded gaze as she waited expectantly for Alec's reply.

"You are correct, but you are thinking with your heart and not your head. Ivy is the second daughter of a lesser noble and she is well past marriageable age. Although she has a good dowry, she comes with no property and is not considered a viable prospect for young noblemen or knights looking to acquire status through marriage. In fact, her prospects are considerably unattractive when one contemplates the list to include elderly widowers or men only interested in the money Ivy would bring them. Ali is her very best hope for a husband who is interested in providing her a stable life and children, even if their marriage will be considered common law by the church. Hopefully, someday, that will change."

Peyton was listening seriously to his explanation. "Did your father even try to find her a husband other than Ali?" she asked. "Or was it simply a quick solution to a greater problem?"

Alec raised an eyebrow slowly. "Ali will probably never be married unless he marries Ivy. And considering Ivy's dreary prospects, it was a logical solution to a great problem, my lady, not a quick decision."

Peyton matched his cocked eyebrow and countered. "Then you are telling me he did not even try. Ivy never had a chance for a respectable marriage and your father chose the easy path by betrothing her to a man that is considered sub-human by the Catholic Church."

He dropped his arm from her then and Peyton saw a flame of rage ignite in the sky-blue orbs. She gazed at him, a chill of apprehension running though her as his expression became one of such deadly intensity that it actually frightened her. She could literally see the fury swelling within him and she realized that her prayers had not been heard; she had indeed offended him. She began to wonder if he was intent on beating her, for his huge body tensed as a snake does before it strikes.

"You will never describe him in those terms again, Lady Peyton. Do you comprehend me?"

She understood his words and the reasoning behind them. Rather than readily agree, as she should have, she was eager to explain that she had meant no harm; she had merely meant to question his father's motives.

"I meant nothing contemptuous, Alec, truly. It's just that…."

He suddenly snatched her by the arm, so brutally that she gasped with pain, and whirled her into the small solar. The door slammed shut with such force that the table rattled and Peyton backed away from him, her apprehension full blown. She had never seen him show an abundance of emotion and to witness his fury, directed at her no less, brought waves of terror.

When he turned to her, his neck was mottled with flush but his expression was impassive. "I forbid you to plead your innocence. If I ever hear another offensive word come forth from your mouth regarding Ali, you will regret the day you were born. Is that clear?"

Peyton stood against the wall by the latticed windows, irritation replacing some of her fear. "Perfectly. If you kindly allow me to explain myself before you tear my head off."

He was standing by a carved cherrywood table, a sturdy piece of furniture that displayed a painted vase from Egypt. One moment the table and vase were whole; in the next they were shattered, crushed by Alec's huge fist in his rage. He kicked the pieces aside, his hands clenched into spheres the size of a child's head.

"You are just like the rest, aren't you? A shallow bitch that cannot see beyond the color of a man's skin," his voice was like shards of ice, cold and biting. "I thought you to be different, Peyton. You nearly had me convinced of the fact. But the truth comes forth and I realize now that you are not. Christ, I tried to stop you from hanging yourself once. I did not want you to give me a reason to hate you. But given enough rope, you are content to condemn yourself, aren't you? If you wanted to ruin your chances for affection in this marriage, my lady, then you have done just that."

She was shocked. Her mouth hung agape at his words and she shook her head feebly. "Alec, can I not defend myself before you denounce me?"

"There is nothing you can possibly say in your defense," he said coldly. "I now see what I am to receive in a wife and you cannot hide the fact."

Her irritation was blooming as her fear somewhat cooled. "Hide what?" she demanded softly. "Why are you so angry that I referred to Ali as sub-human? In fact, you…."

He exploded, hurling the heavy hide-covered chair into the wall as if it were constructed of rotted wood. Peyton's hands flew to her mouth and she ducked as a piece of the smashed cherrywood table came sailing in her direction. Irritation dissolved, her fear consumed her as she covered her head to protect herself from a portion of the table that exploded against the stone wall behind her. A heavy splinter speared her hand, sending rivers of bright red blood streaming down her arm and onto her gown.

But she did not flinch from the pain, only from the terror of Alec's rage. Shaken and verging on tears, she opened her eyes to see Alec's boots directly in front of her.

Her ashen face turned upward. Eyes glittering like the deadly reflection of a broadsword stared down at her and she swallowed the dread that threatened. Even if he did not want to hear an explanation, she was going to deliver one before he tore her in two. And she was positive from the look in his eye that murder was on his mind.

Her voice was tight. "Was it worse that I described him as sub-human when you yourself referred to him as half-man and half-beast? I delivered the term as an interpretation of the church's stance, not my personal opinion. I did not use the term to flagrantly insult him, Alec."

He stared at her. Slowly, she saw his expression loosen. The muscles suddenly went slack with understanding and horror at what he had done, a man who took such pride in his self-control. He'd never lost his composure as he had just done and he was mortified because he believed her. It was simple, it was factual. Christ, he so desperately wanted to believe her.

Peyton's initial reaction had been usual, though somewhat mild. Even Ali had alluded to the fact. And watching Ivy's gradual acceptance of the ebony soldier had not been an easy thing for Alec; he couldn't help but doubt her sincerity. He had seen her kind of "acceptance" before; or so he thought, and he was unwilling for his friend to be pitied by yet another woman. As the hours passed and Ivy grew more and more comfortable with Ali's appearance, Alec found himself growing more willing to believe in spite of his natural reserve. More than anything he, like Ali, wanted to believe. He realized that he did believe.

Gazing down at Peyton's pale face and bloodied hand, he could only remember regretting one other incident with greater sorrow; when he had mistakenly gored his brother. Although he had not meant to hurt Peyton, he had nonetheless. Just as he had not meant to kill his brother.

Mayhap that was why Alec maintained such classic composure in the face of almost anything; the few times he had lost his control and acted rashly, the consequences had been severe. Remorse and sorrow swept him.

"Oh, Peyton," he whispered. "I…. oh, Christ," he sank to the floor in front of her, his face etched with despair. "Forgive me. You are right, of course; I should not have overreacted."

Peyton stared at him, her terror replaced by a deeper sense of ache and offense. She was reduced to a huddled ball by Alec's rage and as the fear died she could only gaze back at him with disgust. Where she had once seen her death in his eyes, she now only saw the greatest sorrow. Unable to respond to his apology, she turned her face to the wall.

Alec was gripped with sadness as she cowered from him. His chest was constricting so tightly that he could barely breath, more anguish than he ever thought possible gripping him. He was a man unused to such volatile emotions and he hated himself for terrorizing her so.

"Peyton, sweet," he said softly. "Get up and let me tend your hand. Come and sit…."

He touched her gently and she lashed out at him, slapping his hand away and splattering him with her blood. "Leave me alone! Go away and leave me alone!"

If he had possessed a dagger at that moment, he would have turned it on himself; surely it would have been less painful compared to the hurt he was experiencing. "Please, love. You can never know how sorry I am for losing my temper, but…."

She kicked at him then, scattering pieces of wood. Her movements were jerky, full of terror and anger. "Go away, you bastard. You will not touch me."

He rose heavily, gazing down at her beautiful red head. "Please, Peyton, do not…. please let me…."

She wrapped her arms over her ears as if to block out his voice, pulling herself into a tight little ball. Her body tensed so terribly that she looked ready to snap and he stepped back, away from her, hoping she would calm were he not hovering over her.

He stumbled backwards, dazed and pained by what he had done, wandering away from Peyton until he bumped into his father's desk. Never taking his eyes off her, he perched himself on the edge of the desk and continued to stare at her, wondering if he could ever make restitution to her for his violent actions. There were no words to describe his torment as he watched her shaking, huddled form.

Time passed slowly, painfully. Peyton remained huddled in a ball and Alec sat frozen on the end of the oaken desk. She did not move or speak; neither did he. He was so deeply shocked at his outburst that he swore silently he would spend the rest of his life making amends to her, whatever it would take. He thanked God that he had still possessed sense enough not to have physically attacked her.

As it was, his father's valuable Egyptian vase with the strange writing had been destroyed, as had a heavy cherrywood table. The upended chair could be repaired, but he seriously wondered if Peyton's wits would ever heal.

"Peyton," he whispered finally. "Please get up, sweetheart. I promise I won't…."

"Go away from me, Alec Summerlin," her voice was a breathy whisper.

He sighed heavily and stood up, wondering if he should not simply force her to sit in a chair so that he could speak with her rationally. She had to understand that he hadn't meant to erupt so violently, but there were deep reasons as to why he had acted so irrationally. Mayhap if she understood his reasons, she could forgive him.

Summoning his courage, he started to move toward her, but his mission was severed in mid-motion.

The solar door opened and Lady Celine poked her head into the room. Her pleasant expression immediately turned to one of horror when she saw the condition of the room, and as her eyes fell on Peyton, panic erupted.

"Alec!"

☙

SOMEWHERE HIGH ABOVE the bailey, a hawk screamed loudly in the warm air. Alec heard it as he gazed across the courtyard, but he did not turn to look as he usually did. He was standing in the very spot Peyton had occupied not an hour before as she cowered in fear of his anger and, somehow, placing himself on the area brought him closer to her. In fact, his thoughts were entirely on Peyton as he waited for his father to speak.

Brian sat behind his great oak desk, staring at the large piece of vellum before him. His handsome face was contemplative, as it had been for the past hour. He gazed at the words on the parchment before him, seeing but not reading. He knew what the words said because he had written them. It was Peyton's betrothal contract.

"Alec," he said finally, his voice hoarse with emotion. "I am afraid you have put me in a difficult position."

"Why?" Alec asked quietly. "Da, I explained to you what happened. I have all but groveled at your feet, at mother's feet, and at Peyton's feet for forgiveness and I am at a loss to understand why you seem to consider my actions so severe."

Brian's brown eyes glared at his son, his heavy salt-and-pepper eyebrows lifting slightly. "You fail to understand? Alec, you could have gravely injured Lady Peyton with your ranting over something as innocent as a term used to describe Ali's race and I am deeply concerned what will happen in the future should she make an even harsher comment. God's Blood, Alec, what if she mentions Peter and you are offended? Will you snap her neck and be sorry for it later?"

"I never laid a hand on her and I never will. You know me better than that."

"I thought I did until this gross display of temper. You scared the girl to death, Alec, and I do not blame her. What in the world possessed you?"

Alec pushed himself off the wall, massive arms folded in front of his chest as he paced the floor contemplatively. "We have been over it. Do you truly wish to hear the same answer again? I mistook her remark against Ali and I raged violently because…. because I was angry that she appeared to be just like all of the other women who cannot see past the color of Ali's skin. But I was wrong. I am glad that I was mistaken in my assessment of the lady's character and I am deeply ashamed of my outburst. What more is it you want me to say?"

Brian's jaw ticked as he listened to the explanation again. Slowly, he shook his head and lowered it to the vellum. "I have come to a decision. Mayhap I have been wrong in my assumption that you and the lady can establish a beneficial marriage. I do not believe Lady Peyton is suited for you and…."

"What?" Alec interrupted with genuine surprise. "Da, what are you..?"

Brian put up his hand sharply and spoke loudly over his son's question. "And I have concluded that I should find a husband better suited for her temperament. She is an outspoken, willful young lady and she will need a husband who cannot be provoked by such character."

Alec's emotionless face took on real emotion. "That's ridiculous. What happened between us was a misunderstanding and has nothing to do with her willful nature."

Brian folded his hands calmly. "I know you agreed to marry her merely to acquire St. Cloven, but I am sure there will be a greater inheritance for you, eventually. You are young still, and I firmly believe there will be other prospects after Lady Peyton. In fact, Lady Caroline Morford was discussed as a possibility even before this situation with Lady Peyton arose."

"As I recall, when you broached the subject of my betrothal to Lady Peyton, you did so because you feared it would be my best, final offer." Alec's shock was turning into an almost panicked anger, desperate to keep what he wanted. "I do not want Lady Caroline. I want Peyton and I shall have her."

"You will do as I say," his father cocked an eyebrow, sitting back in his chair. "I am afraid that I cannot, in good conscience, allow your marriage to Lady Peyton to take place."

Alec visibly tensed. "Why not?"

"I thought I made myself quite clear. You and Lady Peyton are not suited for one another. I believe Lady Caroline will make an adequate spouse, for she is docile and obedient and…."

"I do not want Lady Caroline," Alec repeated, his voice a growl. "Lady Peyton will be my wife."

Brian's eyes flashed with fury. "Listen to me well. Alec, you are the most controlled man I have ever had the fortune to know. I have never seen you become truly enraged, or truly happy, or truly sorrowful. You, my son, are the very model of a man who is in complete control of his emotions; even King Edward has made comment of your self-control," he rose slowly. "It concerns me deeply that this woman has the power to cause you to lose yourself. 'Tis not this one incident that causes me concern but, if you recall, you brought her back to Blackstone only yesterday morning unconscious. You said it was an accident, yet she says you were less than gentle with her. I shudder to think what will happen should she provoke you again and I cannot allow the death of your wife to be on my hands."

Alec was stunned. "Do you truly think I would murder her? I would sooner kill myself than harm her and what happened yester morn was indeed an accident. I was wresting her onto my horse and she fell and hit her head; nothing more."

"So you have said. And rationally speaking, of course you would not kill the lady. But the destruction of this room is testimony to the fact that she can bait you into the realm of irrationality and therein would lay her murder."

Alec shook his head in disbelief. "If I had a history of brutality, then I could understand your reasoning. But you better than anyone understand my attitude against violence. Peyton could never provoke me into such insanity that I would kill her."

Brian's gaze lingered a moment longer on his son before looking to the parchment again. Aye, he knew Alec better than anyone, which was why his son's display of temper frightened him. Alec never lost his temper. He had been so positive that this marriage would be mutually advantageous, but after witnessing the destruction of his solar, he was forced to admit that mayhap the friction between Alec and Lady Peyton went far deeper than mere indifference.

When he had seen Alec embrace the lady yesterday during their engagement celebration, Brian hoped that all was finally well. But he could see that he had been mistaken; he knew he could not allow the marriage to take place, for the health of Lady Peyton and for the emotional stability of his son.

Brian picked up his quill. "The invitations to your wedding will be rescinded immediately and the lingering few guests from the engagement party will be sent on their way," he began to scratch on the vellum before him, avoiding Alec's searing gaze. "The Warringtons have petitioned for the lady's hand. I shall invite them to Blackstone to draw up the particulars of the marriage contract. I shall find you another bride."

Alec was angered in addition to being shocked. "You never told me that the Warringtons petitioned for her. Moreover, you said that there has been an ongoing feud between the de Fluornoys and the Warringtons."

"There is. But if Lady Peyton marries the young Warrington pup, I will no longer have any reason to worry over the smoldering disharmony," he eyed his son, almost guiltily. "And I never told you they appealed for her hand because I was selfish. I wanted the lady for you and as reluctant as you were I thought it best not to tell you she had other offers."

Alec did not reply for a moment. When he did, it was in a tone Brian had never before heard. Like the voice of God. "She will marry me, father. I want her."

Brian raised his head to his son. "You mean you want St. Cloven. Lady Caroline is heiress to Burghley Castle, a far sight larger than St. Cloven, and since her betrothed died of a fever last spring she is mateless. With a little persuasion I am sure…."

"You obviously misunderstood. I said I want Lady Peyton, not St. Cloven."

Brian turned from him coldly. "The matter is closed, Alec. I have no more time for you; I must send out missives canceling tonight's ceremony."

Alec was beyond anger. His mind was literally swirling. Yet as muddled as his brain was, he knew one thing for certain; there was no doubt that Peyton would be his wife. Without so much as a hind glance, he quit the room.

The first person he came into contact with was Ali in the foyer. His friend's face was grim.

"What happened, Alec?"

"Where's Peyton?"

"Your mother and her sister took her upstairs. Damnation, what did your father say?"

Alec's jaw ticked and Ali knew that was not a good sign. "Outside with me."

The two men marched outside, crossing the massive bailey and passing into the stable yards. Alec did not stop until he had reached his destrier's stall and he was not surprised to realize that his anger had intensified during their short walk.

"Father plans to nullify the betrothal and I will not allow it. I plan to marry Peyton regardless."

Ali let out a long hiss. "I have never known your father to overreact, Alec. But then again, I have never known you to destroy a room. What in the hell did she say that caused all of this?"

Alec eyed him a moment. "Nothing of consequence, for it was all a gross misunderstanding and I shall regret my actions until the day I die. God forgive me for harming her, however unintentionally."

Midas, Alec's huge silver warhorse, poked his head out of his stall and nibbled at Ali's hair. "I know you did not mean to injure her. But she was quite hysterical and your mother was beside herself. Frankly, I am shocked by the entire event, for I have never known you to…."

"Enough, Ali. I know my mistake and I shall forever grieve my lapse. But what remains now is that I cannot allow my father to marry her to another."

Ali shook his head, snorting ironically. "At first you did not want her. And now you refuse to let her go? Most puzzling, my friend."

Alec's jaw ticked and Ali watched with amazement; he had never seen Alec so emotional. "What do you plan to do?"

"Explain my actions as best I can and then marry her," Alec replied quietly.

Ali leaned back against the stall, shoving Midas' great head away. "You intend to force her into this marriage? Do you want St. Cloven so badly, Alec?"

Alec raised an eyebrow, staring pensively at his boots. "Nay, I do not want the manor as badly as I want its lady. I cannot explain my feelings, Ali. All I know is that I must have Peyton as my wife. I think.... I think I need her."

"You need a woman who incites you into acts of destruction?" Ali peered closely at his friend. "I have never known you to act in this manner. Obviously, she is very beautiful, but I fail to see why you need to marry her. It's not.... not because her hair is the color of Peter's, is it? Do you somehow see your brother..?"

"Christ, no," Alec waved him off irritably, pacing aimlessly to Midas' great head and tickling the horse's silk nose out of pure habit. "Oh, hell, Ali. I do not know why I need her. But I do, and I shall have her."

Ali thought on his words a moment. "Very well, then," he said decisively. "So you will marry her. What do you plan to do now?"

"I must talk to her," Alec mumbled, staring at his horse as the animal nibbled at the wood of his stall. "And then I will spirit her away to Ely where we shall be married. Tonight."

"Tonight?" Ali lifted his eyebrows.

Alec was silent a moment, deep in thought. Then he straightened, facing his friend. "Go to my bower and grab a large satchel and stuff it with anything you can get your hands on; clothes, food, anything else you can manage. I shall walk around to the window and you will drop the bag to me. Then, you will go and retrieve Peyton and bring her down here to the stables. Make sure Ivy does not come with you; I want Peyton alone."

"And then what? You plan to remove her to Ely? What if she makes a reluctant bit of baggage on the back of your horse? She shall alert the entire fortress and your father will have your head for trying to abduct her."

"She shall not be reluctant, I promise you. Now go and do as I have asked; I have no time to waste."

Ali hesitated a brief moment, gazing at his friend in the weak light. He had never known Alec to act rashly and was frankly astonished. Alec had said he needed the Lady Peyton; since when did Alec need anyone? But he understood somewhat; after all, he himself was certainly beginning to need Ivy in an odd sort of way. Aye, he understood what it was to need someone.

"Alec," he said softly. "Is she truly worth this trouble? Would it matter if she were to marry another? You would forget about her in time. After all, 'tis not as if you are in love with the woman."

Alec's head snapped to his ebony friend, his eyes glittering strangely. Ali could almost read the emotions in the sky-blue depths as Alec attempted to discern what, exactly, he might be feeling. He found that he could not adequately put his thoughts into words; he wasn't even sure if the correct words existed. He wasn't in love with her.

He couldn't be.

After a moment, Alec simply turned his head away. "Nay, I am not in love with her. But I want her just the same."

CHAPTER EIGHT

PEYTON WAS SETTLED in an overstuffed chair, seated by the narrow windows of her bower as Ivy read from a book of poetry. Jubil, sleeping off her thorn apple trance, had been carried to the bed by servants and currently lay in boneless limbo. Lady Celine had left Peyton to rest some time ago and the room was still except for the drone of Ivy's voice. But Peyton wasn't listening; her thoughts were still on the events earlier that day.

Her wrapped hand reminded her of the injury dealt by Alec's fury and her confusion was consuming; a deep ache in the pit of her belly told her that she was feeling far more than anger and fear at Alec's actions. It told her that her injury went deeper than the cut to her hand.

Somehow, he had managed to injure her feelings as much as she tried to keep herself protected from him. Without realizing it, Alec had seeped into her emotions. With the damage dealt by the loss of James, her bewilderment was almost more than she could bear.

"What did you think of that prose?" Ivy broke into her thoughts.

Peyton was jolted from her stupor. "I am sorry, Ivy. What were you saying?"

Ivy lowered the book, compassion in her eyes. "Nothing, darling. How do you feel?"

"Well enough, I suppose," Peyton said. "Why aren't you with Ali? Surely he is missing you."

"He shall survive," Ivy said with a faint grin. "I thought you needed me more, but I suppose I was wrong."

Peyton returned her sister's smile. "I do too need you, you silly wench. But your reading is putting me to sleep."

"So sorry." Ivy slapped the book closed and tossed it onto the bed. She eyed her sister a moment. "Tell me how you truly feel, Peyton."

Peyton shook her head faintly, toying with the material of her gown. "Angry. I want to go home."

"Peyton…. he did not strike you, did he? Lord, He is such a large man he could easily…."

Peyton shook her head more firmly. "He never touched me. He did not have to."

Ivy sighed with regret. "Ali says he has never known Alec to raise his voice much less display his fury. He is quite shocked by the whole event."

Peyton refused to be pulled into the reasoning for Alec's outburst. Her gaze lingered on her sister a moment, seeking to change the subject. "Are you planning to go through with this marriage to Ali?"

Ivy followed her sister's lead, her expression turning soft. "He shall make a considerate, wise husband. And a fine father to our sons. I believe I am satisfied with the arrangement."

Peyton nodded faintly. "You have accepted him completely, then?"

Ivy smiled. "I suppose I have. And I want you to accept him as well. It is extremely important to me, Peyton."

Peyton held up a hand to silence Ivy's plea. "Say no more, darling. My bout with ignorance was a short episode and I apologize for the hateful things I said about him. If you have accepted him, then I have, too," she shifted in the chair, wincing when her bandaged hand brushed against the wood. "Then you and Ali are to be married tonight. What gown do you plan to wear?"

"The emerald silk," Ivy's gaze was on her sister's linen-wrapped hand. "What are you going to wear?"

Peyton's mood darkened as her gaze returned to the window.

"Black."

"Black is striking on you, darling, but I thought the ivory silk would be better with your hair," Ivy's tone was laced with sarcasm. "Besides, I should have thought…."

A sharp rap on the door disrupted her sentence. Ivy rose from her chair and threw open the door, not surprised to find Ali in the doorway. His ebony face tender on his future wife.

"Greetings, sweetling," he said softly. "How is your sister faring?"

"Well enough, considering," Ivy replied, matching his smile.

Ali's gaze roved her lovely features a moment, still reeling with his good fortune. He was amazed that every day, every hour, brought increasing acceptance from his betrothed. It was as if he were living a dream; he kept expecting to wake up and discover it all to have been a wonderful fantasy.

"Might I speak with your sister, sweet?"

Ivy stood back and motioned him into the room. Peyton turned her attention to the black soldier and he smiled.

"Greetings this day, demoiselle. How is your hand?"

"Aching a bit."

"And your head?"

"Except for the lump, it is well."

Ali nodded with satisfaction, noting that she had changed from her blood-stained gown into a garment of bright yellow linen. It was a beautiful dress of soft layers, very flattering to her white skin. Her glorious red hair was pulled off her face with a matching ribbon and he thought she looked particularly fragile this day. But he had come for a reason, not to gawk at the lady's beauty.

"I have been sent to escort you, if you would be so gracious as to accompany me."

Without question, Peyton rose and followed Ali to the door. Ivy, seeing that she was about to be left alone, looked rather sad until Ali stroked her cheek gently. "I shall return for you shortly, sweetling."

Peyton, in spite of her depressed mood, saw an opportunity to taunt her sister and she would not pass it up. Ali's tone was so sickly sweet that she could not resist mouthing "sweetling" to her sister as the soldier preceded her into the corridor. Ivy made a menacing face and stuck her tongue out, bringing a smile of genuine humor to Peyton's lips. White or black, Ali was a man and Peyton was compelled to tease Ivy as if he were any other suitor.

She did not utter a word of inquiry as the dark soldier took her outside into the late afternoon heat, and she still did not voice her puzzlement when he took her into the stable yards. Not until he led her into the quiet dimness of the livery did she look to him questioning.

"Ali, why have you brought me here?"

He smiled gently. "Someone wishes to have a word with you, demoiselle."

Her brow furrowed just as Alec stepped from the shadows. He was dressed in a heavy traveling tunic and a leather overvest. In fact, he was dressed exactly as she had seen him the morning he had found her in the woods.

"Greetings, my lady," he said softly.

Immediately, her pulse began to race but she held her ground, refusing to allow him to see how apprehensive she was. She stared at him a moment before turning to Ali.

"Is this why you brought me here? I have nothing to say to him."

"But I have a good deal to say to you," Alec said softly, gently. "Would you allow me the privilege before you turn your back on me?"

"Why?" she spat, making sure to meet his eye. "You would not give me the courtesy of explaining myself before you were breaking tables and hurling chairs. Why should I show you any consideration at all?"

"Because you are far more gracious and wise than I am, my lady. I only ask a brief moment of your time. Please."

She was shaking with emotion, gazing bitterly into his blue eyes. Her taut body and angry expression told him that she was still furious with him, as well she should be, and he fought the urge to drop to his knees and plead for mercy.

Peyton tore her eyes away from his sorrowful orbs and studied his clothing. As her attention was occupied, Alec motioned Ali away with a faint nod and the soldier discreetly vacated the stable.

"Where are you going?" she asked after a moment.

"Away," he replied honestly. "But I wish to speak with you before I go."

Away? Suddenly Peyton did not like the idea of him leaving. Where was he going? Angry or not, confused or not, she did not want him to leave.

"Speak then," she said shortly.

His gaze lingered on her a moment and she felt the familiar heat from his attentions, but she ignored it. This was not the time for such feelings, as delicious as they could be.

Alec knew this was probably his one and only chance to apologize and he chose his words carefully. "Although I know my actions this day were inexcusable, mayhap you will allow me to give you a bit of insight. As I said before, the church considers Ali less than a man and therefore will not admit him into knighthood. In fact, the only people who ever considered Ali an equal are the men he served with as a warrior, men who have seen his bravery and brilliance. Women, on the other hand, have been very cruel for the most part," his voice softened. "Ali and I grew up together, fostered together, and I can honestly say I never knew an English lady who looked at Ali as a man. They considered him a freak, something to be laughed and gawked at. I remember one time at a celebration at Roby Castle in Yorkshire, Ali approached a young lady and asked her to dance. She immediately laughed in his face and announced quite loudly that she did not associate with apes. Her friends joined in the laughter and began mocking him terribly. Ali simply smiled, bowed crisply in thanks, and walked away. I wanted to kill the wench, but Ali let the insult roll off his back as if it mattered not. But it mattered a great deal."

Peyton listened, her heart aching for the black warrior even as her anger at Alec faded. She could see that simply speaking on the subject upset Alec a great deal.

"A few years ago, after we returned from the Holy Land, he fell in love with a woman who lives not far from here. She was the only woman who showed him a small amount of kindness and, of course, he was smitten. Ali even went so far as to ask for her hand, but her father refused cruelly. When Ali asked her to run away with him to be married, she told him that although she was fond of him, she could never marry him because he was not a true man. It would seem that she was only kind to Ali out of pity," he leaned against the wall, his expression pensive. "The only women Ali was able to associate with were women who were paid for their services. He lost his innocence to a woman of forty-some years who carried the French pox. Ali still bears scars from the disease."

Peyton was completely calm by the time he finished, gazing at him openly and without hostilities. He met her eyes and smiled weakly. "I suppose what I am trying to say, although not entirely adequately, is that I overreacted to your statement simply because I have grown accustomed to women describing Ali as a beast. And I was angry with you for deceiving me into believing that you could mayhap learn to see him as I do. I saw hope in your manner, in your actions. I wanted to believe it was possible."

She crossed her arms thoughtfully. "Alec, I will admit that his skin color shocked me at first; it was difficult not to react to his darkness in a land full of white-skinned people. And I will further admit that I had my own doubts as to whether or not he was a true man. But I have been witness to his intelligence, I have learned to trust my sister's opinion of him, and I have discovered that there is indeed an authentic man beneath the ebony skin. Certainly there is a wide collection of men I would refer to as beasts, but Ali is not among them."

"I realize that now," his voice was a whisper. "But I reacted to you as I have so wanted to react all of these years to every woman who has ever seen Ali as though he were some sort of monstrosity. But I knew deep in my heart that you are not like them in the least."

"But you have grown used to them and, therefore, reacted accordingly and assumed I was of the same shallow traits," she supplied quietly. "I have already admitted that I did share some of those qualities. But I would like to think that I can overcome them."

He nodded, meeting her gaze with a look of sincere remorse. "I called you a bitch, Peyton, and I am deeply sorry. The term is the very farthest from the truth."

She continued to gaze at him a moment, feeling a deep sense of understanding for his earlier actions. In truth, she hadn't been the target; it had been all of the women she represented. Above all of the terror and confusion his rage represented, she deeply admired Alec his devotion to his friend.

"You are so wrong," she said softly. "I can indeed be a bitch when the mood strikes me. Ask Ivy."

His weak smile returned more genuine than before. "I choose to disbelieve you. You are stubborn, aggressive and willful, but you are not a bitch."

Her eyebrows arched. "Stubborn, aggressive and willful? And, pray, what else? I had no idea you thought so highly of me, Sir Alec."

He could feel relief flooding him at the beginnings of the raillery they seemed to share. He was nearly weak with hope that mayhap she was willing to forgive him and grateful to realize that she was not only beautiful, she was rational and perceptive as well. Only a good deal of understanding and intelligence would have been able to comprehend what he had attempted to explain in his own defense.

"I do indeed think highly of you, my lady," he said softly. "Much more than you know."

She smiled faintly, feeling terribly relieved that she understood his reasons for his rage but now terribly concerned that he was leaving. She again indicated his clothing.

"Tell me where you are going."

He pursed his lips thoughtfully and she found herself staring at his delightfully smooth, masculine lips. Lips that made her feel more wonderful than she had ever dreamt possible.

"There is a bit of a problem that concerns us both, my lady. After my display this afternoon, my father is intent on dissolving our marriage contract."

Peyton's face went slack with shock. "He is? Why on earth?"

"Because he fears for your safety. You see, my lady, there has never been a man or woman who could provoke me beyond reason, which is exactly what happened this afternoon. My father fears that eventually I will harm you in some way if you indeed possess the power to bait me senseless."

She stared at him, her sapphire blue eyes endless. "You would never harm me, would you?"

His face washed with indescribable softness. "Of course not. I would kill for you, or die for you, but I would never touch a hair on your beautiful head in anger."

She cocked her head, her brow creased with puzzlement. "You would die for me?"

"Without hesitation."

"But why?"

He smiled gently. "Why not? You are worth dying for."

She appeared genuinely stunned, averting her gaze. "James never even declared such devotion," she murmured, more to herself.

Alec heard her but he did not respond. Suddenly, a seed of jealously formed deep within his heart at the mention of her former love and he was shocked. He wasn't envious of a dead man, but he realized that he wanted Peyton to speak of him with the same adoration. It wasn't so much the words as in the tone, and the more he thought on it, the more he became aware of how very much he wanted Peyton to speak of him as fondly.

"Father plans to betroth you to Colin Warrington in the hope that a marriage will ease tensions between your respective families."

Peyton's eyes bugged wide and her creamy cheeks flushed brightly. "Colin Warrington! Never! I would sooner kill myself than wed that ill-mannered dog!"

"Then I take it that in spite of my tantrum, you would rather marry me?"

"I would marry the Devil himself before marrying Colin Warrington!"

He gave her a quirky smile. "I am afraid the Devil already has a wife. Will I suffice?"

She eyed him a moment. "If you promise never to rage again in my presence, I shall consider it."

He lost all of his mirth and dropped on bended knee before her. It was a swift, graceful motion that startled her; before she realized it, Alec was kneeling beautifully and her right hand was neatly tucked into the fold of his closed palm.

"With God as my witness, I swear to you that I shall never again display such appalling manners. I may lose my temper and I cannot promise that I will never again speak a harsh word, but I vow this day that I shall never again rage against you."

She was astonished at the passion of his statement. She felt her guard lowering and it was further melted by the candor of his demonstration. This was the Alec she had come to know, the gentle giant with a heart deeper than a well. A soft smile creased her beautiful lips.

"I believe you, my Alec," she whispered. "Aye, I would marry you over Colin Warrington. And the Devil."

He brought her hand to his lips and excitement jolted her so that she involuntarily gasped. Her left hand went to his head tenderly as his lips thanked her gently for her compassion. His kisses covered her hand and moved to her wrist as Peyton continued to gently touch his cropped hair, thinking him to be entirely too handsome and chivalrous for his own good.

Before she realized it, he had pulled her into a snug embrace against his hard chest and she found herself gazing down into his sky-blue eyes as his chin rested on the swell of her breasts. It was remarkable that they were hovering so close to one another and not giving in to deliciously hot kisses; instead, they gazed deeply into each other's eyes, rejoicing in the fact that all was well between them once again.

"I thought I had destroyed everything we had established between us," he whispered, his breathing noticeably ragged. "I am so very sorry for what I did, Peyton. I never meant to hurt you."

"You did not, really," she answered with equal breathlessness. "But you frightened me. Lord, Alec, you are so massive that you could easily tear me apart were you so inclined."

He kissed the palms of her hands as they gripped his head, especially the bandaged hand. "I did indeed hurt you as there is the proof. But I never meant to, truly. You are most gracious to forgive me my transgression."

She smiled giddily, her insides quivering with their close proximity. "This time only. Next time, I shall brandish a mace and aim for your head."

"And I would stand stock still to better your focus," he agreed earnestly.

"My aim is true, my lord. I would not need…."

He cut her off with a bruising kiss. She responded with eager whimpers, encouraging him. He licked at her lips and she answered by opening her mouth to him, but he suddenly stopped.

"I would hear you call me by my name, always," he whispered, his hot breath on her face driving her weak for the want of him. "Say it."

"Alec," she breathed.

He kissed her fiercely, his tongue delving into the sweet depths of her mouth before withdrawing sharply. "Not that way. The way you said it before. Possessively."

She had no idea what he was talking about. "What do you mean?"

Again, he slanted his lips over hers harshly, suckling and licking her until she was gasping with desire. "Say it."

"What?" she demanded with as much force as she could muster in between feverish kisses.

"My Alec. You will address me as your own."

"My..?" she began, but he quelled her inquiry with kisses forceful enough to turn her body to jelly; her knees had long since given out and he fully supported her against him.

"Say it."

She grinned at him, a wonderful sort of gesture that made him respond in kind. "*My Alec*. My darling Alec."

She beat him to the kiss this time, planting her delightfully supple lips onto his eager mouth. His gloved hands entwined themselves in her hair and they lost their balance, toppling over onto a large pile of fresh straw.

The stable was deserted and quiet, as the servants were eating their evening meal. In the darkened corner of the livery, Alec rolled Peyton on to her back and continued to ravish her thoroughly. She gasped with the new passion he had so quickly aroused in her on the very first day they had met, clutching him tightly as his mouth drove her insane with desire.

The straw beneath them crunched softly as he moved for the stays on her gown. Even as his mouth fused with hers, she could feel him removing her surcoat, pulling it down her torso and practically tearing it free of her legs. She heard the garment land with a soft rush in the straw next to them as he went to work on the more restrictive shift.

Peyton did not even realize he had completely stripped her when he suddenly paused in his onslaught to unstrap the studded leather belt from his narrow waist. In a fury, the belt and tunics came off, and she watched him through dazed eyes as he lowered his hose. Somewhat regaining her senses, she noticed in the weak light that he had the most magnificent chest she had ever seen. Broad and nearly hairless, it was tanned golden and smooth and her breathing grew more rapid at the sight. She'd seen men's bare chests before, rarely of course, and she knew without a doubt that Alec possessed the most extraordinary form she had ever seen. It took her breath away as she gazed up at him, absolutely flawless.

He paused in his rush when he saw that she was watching him.

Suddenly, he seemed apologetic and he leaned over her, bracing his thick arms on either side of her body.

"I know.... we should not do this, sweetheart, but I cannot help what I feel. I must have you."

"And if I were to refuse you at this moment?"

He paused. "I would put my clothes back on, I suppose."

She brushed a stray lock from her face. "Then put them back on. I am not your wife yet and you may not do as you please with me."

He stared at her and sat back on his heels. His gaze lingered on her a moment longer before he glanced around in search of his tunic. Just as he located the garment and reached a hand to it, she stopped him.

"You would really put your clothes back on?" she asked with a hint of regret.

"I will not force you."

The setting sun cast a warm glow into the darkened stable, bathing her beautiful body in an orange light. Her eyes roved over his superb form, coming to rest on his freed manroot. It was absolutely enormous and she sat up, studying him without embarrassment. Being a proper maiden she should have been mortified, but she found that she was not the least bit ashamed. After all, Alec's entire body was glorious and his manhood was simply another portion, like an arm or a leg, albeit a very personal portion.

"You say it will fit?" she asked timidly.

He looked down at himself, tunic in hand as he prepared to dress. "Undoubtedly."

She turned her gaze to him. "I have never seen.... that is, I have seen horses and bulls rutting, but I have never seen a rutting man. Are they all as large as you?"

He smiled. "Nay, they are not."

She tilted her head thoughtfully. "Are you sure it will fit?"

He chuckled softly. "Sweetheart, the children you bear will have heads and bodies considerably larger than my manhood. You, dear lady, are built by virtue of nature to accommodate a man between your legs. I promise you that I will fit."

She nodded, pondering his statement and discovering that it did indeed make sense.

"Are you afraid?" he asked gently, sensing her reluctance.

"A bit," she replied honestly, lifting her gaze to meet his and he could see a faint mottling of flush in her cheeks. "This will hurt, will it not?"

He tossed the tunic aside. Gracefully, he lowered himself and pushed her onto her back in the same motion. His great body half-covered her as he pushed bits of stray red hair behind her ear.

"I am told that it most always uncomfortable the first time for a maiden," he said softly. "I suppose we will find out."

She gazed back at him, lifting a timid finger to trace the line of his smooth lips. "Have you never bedded a maiden before?"

"Never. I am quite new at this."

"But you have learned from other women to be gentle, have you not?"

He could read her rising apprehension and sought to comfort her. Yet he, too, was apprehensive. When he said he was new to this, he meant in nearly every aspect.

"Have I ever been rough with you, Peyton? Have I ever demonstrated anything other than complete gentleness whenever we have touched?"

"Oh, Alec, you have been entirely tender always. Your touch is as gentle as a lamb's."

"Then I shall be gentle in this endeavor as well," he dipped down and kissed the bridge of her nose. "Shall we continue?"

"That depends. Is your father intent on marrying me to Colin Warrington?"

Alec's soft face tensed. "Mayhap. But the marriage will never take place, for I intend to wed you myself this very night."

"But…. I do not understand. How can you marry me if your father would dissolve the betrothal?"

"Because I intend to take you south to Ely tonight and marry you."

"Oh," she looked slightly astonished by the declaration and he smiled tenderly.

"Is this not acceptable? Either that or you marry Colin Warrington. I will allow you to choose."

She raised an eyebrow. "Some choice. Allow me to contemplate this a moment, if you would."

He lowered his head, his lips lingering directly above her delicious mouth. "Time has expired, my lady. I have made your decision for you."

His lips clamped down and Peyton reacted instantaneously, winding her arms around his thick neck as if she were clinging to him for her own life. Instinctively, she trusted him completely. He had always been gentle with her and she had no reason to believe that this would be any different.

She eagerly anticipated every move he made, moaning softly as his hot lips suckled her breasts eagerly. His suckling motion created a fire between her legs, a sensation she was coming to associate with Alec's touch. She wondered what magic he possessed that caused her to react in such a manner when James, a man she loved, had never provoked such a wanton response. Was it at all possible that she was coming to love Alec and not even realize it?

Alec lapped the sweetness of her breasts, his passion and lust growing by leaps and bounds. His great hand moved down the curve of her torso, delighting in the silky skin. She had the most incredible skin, silky and smooth and flawless.

When his hand reached the softness of her tender inner thighs, she reflexively startled and he caressed her soothingly, whispering comforting words in between scalding kisses.

Peyton heard the words, calmed by his gentle manner and tender touch. But she couldn't help but stiffen when he fingered the red curls between her legs. Even with her natural fear, Alec was pleased to discover that she was slick with moisture and he plunged his tongue into her navel with relish.

Peyton gasped with surprise and he laughed low, bringing himself up to face her as the straw beneath them crackled and scratched. He gazed deeply into her eyes, emotions such as he had never known running rampant. He would be her first and, barring his death, her last lover. And the same would be said for him.

He was so excited that he was trembling as he slanted over her lips once again, with less force and far more emotion. His movements were slow and erotic, all-consuming and bold as his big legs parted her thighs gently but firmly. She opened her legs to him, her passion keeping rein on her maiden's apprehension. She knew she should be terrified of what they were about to do, but she found that she wanted him to touch her, to teach her the heights of passion he had promised within his feverish kisses and tender touch. Aye, she should very well be scared witless. But within the warm folds of his massive embrace, she could only want for more to satisfy the raging desire that surged within her.

Her mind was completely void of any feelings or thoughts other than those of Alec and his magic. When his fingers danced delicately over the thick lips of her private core, she gasped with excitement. A touch she should have shied from, she wanted desperately.

James had never worked such miracles within her soul and she should have felt guilty for giving herself so freely to another man, but she found she wasn't guilty in the least. With each touch, with each kiss, Alec buried James deeper and deeper within the recesses of her mind.

He removed his fingers and Peyton felt his arousal pushing at her, seeking her promised treasure. She was desperate to feel him inside her, wondering if she would find the relief she sought the moment he entered her. Would her passion be sated? Would her desire crest, leaving her weak and satisfied? She truly wasn't sure what to expect, of what sort of pleasure lay in store as he entered her slowly. She only knew for certain that she needed him within her.

Alec tried to bank his frenzy, God only knew, but when she awkwardly pushed forward with her hips, his control slipped and he drove hard. Peyton gasped loudly into his mouth and he drove again, and again, and she cried out softly with the pain of possession. His passionate kisses drowned out her moans, acutely aware of her tightness around his enormous manhood and he knew he had to be hurting her terribly. But his own ecstasy was so tremendous that he almost did not care. He'd found Heaven.

She shifted underneath him in an attempt to move away, but he held her tightly and thrust one last time, seating himself to the hilt. Never had he experienced anything more magnificent. Peyton tore her mouth away from his raiding lips and drew in a long, ragged gasp. The hot, stinging pain radiated throughout her groin and into her legs and she was positive that he had injured her, yet in the same breath, she had never felt anything so incredibly private or wonderful.

It was a peculiar delirium she struggled with as he held her tightly, not moving as they both became accustomed to the very new experience. She could feel his massive root throbbing inside of her, anxiously awaiting the opportunity for release. But Alec held still, clutching her tightly.

Her nails had dug bloody crescents into his shoulders as she held onto him, waiting for the pain to subside. Her rapid breathing filled the dim stable and she was highly aware of his tremendous weight and size upon her. He lay so still that she would have wondered if he was even alive but for his heavy breathing. When she opened her mouth to speak, he suddenly raised his head and his lips claimed her once again.

Peyton forgot the pain. Alec began to stroke in and out of her, a bit unskillfully and on more than one occasion dislodged himself completely, but the more he practiced, the better he became. She began to meet his thrusts, their bodies clashing with fired intensity so hot that she was sure their passion would ignite the straw beneath them.

And as her pain faded, another heat took hold and began to build. Every time their bodies met, it was as if the heat increased and she began to live for each successive thrust. She was seeking what only Alec could satisfy, although she had no idea what that might be, until he suddenly thrust so firmly that her teeth rattled and she heard him moan her name softly. She felt him pulsing within her and suddenly she was plummeted over the threshold of passion, her first climax coming so hard that she began to sob. Wave after delicious wave swept her, slowly fading away until she was only aware of her pounding heart.

The straw softened Alec's enormous weight on her and he was thankful. Lying atop her glorious body, he couldn't have moved if God himself had demanded it. But his lethargy was more than simply his need being satisfied; it was equally due to his emotional shock.

He was imminently grateful that he had never seen his way to bed another woman; it made coupling with Peyton all the more magnificent. He could not imagine the words that would adequately describe what he was feeling, so many emotions swirling within the warm-hazed field of his mind that he couldn't grasp a single one. He was feeling more than he ever had about anything in his entire life.

"Are you well, sweetheart?" he asked softly.

Jolted from her dozing state, Peyton opened her eyes slowly to stare at the rafters of the stable. Alec's great head lay near her shoulder, pillowed by the straw.

"Aye," she whispered.

His hand came up to stroke her cheek and she turned slightly to see him gazing at her tenderly.

"But I hurt you," he said quietly.

"The rapture outweighed the discomfort," she assured him.

He smiled, fingering her red hair. "You are entirely brave, my lady. Your courage awes me."

She returned his smile, moving to touch his clefted chin and square jaw. "And your strength and power amaze me, my Alec. 'Twas the most magical moment of my life, I think."

He kissed her hand as it brushed by his lips. "And mine. How fortunate I am to have you."

She shifted slightly, crunching the straw, and put an arm behind her head. "I wonder if it will always be like this for us. Has it always been as wonderful for you, every time?"

He gazed at her a moment. "Nay. Just this once."

"It has only been wonderful this one time with me? You have never before achieved such bliss?"

"Nay," he shook his head, his voice a whisper. "I have never done this before."

Her eyes widened and she suddenly attempted to sit up. Alec was forced to roll off of her delicious body as she propped herself up on an elbow. "You have never…. Alec, do you mean to tell me that you have never had a woman before?"

"Never in the literal sense."

Her mouth opened in surprise. "How old are you?"

"Thirty-two years."

"And you have never bedded a woman?"

He shook his head faintly. "I have done everything to a woman that can be done except penetrate her, and I have had everything done to me as well. I have probably done some things that even seasoned men have never heard of but I have never entered a woman as I entered you. I have never made love before."

Peyton stared at him in disbelief, shocked at his confession. But as her shock settled, a most wonderful sense of euphoria filled her to think that she had been the very first woman he had made love to. An amazing smile graced her lips, one of utter happiness and astonishment.

"Alec, you are a virgin?"

"Not anymore."

She laughed. "Nor am I. Alec…. I am speechless. I thought certain you had…. well, you certainly knew what you were doing."

He kissed her, hard, cutting off her words. Properly silenced, he grinned and brushed bits of red hair out of her face.

"Now, my lady, it would appear that we have a bit of a problem. It is usual to consummate the marriage after the ceremony, and it would seem that we have completed events out of order. 'Tis most logical that we dress and ride for Ely immediately to correct the situation."

Her smile faded. "I should have stopped you as I have done before, but I couldn't seem to.... I did not want to," she flushed slightly, lowering her gaze from him. "Will your father be terribly angry that you have disobeyed him and married me?"

He kissed her again, twice, and sat up in search of his clothing. "Most likely. But he shall overcome his fury. Moreover, when I tell him that you seduced me, he shall quite agree to our union."

"Seduced you?" she repeated with outrage, sitting up next to him. "Why, you practically ripped my clothes off of me, you brute. How dare you say that I seduced you."

He grinned at her, turning to kiss her soundly as he snatched his tunic. "Lady, you seduce me simply by your presence. I am a weak man at the sight of you."

She blushed at his compliment, averting her gaze again. As she turned her downcast eyes to the straw, her gaze came to rest on her blood-smeared thighs and she gasped. Concerned, he looked to the source of her distress.

"I shall get you some water to wash that off," he said softly.

"But...." she wiped at the spots with her hand. "You hurt me, Alec. I am bleeding!"

He stood up, pulling up his hose. "Sweetheart, I did not hurt you and 'tis completely natural for you to bleed a little during the loss of your innocence."

She glared at him doubtfully. "I realize that, only I did not expect to see quite so much.... blood. You did not bleed as well, did you?"

He laughed low in his throat. "Nay, love. Men do not bleed when they lose their virginity. Just women."

She closed her thighs and hugged her legs, watching him pull his tunic over his head. "Alec?"

"What, sweet?"

She did not answer for a moment and he looked at her expectantly as he straightened his tunic. Seeing his attention, she blushed and lowered her gaze. "I…. thank you."

He half-grinned, snatching his leather over tunic from the dirt floor. "For what?"

"For waiting."

He stopped his movements, leather tunic half-way to his head. After a moment's contemplation of what she meant by her short answer, he continued to pull the tunic over his head.

"You are welcome."

She lifted her gaze again, watching him dress. "I suppose what I mean to say is that I am glad you waited for me. Sometimes I think it is rather unfair that the woman is expected to remain a virgin until marriage and not the man. I feel better knowing that no woman has marked you before."

"Lady, not only have you marked my heart, you have tattooed yourself onto my body," he touched his shoulders with a grin. "I am verily proud of my battle wounds."

Her eyes widened with astonishment. "I have marked your heart?"

His humor faded and she could see his confusion as he reached for his studded leather belt. "Of course you have," he said softly. "Why do you think I am willing to defy my father to marry you?"

He was being completely honest in spite of his confusion and she felt a surge of courage. As puzzled as she was by her conflicting feelings and her love of James, deep down, she knew the truth.

"I think you have marked me, too," she whispered.

He looked at her, the porcelain face and incredible hair, and felt a rush of joy at her admission. But he was still frightened and confused; this woman had power over him and that scared the wits from him. It frightened him that his heart could so easily control his head.

A tin cistern of water was a few feet away. He retrieved a handkerchief from his traveling satchel and dipped it in the water, bringing it to Peyton. He turned away as she quickly washed away her blood, and then moved to the stable door to watch the activity of the castle as she dressed privately.

It was still quiet on the grounds as the sun set and his mind moved ahead quickly to the journey that await. Peyton approached him, shaking the straw from her hair and he smiled at her, picking out bits of chaff from the golden-red tresses.

"I shall saddle Midas and we will be on our way," he said quietly. "There should be a comb in my satchel for your hair."

She cocked an eyebrow, eyeing the large bag on the floor near the wall. "You were certainly confident that I would agree to your proposal. Pray, what else is packed for me?"

"I do not know," he replied, moving to Midas with a bridle. "Ali packed the bag."

"Good lord," she muttered, digging through the bag. Tunics for Alec, some sort of rough garments for her, soap, a heavy cloak, a battered metal mirror and a tortoise shell comb. "Where did he get this clothing? 'Tis nothing of mine."

"He made do with what he could collect." Bridled, Midas stood still as Alec swung a heavy woolen saddle blanket onto his silver back.

Peyton continued to dig about in the bag and finally stood up, brushing off her hands. "Unacceptable. I would gather my own things."

"There is no time, sweetheart." The saddle Alec placed on Midas must have weight one hundred pounds, but Alec lifted it as if it were made of fluff. Peyton watched him, marveling at his strength. She couldn't have managed to move the saddle much less lift it.

"I will only take ten minutes. Can we spare ten minutes?"

He slanted her a gaze as he cinched the straps. "Peyton, if we are discovered there will most like not be a marriage this night, if ever. The longer we remain, the better the chance of us being detained. We must leave as soon as my horse is readied and we cannot spare even a moment longer."

She frowned at him, realizing he was most likely right. Resigned and pouting, she retrieved the comb from the bag and combed the straw out of her considerable mane.

He concentrated on preparing his horse, every so often glancing at her bright head and hardly believing what he was about to do. He was about to elope with a woman he never wanted in the first place. He shook his head at the irony, knowing how very wrong his father was; they were perfect together in every way and nothing short of death could force him to relinquish her.

He was nearly finished with Midas when Peyton suddenly dropped the comb and rushed to him. "Alec! I think I hear someone coming!"

He grabbed her, pulling her into the shadows of Midas' stall and motioning for her to remain hidden. Then, casually, he returned to his horse and finished his task just as Jubil rounded the corner to the stable. Alec looked to her with some surprise, eyeing the bag in the woman's hand.

"My lady," he greeted. "What are you doing out here in the stables?"

Jubil entered the dim livery, her gaze darting about. "Where's Peyton?"

Alec stopped fumbling with his saddle and leaned an arm on his horse. "What makes you think she is here? As you can see, I am preparing to leave and…."

"She is going with you, of course," Jubil finished for him. Then she called out: "Peyton, sweetheart? I have brought you a bag!"

Alec would have liked for Peyton to stay out of sight as long as he deemed necessary, but Peyton had a mind of her own. Her luscious red hair glistened in the weak light as she moved out of the stall and stood next to Alec.

"Why did you bring me a bag?" she asked her aunt.

Jubil thrust the leather and canvas satchel at her niece.

"You will surely need clothing for your journey."

Peyton raised a slow eyebrow. "What are you talking about? Jubil, are you flying again?"

"Nay, sweetheart, not at all," Jubil said softly. "I overheard Lord Summerlin and his wife speaking about your possible betrothal to Colin

Warrington and I knew that Alec would not let you go. I could only assume that he was taking you away this night, since Lord Summerlin is already drawing up a contract between you and Warrington."

Peyton felt a stab of distaste at the thought and looked to Alec for his reaction. As usual, his face was expressionless. "Did my father say he had already created the betrothal contract between Peyton and Warrington?"

"He was attempting to complete it, but your mother was most resistant to the idea," Jubil said. "She seems to think that you and Peyton belong together, in spite of everything."

Alec cocked a contemplative eyebrow, his only response. Jubil was staring at the man openly but managed to tear her eyes away long enough to look to her niece. "Ivy is being readied for her wedding, Peyton, and she is frantic to find you. Ali cannot keep her uninformed much longer and I would suggest that you leave immediately."

Peyton's eyes suddenly stung with tears as she realized that she would miss her sister's wedding. With a heavy sigh, she nodded reluctantly and Alec put his hand on her shoulder, sensing her thoughts.

"Come on, sweetheart. 'Tis time to leave," he glanced at the older woman. "I will trust you with our secret, then. Not a word, Aunt Jubil, and I shall be grateful."

Jubil blushed at the use of her name. "Lucifer himself could not wrest it from my mouth."

He nodded confidently in reply, turning to Peyton. "I want you to exit via the servant's gate near the kitchens and meet me out in front. I must take Midas through the gates, as he is far too large to pass through the tunnel entrance."

"But what if your father sees you?" Peyton asked. "Won't he try to stop you?"

Alec shook his head. "I doubt it. After the conversation we had earlier, he shall most likely think I am going off to sulk."

Satisfied, Peyton nodded and Alec led Midas from his stall, clutching her with his other hand. Jubil moved briskly to her niece, digging through the bag she held.

"Your cloak, sweetheart," she said, swinging a heavy brocade cape over Peyton's shoulders. It was a beautiful forest-green, lined with brown rabbit and nearly too hot on this warm night. But there was dampness to the air and she would be grateful for the protection later. Alec watched with approval as Jubil secured the cloak, oblivious to Peyton's protests that it was too warm to wear.

"You will need the cloak to protect you from the night," he said with a faint smile, casting a glance at Jubil. "Thank you, my lady. Your foresight is appreciated."

"My pleasure," Jubil smiled openly at him and Peyton shook her head.

"Traitorous cow," she muttered. "You would do anything for him regardless of my feelings, would not you?"

"He is to be your husband," Jubil said firmly. "We must obey the master, mustn't we?"

Peyton snarled her lip at her aunt as Alec snickered. Outside the stables, the servants were beginning to return from their evening meal and Alec tossed Midas' reins on to the pommel of the saddle.

"Go now," he whispered to Peyton. "I shall meet you out in front."

Peyton peered out into the stable yard. "But all of those servants are going to see me. Won't they tell your father that I ran off – again?"

Alec started to reply but Jubil interrupted. "They'll not see you, sweetheart."

With that, Jubil left the stable and strolled through the yard toward the castle. Suddenly, she let out a rousing yell and launched into the loudest song Alec had ever heard outside of a tavern. Instantly, all of the servants in the stable yard turned to the thunderous source of the tune and watched the woman with great curiosity. Peyton, knowing that the time was upon her to depart while the servants' attentions were occupied, pulled the cloak about her and started for the stable door.

But Alec grasped her before she could take a full step, planting his delicious lips firmly on her own. The warm, lingering kiss made her toes tingle. He pulled away, grinning.

"For luck," he whispered.

Her cheeks flushed, she returned his smile shyly and slipped from the livery. Alec watched for several moments as she moved silently across the courtyard before mounting Midas and riding unmolested from the bailey of Blackstone.

CHAPTER NINE

THE VILLAGE OF Ely sat nine miles to the southeast of Blackstone on the plain of Fenland, sometimes alluded to as the Isle of Ely in reference to the days when the entire region was an untrained marsh. Bordered by the River Ouse, the hamlet was asleep for the most part as Alec entered the outskirts. It was an unremarkable little town until one lay sights on the Norman cathedral that dominated the skyline; a most remarkable structure with towers that soared to the sky like fingers reaching for heaven.

It was an hour before midnight as Midas' hoof-falls echoed against the cobblestone toward the cathedral. They passed a tavern and Peyton studied it intently, listening to the singing and laughing and wishing that Alec would take her inside simply so she could see what it was like. Having barely ventured from the confines of St. Cloven, she was understandably curious.

A couple of knights came stumbling through the front doors and immediately made comment of Midas as they rode past. Alec ignored the whooping and hollering, even when the men yelled their highest bid for the magnificent destrier.

Peyton kept the hood of her cloak over her head protectively, shielding her face from the loud men and feeling a good amount of apprehension. She was afraid they would try to steal the horse from underneath them and Alec was unarmed but for his crossbow and a dagger. He wore no sword, something she considered most strange. Suppose he was called upon to defend them both; he would have no ready means of protection. Suppose they fell into danger somehow? Suppose..?

"Why is it that you do not wear a sword and armor?" she asked.

"As I told your sister, I gave up knightly pursuits long ago."

"But why?" she turned to look at him. "What if I were to need defending, Alec? You have no sword to accomplish this."

He grinned in the moonlight. "God help the man who provokes you, my lady. You are the last woman in the world who needs defending."

She scowled reproachfully. "You know what I mean. You are certainly not past your prime, and I know you fought with Edward on the Seventh Crusade. Why is it you do not bear arms anymore?"

His smile faded and he looked away after a moment. "I choose not to."

She stared at him, perturbed that he was avoiding her question. She had a right to know, after all. If she was to be his wife, then she would know why he chose not to bear a sword like most husbands. But it was obvious that there was far more to her question than a simple answer. Irritated, she turned away.

The cathedral loomed before them momentarily. Alec reined Midas to the monastery that bordered the monstrous church and dismounted, pulling Peyton off with him. Taking her hand, he led her to the carved oaken door and rapped heavily.

A short man with thin hair answered, dressed in coarse brown wool. His eyes widened slightly at the sight of Alec, surely the largest man he had ever beheld.

"How may I help you, my lord?" he asked in a soft voice.

"My lady and I wish to be married this night. I would speak with the Monsignor."

The monk beckoned them inside. "Leave your sword at the door, my lord, and follow me."

"I bear no sword," Alec said, almost stiffly.

The monk merely nodded his head and moved silently down the narrow hall. Alec, for his massive size, kept bumping into wall sconces and rosaries as he followed, thankful when the little man stopped and motioned them into a room. Alec ducked underneath the door frame as he entered the small chamber.

"You will wait here, and I shall summon Father Lenardon."

"He is the Monsignor?"

"He is my superior and capable of transacting such business as you seek," the monk closed the door softly.

Peyton removed her hood and glanced about the small, vacant chamber. "I feel as if I am in prison."

Alec gazed at the meager furnishings and whitewashed walls, clean but worn. "I see your point. I myself feel as if I have just entered an abode meant for midgets," he motioned to a small stool. "Sit, sweetheart. We could be in for a long wait."

She shook her head. "My backside is sore from so much riding," instead, she pressed her back against a wall to stretch out the muscles. "I wonder if your father realizes that we are both missing."

"If he doesn't by now, he will shortly," Alec fumbled with his thick leather gloves, loosening them. "But there is naught he can do, even if Jubil tells him what she knows."

"He shall be angry," Peyton said softly.

"He shall get over it," Alec shrugged. "Especially when he sees his grandson next year."

She smiled, a delightful flush mottling her cheeks and he went to her, taking her face between his huge hands.

"I pray that the past few hours of riding have not made you overly sore," he said with a tender smile.

"Not overly," she replied, her eyes locking with his. "'Tis a bit tender to walk, but nothing more. I am sure it will be gone by the morrow."

"And I promise I will not aggravate you until such time as you are properly healed," he said with a twinkle to his eye. "It may kill me, but I shall valiantly adhere to my vow."

She put her fist into his stomach playfully and pulled from his grasp. "You are a vulgar beast, Alec."

He pretended to rub the spot where she had weakly punched him. "And you, my lady, are enticing beyond reason."

Abruptly, her smile faded and she turned away. Alec saw her expression harden and he was puzzled. He reached out and grasped her arm gently.

"What is it, sweetheart? What did I say?"

She pulled free and moved away from him. "Nothing, Alec."

He followed her, grasping her chin gently and forcing her to look at him. "If there is one thing I will demand in this marriage, it is honesty. What did I say to upset you so?"

She heard her own words echoed in his voice and she sighed with resignation. A terribly clever man, her future husband. Slowly, she sat on a sturdy little stool.

"James used to tell me I was indecently enticing," she murmured, turning to him after a moment. "You simply reminded me of him, that's all."

He gazed down at her, again feeling the peculiar stab of jealousy he had experienced once before. The more he pondered her statement, the more he needed to clarify the entire Deveraux relationship. It was as if something inside him demanded to know what, exactly, he was up against. He'd not particularly cared until this moment.

"Did you love him terribly, Peyton, or were you simply resigned to the fact that he would be your husband and felt a duty to be fond of him?"

Instead of becoming angry, a painful expression washed her features and for a moment he thought she was going to cry. "I loved him. Love him, I mean. I was looking forward to spending my life as Lady Deveraux until all of my dreams were destroyed by the point of a spear-tipped joust pole," she lowered her gaze, remembering the event once again but, strangely, without the wrenching pain that usually accompanied the memory. "Do you know that the spear went all of the way through him? By the time I reached him on the field, he was laying on his side and six inches of the spear protruded from his back. I tried to hold him but…. it was awkward. I could only cradle his head."

"I am surprised that the marshals allowed the spear-tipped pole to be used. They ceased using those poles long ago; in fact, I have never competed against anyone who wielded a spear-tipped shaft."

Peyton turned her pensive face to him. "As I said, the knight had broken his primary pole and they allowed him to use his spare. Have you competed in many tournaments?"

He eased his enormous body onto the solid oak table, scrubbed until it was nearly bleached pale. "Quite a few. Peter and I used them as personal competitions, each man trying to out-do the other."

She found it surprising to hear him refer to his mysterious, deceased brother. "And who won?"

Alec smiled as if remembering the rivalry. "Me, most often, which thoroughly angered my brother. He was two years older than I and convinced that the eldest should always be the victor," he chuckled softly. "I remember one year at a tournament in Cheltenham I won both the melee and the joust competitions. Instead of congratulating me, Peter tried to punch me in the nose. As our father stood by in horror, we wrestled about until another knight, the man I beat in the melee, shouted encouragement to Peter. My brother promptly stopped our brawl, calmly walked over to the other knight and knocked out four of his teeth. It would seem that only Peter had permission to provoke me in a fight and no one else."

She smiled, forgetting her sorrow as she was drawn into his recollection. The mood was light and comfortable and she felt comfortable asking him a most discomfiting question. After all, she was to be his wife, was she not? Surely he would not fault her for wanting to know.

"How did Peter die, Alec?"

His smile faded. Stone-faced, he stared off into the dimness of the room, his gaze averted from Peyton and she was suddenly sorry she had asked. He had told her quite firmly that he did not speak of his brother and she should not have pushed. Yet…. she felt as if she had to ask. He was to be her husband, yet she knew virtually nothing about him. This man who did not bear a sword, who refused to wear armor.

"I am sorry," she whispered. "I know you do not like to speak of him. Forgive me for asking."

He continued to stare off into the room a moment longer before turning to her, his face masked with pain. Immediately, she stood up and wrapped her arms around his thick neck, pulling his face into her soft shoulder. He responded instantly, embracing her in massive arms.

"'Tis a natural question, and I will answer you," he whispered against her. "But it is difficult…."

"Then do not," she shushed him quietly. "You do not have to tell me."

He pulled his face from her silken flesh, instead, Peyton ended up resting her head on his great shoulder as he stroked her hair absently. As if it was she who needed comfort. But he eventually spoke.

"When Edward, then the prince, embarked on the Seventh Crusade, Peter and Ali and I were sent ahead to secure a particularly valuable garrison that would have made the seizure of Acre more simplified, if such a thing is possible. Being young and eager, we went willingly in a group of thirty knights that constituted the advance party for the prince. I led the assault group, and Peter and Ali acted as my generals. It was a well-formed group of brave men that took shelter in an abandoned fortress a few miles from Acre, and from there we launched raiding parties into villages to weaken the Muslim resistance for Edward's approach," his voice grew soft. "I was twenty-one years old at the time. I thought I knew everything and I furthermore believed that the abandoned fortress where my knights were hiding was a perfect refuge the Muslims would never find. Not only did they find us, but they attacked our garrison with three hundred men and caught us completely unaware. There was nothing to do but escape. Peter died when I thought he was an adversary and killed him myself."

Peyton's eyes widened and she raised her head from his shoulder, staring into his sky-blue eyes. "You killed him? Good lord, Alec, what happened?"

"It was dark in the catacombs where the knights had retreated," he said quietly. "It was explicitly understood that when we traversed the catacombs, there was to be an established signal to identify you as an ally. In the midst of the panic of retreat, Peter did not give the signal, whether he simply forgot or did not feel it to be necessary anymore, I do not know. I heard him coming and waited for him, thinking him a foe. When he appeared in the darkness, I jumped from the shadows to gut him."

Peyton's mouth opened in shock and sorrow. Gently, she touched his face as he struggled to maintain his calm. "Oh, my Alec, I am so sorry. No wonder you do not want to speak of it."

Alec had been struggling with Peter's death for twelve years but, suddenly, he found a great deal of comfort in Peyton's sweet touch. He had never allowed anyone to comfort him in his grief, not even Ali, because his brother's death had been his burden alone to bear. No one had been able to ease his sorrow with a word or a gesture.

He had always maintained his emotionless facade when thinking or speaking of Peter; at least, he tried to. But as Peyton caressed him softly and kissed his cheek, he suddenly felt his twelve-year-old dam crumbling like the mighty walls of Jericho. Piece by piece, it began to dissolve and he suddenly grabbed Peyton against him, burying his face in the swell of her bosom.

He couldn't keep his grief to himself anymore; he needed to be absolved somehow, and Peyton was offering her comfort. He hadn't known this woman but a few days and already he felt as if he had known her a lifetime. He began to realize exactly what he had meant when he told Ali that he needed her; mayhap his uncanny sixth sense was speaking to him, allowing him to release himself in this woman's arms. All he knew was that, somehow, she promised assuagement if he would only submit.

"I killed him!" he whispered into her flesh.

Peyton clutched him fiercely. She hurt so terribly for him; as huge and mighty as he was, he was not beyond agony of the heart. It was the only threat his physical power could not overcome.

"It was an accident, darling, an accident," she whispered fervently. "You had no way of knowing it was your brother."

He coughed, a great guffaw of pain and anguish. "But why did not he use the signal? I shall never understand 'til the day I die! I have never understood!"

"As you said, mayhap he forgot in the heat of excitement," she said soothingly, stroking his head, the back of his neck, his shoulders. "In any case, do you think if the situation were reverse, Peter would have acted any differently? What if it had been you racing down the dim corridor, too frightened to remember a pre-arranged signal? Do you think Peter would have identified you first before striking? Of course not. He would have struck first to preserve his own life, which is what you did. You cannot berate yourself for your own sense of self-protection."

He did not say anything for a moment, clutching her tightly against his massive body. In fact, Peyton could barely breathe, but she ignored the discomfort. Alec was demonstrating his anguish and if it eased him to hold her tightly, then so be it. She was content to offer what comfort she could.

Alec had heard her words before, coming from Ali's lips, from his own father. But suddenly, they made a good deal more sense coming from Peyton. Mayhap it was because she was far removed from the situation and had a clearer vision of the circumstances. The same opinion coming from Ali and his father had been simply words intended to ease his guilt, but coming from Peyton, they actually meant something.

He lifted his great head, gazing at her and feeling tremendously frail in her arms, as if she held all of the answers he had been searching for all of these years. "Are you always so wise?"

She smiled, touching his face. "Always, darling."

He smiled feebly and returned his face to her breast again, feeling weaker emotionally than he had in years. It was as if something had been lifted from him, or drained out of him. In any case, he felt a sense of relief that was both unexpected and gratifying.

"Is this why you refuse to live as a fighting man anymore?" she asked softly.

He nodded faintly. "I lay down my sword the moment I killed my brother and I have not wielded it since."

Peyton kissed the top of his head tenderly. "My poor Alec. Do you know my aunt heard a silly tale that you were called The Legend because of your skill with a blade?"

"Silly or not, it is nonetheless true. I was knighted at eighteen, a full three years sooner than most knights because I was far more skilled than most seasoned warriors. Peter was knighted a year later at twenty-one and I swore he never forgave me for having the audacity to be knighted before him. Any reputation I achieved was before the tender age of twenty-one."

Peyton smiled vaguely. "You are indeed a great warrior, then. England lost a mighty son when you lay down your blade."

He was silent a moment. "A hell of a lot of good my knightly skill did me. I led Edward's advance party into ruin and I killed my own brother all in the same day. I was far too confident for my own good and it led to nothing but destruction."

"You were young, my Alec," Peyton said softly. "You are far too harsh on yourself. Men are allowed mistakes, sometimes great ones, but they must continue on."

"Alec Summerlin is not allowed mistakes."

"By whose decree?" she demanded softly.

"Mine."

They remained as they were for an endless amount of time. Peyton continued to hold and caress him as if he were a small child needing solace, and somewhere in the process began to hum softly. It was an old lullaby, something her father used to sing to her when she was very young, a gentle melody that reminded her of happier days. She hoped it would remind Alec of happier days, too. She had a sweet, clear voice and he closed his eyes as she hummed to him, knowing the tune from his childhood. Coupled with the warmth of her body and the contentment he was experiencing, it was enough to lull him into an emotionally-spent doze.

Peyton felt him relax in her arms but she continued to hum, to maintain the peaceful mood. Lord only knew that he had been struggling with guilt for twelve years with barely a moment's reprieve. In her arms, she wanted him to feel safe for the moment.

Peyton was sure she had been standing for hours with Alec leaning against her soft bosom when there was a sharp rap on the door. She moved to wake Alec, but he was already out of her arms and bolting to his feet, six and a half towering feet of muscle and flesh. She was amazed that he had come alert so quickly as he bade the caller to enter, but not before grasping Peyton's hand in his own.

A tall, thin man entered the room, followed by the monk who had gained them entrance to the monastery. He eyed the lady and her knight.

"I am Father Lenardon," he said in a soft-pitched voice. "I understand you wish to be wed."

"That is correct," Alec replied evenly. "My lady and I wish to be wed this night."

The monsignor raised an eyebrow. "There is more involved than a simple ceremony, my lord. I must have permission…."

"There is no one to give permission, Father," Peyton said quickly. "I am an…. orphan. My father died six months ago and I have no living relatives."

"And I am prepared to pay a handsome sum," Alec put in on her heels, so as not to give the priest time to deny their request. "We have ridden a very long way and wish to be on the road again soon, properly wed in the eyes of God and England. Will you do this for us?"

The monsignor looked them over, head to toe, as if to determine the truth of their statements. "Your lady is not a fugitive or a captive?"

"Of course not," Peyton said irritably, then quickly added, more politely: "We simply wish to be married, Father."

Truthfully, there was nothing more the deacon could say. It was not uncommon to perform quick marriage ceremonies to those whose circumstances required it, and he was always pleased to marry a couple rather than have them commit sins of the flesh outside the bonds of matrimony.

He glanced at Peyton again, who certainly did not look the part of a fugitive or captive. The hulking knight next to her was the largest man he had ever seen and he had no desire to provoke his temper by a refusal. Better to get it done with quickly so they could be on their way.

"Very well then," he said. "Follow me."

Peyton felt a distinct tingling in her stomach to realize the monsignor would indeed marry them. In a short amount of time she would be Lady Summerlin, a title she found she would be proud to bear. Almost more than Lady Deveraux; aye, more than that even.

They followed the monsignor and the monk down the narrow hall and into a dimly lit chapel. Banks of expensive tallow candles burned dimly and two oil lamps blazed by the gilded altar. The monsignor moved to the other side of the altar and motioned Alec and Peyton to stand in front of him.

Kissing the scarlet silk mantle offered to him by the monk, the monsignor donned his cape of office as the monk and another brother moved to prepared a few necessary items for the ceremony.

The monsignor wasted no time. Draping the scarlet mantle about his shoulders, he made the sign of the cross before the couple and began to intone the marriage mass. Peyton tried to listen to his words, his monotonous tone, but her attention was continually diverted by the fact that she was actually getting married. It was happening so quickly that she could scarcely believe its actuality, and even though Alec wasn't touching her, she could feel his body heat like a roaring blaze. This man whom she had come to know more intimately than she had ever known anyone in her entire life was to be her husband. Not James, but Alec.

The priest droned onward and recited a prayer, to which Alec crossed himself and murmured a response. Swiftly, he knelt and pulled Peyton with him, who made the sign of the cross and mumbled her response a split second later. She was supposed to close her eyes, for the monsignor was repeating a marriage invocation, but she couldn't seem to keep her lids sealed.

The enormity of the entire situation was weighing heavily on her and she was having difficulty concentrating. She always thought her wedding would be a huge affair, full of flowers and music with Ivy by her side. Instead, she found herself in a chapel in a distant city being married by a man who appeared to be running a race to conclude the marriage sacrament.

But the evidence remained; she was getting married. In fact, she was already married. Married to a man she felt closer to in three days than she had felt with James during the ten years they had known one another. She wondered seriously why she and Alec were so comfortable with one another, as if each understood the other's character without question and accepted it as such.

It was odd and wonderful, and she almost did not feel as if she were betraying James anymore. Certainly he would want her to be happy, would not he? Or had he expected her to play the part of the devastated lover for the rest of her life? Knowing the man as she had, he could be selfish and petty. But she refused to believe that he would have demanded she remain true to his memory.

Even if an order for faithfulness had been his dying declaration, she realized she would have willingly betrayed him for Alec.

The monsignor made the sign of the cross again and Alec rose, gently pulling Peyton to stand beside him. The priest mumbled a binding prayer and bade the couple to drink from a common chalice. The wine was vinegary and tart, and Peyton gazed deep into Alec's eyes as she took a healthy swallow. They continued to stare at each other as the monsignor said the final blessing and informed the new husband that he was allowed kiss his bride. Lady Peyton de Fluornoy Summerlin received a chaste kiss from her husband.

Alec gave her a wink and immediately thanked the monsignor, paying the man with a twenty mark gold piece and five additional one mark gold pieces. All in all, an extremely expensive ceremony and Peyton watched him through somewhat dazed eyes; she could hardly believe they were actually wed even as the evidence of that bought union exchanged hands.

A lesser brother drew up the marriage contracts, one copy for Alec and another copy for the church's records. Peyton was able to sign her name to the church's register, having to ask her new husband how to spell his last name. She nearly spelled it Summerlyn, much to his amusement, but he commented that he liked the spelling better that way. Without further delay, he escorted his wife from the church out into the dark night, the freshly sanded marriage contract clutched carefully in his massive fist.

"What now?" she asked as he untethered Midas.

"That will depend on you," he said, fumbling with the reins. "We can either ride back to Blackstone and face my father's wrath immediately, or we can steal away for a few blissful hours at an inn."

She smiled. "I choose the inn."

He matched her grin. "I thought so."

He lifted her onto his horse and mounted behind her. "I know of a quiet tavern near the edge of town. The proprietor and I are old friends."

She yawned happily, the events of the night sinking in and a healthy joy settling. "Well and good. He can keep you occupied for the rest of the night while I sleep."

He raised his eyebrows. "I think not, Lady Summerlin. You will occupy my attention, asleep or not."

"But you promised to leave me alone to recover."

"I lied."

She giggled as Midas clip-clopped down the cobbled road.

Alec reined his horse in front of a bustling tavern, eyeing the establishment as he dismounted. Peyton, too, looked surprised at all the activity.

"This is your quiet inn?" she asked.

He shrugged feebly and pulled her off the charger. Gathering their two satchels as well as his crossbow, he took Peyton's arm and led her inside.

The common room was warm and fragrant, smelling of roasted meat and old ale. Smoke from the blazing hearth cast a faint fog in the room, shrouding the occupants like a mist. It was a busy place, full of ladies and knights, men-at-arms and loud whores, and Alec drew distinct stares with his enormous presence as they made their way into the depths of the noisy room. His sky-blue eyes grazed the room for his friend, but the man was nowhere to be found until a whooping shout pierced the air.

"Alec!" came a boom. "I thought it was you, you blond devil!"

Alec and Peyton turned to see a large man bounding toward them, almost plowing over a serving wench in his eagerness. Peyton instinctively stepped back, pressing against Alec as the man came upon them; he was nearly as large as Alec with unkempt black hair and black eyes like polished onyx. A well-manicured beard was the only characteristic that singled him out from the rest of the shabby crowd and he reached for Alec's hand, pumping it hard in greeting.

"How is it that you have come my way?" he said happily. "God's Blood, it's been at least a year since I have seen you. And where's that black bastard Ali? The whoreskin still owes me five gold pieces, you know."

Alec grinned broadly. "Always a pleasure to see you again, Simon. You certainly know how to make a man feel welcome."

"Welcome? Ha!" Simon snorted loudly. "I practically owe you this damn hovel, with all of the gambling you and I used to do…." his eyes suddenly fell on Peyton and his eyes widened, clearing his throat in surprise. "Oh…. my. Who is this exquisite creature and what in the hell is she doing with the likes of you?"

"This is my wife," Alec replied, answering both questions and feeling a good deal of pride at the announcement. "Peyton, this is Sir Simon de Clerc. Simon, this is my wife, the Lady Peyton Summerlin."

Peyton bobbed a curtsy as Simon's eyes opened wide with astonishment.

"A wife?" he repeated. "God's Blood, Alec, you have actually taken a wife? And look at her; my God, she is beautiful. I am completely speechless."

"Good," Alec replied with a smirk, glancing about the room. "Is business so good that you would not have a room to spare us?"

"Never!" Simon declared. "My very best room is still available because no one here can afford it. It's yours for the night, free of charge."

"Naturally. And we expect a full meal, also free of charge. I will consider it your wedding gift to us."

Simon bowed deeply. "Naturally. I shall send up the best fare I have to offer."

"Better than that, I hope," Alec slanted the man a distrustful gaze. "Point us in the right direction so that I may remove my wife from this ribald atmosphere."

"Can't we eat down here?" Peyton asked, tugging on his sleeve. "I have never been to a tavern."

"Would you be so good as to eat with me?" Simon asked hopefully, looking to Alec. "Come, come! I have a cozy table by the hearth. Surely you will not deny me your company after all this time?"

Alec passed an uncomfortable glance at the room once more, but the expression on Peyton's face made his decision for him. With a slight nod, he allowed Simon to lead them over to a large table where three wenches were eating loudly, drinking like men. Simon promptly removed the women, all but kicking them from the table. Scolded and humiliated, they passed challenging glares at Peyton as they retreated.

"Have you something to say to me?" Peyton immediately bristled at the harsh looks. "It shall be your last statement before I rip your tongue out and wrap it around your neck!"

Simon laughed loudly as Alec pulled his wife to sit, but Peyton was still riled and glared daggers at the trashy women as they disappeared into the kitchen.

"God's Blood, Alec, I like her already," Simon declared, bellowing for food and ale with the same breath.

"Turn around," Alec rumbled to his wife. "Behave yourself."

"Did you see how they looked at me?" she demanded, still outraged. "Why did they do that when I did nothing to warrant it?"

He sighed and leaned close to her. "They are simply jealous of your beauty, sweetheart. You must learn to deal with such hostilities calmly."

Somewhat sated, Peyton accepted the cup of ale offered by Simon and took a deep drink, immediately choking on the swallow. Simon looked concerned.

"What is it, Lady Summerlin? Is something wrong with the ale?" he asked earnestly.

She made a face, pushing her cup away. "Nay, my lord, nothing abnormal…." she licked her lips and shuddered. "Where did you purchase this ale?"

"From a man in Mildenhall," Simon replied. "He brews it especially for me. Is it not acceptable?"

Peyton cast a helpless glance at Alec, who was smiling faintly at her over the rim of his cup. "Why on earth would you purchase ale from a man in Mildenhall when the very best ale in the realm comes from St. Cloven?" Alec demanded.

"St. Cloven! Pah!" Simon snorted. "The best ale in all of England, but too damn expensive. My customers' lowly palates do not require such extravagance. Were I to purchase St. Cloven ale, I would go broke because no one could afford it."

Peyton and Alec exchanged grins. "No more, Simon. I happen to know the lord of St. Cloven personally and I will see that you are treated most fairly," Alec said.

"Truly?" Simon said thoughtfully. "Do you think I could purchase St. Cloven ale for what I am paying now?"

"What do you pay now?" Peyton asked.

"Forty pence a barrel."

Peyton considered that price. St. Cloven ale was priced nearly three times higher. "Would you purchase ale from St. Cloven for sixty pence a barrel if, for every two barrels you purchased, a hogshead-barrel was given to you without charge? You could conceivably purchase five barrels for the price of four, ten for the price of eight, for nearly the same price you pay your present supplier for his inferior ale. The quality of St. Cloven's drink would overshadow the slight increase in your cost."

Simon scratched his chin. "Aye, I would do that. Were word to spread that I supplied St. Cloven ale I would likely have more business than I could handle."

"Done," Alec said firmly, his gaze warm on his wife. Not only was she beautiful and brave, but she had a head for business and that pleased him immensely.

"How can you do this, Alec?" Simon queried. "Did your father annex St. Cloven, perchance?"

Alec smiled and took a healthy drink of the bitter ale. "I married it."

Simon stared at him a moment before turning an astonished expression to Peyton. "*You* are St. Cloven ale?"

Peyton felt Alec's hand on her back gently. "I am Lady Summerlin, formerly heiress to St. Cloven."

Simon's mouth went agape with surprise and he slapped himself on the cheek as if to regain his senses. Then he laughed. "God's Blood! I have ties to St. Cloven!"

The food came then, great trenchers of roast pork and gravy, huge chunks of fresh bread, butter, and boiled carrots and apples. Peyton dug in with gusto and ate until she could hold no more, but her voracious appetite could not compare with Alec. He must have eaten half the pig as his wife wallowed in over-stuffed misery.

"Tell me, my lady, how did you come by your name?" Simon asked, his mouth full of food. "'Tis a man's name, usually."

Peyton sighed with contentment as her food settled. "'Twas my mother's maiden name and she swore she would give one of her children the name, male or female. The Peytons come from the Isle of Arran in Scotland. They still inhabit Brodick Castle on the island, although I have never been there. I understand it is very lovely."

"Scotland is a wild land," Simon agreed, eating loudly. "But it breeds the most beautiful women. Wild, delightful women."

Alec lifted an eyebrow, unwilling for Simon to pursue that particular line of conversation. "You have only to look at my wife to know that Scotland does indeed breed beauties. Her sister is to be Ali's wife, by the way."

Simon smiled broadly. "Ah! The black lad did indeed find a mate. You know, Alec, the only time I ever saw Ali comfortable with a woman was in the Holy Land where all of the women were nearly his color. I thought he might find a Saracen bride."

"He was far too young for a bride at that time," Alec said softly. "Lady Ivy has accepted him as her husband and it is a most agreeable arrangement."

"No doubt." Finished, Simon sat back in his chair and belched loudly, stretching his huge body. "Imagine that I know two men who are related to St. Cloven ale. 'Twill prove to be a gold mine for me. My lady doesn't have any more unattached sisters, perchance?"

Peyton shook her head. "Nay, my lord. There are only two of us."

"Pity. Imagine what I could do if I were married to St. Cloven," he raised an eyebrow at her. "You would not consider leaving Alec and marrying me, would you? I would be more than happy to dispose of your husband."

She grinned and Alec pulled her chair over to him, putting his arm around her shoulders. "I might reconsider my vow and wield a sword if I thought you to be serious. You'd not take her without a fight."

"In that case, I recount my offer. I would sooner go up against the Devil himself than meet you in a swordfight."

Peyton leaned against Alec, content and happy, basking in his heat. It occurred to her that Simon had seen Alec fight at one time and she was curious to know the man's complete opinion of Alec's skill.

"He is a great knight, then?" she asked.

Simon's eyes glittered at Alec through the smoke. It was the first time all evening he seemed to calm somewhat. "Do you not know the man you married, my lady? There was no better knight in the entire realm."

"Simon...." Alec shook his head faintly, modestly toying with his cup.

Simon grinned, propping a huge boot on the table and knocking his empty trencher to the floor. Underneath the table, fat dogs scuffled for the scraps and Peyton raised her legs to avoid being bitten.

"Lady Summerlin, your husband was beyond magnificent when it came to swordplay. There was not a man in the entire civilized world that could best him. When he competed in tournaments, the melees were always decided before the combatants ever took the field. Everyone knew that Alec Summerlin would triumph, although there were those of us who were foolish enough to take our chances against him. Aye, there was none more brilliant," Simon chuckled at Alec's demureness. "Stop acting the blushing maiden, Alec. You know full well your skill and power. When England lost you, she lost her most powerful warrior since Galahad."

"Galahad?" Peyton gazed at her husband, who merely took another drink of ale.

Simon was enjoying Alec's embarrassment. "Certainly. But I doubt even Galahad could have held the position against the raiding Muslims those years ago. Nothing short of God could have defended thirty English knights against hundreds of barbarian soldiers."

What had promised to be a glorious tale of Alec's strength suddenly turned uncomfortable as Simon referred to the fallen fortress. Peyton turned to her husband to gauge his reaction as Simon continued on, fully aware of the tender memories.

"There were very few of us left alive to escape the initial onslaught," Simon sat forward, his eyes intent on Peyton. "On our retreat we ran headlong into a patrol of Muslims, fifty barbarians against eighteen English knights who had just fled for their lives. Your husband was magnificent as he engaged man after man with only his spear and dagger. It was a sight to behold, indeed, for he killed thirteen men on his own while the rest of us struggled with two or three. 'Twas the last time I saw The Legend in action."

"He was magnificent, then?" Peyton repeated in awe.

Simon smiled with satisfaction. "Indeed, madam. Alec could fight God himself and win." Sighing, he gazed at Alec fondly. "Edward has never given up hope that The Legend would forsake his vow and take up campaigning again. With the trouble Edward has from the Llewellyn ap Gruffydd and the Scots, he is sorely in need of Alec's power. I shall wager he shall never stop begging you to join him, Alec."

Peyton again turned to Alec with a faint smile of admiration when she saw that he was not smiling; in fact, his expression had turned to stone. She well remembered the personality trait she had learned to hate, but this time she did not to shy away from him. Knowing what she did of his past, she realized the facade was an act of self-preservation. She raised her hand and clutched the arm that rested on her shoulder, reassuring Alec silently that she understood his torment.

"Alec is no longer a fighting man, but lord of the manor," she said quickly, changing the subject. "You will have to come visit us at St. Cloven. Ali and Alec have grand plans on renovating the keep and I promise it will be a magnificent place when they are finished."

"Ali is a grand designer," Simon took the bait and followed her lead. "I understand he did a great deal of the planning when Lord Brian added a south wing to Blackstone."

"Ali has a mind for dimensions," Alec said quietly, draining the last of his cup. "He can figure exact measurements of the most prolific proportions and they are always correct. I have never known him to be wrong."

His voice was faint and Peyton felt a distinct melancholy settle. Now that they were fed, her fatigue was increasing and she gently tugged on Alec's sleeve.

"I am tired, Alec. Can we retire?"

"Certainly," he set down his cup. "I shall escort my lady wife to our chamber and return to our conversation, Simon. Stay where you are."

Simon nodded, focusing on Peyton. "'Twas a pleasure to meet you, my lady. And remember my offer should you ever tire of The Legend."

She glanced up to her husband. "Hopefully, he will keep me properly entertained and I shall never tire of him."

Simon snorted a chuckle, properly contrite when Alec cast him a menacing glare. He continued to watch as Alec escorted his wife through the sea of men and wenches, wondering how Alec had been fortunate enough to wed such a beautiful woman. Not that he did not deserve it, of course; 'twas only right, considering Alec was the greatest knight in the realm. At least, he had been at one time.

Simon's finest room was not much to the eye, but it was clean and comfortable and Peyton was sorely feeling her exhaustion as Alec set the satchels to the floor and tossed their cloaks over a chair. She immediately tossed back the bedrug and threw herself on the mattress, clothing and all. Alec grinned as she jerked the cover over her head.

"You are not even going to undress?" he mused. "My, my, you must be fatigued."

She sighed heavily, with contentment. "Do not be long. I shall expect you to join me shortly."

"Aye, General."

"And tell a serving wench that we will expect a morning meal at sunrise."

"Aye, General. Anything else?"

She grunted and he chuckled softly, moving for the door. "Good night, sweetheart."

"Good night, my Legend."

In faith, he was exhausted as well, but he was also eager to finish his conversation with Simon. The man had been invaluable support during the long months in the Holy Land and Alec considered him a good friend. Furthermore, were he to retire with Peyton, he was positive he would not be able to contain himself and he had promised that she would be allowed time to recover. He did not want to break his promise; Christ, he might stay downstairs all night in that case.

Peyton heard him leave, nearly asleep. The bed was comfortable to a fault and as she drifted off, she suddenly remembered that she had neglected to ask him what time they were to leave. After all, she wanted to rise and bathe in plenty of time to return to Blackstone and she wanted to make sure there was hot water available for her toilette.

She rolled onto her back, debating whether or not she should go downstairs and ask him, but she did not want to leave the comfort of the bed. It was warm and wonderful and her eyes closed again as she pondered her predicament. But she forced her eyes open, determined to seek her answer so she could sleep with confidence. And besides; she had to use the privy terribly and she did not see a chamber pot in the room. With a grunt, she heaved herself from the bed.

Somehow, the common room was smokier and louder than she remembered. She immediately spied Alec at the table near the hearth with Simon, a large pitcher of ale between them. Two serving wenches were hanging all over Simon, and Peyton thought it fortunate that the women were staying away from Alec, lest she be so inclined to tear their hair out by the roots.

It was amazing how protective she was of him already, but not so amazing considering the soul-baring that had occurred between them. She felt a distinct need to protect him from those who would be a physical threat or a deliberate temptation.

She descended the stairs and began to weave her way towards her husband. His back was to her and she was focused only on his blond head, smiling weakly at Simon when he caught sight of her. But her forward momentum was halted as a mailed arm reached out and grabbed her, and Peyton suddenly found herself sitting in an armored lap.

"Look what I have caught!" the knight crowed happily. "The most beautiful wench in Ely! Where have you been hiding yourself, lass?"

Peyton balled her fist and struck the knight squarely in the face, releasing his hold. As she struggled from his lap, a giant hand suddenly reached down and pulled her free. Startled, she looked up to see that Simon had hold of her protectively as Alec plowed into the unfortunate knight.

Peyton watched with amazement as Alec finished the man in two powerful blows of his massive fist; one to the face, and another to the side of the head. In the next second, the unconscious knight lay in a heap upon the floor.

Instantly, his companions were on their feet, four against one, and Peyton gasped as she tried to pull free of Simon's grasp.

"No!" she cried, yanking free and planting herself in the deadly position in front of her husband as if to act as his shield. She assumed the knights would think twice before driving their swords into the guts of a young woman. "No fighting! He is unarmed!"

"He should have thought of that before he injured Graf!" one man snarled. "Prepare to meet thy God, giant."

Alec tried to remove her from the line of fire, but Peyton refused to budge. "You will not touch him! Had your companion not been stupid enough to grab another man's wife, he would not have been injured. Now, sit and I shall pay for your food and drink; lodgings, too."

The knights looked to one another, pondering her words, but they had not sheathed their swords and Peyton refused to move from her defensive position.

"Does your wife always fight your battles for you, giant?" a second knight sneered.

"Be glad that she has," Alec's voice was like thunder. "She has spared your life this night."

The four knights laughed heartily and Peyton began to worry; if Alec continued to provoke them, surely she could not prevent the coming battle. She cast her husband a menacing glare, but he ignored her. He was watching the four knights as a cat watches a mouse.

"You talk bravely for a man who does not bear a sword," the second knight said again. "You do not even wear armor."

"I do not need armor or a sword to prove my manhood," Alec replied smoothly. "Now accept my wife's offer for restitution and sit down or commence with your battle. I shall not stand here all night."

Peyton let out a sigh of frustration. Before she could control herself, she turned to her husband. "I am trying to save your hide, Alec. Would you please stop antagonizing them?"

He actually smiled at her. "I am not antagonizing them, love. I am simply trying to help them decide what course of action to take."

Infuriated, Peyton returned her attention to the knights. "Sheath those swords 'else I shall shove them down your throat. There will be no battle here tonight."

"Lady," the first knight said slowly. "Although you are most delicious to observe, I grow weary of your unruly tongue. Take a seat and let the men work out their differences."

Alec side-stepped Peyton, drawing the knights' attention away from his wife. Before Peyton could follow him, Simon had a firm hold of her and clapped a hand over her mouth when she tried to protest.

"You take your life in your hands speaking to my wife in such a manner, little man," Alec said quietly. "Apparently you learned little from your colleague's mistake."

Four swords glistened in the weak light and Peyton's eyes widened fearfully; she knew precisely where the confrontation was leading and she was terrified. Simon released her from his grip and wandered away, leaving her standing alone as the room full of patrons quickly vacated; there was not a person in the stuffy hall who did not sense the coming battle.

A real fear gripped her; she had visions of Alec's guts coating the stone floor and in the same instant, horrible flashbacks of James' gored body slammed into her mind. She whimpered softly, hands to her mouth; it had nearly killed her to watch James die in her arms and she was positive that if Alec were to die in her presence, she would never recover. She would not want to live.

"Alec…," she whispered desperately, tears beginning to well within her great sapphire eyes. "Oh, God, no…."

He heard her, but he was focused on the four men in front of him. His uncanny sixth sense told him they were preparing to strike, and he braced himself as he drew their attention away from Peyton. He wanted her out of the range of the broadswords.

"Come now, lovers," Alec said provocatively. "You were so brave. Has your courage shriveled like your manhood?"

"Bastard," one knight spat, and suddenly the air was filled with the whoosh of arcing broadswords. Peyton screamed and jumped back, nearly tripping over a table, but her eyes never left her husband. She was positive that she was about to witness his demise.

The two knights closest to Alec brought their swords down in unison; Alec lashed out a huge booted leg and caught the first knight in the wrist hard enough to dislodge his heavy sword. Before the blade clattered to the floor, he brought up his hand and with an amazingly deft maneuver managed to disarm the second knight. Another broadsword went sailing.

Before the two attackers had time to react, Alec drove his fist into the second knight's face, immediately turning to drive his thick elbow into the face of the first. Like two weakling knaves, the men went down in a heavy crash of armor just as the third and fourth knights upended the table in their haste to reach Alec.

Peyton barely had time to comprehend the happening of the events. She stood, terrified and amazed, as Alec effectively disarmed the third knight and then used him as a shield against his comrade, who mistakenly gored him. As the fourth knight struggled to remove his broadsword from his companion's belly, Alec balled his massive fist and smashed the man's jaw into fragments. Writhing in pain, the last foe fell to the floor as blood erupted from his shattered mouth.

Simon came flying back into the room, his heavy sword arcing high in Alec's defense. But he came to a skidding halt when he viewed the carnage before him; five injured knights littered his floor and he looked to Alec with disappointment.

"You did not even wait for me?" he asked, dejected. "How could you do that to me, Alec? It has been ages since we last fought together."

Alec turned to his friend, not so much as a bead of sweat on his brow. "I tried to save one for you, but alas, I could not control myself. So sorry, old man."

Peyton stood a few feet away, her hands over her mouth in shock. Initial shock fading, relief flooded her body and she began to tremble violently. She was dazed, angered, panicked; everything she could possibly feel. All she could imagine was Alec's gored body lying on the floor, lifeless and pale.

Bile rose in her throat and she knew she was about to become ill; in a valiant effort to spare her dignity, she attempted to make her way to the privy. Two steps into her retreat, however, she realized her effort would be in vain; her weakened legs gave way and she stumbled to her knees, vomiting her dinner all over Simon's dingy stone floor.

Alec was next to her instantly, pulling her hair away from her face and clasping her body firmly. She retched and retched until there was nothing left, and still she retched more. She fought to catch her breath as her vision dimmed momentarily.

"Easy, sweetheart, easy," he whispered softly. "You are overwrought. Let me help you…."

"No!" she rasped, twisting away from him.

His eyes were wide with concern. She waved him off, attempting to retain her last scrap of decorum as she hastily mounted the stairs. He bound up the steps after her, leaving the clean-up to a still-disappointed Simon and his stunned employees.

Peyton stumbled into their room, bolting aimlessly to the opposite side of the chamber as Alec stormed after her. He reached for her once again, but she lurched out of his range.

"Nay!" she gasped, bumping into the wall. "Do not touch me!"

He was truly concerned for her. "You are exhausted, sweetheart. Come lie down."

She shook her head vigorously, tears springing into her sapphire eyes. "How could you do that to me, Alec? How could you?"

He stopped trying to pursue her and paused, a puzzled look on his features. "Do what, love? I was merely protecting you from a band of ruffians."

Tears spilled and a great, anguished choke bubbled up. "Did you really think I wanted to see you fight those men? Why do you think I was trying so desperately to calm them with reason? I did not want you to fight them!"

His brow furrowed slightly; he simply did not understand her trouble. "But…. I am unharmed. They could not have killed me."

She began to sob; deep, angry, frightened sobs. "Do you think I wanted to see you gored like James, right before my eyes? How dare you fight in my presence when you know…. you know that…."

She trailed off, overcome with wracking sobs. His heart broke as he understood her terror and he cursed himself silently; of course it never occurred to him that a skirmish might upset her because she had seen her betrothed gored before her eyes and had been unable to prevent the event.

Indeed, she had made a strong attempt to calm the situation in the common room with reason and pacification. Although she'd had no control over the situation that had claimed Deveraux, she had grappled for command over a situation that could have just as easily claimed Alec. She simply couldn't stand by as her worst nightmare was replayed before her disbelieving mind, and in his confidence he had worked against her.

Immediately, he went to her and she did not resist. Instead, she clutched him tightly as he lifted her off the ground and cradled her in his massive arms.

"I am sorry, sweetheart," he kissed her red head. "I never thought.... forgive me, my sweet. I was horrible and inconsiderate."

"Aye, you were," she sobbed into his shoulder. "I shall never forgive you if you do that again. Do you understand me?"

"Perfectly, love."

He carried her to the bed and sat down, rolling onto his back and taking her with him. She clung to him as if to never let him go and he held her tightly as the feathered mattress swallowed the both of them. Her sobs were muffled in the barrier of his leather overtunic, filling the heavy silence of the room as Alec listened, feeling like a fool for not being sensitive enough of his wife's feelings.

But as he listened, the familiar jealousy began to creep into his chest; was she crying for James' memory, or because she feared for Alec's life? Certainly it wasn't the time to question her, but he found the question weighing heavily on his heart. Why should he be comforting her if she was weeping for another?

"Do you weep because I frightened you?" he asked softly, feeling terribly selfish for voicing his thoughts.

"Of course!" she snapped, wiping at her nose. He released one arm from her and handed her a linen towel that was placed on the table beside the bed. She accepted the linen and blew her nose hard, wiping at her face.

"Then you do not weep for a memory?"

She eyed him, her lids red and swollen. "Wh-what memory?" she hiccupped.

He gazed up at her, thinking her to be terribly beautiful even when she cried. "James. Do you weep for your dead lover or for your husband's life?"

Immediately, the tears stopped and she stared at him as if she could not comprehend his words. Slowly, her cheeks flushed an angry red and she shifted herself away from him.

"I weep because I did not wish to see you speared," she said coldly.

"I am past weeping for the man I loved."

A flash of emotion rippled across his controlled face and he vaulted off the mattress. His jealousy bloomed at her words, angered to hear that she loved another man. But he had always known she had loved her betrothed; why should her repeated declaration upset him so? Unbalanced, he moved for the door, anything to be free of her presence and his confusion.

"Then go to sleep and try to forget. And dream of your dead love if it comforts you." He could scarce believe he added the last sentence, purely out of spite.

Peyton glared at him, confusion and anger of her own filling her full. Her response was borne purely from malice, for she had no doubt that he had meant to hurt her with his unfair questions. "It does, thank you. I am glad you understand that." Once, the statement had been true. But no longer.

Stung, Alec threw open the door and slammed it heavily in his wake. Peyton continued to stare at the door, her chest constricting with bitterness and puzzlement as she pondered their exchange of words.

Why couldn't she have been honest with him and tell him that the reason why she had become hysterical over the brawl was because she couldn't stand to live without him? Why couldn't she have been honest with him?

Exhausted and sick, she fell back on the pillow and closed her eyes, feeling more confusion and ache than she ever had.

When she dreamt, she dreamt of Alec.

CHAPTER TEN

THE MORNING DAWNED heavy with a humid mist and Peyton was glad for the protection of her nearly-shunned cloak. It kept the moisture from her face as she and Alec plodded along the deserted road, no more than three of four words spoken between them all morning. He was brooding and silent and so was she, each puzzled by their feelings and unspoken truths. What should have been their wedding night had been an empty, desolate thing.

Alec had consumed far too much of the cheap ale after leaving Peyton alone in their room and was sporting a horrible headache. Every blow of Midas' hooves intensified the ache, matching the pain in his heart. His mood was as gray as the weather.

The road was void of activity, not even a peasant crossing their moody path. Alec's arm around his wife's slender waist was unmoving and uncomforting, and Peyton would have rather walked than face his coldness. But she was showing signs of coldness herself, confused with the turn of events the night before and increasingly curious as to where he had spent the night. He certainly hadn't slept with her.

She shifted on his hard thighs and his grip unconsciously tightened to prevent her from falling off the horse. She stiffened when he reacted to her movement, for her anger had not abated in the least since last night and she hoped her taut body would convey her fury. For good measure, she attempted to sit forward and put a barrier of separation between their bodies, but unfortunately, there was nowhere for her to go on the limited saddle.

"If you shift any further, you are going to fall off," his voice was cold. "Remain still."

"I want to walk," she snapped irritably, trying to wriggle free. "Let me down."

"Nay, lady, for it will only slow our return. You will continue to ride with me."

She did not want to be cradled against his stiff body any longer and her struggles increased. "Put me down, Alec, I demand it."

Instead of refusing, he suddenly removed his arm and she fell to the ground, landing on her bottom. Grunting with the dull smarting on her backside, she rose to unsteady feet as Alec reined Midas to a halt several feet away.

His gaze was unreadable. Before she could rage at him, he turned Midas down the road and continued on.

Peyton watched him ride down the deserted road, wondering to what lengths his anger would go. Would he leave her if she were to fall far behind? Or would he demand she remount? Feeling the need to test him, for whatever reason, she sat down on a stump and continued to watch as Alec and Midas rode out of view.

So he would leave her. Miffed, she angrily batted at her skirt where bits of leaves clung to the material. The night's events repeated themselves in her mind, thoughts of Alec's warmth as he introduced her as his wife, how his hand never left her even as they ate supper. His voice had been tender when he spoke to her, his manner affectionate and kind. And, he had bared his soul as they waited in the private chamber of the monastery. The protectiveness, the attachment she felt for him, went beyond words. Not even James had warranted such strong emotion and she wondered why she should feel so strongly toward Alec when she professed to love James. Mayhap she hadn't loved James after all. Mayhap, in truth, she loved Alec.

Her sapphire blue eyes gazed down the road, barren since Alec had disappeared. Why couldn't she have told him the truth last night, admitting her true feelings? The only time James had ever entered her mind during the scuffle had been when she feared that Alec would end up impaled in the very same fashion. Other than that brief recollection, she'd barely thought of the man at all since her introduction to Sir Alec Summerlin.

She closed her eyes with regret; she had been so wrong to reprimand him when he had only meant to protect her. Her fear had raged and she had snapped at him when she should have thanked him. Gathering her skirts and swallowing her pride, she commenced down the road after her husband, hoping he would forgive her rash nature.

Not five minutes later, she met Alec as he back-tracked his steps. His gaze upon her was emotionless as always and she swallowed hard, summoning the courage to apologize for becoming angry on their wedding night.

"Are you ready to ride?" he asked.

She watched him for a moment. "Do you hate me overly, Alec?"

He met her gaze, pure blue to sapphire blue. "Nay, I do not."

"But you are angry."

His gaze faltered for the first time and he looked away, studying his hands, the scenery. "And I should not be?"

She shook her head. "You have every right to be furious. I am sorry I scolded you, and I am sorry for what I said. And.... and I do not dream of James anymore."

His expression was guarded. "It matters not to me."

Rebuffed, she lowered her gaze as hot tears filled her eyes. She was attempting to apologize to the man and he was being most stubborn about it. Hurt by his indifference, she pushed past him and continued down the road. Behind her, she could hear the clip-clops of Midas' hooves as they followed.

She walked for some while, wiping the tears that streamed down her face as Alec pursued at a safe distance. She was angry that he rejected her apology, angry that he did not care about her feelings. He had said once that he cared not if she loved him; he simply wanted a wife who was pleasant and obedient.

She tried to reinforce her bravery, determining if obedience and appearance was all he wanted out of a mate, then she would oblige him. No love, no real warmth or affection. She would strive to give him what he demanded in a spouse. An efficient machine, the perfect chatelaine.

…. but how could she live with the man and not become attached to him? She was already dangerously attached to him.

"You do not dream of him anymore?" she heard his voice behind her, barely audible.

She refused to respond and risk greater hurt. She had no desire to speak with him at the moment, at least not until she regained her composure.

Suddenly, Midas charged past her and blocked the road. She stopped, refusing to look at Alec as he dismounted his charger.

"Tell me that you do not dream of him anymore," he said quietly.

"What do you care?"

He did not say anything for a moment. "You are my wife. I shall not have you dreaming of another man."

She let out a choke of disbelief, amazed at his selfishness and arrogance. "Is that all you care about? That I am your wife and you fear the memory of a dead man? Good lord, Alec, are you so self-centered and insecure?"

"Nay," his voice was a faint whisper. "You are my wife and…. I do not wish to share you. If you dream, I would have you dream of me."

"I did dream of you!" she cried, her voice shaking with emotion. "Dreams were all I had last night as you saw fit to vacate our bed in favor of…. other arrangements."

"I did not retire at all last night. Simon and I spent the entire night recollecting the days of glory."

She shook her head in exasperation and pushed past him again, resuming her walk. "No more, Alec. I am weary of this conversation."

"Peyton," he called after her, his tone almost pleading. "Do not walk away. Please…. I am sorry. I did not mean what I said when I told you to dream of your love."

"Aye, you meant it," she came to a halt. "You knew exactly how to hurt me and you did. How would you feel if I brought up Peter maliciously? 'Twould be salt on an open wound."

He lowered his gaze and she could see his jaw ticking. "I am sorry. I was angry and I should not have said what I did."

She moved toward him, slowly closing the distance. When she was directly in front of him, she put her hands to his face and forced him to meet her bejeweled eyes.

"Listen to me well, husband. Last night, I was fearful for your life. I could see your guts spilled on the floor as you fought those knights and it frightened the wits from me. Alec, were you to die, I would never recover and the passion of my feelings has nothing to do with James," she lowered her voice as she witnessed the soft expression on his face. "I lived through James' death, my Alec. But I would refuse to survive yours. There would be nothing left to live for."

His mouth worked as if he was attempting to reply, but he gave up. "Oh, Peyton," he whispered, his great hands rising to grasp her face. "I…. oh, Christ…."

His lips slanted over hers before he could finish his sentence. Peyton caved into him, feeling his warm arms embrace her protectively, the heat from his body saturating her. Once angry and bitter, her feelings evaporated at his touch. Tongues plundered and tasted until they were both panting from passion.

"I missed you terribly last night," he breathed, his mouth suckling on her jaw line.

"I missed you too," she whispered. "You were magnificent in the fight against those knights, my Alec. You certainly do not need a sword if you can defend yourself with your wits and strength."

"I have had to compensate," he rasped, dragging his mouth over her neck. "Christ, sweetheart, I want you right now."

"Now?" she repeated. "But there's nowhere…."

She was in his arms, aloft from the ground. He carried her across the road and into a bank of dense foliage.

"We do not need a bed," he said hoarsely.

He propped her against a tree and supported her with pressure from his hips as he fumbled with her gown. Uncertain but hot with passion, Peyton threw caution to the wind and helped him hike up her skirts. His hands groped her, kneading her sweet flesh as his mouth repeatedly plundered the honeyed depths of her mouth.

She was sure she would swoon from his insistent onslaught as he grasped her thighs and wound them around his waist, but it was a most pleasurable form of discomfort as the world around her faded. She gripped him tightly as his hands left her long enough to lower his leather breeches, then cried sharply with bliss as he grasped her buttocks firmly.

"Are you sure you are not too sore?" he breathed in between fevered kisses.

She could only nod, eager to feel him inside her at once. "Now, Alec," she gasped.

One hand on her bottom, the other possessively on her breast, he guided his great manhood into her drenched sheath, sliding nearly half his length instantly. Peyton moaned from the pleasure-pain of it, driving her hips forward to meet him. Their hips gyrated against one another as his massive organ found its seat and they began the primal mating rhythm.

Alec climaxed almost immediately. Peyton felt him throbbing within her, so highly aroused that his spasms threw her over the brink and she cried out, gripping his shoulders so tightly that she swore she was tearing his tunic to shreds. The delicious convulsions she had been introduced to yesterday had returned and she latched onto his lips as their passion slowly faded. No words were spoken as their kisses cooled from hotly passionate to warmly affectionate, wordless reminders of the fondness they were rapidly coming to feel for one another.

"Christ," he mumbled, nibbling her lower lip. "What you do to me, lady."

She grinned and he kissed her teeth, matching her smile. "We should be on our way," she said softly.

"We should?" he suckled her chin.

She snickered softly, regaining her tattered senses and pushing against him. "Aye, we should. Enough for the moment, Alec. We will have tonight."

He snorted. "If I am not thrown into irons."

Her eyes widened with apprehension. "Your father would do that?"

He pecked her on the tip of her pert nose and gently lowering her to the ground. "Nay, he would not. But I am sure to receive the scolding of my life from both of my parents."

She brushed off her skirts and shook the chaffed bits of bark from her cloak. She was uncertain as to how she should respond, knowing she certainly shared in the blame for their actions. Were there to be any punishment, she should be equally dealt with.

Next to her, he had secured his breeches and straightened his tunic. His hands were still covered with his great leather gloves, as they had been all along, and he examined his hands with a smirk.

"I did not even bother to take them off," he raised them to his nose and inhaled deeply, with great relish. "Ah, sweetheart, they smell of you, musky and spicy and womanly. I shall surely never remove them now."

She flushed and turned away from him, shaking her head at his crude comment. He caught up to her with a grin and they exchanged glances, his tender and hers reproving. Laughing softly, he grasped her hand gently and escorted her to the road where Midas was grazing contentedly on a cluster of buttercups.

☙

IT WAS SHORTLY after the nooning meal when the looming structure of Blackstone appeared on the horizon. Peyton felt her anxiety level soar at the sight, wondering what sort of chaos had transpired since their flight to Ely. Had Ivy and Ali wed? Or had Sir Brian punished them both in a fit of anger? And was Alec's father waiting at this very moment, in fact, for the precise moment when they passed through the gate in eager anticipation of severing his son's head for his disobedience? Swallowing hard, she hoped her courage would hold out in the face of Brian's undeniable rage.

There were several soldiers on the battlements, shouting to their comrades down below and Peyton heard Alec's name at least twice. By the time Midas danced in through the open gates, Ali was there to greet them.

"Alec, thank God you have returned," he said in a low voice.

Alec sensed Ali's urgent manner but refused to give in to the tension. "'Tis good to see you too, lover," he said with their usual banter. "Meet my wife, the Lady Peyton Summerlin."

Ali closed his eyes a brief moment as if to ward off the horror of the introduction. "Then you did marry her."

"Of course I did, I told you I would," Alec dismounted his steed and eyed his friend. "And what of you? Are you a husband?"

Ali's nostrils flared. "I am not."

Alec raised an eyebrow, feeling the seeds of concern take root. "And why not?"

Ali's jaw ticked and he looked distraught, far more upset than Alec had ever seen him. "Damnation, Ali, what's wrong?" Alec demanded softly.

Ali took a cleansing breath. "Your father suspected that you had abducted Lady Peyton for the purpose of forcing her into marriage. He knew that I was a party to your secret and tried to coerce me throughout the night to tell him of your whereabouts; naturally, I refused. Knowing that Lady Peyton would be your wife upon your return to Blackstone, he dissolved my betrothal to Ivy and pledged her to Warrington in her sister's stead."

Peyton heard everything. With a shriek, she slid off Midas. "My God, Ali, where is she?"

"In her bower. Awaiting her groom, who should be arriving late tonight."

Alec's gaze drifted to the structure, black and foreboding. His characteristically emotionless face was dark with the turn of events.

"Alec, she cannot wed Colin," Peyton grasped his arm. "You must talk to your father!"

"There is more," Ali continued, his voice dull with emotion and fatigue. "Rachel went into labor last night. She is still laboring to bring forth a child Pauly believes to be dead and your mother is beside herself."

Peyton put her hand to her head, closing her eyes and saying a brief prayer for the slight, dark-eyed woman. With tension and crisis surrounding them like a fog, she felt Alec's arm go about her comfortingly and she collapsed into his warmth and strength. Yesterday, they had only been concerned with themselves and no one else, and Peyton suddenly felt very guilty and selfish. Tears stung her eyes with the enormity of the situation as she looked to Ali.

"Ali, I am so sorry," she whispered. "Had I not gone with Alec, you and Ivy would now be married."

He smiled weakly. "We shall be still. I plan to do what Alec has done; abduct my bride."

Alec shook his head faintly. "It will not work. The church will not marry you, merely a lawyer, and therefore your marriage to Ivy could be dissolved on the grounds that it is a common law union."

Ali's ebony eyes flashed. "She is mine, Alec. Believe me when I say I have made the woman mine in every sense of the word and I will not stand by while she weds Warrington."

Alec drew in a deep, slow breath, comprehending Ali's meaning and knowing his disappointment all too well. He had been able to remedy his situation, but Ali was helpless and anger suddenly tore at him.

"Ali, take my wife into your safekeeping, please," he gently removed Peyton from his waist and placed her hand in Ali's. "I am going to speak to my father. You will bring my wife inside in a few minutes, but allow me a brief time alone with him first."

"Be mindful that he is in a bitter mood. I have never seen him so dark, Alec."

Alec did not reply, crossing the bailey with his proud, strong gait toward the entrance. Peyton and Ali watched a moment before turning to look at each other, silent words of apology and question and apprehension filling the space between them.

Ali smiled faintly. "So you are Lady Summerlin now? Congratulations, mademoiselle. May your union be blessed."

Peyton glanced at Alec as he disappeared into the castle. "I am beginning to believe our marriage is already cursed," she turned back to the ebony soldier. "How is Ivy faring?"

His smile faded. "Despondent. I have been not allowed to see her since early this morn."

Peyton sighed with regret, wondering when the situation suddenly careened out of control. When she had left with Alec yesterday, it seemed as if they were to be the only people affected by their decision and she could see how their rash action was collapsing. Ali was affected, and Ivy, and the damnable Warringtons were being drawn into the circumstance. Having eloped was hazard enough, but now with the added concern of Rachel's dead child, it would seem that the Summerlins had more to deal with than ever before.

But she did not regret her decision to marry Alec. And she knew he did not, either. Were she to repeat that moment in time, she would have done the same again.

Ali tucked her hand into the fold of his elbow and they began to stroll towards the castle, a leisurely pace to allow Alec time to deal with his father. And with the turmoil of the past night, the inner sanctum of the castle was far worse than the ninth level of hell.

ALEC STRODE INTO his father's solar without bothering to knock. Brian was at his desk, his handsome face scrutinizing a sand-colored piece of vellum before him. When he heard the heavy boot falls he glanced up, surprise and rage washing his features.

"Alec!" he exclaimed.

"What is this I hear? You plan to wed Lady Ivy to the Warrington pup?"

Brian was up from his desk, moving towards his son as if to wring the living daylights out of him. But he came to an unsteady halt instead, no fists forthcoming even if he was mere inches from his son's face. "Where's Lady Peyton?"

Alec was undoubtedly cool, cooler still in his outrage. "My wife will be joining us shortly."

Brian's face mottled red underneath the silver and black beard and he turned away, dragging a hand over his face in a wretched attempt to control his fury. "Dear God, you married her. You married her after I dissolved your contract!" he whirled to his son, jabbing a thick finger at him. "You had no right, Alec! No right whatsoever and I swear to you that this is not the end of it. You were wrong to disobey me."

Alec raised a slow, deliberate eyebrow. "I took what was mine and there is nothing you can do about it. The marriage contract is in my saddlebags and the union was consummated. She is my wife in the eyes of God and by the laws of England."

Brian marched toward his son again. "By God, what have I ever done to cause you to go against me? Have I wronged you somehow? Have I humiliated you, cursed you? Why would you do this?"

"Because I want her," Alec replied honestly. "Why are you so angry when I have forged a powerful alliance with St. Cloven, to say nothing of the Summerlin heirs Peyton will bear."

Brian blinked sharply as if he had been struck. All of the color drained from his face and he suddenly looked very old and very tired. Turning somewhat unsteadily, he meandered to his desk and perched his wide bottom on the pointy edge, his brown eyes gazing pensively into the space of the room.

"'Twill be the only heirs the Summerlins are to have," he said hoarsely, shoulders sagging. "Pauly says that Rachel's child is dead."

The fire had gone out of the confrontation and Alec was deeply sorry for the heartache he had caused his father. It was an added problem the man did not need, but he did not regret his action in the least. Still, he was remorseful for the turmoil he had brought down upon Brian's shoulders. He and his father had always been exceedingly chummy and it pained him to see disharmony between them.

"Ali told me," he replied quietly. "The child has not been born yet?"

"Not yet. It's been over eighteen hours and there has been little progress in the birth."

Alec sighed, moving to sit beside his father. Now that the initial hostilities and anger were aired, it was easier to focus on the true catastrophe happening within the walls of Blackstone. A marriage, as significant as that was, was nothing compared to the perpetuation of the family line.

"Pauly could be wrong, you know," he said to his father.

Brian snorted softly, sadly. "Mayhap. But the fact that the child is nearly two months early is another strike against it. Remember last year when she bore a daughter nearly three months early? The child lived naught but a few hours."

Alec was truly sorrowful for Rachel and for his father. All the man wanted out of life was a grandson, an heir to carry on the powerful Summerlin name.

"Is mother with her?" he asked softly.

Brian nodded dully. "Your mother has not slept since the labor began. She is nearly at her limit and Paul is only capable of wailing and carrying on like an idiot. He is asleep now, thankfully, but I have had my hands full keeping him calm."

Alec watched his father, the man whom he most wanted to be like when he was a young boy. There was still a portion of that little boy buried deep within, the son who wanted to be a powerful knight like his father, still so desperate to please him.

"I am sorry to cause you so much unrest, Da," he said quietly. "But I believe my marriage to Peyton will be most favorable and strong. I will make you proud of me, have no doubt."

Brian turned to look at his son, still in his view the most powerful knight in the realm. God, how he loved him. "You have never disappointed me, Alec. You have been the cause of a good deal of insanity and torment, but you have never shamed me," he slapped his fair-haired son gently on the cheek. "Yet you will know how displeased I am with your actions. I made it quite clear that Lady Peyton was betrothed to the Warrington boy and it was not your right to act as you did."

The mood between them was calm and rational and Alec felt a good deal less defiant, simply the need to make his father understand his reasons. "I want her, Da. I have never wanted a woman in my life, but I want her. Is that so difficult to understand? She gives me a peace and comfort I have never known," he lowered his gaze, studying the cracks in the floor. "I told her of Peter and as I did, I suddenly felt as if some of my pain had been eased. 'Tis difficult to describe, but it was a cleansing experience. I.... I need her. I have never needed anyone in my life as I need her."

Brian was focused on his son, amazed at his confession. He'd never heard words of such depth come forth from his emotionless son and he was touched. "Then I am glad for you, Alec, truly," he said quietly. "God only knows the guilt you have harbored these twelve years. If your wife helps ease your anguish, then I could ask for no greater pleasure."

Somewhat embarrassed at his admission, even if the listener was his father, Alec gazed at the floor pensively for a moment before looking to the burly man with a sheepish grin. "But you are still angry."

Brian raised a sharp eyebrow and growled. "Had I the strength, I would take you over my knee. You have put me in a very awkward position."

Alec's grin faded. "You cannot be serious about marrying Ivy to the Warrington whelp."

"With Peyton married, Ivy is the logical substitution."

"Have the Warrington's already agreed to her?"

"They consented early this morning, which is why they are on their way to Blackstone to complete the contract."

Alec crossed his massive arms thoughtfully, eyeing his father. "She is no longer a virgin. They will not want her when this becomes knowledge."

"My God," Brian's face twisted as if in great pain. "I knew it. Ali would not tell me, but I suspected as much. Especially after your mother told me of Lady Ivy's…. er, mark. Damnation!"

"Then you now know it as fact. Surely you cannot promise a compromised woman in marriage."

Brian opened his mouth to utter a reply when there was a soft rap on the door. He and Alec turned to the door as it opened quietly and Ali poked his head in.

"Alec?" he began hesitantly. "I have brought…."

Alec waved him in. "Come in, all is well."

The door opened wide and Ali entered, leading Peyton by the hand. Peyton, flushed and nervous, kept her gaze lowered until Alec reached out and took her from his friend.

"It's all right, sweetheart," he said softly. "Greet my father."

Peyton raised her eyes uncertainly to Brian, who merely gave her a weak smile. He could see her doubt and fear and knew for a fact she was an innocent in Alec's determined scheme. Poor naive child, he thought. Little did he realize the truth.

Brian held out his arms to his newest daughter. "Come here, love, and let me see if you taste as good as I remember," when she responded to his embrace, he kissed her on the cheek and smacked his lips. "Indeed. Better by the day, like St. Cloven ale."

Peyton managed an embarrassed grin as Alec pulled her into his gentle embrace. "We cannot age it too long, my lord, else it will be too strong and bitter," she said.

"Undoubtedly." Brian rose and went to an ornate wooden table etched in gold leaf. Upon the table were two large pitchers, and he poured amber liquid into four glasses. "I do believe that in the six months you have been managing St. Cloven, the ale has never been better. Do you not agree, Alec?"

Alec took a proffered chalice and handed it to his wife, taking the next for himself. Ali took his cup silently and moved to the distant wall, his expression guarded. He was still too wary of Brian's intentions with Ivy to be chummy with the man.

"Absolutely," Alec smiled at Peyton and took a healthy drink of his goblet.

Peyton followed suit, the familiar tang of St. Cloven Dark Ale bathing her tongue. Two more swallows of the liquid had her courage returning as well as her voice. Brian had resumed his seat behind his desk, pondering his surroundings distantly as they drank their ale in silence.

"My lord," she said, setting her goblet down. "Is it truly your intention to marry Ivy to Colin Warrington?"

Alec expected her to ask such a question and turned expectantly to his father, waiting for the correct reply. Brian, however, did not respond instantly. He continued to sit and contemplate his ale.

"If you will forgive me, my lady, that is none of your affair," he said after a moment. "With your father dead, 'tis my duty to find your sister a suitable husband and…."

"And Ali is not suitable?" Peyton demanded, bordering on outrage. "He was quite suitable not a day ago. Why is he no longer suitable?"

Brian looked at her, then. "Ali is not an heir. Your sister will become lady of Wisseyham Keep, a substantial manor with a good deal of investment in cattle and, in that respect, Colin Warrington is a more suitable mate."

"Colin Warrington is a pig," Peyton said flatly, forgetting to whom she was speaking. "He is a disgusting, filthy man with the morals of a barbarian. Obviously, my father never fully divulged the extent of the de Fluornoy-Warrington feud, else you would not make such a ridiculous statement."

Brian lifted an eyebrow at her insolence. "Mind your tongue, lady."

Peyton was never one to back down from a confrontation and with her sister's happiness at stake she would push her manner to the very limits of respect.

"Gladly, but first I will tell you exactly what Colin Warrington is capable of. He and his father used to delight in burning fields of our barley to sabotage our livelihood until we hired soldiers to stand guard on ripening fields to discourage such actions. When they tired of burning our crops, they moved to harassing our villeins. They would abduct children from their parents only to leave the children to fend for themselves miles away from the village, three and four-year-old children forced to find their way home. More than half that were abducted never saw their way home, my lord. Some simply vanished, and still others were eaten by wild animals. Still other half-starving children somehow found their way to St. Cloven, where we would feed them and try to nurse some health back into their starving little bodies," her eyes stung with tears from the memory of the tragedies, horrors she had forced away because the remembrance used to bring on nightmares.

The mood of the room grew somber as she continued. "But they were not sated with their sadistic lust; not yet, anyway. They progressed beyond simple abduction to raping young girls, threatening to kill them if they told who had deflowered them. Eleven, twelve, or thirteen years old; it did not matter to them. I know for a fact that there are at least four Warrington bastards roaming the village of March, one birthed from an eleven-year-old girl. But we could never prove anything, for the victims were too frightened to point a finger."

Brian did not look particularly stunned, merely sickened. His handsome face was dark and icy, a distinctly frightening countenance, but Peyton did not pause to contemplate his expression; she was concerned only for her sister's future. After a moment, Brain tore his eyes away from her and scratched his beard roughly. "Why did Albert not ask for Summerlin assistance?"

Peyton smiled thinly. "Because like you, my father had a great deal of pride. He did not want others to be involved in a problem he never lost hope of solving on his own. Even.... even after Nigel raped Jubil one day when she was in the woods gathering ingredients for her potions. Fortunately, Jubil was intoxicated at the time and remembered little, except that she kept recalling Nigel's face looming over her. Never again wonder why father was such a recluse; he indeed kept to himself. But he was distrustful with good reason."

Brian was staring at her, digesting her words, and Peyton noticed the pale, faintly bluish ring surrounding his lips. His expression was open and unguarded and she prayed that he was reconsidering his stance. She continued to gaze at him, even as she felt Alec's comforting hand on her back. He simply had to understand.

Finally, Brian sat forward with a grunt and folded his hands on his desk deliberately, his brown eyes transformed from soft to piercing. "Do you swear to me that this is true?"

"She would not lie to you," Alec cut in, incensed.

Brian held up a sharp hand to silence his son, his eyes never leaving Peyton. "Answer me."

"I swear it upon the word of our Lord," she said without hesitation. "Ivy and Jubil will confirm my story if you wish."

Brian stared at her a moment longer, a throbbing vein in his temple drawing Peyton's attention. When he spoke, his voice was low. "Ali, you will ride to Northampton immediately and retrieve Lord Finchamp of Dowling Street. He is the lawyer who agreed to marry you and Lady Ivy. You will bring him here posthaste."

Ali leapt into action, not even bothering to thank the man before he was bolting from the room. Peyton felt her entire body go limp with relief and she proceeded to down the entire contents of her chalice without a pause.

"If he hurries, he can return before the Warrington's arrive," Brian rose from his chair, mumbling to himself like an old man. "I have got to see if there has been any progress made on the birth of my grandchild."

Alec watched his father retreat from the room, knowing how impotent and weak he must be feeling in the face of his insolent children and a life that was intent on eluding his control. When Brian disappeared into the dim depths of the foyer, Alec turned to his wife, who was on her second cup of ale.

"Easy on that, love," he said softly. "I shall not have my drunk wife bouncing off the walls."

She gave him an irritable look and drained the cup. "I drink for a living, Alec. I have not been drunk in years."

"How unfortunate. I was hoping you would drink yourself into a stupor and I would be able to take advantage of you."

She smiled, feeling contentment as the warmth of the ale began to fill her. "Thank God all is working out well. Ali will marry Ivy, I have married you, and we will all return to St. Cloven to live happily ever more."

He smiled faintly in agreement. "You make it sound as if we will have a perfect life together."

"I would hope we will have a pleasant one, anyway. With my bold tongue and your considerable anger, 'twill be anything but perfect."

"I do not have considerable anger," he moved to her, enveloping her in his muscular arms. "'Tis only irritation you see."

She cocked an auburn eyebrow. "Irritation that kept you out of our bed on our wedding night. Irritation that caused you to tear this room apart and very nearly me with it. Irritation indeed."

He tried to kiss her but she dodged him, twisting from his grasp. "Not now, Alec. I would go see Ivy and tell her the good news."

He followed her about as she tried to move out of his range. He reached out to grasp her arm, only to have her slap his hand away. He grabbed at her skirt and she yanked the fabric from his grasp, squealing with laughter when he rapidly snatched at her with the other hand and succeeded in grabbing a handful of red hair.

Gently, he pulled her against his taut chest, winding the liquid fire strands around his powerful hand and cupping the back of her head.

"You will never escape me, wench," he purred.

"I was not trying to escape you," she replied, feeling the wickedly warm sensations of desire bubbling within her chest. "I was merely trying to elude you because you know as well as I that we are no longer satisfied with mere kisses, and there is no privacy for.... that."

"What?" he whispered, his mouth descending on her lips.

She bent her knees, slouching low and trying to evade his probing mouth, but he merely wrapped an arm around her waist and hoisted her up to his level.

"Nay, Alec, not now," she protested weakly, grinning as she turned sharply away from his seeking lips.

"I merely wish to taste, my lady," he whispered, his hot mouth latching onto her neck.

Instantly, she felt herself giving in to him, but she fought against the overpowering passion that he so easily elicited. "Please, Alec, no! I cannot.... I am still tender from yesterday and this morn."

His kissed her neck but a brief moment longer before pulling back with a heavy sigh. "I am a savage beast, I know. But I simply cannot help myself when I am around you. 'Tis your own fault for creating such a monster with your beauty and sensuality."

She smiled, kissing his lips sweetly. When he moved to respond intensely, she avoided his pursuing lips and put her hand over his face to stop the onslaught. "Put me down, please."

"One more kiss and I shall," he mumbled against her palm.

She glanced at him, giggling to see that her fingers had plastered one eye closed while the other sky-blue eye blazed brightly at her. "No more. Please? I would go see Ivy now."

He sighed and twisted his lips reluctantly, but he did as she asked and lowered her to the ground. She continued to grin as she straightened her surcoat.

"Thank you, darling."

He raised an eyebrow and grasped her hand, leading her from the room. "I would respond that obeying your request was my pleasure, but it was not. You are a cruel woman to deny your husband a simple kiss."

She eyed him. "A kiss is not such a simple thing between you and I, my Alec."

THE DOOR TO the bower was bolted from the inside. Peyton rapped softly, calling for her sister to open the door. After an eternal pause, the panel opened and a hand suddenly came flying out at Peyton, catching her in the jaw with a sharp slap.

Peyton stumbled back as Ivy propelled herself from the archway, oblivious to Alec's presence. He reacted instinctively, grasping his sister-in-law about her considerable waist as she charged his wife.

"Why did not you tell me what was going on?" Ivy raged as Alec restrained her. "Do you realize what you have done to me?"

Peyton, hand on her cheek, stood a safe distance from her raging sister. "Everything is as it should be, Ivy. Ali is riding to Northampton for the lawyer as we speak."

As if by magic, Ivy's struggles ceased and her blue eyes widened. But Alec did not let go of her just yet; the woman was amazingly strong and she had dealt his wife a heavy blow. And he wasn't entirely certain that she would not charge her sister again.

"What.... what do you mean?" Ivy breathed. "Ali went to Northampton?"

Peyton nodded. "To fetch the lawyer. Lord Brian seems to think you two will be married before the Warrington's arrive this eve."

Ivy's strength fled and Alec found himself supporting her. He and Peyton managed to steer her back into the bower, directing her into the nearest chair. Alec went to pour her a large draught of ale as Peyton patted her shoulder comfortingly.

"I am sorry, darling, truly," she said softly. "We had no idea Lord Brian would react this way. It never occurred to either of us that he would betroth you to Warrington in my stead."

Ivy took a deep, ragged breath to steady her reeling head. "Nor did it occur to me," she grasped her sister's hand tightly. "I am sorry, Peyton. I should not have lashed out at you as I did, but I have spent the entire night worrying and crying and.... oh, Christ, I am so sorry. You are wed, then?"

Peyton smiled. "The Lady Peyton de Fluornoy Summerlin."

Ivy managed a weak smile before her eyes fell on Alec, tall and strong, as he handed her the chalice of ale. "Thank you, dear brother. I do apologize for whacking your wife."

He raised an eyebrow, the corner of his lips twitching. "We would duel come the dusk were I not so afraid that you would best me."

"Coward," Peyton muttered.

"Indeed," Alec grasped her chin gently and studied the red welt on the creamy skin, almost a perfect handprint.

Ivy swallowed, embarrassed as Alec observed her handiwork on Peyton's face. She thought it best to change the subject before he changed his mind and decided to call her out. "How is Ali faring? I have not seen him since early this morn."

"He is exhausted but well, considering," Alec replied, seating his large frame on the edge of the bed. "I am positive at this moment he is riding like the wind to reach Northampton. Hell, the horse probably isn't fast enough and he is racing on foot."

Ivy giggled, relieved, feeling a good deal of comfort and satisfaction. A most pleasurable end to a most horrible night, an end she thought never to see. "What made your father change his mind, Alec?"

Alec glanced at his flame-haired wife. "A close relative was most persuasive on your behalf."

Ivy gave her sister a long look. "I am afraid to ask. Did you attempt to garrote your father-in-law? Or was it the threat of skinning him alive that caused him to change his mind?"

Peyton gave her sister an irritable look and moved toward Alec. "Nothing of the kind. I simply told him of the Warrington's true nature and it was enough to convince him."

The humor faded from Ivy's expression. "That was my biggest fear, you know. Being thrown into the den of debauchers, alone."

Peyton's humor vanished as well. "Worry no more, darling. Lord

Brian is a wise and sensible man."

Alec's thick arm snaked out and grasped her around the waist, pulling her onto his lap. "Only last night he was Lucifer incarnate. My father seems to be a great many things to a great many people."

Ivy watched her sister and her new husband, marveling at how well they were getting on. Their beginning had been so terribly rocky that she never truly thought she would see this level of fondness between them. It was readily apparent that there was a great deal of affection and she sincerely hoped that somehow Peyton had been able to put James out of her mind. From the way she was looking at Alec, it would seem so.

"When will we return to St. Cloven?" she asked after a moment.

Alec turned his attention to her briefly before returning to Peyton. "Tomorrow, most likely. Ali and I must pack our possessions and then we may leave."

"We do need to return as soon as possible," Peyton said, her arms wound around her husband's neck affectionately. "We have an entire lot of pale ale that should be ready for sale. I must get back and determine its readiness."

"Do you not have a master brewer to attend to that?" he asked.

"Of course. But I have the final decision."

He almost added that her duty was past tense, at least until he learned the intricacies of ale making, but he bit his tongue. It occurred to him that his wife was intelligent enough to continue her position as master ale administrator without his interference. After all, she had been born into it, as he had not been, and knew the details and workings far better than he. Moreover, the reputation of St. Cloven's ale had not suffered in the least since Albert's death; if anything, it had increased in quality.

Aye, he decided firmly, the best thing would be for him to allow his wife to continue with her duties. He was smart enough to know wherein her strengths lay.

"Then we shall leave tomorrow," he said decisively. "As it is, I want to make sure St. Cloven's stables are well equipped to handle my brood of horses before I transfer them from Blackstone."

"Horses? What horses?" Peyton asked.

"My Saracens," he replied. "I collected three mares and a stallion when I was in the Holy Land. I have been breeding the mares to the destriers and have developed several incredibly strong and swift animals. I have already sold two of them to the king for his private stable at a considerable price, and in turn I have several nobles breathing down my neck to purchase my next crop of foals."

"Horses and ale. What a smelly combination," Ivy snorted. "You two will certainly be a pair, one reeking of manure and the other of liquor."

Peyton shot her sister a hostile glare, though exaggerated, before refocusing on her husband. "You never told me that you bred Saracens."

"Not exactly bedchamber talk, darling," Ivy said before Alec could answer. "I doubt that was foremost on his mind when he took you to bed last night."

Alec actually grinned. "Your sister's right, of course, and it never came up in casual conversation."

Peyton shrugged in agreement, hearing her sister snickering over her shoulder. With a sly glance, she looked to Ivy. "You are in no position to laugh at me for not knowing everything about my husband, considering the fact that you are unwed and no longer a maiden. I do not suppose you and Ali have done much talking, either."

Ivy did not flush, as she should have. Instead, she gave her sister a bold, seductive look. "He said that you once asked if he was black all over. I can confirm that he is."

Alec rolled his eyes at the bawdy turn in conversation. "I am sure he does not wish for that to become public knowledge, Ivy."

"I am not the public," Peyton said indignantly.

"Nay, you are not, you are my wife, and I shall not have you privy to such personal knowledge as another man's body characteristics," he cast a stern eye to Ivy. "You will keep such facts to yourself. You will not tantalize my wife with tales of your all-black soldier."

Ivy laughed at him, as did Peyton. Alec tried to remain stern, pulling Peyton closer and burying his face in her neck lest they see that he was on the verge of grinning. Peyton patted his head as if he were a child.

"I am afraid we have embarrassed him with our bold talk," she told her sister. "He shall never recover."

"Poor, poor Alec," Ivy clucked. "Tell me, Peyton. Is he white all over?"

Peyton opened her mouth and Alec's head came up. "Not a word," he threatened. "That is something your sister will have to ponder the rest of her life. Now, the both of you, cease this line of talk. I am terribly unnerved by the entire thing."

Peyton and Ivy grinned at each other. "Poor innocent pup," Ivy said soothingly. "Of course we will speak of something else that will not upset your delicate balance. Let's talk about breeding."

"Breeding!" Alec boomed. "Not a chance!"

"Horse breeding, Alec," Ivy insisted, losing the battle against her giggles. "Won't you tell us about it?"

"No," he said flatly, swatting his wife's behind when she leapt from his lap in a fit of snickers. "It's a secret. Not for your fragile feminine ears."

Peyton shook her head as Ivy begged and Alec refused, moving for the wardrobe and thinking on changing into a fresh gown. She continued to dig through the wardrobe as Alec and Ivy bantered until she suddenly realized that something was missing from their room. Someone was missing.

"Ivy, where's Jubil?"

"She went out after the nooning meal to scour the countryside for new ingredients," Ivy replied. "She took a knight with her – what's his name? Toby? He looks a good deal like you, Alec."

Alec raised an eyebrow, the mirth gone from his expression. He did not say anything for a moment, a distinct give away, and Peyton turned to look at him intently from her position by the wardrobe.

"Is he a cousin?" she asked.

He sighed and shook his head. They would both hear the truth soon enough; better to hear it from him. "He is my half-brother."

Peyton looked at him in surprise. "You father's bastard?"

"Nay," he replied quietly. "My mother's."

Peyton's eyes widened further and she glanced at Ivy, whose face was a mirror of her own. "Your *mother's* bastard?" Peyton repeated.

He nodded faintly, rising from the bed with popping joints. "Toby was born while my father was away, fighting with King Henry. I do not know who his father is and I never asked."

Peyton, brow furrowed with puzzlement, turned back to her wardrobe. "He is a very handsome man. Except for his shorter height, he looks a good deal like you."

Alec appeared lost in thought a moment longer before glancing at his wife. "He is a good lad. My father allowed him to return to Blackstone after fostering because my mother missed him terribly. Especially after the misfortune of Paul and the loss of Peter, my father would not deny my mother her living flesh."

Peyton drew out a golden gown, her movements slow and thoughtful. "Your father is a saint, Alec. I would not be so generous."

Alec shrugged. "He is a decent man, far more than most. As I said, I do not know the entire story regarding Toby's birth and most likely never will. But, if you please, this knowledge goes no further."

Ivy nodded solemnly as Peyton laid the golden gown on the bed. Alec eyed it with approval. "A magnificent piece. You will outshine the sun."

"It's not for me, it's for Ivy," she said firmly. "'Tis the dress she will be married in."

Alec smiled faintly, glancing to his sister-in-law. "In that case, Ivy, you shall outshine the sun."

Ivy stood from her chair, brushing her fingers over the burnished gold. "How long does it take to ride to Northampton?"

"With luck, he shall return in three or four hours," Alec replied, noting the wistful tone of Ivy's voice. "Have no fear, Lady Ivy. He shall return dragging the lawyer by his hair if it is the fastest way."

From outside the thick stone walls there came a shouting, a chorus that was picked up by several other soldiers. Alec moved to the latticed windows, feeling the heat of the day grasping at his face as he gazed out over the bailey.

"What is it?" Peyton asked him.

He shook his head vaguely. "I am not sure. It looks like…." he suddenly broke off, taking a long look before whirling on his heel and marching for the door. Ivy and Peyton watched his sharp movements with concern.

"What is it, Alec?" Peyton demanded again.

To her distress, his face was as hard as stone. When he spoke, his tone was like ice. "It looks as if the Warrington's have ridden even harder than Ali. They're early."

The sisters gasped and dashed to the window even as Alec jerked open the door. But he paused a moment, anticipating their reaction. He was far more concerned with their mental state than the anger that would surely come from the scorned family.

"Blue and black," Peyton murmured. "The Warrington standard. See the preying cat?"

Ivy nodded. "Look! My God, there's Colin Warrington himself in the very lead."

Peyton jostled for a closer look. "Look at the pea-brained lout! And, Good Lord, Nigel has lost a good deal of hair. The last I saw him, he had a crown of sandy blond hair. Now it looks as if a blind man tried to shave his scalp."

Satisfied to see that the appearance of the hated enemy had not turned either woman into hysterical females, he closed the door behind him and proceeded down the corridor.

Truthfully, their reaction did not surprise him; he was coming to learn that the de Fluornoy women were made of much stronger elements that most other females. Their bravery and gumption pleased him deeply, and he was far better able to focus on the coming conflict that was undoubtedly brewing.

His wife's scorned suitor.

CB

BRIAN AND LADY Celine were caught up in the turmoil of Rachel's labor and Alec could hear the woman moaning as he stood outside her bower, relaying the arrival of the Warringtons to his father.

Brian, pale-lipped and sweating, seemed to be having difficulty grasping the turn of events and Alec was concerned for his father's sanity. He knew how desperately his father wanted a grandson, but the man was acting as if it were his very own child being born. Lady Celine, pale and drawn, made a brief appearance in the corridor and did not so much as utter a hostile word to Alec regarding his elopement. All of her energy, too, seemed to be focused on the impending child and she quickly disappeared into the bower when Rachel emitted a particularly pathetic groan.

It was plain to Alec that his father was incapable of handling this tense confrontation at the moment and he hastened to assure his father that he would handle the Warringtons until Brian's composure returned. While his father retreated to his bower to freshen-up and regain his senses, Alec found himself down in the foyer preparing to greet the most unsavory guests.

Toby met him in the doorway, his young face flushed from the heat. "The Warringtons are early. We have not prepared…."

Alec cut him off. "I know. Where's Jubil?"

Toby blinked at the change of subject. "Upstairs, I suppose. We returned a few minutes ago. What about the Warringtons?"

Alec watched the small procession enter the bailey, particularly scrutinizing the two men astride lavish chargers. The father and son dismounted, conversing between themselves and studying the interior of the bailey. Purposely, Alec let them wait.

"Toby, find Jacques and Horatio. Tell them to hasten the preparation of the chambers in the west wing for the Warringtons."

"But those are the smallest, dingiest rooms in the.... oh," Toby suddenly grinned, a gesture much like his older half-brother. "Anything else?"

"Notify the kitchens that our guests are early. Tell them we will delay dinner for three hours after the usual time."

Toby continued to grin. "How terribly inconsiderate. Shall I also have the stewards provide the bedchambers with shackles and chains?"

"Not at the moment," Alec returned crisply. "Nails in the mattress shall suffice for now. Get moving, lad."

Toby dashed off and Alec continued to watch the Warringtons as they waited for a Summerlin to extend a welcome. One of the lesser stewards had already greeted them and Alec watched the servant bow and scrape before Nigel, knowing that the excessive delay was becoming intensely embarrassing. But he continued to linger in the doorway unobtrusively, forcing the Warringtons to wait.

A figure suddenly appeared beside him, resplendent in a bejeweled shade of sapphire that matched the intense color of her eyes. Alec instinctively reached out and grasped his wife's arm.

"What are you doing here?" he demanded softly.

Peyton looked quite innocent. And quite determined. "Your mother is unable to attend her guests and I, as your wife, shall greet them in her stead."

Alec let out a hiss. "Do you think that entirely wise?"

"Of course," she said briskly. "What are you waiting for?"

He gazed down at her, from head-to-toe the loveliest woman he had ever laid eyes on. It was enough to melt him to the core.

"I cannot say that I agree with you," he said softly. "Especially in light of the fact that one of our 'guests' happens to be a spurned groom."

Peyton's brilliant eyes trailed to the bustling bailey, dust swirling through the air and clinging to the clothing of their visitors. "I am not concerned in the least with Colin Warrington's feelings, Alec. I am your wife, as I should be. If Colin cannot accept the fact, it is his misfortune."

Alec could force her to return to her room, of course, as he suspected he should. But something deep in his soul wanted the Warringtons to see her, to know that she was his, and to know how proud he was to have her. His intention was not to flaunt her in their face as one would a coveted prize; precisely, he wanted them to see that he considered her far more than a trophy. He considered her the only woman worthy to be his wife.

"All right, then," he said quietly. "But you will allow me to do the talking. Do you comprehend me?"

"Aye," she nodded, although he wondered if she meant it.

But he did not press her for her vow to curb her tongue. Instead, he tucked her hand into the crook of his elbow and stepped into the bailey.

Colin and Nigel were riveted to her from the moment she exited the castle and Alec felt himself stiffen at the attention. But he maintained his outward calm, approaching with Peyton on his arm and eyeing the Warringtons as if they were a lower life form.

"My lords," he said in his low, rich voice. "I am Sir Alec Summerlin and this is my wife, the Lady Peyton. I bid you welcome to Blackstone."

Colin and Nigel barely looked at him; they were entirely focused on Peyton as she curtsied with polished grace.

"Where is your father?" Nigel asked, his tone cold.

"Indisposed," Alec replied with equal hardness. "Your party is early and he has more pressing duties to attend to at the moment."

Nigel continued to stare at Peyton, who kept her gaze properly averted. "You are looking exceptionally well, Lady Peyton. I haven't seen you in many years."

She merely nodded and Nigel made a move toward her, extending his hand. Alec saw that he was moving to grasp her chin, to force her to look at him, and he pulled her out of the man's range.

"That," he growled, "would not be a wise move, my lord. No man touches my wife but me."

Nigel looked to Alec, his blue eyes narrowing. "Considering you are speaking of stolen property, you are hardly in a position to make demands. Lady Peyton was meant for my son, as you well know, and I cannot tell you how displeased the House of Warrington is at this blatant thievery."

"Lady Peyton was originally intended for me, my lord, but you had no way of knowing that when you sent your missive requesting her hand. Plans for our marriage had already been made some time ago."

Nigel snorted, his eyes trailing to Peyton once again. This time, she was looking at him openly, hostility simmering in the depths of the sapphire blue eyes. He smiled thinly. "It certainly did not take you an over amount of time to find another husband after the death of Deveraux. As I hear it, the two of you were inseparable. You were at the tournament in Norwich when he was killed, were you not? How tragic for you."

To her surprise, Peyton did not flinch. She felt a good deal of anger at his attempt to upset her, but none of the hollow grief she associated with James' death. It was amazing that she wasn't dissolving into tears at the mere sound of his name.

"Indeed," was all she said.

Alec did not look at her, his fury rising over Nigel's bid to unnerve her. But he was immensely pleased that she did not respond to his jibe, as he had asked her not to. She was silent, as promised, allowing her husband to handle the situation.

Nigel laughed softly at her lack of reaction. "Surely with all of that red hair you cannot be so cold-hearted. I express my condolences for the passing of your beloved betrothed and all you can say is 'indeed?' Shocking."

Her composure slipped somewhat, replaced by building anger. When she spoke, it was with carefully measured tones. "I neither want nor care for your condolences, my lord. I am here on behalf of my husband's mother to bid you welcome to Blackstone, not to hear your prevaricating blather."

Alec almost smiled, but he fought it. Nigel raised a disapproving eyebrow at Peyton's tone as Colin stepped forward, appraising her as if she were a prize mare.

"Let us hope that your new husband is able to impart some manners into your refractory nature," he said in a low voice. "Be glad, in that case, that you did not marry me. Beauty or no, I would have taken your hide off at the first sign of insolence."

Peyton's beautiful face glazed with animosity. Good lord, how she hated this man! Certainly she had promised Alec that she would not speak overly, and until this point she'd handled herself exceptionally well. But to stand so close to the hated Colin Warrington eroded her will power and she couldn't resist jabbing his arrogance.

"You are not man enough."

Colin twitched menacingly in her direction. Alec was driving his fist into the younger Warrington's face before he took another breath, sprawling the man on the dirt in less than a second. Nigel yelped and shielded his son protectively as Peyton pressed herself to Alec, struggling to stop him from doing any further damaged to Brian's guests.

Throughout all of Peyton's pleading and Nigel's protests, Brian chose that moment to exit the castle, taking a mere two steps onto the loose dirt of the bailey as the horrific scene unfurled before him.

"Alec!"

CHAPTER ELEVEN

"YOU DID NOT have to hit him," Peyton said softly.

Alec stood by the windows as a soft breeze caressed his heated face. A second cup of St. Cloven Dark Ale rested in his massive palm and he could feel his wife's warm hand on his arm.

"He was a threat to you," he said simply.

Peyton laid her cheek against his broad back, winding her arms around his narrow waist. "He was no threat to me, my Alec, not with you as my protector. You truly did not have to strike him."

He shrugged, his only answer, and drained his cup. She felt his huge palm enclose her two hands clasped at his waist. "I suppose I should retreat downstairs and apologize for my rash actions."

"Nay, darling, you will stay here until your father sends for you," she replied evenly. "Your father will do a better job of calming the Warringtons without your presence. Let them cool before you go charging in."

He contemplated the world outside his chamber window a moment longer before turning to capture Peyton in his arms, breaking a smile at the sight of her lovely face. "I do not charge."

"Aye, you do," she said firmly, winding her arms around his neck. "You do indeed charge and you are faster than a bolt of lightning. I never saw you move and suddenly, Colin was writhing in the dirt."

He lifted his shoulders. "As I have said, I have learned to compensate because I no longer carry a sword. I have learned to fight with my hands and feet. I simply must be quicker than anyone else because a man with a blade is given a heavy advantage automatically. If I do not move faster than my enemy, my life is forfeit."

She sighed and shook her head, eyeing him with disapproval. "You father did not need this added stress, you know. He has enough to deal with."

Alec looked remorseful for the first time. "I realize that. But I was defending you and I do not regret my protective instincts. Had I not moved, he most likely would have injured you somehow."

She smiled. "I am not afraid of him, my darling. Not with you to defend my honor."

He smiled weakly and she pinched him lightly on the cheek. He caught her mirth and squeezed her tightly, brushing her lips with his own a couple of times before slanting over them hungrily.

To think of Colin Warrington in possession of such sweetness and beauty drove him crazed with fury, emotions he funneled into his kiss and in no time he had her aloft in his arms, heading for his bed. Peyton sensed his passion, fed off it, and her own lust quickly blossomed.

But their desire would have to wait. Just as he reached the bed, there was a heavy rap on his door and he tore his mouth away from his wife reluctantly.

"Who comes?" he demanded.

"'Tis me, Alec."

Peyton looked at him questioningly as he lowered her to the ground. "Toby," he told her, moving for the door.

Toby looked embarrassed for his intrusion as if he had known exactly what they were doing behind the closed door.

"Your father requests your presence in the solar," he said softly, his blue eyes passing to Peyton shyly. "And I am to take your wife to assist your mother."

"Rachel still has not delivered?" Alec asked, concerned.

Toby shook his head. "Not yet. Your mother is exhausted and your father requests that your wife relieve her of her duties while she rests."

Peyton nodded firmly. "Of course," she said, although she was unnerved by the prospect; she'd never attended a woman in birth. Other than a horse, she'd never even seen a birth and she was horrified and fascinated by the mysteries it held. But in the same breath, she also felt a sense of maturity. As if being a wife entitled her to the privileges of seasoned, knowledgeable women, and she was anxious to join their ranks.

Even though she was aware that the child was most likely a stillborn, she was nonetheless willing, and frightened, to accept the challenge. Lady Celine was depending on her assistance and she would not disappoint. 'Twas her duty, as Alec's wife, and she was eager to prove her worth to the House of Summerlin in an attempt to offset the impulsive action of their elopement. She had every intention of bravely meeting her new duties, no matter how potentially disturbing they might be.

As they moved for the door, she fought back her natural apprehension and turned to her husband. "Are you going to be all right without me?"

"Yes, love, I shall be fine," he assured her, bordering on mockery.

She raised an eyebrow at him. "Do not be glib. I am serious."

"As am I," he grinned, kissing her sweetly on the cheek. "Toby, take good care of my wife."

"Aye, my lord," Toby replied softly.

Alec's boot falls faded down the hall and Peyton turned to Toby, scrutinizing his features for traces of Alec. She saw a good deal of her husband in the muscular young knight, only three years older than herself. Toby caught her open appraisal and knew instantly that Alec had told her of their blood relations. Usually shy and reserved, he found himself studying her in return. Christ, she was a beautiful creature.

"May I show you to Lady Rachel's room?" he asked respectfully.

She nodded, taking his proffered arm. "Thank you, sir knight."

He smiled, blushing brightly. "My pleasure, Lady Summerlin."

CONSIDERING ALEC HAD righteously pounded the man, Colin did not look overly bruised. There was a huge swollen nodule on his jaw, but other than that he appeared in good health. He stood in Brian's solar with a cup of fine St. Cloven ale in hand, disdainfully watching the activity in the bailey as Baron Rothwell and his father conversed tensely.

Alec's blow could not have come at a worse time. With Nigel outraged at Peyton's marriage, it certainly had not helped matters that the new husband had pummeled the would-be suitor. Nigel forewent any casual greetings, delving directly into his protests that Colin had not been given a fair chance to win the fair maiden's hand and furthermore stating his displeasure that Ivy had been offered as compensation.

Brian, irritated with the man's commanding attitude and haughty manner, informed him with a shade of satisfaction that Ivy's offer had been withdrawn due to a previous betrothal contract Albert himself had made, an arrangement Brian had been unaware of until most recently. A lie, of course, but it was a falsehood that would hopefully deter Nigel from an all-out declaration of war. He was angry enough to have lost the heiress, but to lose the sister as well was a considerable insult.

Brian sent for Alec early into the meeting simply for the fact that Alec's presence could not infuriate Nigel and Colin any more than they already were; moreover, Alec was a calming influence on his father and Brian was not entirely in control of his emotions at the moment. Alec's elopement and Rachel's labor had him on the edge. When Alec entered the solar, characteristically in control of his outward composure, Brian felt a good deal of relief.

Other than a disinterested glance, Colin paid Alec little attention. Nigel, however, spent a good deal of time glaring at the massive man as he vigorously protested his treatment from the entire House of Summerlin. Alec dutifully apologized for his lapse in manners but did not go so far as to apologize for the action of striking Colin. From the look on his son's face, Brian knew there was no amount of pleading that could convince him to apologize for preserving his wife's safety.

And it was also readily apparent to Brian that Alec's body was tense even if his expression held firm, an unusual state for his son to acquire. He was well aware that the taut stance was on behalf of his wife, and further on behalf of Ali and Ivy. With Colin in the room, Alec was very much on his guard, but it was more than that; Brian sensed a good deal of animosity.

He was extremely unnerved by the emotions radiating from Alec; he'd never known Alec to radiate any sort of emotion and it made a difficult situation all the more trying. He had hoped that Alec would inject a certain amount of control into the setting; obviously, he had been wishing for naught and he felt his superior hold slipping.

"Tell me, my lord," it was the first time Colin had spoken since entering the solar. "Is the Lady Ivy already married?"

"Nay," Brian replied. "We have planned the ceremony for this evening."

Colin turned away from the window, his large green eyes glittering. Alec studied him; he was tall and muscularly lean, not unattractive in the least. He would have been handsome had it not been for the simple fact that evil seemed to emit from him like a vile smell.

Alec remembered coming upon Colin once or twice in his youth, before he was sent away to Northwood to foster, but little beyond that. They had never remotely been friends, mostly for the fact that Colin seemed to have a hostile attitude toward Ali. Alec possessed a vague memory of a five-year-old Colin Warrington calling Ali a hairy demon. It was a recollection that still bore weight.

"Who is she betrothed to?" Colin asked.

Brian folded his hands on his desk, his face calm and steady. "Ali Boratu."

"The black beast who calls himself a man?" Nigel said incredulously. "God's Balls, Summerlin, you might as well have married her to a horse!"

Brian waited for Alec to tear both Nigel and Colin limb from limb and was mildly surprised when no rage was forthcoming. A glance at his son showed his face as unreadable as always, yet the veins in his neck were throbbing distinctly.

"Ali is a decent man with some wealth and a most fitting mate for the second daughter of a lesser knight," Brian explained evenly. "The betrothal has been inked for quite some time."

"Then why did you offer Lady Ivy in Lady Peyton's stead if she was already betrothed?" Nigel demanded, a balled fist on his thigh.

Brian blinked slowly in a show of lagging patience. "As I told you, I was unaware that Albert had arranged a marriage contract between Ivy and Ali. The transaction was made through Ali's father, Olphampa."

"How long ago?" Nigel insisted.

"I am not sure. It occurred after Ivy lost her innocence to Ali."

Colin looked at his father, the men exchanging shocked glances. After a moment, Nigel looked to Brian, considerably less combative. "Nonetheless, if they are not married, the contract can still be broken. My son, as heir to Wisseyham Keep, carries a far more attractive inheritance than a mere soldier."

"She carries his child," Alec chimed in emotionlessly. Lie or not, he would not allow Nigel to negotiate the point.

"Nothing a brew of parsley cannot take care of," Colin addressed him impassively, his evil eyes bright. "Something I have heard her insane aunt can administer quite well."

"I will not condone an abortion," Brian said sharply. "The church frowns upon such action, as you well know. The dissolution of Lady Ivy and Ali's marriage contract is not up for discussion and I do apologize that you have come a long way to face disappointment."

Nigel sat very still, pondering Brian on the other side of the desk. The room itself stilled as the future was mulled over by the four men and Alec began to hope that the meeting with the Warringtons would draw to a relatively bloodless close. The sooner they were out of Blackstone, the better for all.

"Might I have a word with you alone, my lord?" Nigel asked, almost politely. "Away from our sons' ears."

Brian glanced at Alec, who shrugged vaguely. It was obvious that Brian was seeking Alec's reassurance that there would be no brawl were the two younger men left alone, and Brian appeared confident that Alec would make no aggressive action, providing Colin was wise enough to keep his mouth shut. Yet it did not go unnoticed by Alec that his father's pallor had changed to a pasty yellow as he rose stiffly from his desk.

"Outside," Brian said shortly.

Nigel rose and followed him out into the foyer. Brian continued into the main dining hall, vacant of servants or soldiers, and indicated for Nigel to take a seat at the end of the long scrubbed table. Nigel glanced about the room, fresh with rushes and scented with dried herbs in earthenware pots. Slowly, he perched on the edge of the bench.

Brian refused to look at him, turmoil wrenching his guts. God help him, he knew what was coming and he knew there was nothing he could do against it. Dark secrets were about to be discussed, secrets he attempted to pretend did not exist.

Which was why he avoided the Warringtons at all costs. Aye, he knew full well of the dispute between Nigel and Albert, and he had heard rumor of the atrocities the Warringtons were accused of committing. It was difficult not to have heard the accusations, being liege of the barony where the crimes were taking place. But he had ignored the rumors, tucking the facts far back in his mind and turning an ignorant eye to the heinous acts. He rationalized his action by convincing himself that if Albert de Fluornoy had not formally asked for his help, then the villeins must be spinning tales to create unrest. Villeins were a stupid lot with an overactive imagination, were they not?

Brian reiterated his reasoning as the years passed until he believed them. He knew he was a coward for not responding to the transgressions, but he simply could not force himself to confront Nigel Warrington. Not when they shared such terrible mysteries.

But now, Nigel was intending to bring forth his darkest nightmare and Brian was sick with it all. Nightmares no one, save Celine, knew.

Nigel saw the man's face, his ashen pallor, and smiled thinly. "Come now, Brian. I shall not bite."

Brian's face was taut. "Get on with it."

"As you wish. You will break the betrothal between Ali and Lady Ivy and wed the lady to my son. Is that clear enough?"

Brian's jaw twitched miserably. "I cannot break the contract. It is set and...."

"It is not set. Nothing is set. I do not care if the bitch has been sleeping with the black animal since she was a child, she shall wed Colin."

"Do not speak of them that way."

"I shall speak of them however I damn well please. I will consider the marriage to Lady Ivy small compensation for the loss of the heiress to St. Cloven. You sorely push my patience wedding the Lady Peyton to your son, Brian."

"What's done is done," Brian snapped softly. "Alec eloped with the girl, legal and just, and there was naught I could do. They were married in Ely, no less, and nothing short of God can dissolve the union. She is out of your reach, as is the Lady Ivy."

"Unacceptable. The lady will marry Colin or certain distasteful matters might not remain veiled in secrecy much longer. Do you comprehend my meaning?"

Brian's brown eyes glared at the man a moment. "Do not threaten me."

"'Tis certainly no threat, brother."

"Do not call me that!" Brian hissed viciously. "Do not ever call me that!"

Nigel smiled sinisterly. "The truth hurts, does it not? I am the bastard of your father's loins. Fitting that my son should reside within your walls, bastard of my loins."

Brian clenched his teeth. "Your revenge is misplaced and sickening. What you did to Celine...."

"I did nothing but comfort her while her warring husband was away, fighting with Henry," Nigel said soothingly, mocking the pain in Brian's heart. "The liaison was of mutual consent, brother. You have known that for twenty-three years and you have no one to blame but yourself for your own neglect."

"'Twas not neglect," Brian said, his voice a hollow echo.

"You seduced her, you bastard. You courted her with lies of my infidelity and convinced her that no one but you would take care of her. While I was away warring for our king, you enticed her beyond reason and confused her with sweet words and falsehoods, and when she showed an ounce of refusal toward your onslaught, you raped her."

Nigel's eyes glittered like diamonds, cold and sharp. "If you choose to believe those reasons, then that is your choice. But Celine and I know the truth. I suspect Toby will too, someday."

Brian refused to reply, his jaw grinding as he studied the moldings on the great hearth. Anything to avoid Nigel's piercing eyes, lest he strike the man down on the spot.

Truthfully, he did not know what measure of control was preventing him from doing so. Was it the fact that he felt a measure of pity for the man, a bastard of noble breeding, never given the same chances in life as his half-brother? Brian did not know why he showed so much restraint when it came to Nigel; mayhap he never would understand. The memory of Celine's liaison with Nigel, or rape as Brian liked to believe, was like an open wound after all of these years. A wound that Brian could not bring himself to tend, and it seemed to ache deeper every time he gazed upon the result of that particular encounter. Toby had no idea the pain he caused Baron Rothwell. Or why.

After several long moments, he spoke. "Why would you seek revenge on me for my father's indiscretions? What have I ever done to you to warrant your hatred?"

Nigel's features twisted coldly. "You have done nothing, my lord, except inherit our father's holdings and titles, deny your blood ties to me, and ignore your relations."

"And you have done nothing but shame the Summerlin name with your villainous acts and despicable horrors. Why in the hell should I acknowledge you?"

"I do not bear the Summerlin name. I bear the name of the man who raised me, my mother's husband."

Brian did not reply for a moment. With a long sigh, he turned from the cold hearth. "Your mother and my father loved each other, Nigel. My own mother was sickly and cold, and your mother's husband was a beast of a man. The fact that our father sought comfort in your mother's arms was not surprising, and neither is the fact that their relationship resulted in you. Yet you know full well why my father could not acknowledge you as his own."

"Would not, you mean," Nigel corrected with restrained bitterness. "He already had his heir. What would he do with a bastard son?"

Brian sat heavily opposite Nigel, the table not the only barrier between them. "To acknowledge you would have been to bring great scandal to two noble households, pure and simple. He could not risk it."

Nigel suddenly brought his fists to bear on the oak table, a loud boom echoing against the vaulted ceiling. "He had to spare his own pride, Brian! He cared not what scandal would ravage the House of Warrington, only the House of Summerlin. He never gave a damn about me, only you."

Brian gazed at his half-brother, two years younger than himself. His eyes were guarded, almost sad. They'd had this conversation before, a few times, and it always ended the same way. Nigel never did understand why William Summerlin refused to acknowledge him as his son, and it cut him deeply. Therefore, his anger, his hurt, was directed against Brian.

"This is not about the Summerlins or the Warringtons, it's about Colin's betrothal," Brian said softly, refocusing the subject. "As I said before, I cannot break Lady Ivy's contract and furthermore, I do not understand why it is so important that I do. There are several eligible young ladies in the province."

Nigel faltered for a brief moment, a peculiar ripple of emotion crossing his features. He did not want any other young ladies for Colin; he wanted a de Fluornoy. He wanted St. Cloven.

"They are not suitable for Colin. As the nephew of Baron Rothwell, surely he is entitled to a woman of equal standing."

"The Lady Caroline Morford is available. Surely she is…."

"A trollop, unfit for my son."

"And Lady Ivy, though compromised, is considered appropriate? You are not making sense."

Nigel's nostrils flared, a far cry from the relaxed man who had entered the room moments earlier. "Lady Ivy will marry Colin or a great many people will be privy to information only a select few know. I swear it."

Brian stared at his half-brother. Again, he wondered why he hadn't killed him before now, seeking the services of faceless assassins and having the man done in. And God only knew why he had spent his life avoiding his bastard blood. He thought, mayhap, if he ignored him, or humored him when so required, that Nigel would remain pacified. But much to his concern, it was increasingly apparent that Nigel would no longer play the game.

Nigel read the hesitation and, suddenly, he felt his advantage rise again. "I would wager to say that Alec doesn't know that I am his uncle, or that Toby is my son. And I would also wager to say that Thia had no knowledge of her blood relations. Certainly Colin doesn't know, for I have never found it necessary to tell him. I wonder how they would react to such knowledge?"

"After the initial shock, they would recover," Brian replied steadily, although the very idea Nigel was suggesting was by far his greatest fear.

In truth, he had no idea how his children would react. And Toby; the lad had never been told who his real father was. How would he respond to the knowledge that dastardly Nigel Warrington was his true father? And, God forbid, what if he should demand to know the circumstances of his birth? How could Brian bring himself to tell the lad he was the result of a rape?

Nigel shifted on the hard bench, rising slowly against his protesting joints. Not only were his joints achier than usual, but his feet were swelling with the gout, and his one desire after this meeting was to retire until the evening meal.

"I shall give you a choice, then," he said quietly. "You may choose your prospects. If you will not marry Colin to the Lady Ivy, then marry him to Thia. Surely your daughter has not found a suitor yet."

Brian stiffened; he'd kill both Colin and Nigel himself before he would allow Thia to fall into their clutches. "That is not a fair choice, Nigel. Thia is not ready to wed."

"She is seventeen years old and of marriageable age," Nigel returned. "Ivy or Thia. Make your choice."

Brian's face darkened as he mulled over his options. To marry his daughter to the Warrington heir was out of the question; therefore, if he failed to pledge Ivy, he had no doubt that the entire province would be aware of ugly family secrets and the Summerlin name would be cast in disgrace.

The House of Summerlin had suffered the blow of Alec's vow to lay down his arms, a scandal that rocked Edward's court to the very foundation simply because Alec had been the best knight in the realm at the tender age of twenty-one. Aye, Brian had withstood the dishonor of a son who was labeled a coward, and the Summerlin name still stood with its pride intact. But if Nigel's dark secrets were to become common knowledge, then there would be no recovery for the distinguished Summerlins.

His jaw ticked as he realized he had one choice, as cowardly as that choice was. Dear God, sometimes he felt so unworthy to be labeled a man. For a fierce knight who had fought with his king and who had braved the searing sands of the Holy Land to battle the insurrectors, he was showing a tremendous lack of bravery against a solitary man. The one man who could ruin him.

"All right," he whispered, his voice barely audible. "Allow me to explain my actions to Lady Ivy before you announce your victory to Colin."

Nigel smiled, a sinister gesture. "How wise, dear brother. How generous."

Brian couldn't bring himself to look at him, the man who would make him appear most feeble and untrustworthy to those he cared for. He couldn't imagine how Ali was going to react, or Alec for that matter. God, he hated himself.

Brian moved past Nigel, leaving the man smirking victoriously in his wake.

☙

ALEC AND COLIN were still standing in the solar, neither man having moved a muscle. Brian motioned sharply to his son.

"With me."

Alec obediently followed his father up to the second floor, to a seldom used room usually reserved for reading or lounging. Alec watched his father with concern, for the man was visibly upset as he paced and scratched agitatedly.

"There is no easy way to say this, Alec. I have changed my mind regarding Ali and Ivy's betrothal. The lady will wed Colin."

"What?" Alec's mouth opened in surprise. "But.... you cannot! You already gave Ali your word!"

"I made no such promise!" Brian shouted. "I simply sent him ahead for a lawyer, but I gave him no assurance that the marriage would indeed take place. After a most involved discussion with Nigel, I see that it is in Lady Ivy's best interests to marry Colin and you will not question my decision."

Alec's face was a mask of astonishment. "Then if I may not question your decision, I will certainly question your sanity. Why in the hell would you change your mind?"

Brian's chest was beginning to harbor the familiar ache that it did so often when he was upset or over-exerted. His hand moved to his sternum as if to massage away the pain. "I have my reasons, Alec," he said quietly, his tone laced with defeat. "You will retrieve Lady Ivy and bring her to my bower. I will leave you to inform your wife and make it clear that I will not tolerate any confrontations from her. She seems to want to pry into affairs that do not concern her."

Over his initial shock, Alec calmed dramatically and fixed his father with a heady glare. "I cannot promise that she will not come storming after you with a dirk in her hand and I furthermore would not blame her. If you expect me to control her, then you must give me a valid reason for your abrupt change of mind. And what about Ivy? Have you considered her feelings for one moment, dissolving her betrothal to Ali, then restoring it, now snatching it away once more? More than likely, she and her sister will both come after you with murder on their minds."

Brian's nostrils flared as the pain in his chest grew. "I cannot.... suffice it to say that I saw Nigel's reasoning in the matter and it makes sense. As I explained to you before, Colin is heir to Wisseyham and in need of a viable consort. Lady Ivy is such a person. Can you not see the advantages of her being chatelaine of Wisseyham instead of playing her sister's shadow at St. Cloven? It is a far more attractive offer for her to become mistress over her own manor."

Alec could only stare at his father, dumbfounded at his reasoning. "She doesn't care about any of that. Da, she is the first woman who has been able to tolerate the color of Ali's skin and.... Christ, what are you going to tell him? He shall go mad!"

"I am not going to tell him anything," Brian said quietly, his lips turning a faint shade of blue underneath his silver and black beard. "You and Olphampa are going to ride out and intercept him. If he is going to rage, let him do it in the open with only you and the wildlife to hear him. When he returns to Blackstone, it will be as a calm man resigned to do the bidding of his liege."

Alec shook his head with disgust, refusing to believe that his father had gone back on his word. His father had always been a man of firm decisions and reason, not at all like the man of confusion in front of him. Alec was not only angered, he was puzzled to the core and he worried on Ivy's reaction, not to mention Peyton's.

Foremost, however, he was grieved for Ali. The man had been treated like dirt for most of his life, but never from his own. It would seem that even Brian was apt to follow the lead of others who had left their footprints on Ali's pride.

Alec gazed at his father a moment, noting the pale color, the shaken state, and he knew exactly where the blame lay. Nigel Warrington must have done or said something terrible to cause Brian to refute a decision of this magnitude, but for the life of him, Alec could not reason what that action might have included. Alec refused to believe that Brian had changed his mind for the very reasons he listed.

The genesis of an idea suddenly sprang to Alec's mind, the beginnings of something pronounced and deep. Were Ali standing in Alec's position and the situation reversed, he knew exactly what Ali would have done without hesitation. And Alec knew without a doubt that he could not allow his friend to be devastated in such a cruel fashion. By a trusted friend, no less.

To hell with the consequences. Ali and Ivy were meant to be together, and Alec would do anything in his power to provide for that wish.

He eyed his father a moment as his plan took root and blossomed. Hopefully, his father would not read his mind as he had done so ably in the past. "Rest a moment, Da. Nigel has you worked up and you are already feeling ill. I shall take care of my wife and her sister until you can calm yourself." Or at least until I can get Ivy a safe distance away from Blackstone.

Brian sank into the nearest chair, his hand still on his chest. "Bring Lady Ivy to me and I shall inform her myself. But…. give me a few moments, if you please. This day has taxed me sorely."

Alec nodded, moving swiftly for the door as his father called to him once again. "I am sorry, Alec. I wish things were not as they appear to be."

It was a queer statement and Alec eyed his father with puzzlement. "And how is that?"

Brian did not look at him. "That I am a weakling, a confused old man. I am not, you know. What I do, I do to preserve the sanctity of the Summerlin line."

Alec's eyebrows furrowed and his hand left the door latch, instead, moving back into the room towards his father. "And what, may I ask, does this decision have to do with the Summerlins?"

Brian shook his head faintly and slouched against the chair. "More than you know, lad. You must trust me on this. Lady Ivy must marry Colin."

Alec's grand scheme to whisk Ivy away was suddenly in peril of being crushed. What in the world did his father mean? "What would happen if she did not?"

Brian closed his eyes, laboring for breath. "Catastrophic things, Alec. Please do not ask me anymore."

Alec was by his father's side, kneeling beside the bear of a man. His sky-blue eyes were questioning. "I must. Has Nigel threatened you? What has he done?"

Brian peeped an eye open and observed his proud, strong son. The sight of Alec's concerned face was almost the shove he needed to confess the sins of the past, but he stopped himself. He simply couldn't bring himself to admit to his son that the Summerlins were less than perfect. That he was less than perfect.

He closed his eye. "Nothing, lad. Get on with my request."

Suddenly, Alec was greatly indecisive. Would spiriting Ivy away jeopardize some secret treaty that his father was struggling to conclude, something Alec was unaware of? He had no idea what that could possibly be, but Brian seemed far more exhausted and serious than Alec had ever known him to be. And that deeply concerned him.

The longer he knelt next to his father, the more uncertain he became. Family came above all else, even Ali, and if Alec's rash action would hazard Brian, then Alec would not be a party to it. No matter how deeply he felt to the contrary.

"Da," he said softly. "Why won't you tell me what Warrington said to make you change your mind? Do you not trust me?"

"With my life, Alec, as you well know," Brian said quietly. "But, truthfully, I cannot tell you. You must trust me on this, lad. You simply must."

"But…."

"No," Brian held up his hand sharply, moving to grip Alec's trencher-sized hand tightly. "No questions. You must trust me."

Alec looked miserable and Brian felt the pain of his secret to his soul. Deeper, in fact. He felt as if an unseen hand was wrenching his guts violently. The look in Alec's eyes was the force behind the unseen hand, Brian realized, and he closed his eyes against him. He couldn't stand to see the beseeching look on Alec's face.

"Go," he rasped.

Alec rose unsteadily, wanting to press his father for the answers he sought. But Brian was weak, as his heart condition often rendered him, and Alec would not harass him. His only hope was that the wedding could be delayed until some sense was pounded into Brian's head.

It was his only hope and a weak one at that. As much as he wanted to take Ivy to Ali, he could not. His father had asked him to trust him, and trust him he would.

Alec opened the door to the small room in time to see Toby marching rapidly down the hall, heading straight toward him. Much to Alec's concern, Toby appeared agitated.

"What's wrong?" he demanded of the younger knight.

"Where's Lord Brian?" Toby countered.

"Resting," Alec passed a glance into the room. "What's happened?"

Toby took a deep breath. "Lady Rachel delivered a dead son a few minutes ago. Lady Celine is with her now, but your wife was present at the birth and she is…. well, she is hysterical, Alec. I returned her to her chamber."

"Christ," Alec muttered, passing another long glance at his father. Brian was looking at him, his pale face even more ashen. Alec waited for his father to bound out of the chair and demand to see the dead infant, as he had with the other two children Rachel had delivered, but instead his turned his head away and Alec swore he saw the great shoulders heave in sorrow.

Swallowing his own grief, Alec softly closed the door. "You mentioned that mother is with Rachel?"

Toby nodded. "Aye."

"Where is Paul?"

"Olphampa and Sula are comforting him."

"What of Thia?"

"With Lady Celine."

Alec nodded shortly, relieved that he was not given the duty of comforting his dim-witted brother. Paul could barely comprehend what was transpiring and there was no talking sense into him. Alec knew this for a fact; he had tried on two previous occasions to ease his brother's grief, but it was beyond Paul's capacity to accept consolation and move beyond his pain. Alec had quite enough pain of his own at the moment.

"Tell Pauly my father is in need of a soothing potion for his heart when the circumstances allow," he said quietly, already moving down the hall with Toby by his side. "Furthermore, I want you to personally see to the containment of the Warringtons; they need watching. As for me, I am going to see my wife."

The men split up at the top of the staircase. Alec continued down the corridor, mentally bracing himself for the confrontation that was to come with Ivy and wondering in a moment of weakness if he should not simply follow through with his original plan. After all, Ali and Ivy could be married and flee until such a time when it was safe to surface again. Mayhap by that time, the Warringtons would forget about the de Fluornoys and time would have healed over any enmity.

Alec was terribly torn; his loyalty to Ali, his loyalty to his father. He had already disobeyed his father's wishes once regarding the de

Fluornoys; were he to do it twice, he wondered if Brian would be so forgiving. Right or wrong, Brian was still his father and as his son, he was obligated to obey.

He was met by Jubil at the door. Her eyebrows rose at the sight of him. "Do you know what you mother did? She forced Peyton to witness the birth of a dead child!"

Alec eyed the woman and pushed his way into the room, his gaze falling on the sleeping form of his wife. Gently, he sat on the edge of the bed and put a soothing hand to Peyton's head, his face terribly tender.

"Jubil gave her a potion to soothe her nerves and it put her to sleep," Ivy said softly.

Alec tore his eyes away from his wife long enough to look at the blond sister, seated in a chair by the bed. Out of guilt, he could not maintain his gaze and turned back to his wife.

"Her eyes are red," he whispered.

"She was hysterical, Alec," Ivy said quietly. "What did you expect? She has never attended a birth before."

Alec stroked the red hair and Peyton sighed raggedly in her sleep. He would have liked to have sat by her all afternoon, caressing her beautiful head, but out of the corner of his eye he could see Ivy and he knew he must deliver the news of her future. The sooner the better, and considering Peyton was passed out like a drunkard, he would be better able to deal with Ivy alone. Kissing the red head tenderly, he rose from the bed and motioned to Ivy.

"I have a need to speak with you," he said softly.

Dutifully, Ivy rose and went to him, her pretty face expectant. Jubil took her place next to Peyton and began singing a faint, sweet lullaby, and Alec recognized it as the same melody his wife had sang to him the previous night in the monastery. The warmth of the memory filled him for a moment, a sweet flicker of time when he and Peyton had been closer emotionally than he had ever been to anyone. But Ivy was waiting and Alec gazed into her blue eyes, faltered on his words, and tried again.

"Ivy, something has occurred," he said softly. He had decided that being honest was the very best option he had, and he grasped her arm gently as he spoke. "My father has been speaking with Nigel Warrington and, needless to say, the man is quite angry over the broken betrothal. However, he and my father agreed on several valid points, one being that you would be an excellent chatelaine for Wisseyham Keep since Nigel is a widow and there are no female relatives to fill the position. Secondly, Colin is heir to a substantial fortune and you, as his wife, would be in a far greater social position than if you were the wife of a mere soldier."

Ivy's face darkened immediately and she jerked her arm free from his grasp. "I do not want to marry Colin. I want to marry Ali and I shall. You said…."

"I know what I said, but that was before my father had a chance to dwell on your future. He feels that he is providing you with the very best possible life by wedding you to Colin, a life of prominence and wealth, whereas with Ali, you would have none of this. He must do as he believes your father would have wanted and…."

"My father hated the Warringtons!" Ivy shrieked. "They pleaded for Peyton's hand several years ago and father refused them outright! He would have never wed me to Colin!"

Jubil overheard everything; it was difficult not to. Swiftly, she rose from her seat by Peyton and stood beside her youngest niece. "She cannot marry the Warrington heir, Alec. She already carries a black son and the child will not fair favorably in the House of Warrington."

Both Alec and Ivy looked at the old woman as if she were mad. Alec almost responded but caught himself, focusing on Ivy in an attempt to calm her before she flew out of control. "I realize what this appears, that my father is weak and easily swayed, and that his word cannot be trusted. But I assure you that this is not the case; my father is a wise, intelligent man and he must do for you as he decides best. You might not agree with him, but given time you will understand his actions."

Ivy was ashen. Her mouth hung open and she took another step back from him. "He has already promised me, hasn't he? He only pretended to relent and sent Ali away on a false errand so that he would be out of the way while the real marriage took place."

Alec shook his head. "Not at all. He was sincere when he sent Ali for the lawyer. However, he has had time to think and has come to the conclusion that 'twould be best that you to marry Colin and become chatelaine of Wisseyham."

"No!" Ivy roared. "I shall not marry him! I shall kill him first!"

Alec was calm, watching the woman work up a wild rage. He kept recollecting Peyton's words, how Colin raped young girls and left children to die, and how Nigel himself had raped Jubil even if they could not prove it. He also remembered the scene in the bailey when Colin had moved threateningly toward Peyton, and it was apparent that he was not a man of mercy or conscience. Even if Ivy could hold her own against him in a fight, he seriously doubted she could survive to a ripe old age in the House of Warrington. Being an aggressive woman was one strike against her, but being a de Fluornoy was a death sentence.

All of Alec's indecision left him. He knew, as he lived and breathed, that he could not be a party to the misery of his wife's sister. Nor could he betray his friend. There was far more to this than he could comprehend and his head was spinning already from the enormity of events, but he could understand one thing quite clearly; Ivy could not marry Colin.

Family loyalty! He turned away from Ivy, clenching his fists as his eyes fell on Peyton. Christ, she was his family now, was she not? She and St. Cloven were his, no matter what his father said or did, even if saving Ivy from the slimy grip of Colin Warrington cast an irreversible shadow on his relationship with Brian.

He loved his father, as much as a son could love a father, but he could not allow such a horrible transgression to take place with his full knowledge. How would he ever explain Ivy's betrothal to Peyton when he himself did not fully understand? His father had asked him to trust him; he did trust him. Undeniably. But in this matter, he trusted his instincts more. He had to remove Ivy before the Warringtons could get their claws into her.

He reached out and grasped Ivy, forcing her to look at him. "Do you trust me?"

Ivy was fully prepared to punch him in the nose and curse him, but the look in his eyes was so intense that she stopped in mid-rage. There was something in his gaze.... "Aye, I do."

His jaw ticked as he released her. "Then pack a small satchel. I shall return shortly and do not let anyone through that door but myself or Toby. Do you understand? Not even my father."

Ivy nodded unsteadily and he moved to the door with determination, his gaze resting on his wife once more as he realized that he was about to commit an offense against his father not merely for the loyalty of a friend, but for the happiness of a newly acquired relative.

He was doing it for his wife. God help him, he was willing to risk everything for her.

The door slammed and the room shook to the rafters. Ivy bolted the oak panel as if to lock out the Devil himself.

CHAPTER TWELVE

PEYTON SLEPT THROUGH Ivy's departure, through Brian's raging, through Nigel's furious protests. Celine, exhausted with the death of her grandson, had taken to her bed ill and was unable to deal with the angry men wreaking havoc in her solar. Only Thia was left to weather the storm by her father's side, gravely concerned for his color and wondering when their peaceful life at Blackstone careened so terribly out of control. However, it was not difficult to isolate the catalyst.

Lady Peyton Summerlin slept soundly as a violent confrontation shook the very walls of Blackstone. Nigel against Brian, curses and shouted words, pleas for understanding and patience; she was completely unaware that she had been the window through which the Devil had entered to do his work. She dreamt once, of Alec, but when she tried to touch him he had vanished. After that, her slumber had been dreamless. Thankfully, no nightmares of dead babies plagued her.

She was further oblivious to Thia Summerlin's dark thoughts of her, the hatred building within the soul of the woman. Thia had been indifferent to Peyton after their confrontation, and she surprisingly thought she might grow to tolerate the woman who stood against her so admirably in a verbal conflict. But listening to her father's exhausted, angry voice and watching Nigel Warrington spew threats, she knew at that moment that she could never tolerate such a disruptive force within the walls of Blackstone.

Everything had been so right before she came. She was beautiful, though not Thia's usual taste. Her taste ran to young serving girls and nubile villeins she could convince to join her in same-sex frolics. No one knew of her strange lusts, the carnal improprieties that she indulged in. Her parents simply thought she hated men because she was afraid of them, and she would allow them to believe what they would. Marrying a member of the opposite sex did, indeed, frighten her. She wanted no part of it.

What she wanted most at this moment, however, was to be rid of her brother's wife. She could deduce from the conversation that Lady Peyton had been the primary objective, and that Lady Ivy had come in second. Thia watched impassively as Nigel spitefully broke a rare Grecian artifact her father had collected in Athens; if there was some way to deliver the Warringtons what they so apparently desired, two problems would be solved quite nicely. Blackstone would return to normal and the Warringtons would have the bitch. All would be well again.

If there was only a way.

ଓ

PEYTON AWOKE TO Alec's pale face. The room was dark but for a small fire in the hearth to ward off the cool dampness and she immediately sat up, rubbing her eyes. He smiled weakly at her.

"It's nearly time for supper, love," he said softly.

She gazed at him sleepily, Jubil's potion still working. Absently, she touched Alec's cheek and looked about the room. "Good Lord, how long have I been asleep?"

He covered her hand as it touched his face with his warm palm. "Several hours. How do you feel?"

"Tired," she yawned. "I feel as if I could sleep for days."

"Eat first. We will retire early tonight, I promise."

She nodded and yawned again, noticing for the first time how drawn and tired Alec appeared. He helped her from the bed silently, none of the usual warmth in his expression. In fact, he seemed unusually withdrawn.

"What's wrong, darling? You are quiet."

He glanced at her, preparing to evade her question but thinking better of it. She would find out soon enough and it was unfair not to prepare her for what was to come. He motioned her to sit at the vanity, and as she picked up her horsehair brush he spoke.

"My father reconsidered his position on the marriage of Ali and Ivy. 'Twould seem that Nigel Warrington was able to convince him that a marriage between Ivy and Colin would be most beneficial for Ivy's sake, and my father agreed."

The horsehair brush clattered to the ground in mid-stroke and Peyton bolted from the bench. "No, Alec! She cannot!"

He put his hand on her arms soothingly. "I know, love, I know," he said patiently. "This is why I spirited your sister out of Blackstone and delivered her to Ali not two hours ago. They should already be married by now."

In his grasp, Peyton relaxed so violently that she nearly collapsed and Alec crushed her against his hard chest. "Oh, Alec," she breathed. "Why has this happened? Why did your father change his mind again?"

"I do not know," he admitted honestly, caressing her. "But I knew that I could not allow the marriage to take place. Needless to say, my father is livid."

She looked at him, her eyes soft. "Did you tell him what you did?"

"He guessed; the man is no fool, especially after our elopement. Furthermore, the Warringtons are outraged and the mood in general is strained."

Peyton gazed at him a moment, moving to stroke his stubbled cheek. "You did this for me."

He met her gaze, blue on blue. "And for Ali and Ivy. How presumptuous of you to imagine that I would risk my hide for you alone."

She grinned and kissed his cheek sweetly. "Thank you, my Alec.

From the bottom of my heart."

He kissed her palm and released her, moving for the pewter ale pitcher near the window sill. She continued to watch his movements, those of a man with a good deal on his mind, and she was grateful that he would risk himself for the sake of her and her sister. She was only just becoming to realize the depths of the man she had married and furthermore realizing just how fortunate she was. A man she had sworn to hate, once. A man she could never hate.

"Where are Ali and Ivy now?" she asked softly.

"Truthfully, I do not know. I told them to stay out of sight for several weeks and then contact me at St. Cloven. If I know Ali, he shall most likely sail to France and wait there."

"Why?"

"To get Ivy out of England," he turned to her, cup in hand. "Since their marriage will only be considered common law, it is imperative that he remove her from the country until the situation stabilizes. Technically, the Warringtons can claim Ivy as stolen property and Ali could be thrown in the vault as a thief."

Peyton gasped, her eyes wide. "They would not!"

He smiled wryly. "From the noise going on in the great hall, I would not be surprised if the Warringtons declared war on all of us. They're righteously outraged, as is my father, and all of the anger is directed at me."

Peyton digested his words, turning away and feeling a good amount of guilt. She knew Alec had acted on her behalf no matter what he said. Aye, she was equally to share in the blame and she knew it. The most logical solution would be to return to St. Cloven immediately and remain until the climate cooled.

"Then we should leave for home right away," she said softly. "The sooner you are removed, the sooner tempers can ease."

He nodded. "You are right, of course. But I hesitate abandoning my family after what I have caused and after the death of the babe...." he suddenly looked at his wife, troubled by his tactless slip. He saw her brow furrow with sadness and gently sought to ease her. "I am sorry you had to be witness to a most distressing event, sweetheart. If there is anything I can do…."

"My mother bore three dead children after Ivy and I were born, all male," she said, swallowing the tightness in her throat. "'Tis not a strange occurrence."

She was trying to be brave and he respected her determination, unwilling to weaken it by extending more apologies. He felt bad enough for his dead nephew, but such was the way of things sometimes. He drained his cup and set it down with a resounding clang.

"Did my mother say anything about our marriage?"

She shook her head, swallowing her sorrow. "Not a word. In fact, she was exceedingly sweet to me. She even kissed me."

He smiled faintly, knowing that his mother supported their marriage even if her husband at this moment was most likely wishing he had never heard of Lady Peyton de Fluornoy. Pleased with her show of acceptance towards his new wife, a bright spot in an otherwise hellish afternoon, he sighed and put his hands on his hips. "If we are leaving for home tonight, we must pack. I shall see about locating Jubil and return her to help you load your bags."

"Where is she?" Peyton asked.

"With Toby, somewhere," Alec snorted softly. "He seems fascinated by her, convinced she's a great sorceress."

Peyton rolled her eyes to let him know just what she thought of her aunt's powers. "Do not let him believe that. She is a mere woman, knowledgeable in herbs and potions, but it does not go beyond that."

"She believes she is a witch," Alec said with a faint grin.

Peyton shook her head, removing a satchel from the wardrobe. "Did she tell you that? Did she also tell you that she is Athena, Goddess of Wisdom? Or her more recent claim is that she is the deity Cybele, the asexual dominate."

His eyebrows rose as he watched her pack, feeling himself calming with the ale in his veins. "Christ, where did she hear about Cybele?"

"Jubil is an intelligent woman, well-read thanks to my father's library. Sometimes, during her trances, she claims she is Cybele and that she is in need of claiming a lover," Peyton shook her head with disgust. "What we have yet to figure out is if she means a male or female lover. In myth, Cybele possessed both female and male genitalia."

"Until she cut off her male organ and became female," Alec finished, remembering his ancient Greek mythology. "And, as I recall, she gained a male lover, became insanely jealous and in turn drove her lover mad. He then castrated himself and died."

Peyton nodded, packing her satchel. "She worries me sometimes, Alec. It seems as if the older she grows, the more unbalanced she becomes."

"She would never hurt you, would she?" Alec asked, wondering if he should seek to repress the aging aunt at some point in time.

"Nay, she would not. But she might inadvertently hurt herself and that frightens me."

Alec pondered her statement a moment before draining his cup and pouring himself more ale. Peyton finished packing one satchel and began stuffing another.

"She said something strange once," Peyton said softly, thinking aloud. "She referred to your sister as the woman with a taste for female flesh. Do you know what she could have meant?"

Alec gazed at her emotionlessly. "Did you ask her?"

"I have not yet had the chance," Peyton turned to the wardrobe and forgot all about her question to Alec. "I am going to string Ivy up by her ankles! She took my bronze satin gown when she knows very well it doesn't fit her. And.... Good Lord, she took the shoes too. They'll be ruined by her fat feet!"

Alec watched his wife rant and curse her sister, deeply relieved that she had forgotten her inquiry about Thia. He wasn't so sure she would like his answer and, for that matter, he would not have liked his answer, either. His younger sister thought she had everyone in the dark about her appetites, but Alec had heard the rumors and once, he'd even seen a smidgen of truth. It was something, however, he did not like to think on.

Peyton packed three large satchels, completely clearing out the wardrobe. Jubil had a small satchel that she hadn't even bothered to unpack in the first place and it sat in a cluttered mess against the wall. Securing it, Peyton put the four bags on the bed and turned to her husband, who was on his fourth cup of ale.

"Aren't you going to pack, darling?" she asked.

He was studying her. In fact, he hadn't taken his eyes off her since he had entered the room and the alcohol in his veins flushed his cheeks and gave him a half-lidded appearance.

"Nay," he answered softly. "I am not going to pack anything. I shall ride to St. Cloven with my wife and the clothes on my back and nothing more."

Puzzled at his response, she lowered her gaze as if to check her baggage again and make sure all was present. She heard Alec set his chalice to the table and his heavy boot falls came near. She wasn't surprised when thick, warm arms embraced her tightly and she could smell the ale on his breath.

"Alec," she gasped as his mouth devoured her neck. "Do not we have to leave? You said…."

"I am fully aware of what I said," he whispered against her. He continued to suckle on her neck as she waited for him to go on with his reply, her passion rapidly flowering. Another few moments and she would not care if he answered her or not.

Just as his mouth reached her lips and she opened her mouth to him, he stopped and gazed at her with seduction-hazed eyes.

"You and St. Cloven are all I have. After this night, I fully expect to be disowned," his expression suddenly went vulnerable and she was shocked by the fragility she read in his eyes. "Do not ever leave me, Peyton. I couldn't stand it."

She touched his face tenderly. "I shall never leave you, my Alec. I promise. St. Cloven and I are all you will ever need."

He was as emotional as she had ever seen him and she eagerly fused her mouth to his, reassuring him that come what may, she would stand by him. He had already sacrificed so very much for her and she would not disappoint him. She couldn't have left him if she wanted to. She loved him.

.... good-bye, James.

ও

ALEC HAD BEEN gone for some time as Peyton paced the floor of her bedchamber impatiently. Jubil, seated by the lancet windows, watched her niece closely.

"Do not fret, sweetheart," Jubil said quietly. "Alec has merely gone to retrieve the horses, not turned tail for the border."

"I know that," Peyton snapped. "But he has been gone a long time. Mayhap I should go look for him. He might have gotten into trouble."

Jubil did not answer; clear-minded today, she wasn't sure how to reply. All she knew was that Alec Summerlin had surpassed even her expectations as a husband. Surely no man had made a greater sacrifice for his wife and her family. She furthermore suspected that Peyton realized her good fortune and was already deeply attached to her new husband, whether or not she realized it.

But Peyton was indeed aware, hence her uneasy manner. Her patience evaporated, she halted her pacing and stared at the chamber door as if imagining herself walking forth in search of her errant husband. Not content merely to envision, she moved to the door quickly.

"I shall find him," she told her aunt. "Wait here, Jubil. For Heaven's sake, do not leave."

Jubil nodded faintly. "Take care, sweetheart. The halls of Blackstone abound with threats."

Peyton slanted her aunt a puzzled gaze; however, the expression was not without some apprehension. She knew her aunt to be free of her stimulants and she pondered the warning. Lacking the time or interest to ask her what she meant, she stole from the room and shut the door softly.

The halls were dim with impending dusk. The torches in their iron sconces were burning brightly with new flame, illuminating the hall as Peyton traversed the stone with soft footfalls. She could hear voices, servants down the corridor, but she ignored them as she made her way to the stairs.

As she mounted the top step, she could hear strains of voices from down below; male voices that caught her attention. She thought she heard Brian, mayhap Nigel, but she could not be sure. The only thing she was sure of was that she did not hear Alec's voice. Silently, she descended the stairs.

The first floor was bustling with servants in preparation for the evening meal. Peyton moved down a narrow corridor, away from the grand hall and Lord Brian's solar, in hopes of locating an exit without having to pass by the two larger rooms. Her intention was to find a servant's entrance and slip to the stables in search of her husband.

The corridor branched off and she took the path to the left, entering a dimly lit passageway. She thought she caught sight of a large door at the far end of the hall and she set her sights on it, knowing from its placement that it must lead to the bailey. The passage was void of activity and the further she traveled, the more hushed it became. It was an eerie silence, cloying and empty, and Peyton heard her footfalls loudly as she moved toward the large oaken panel.

In her quest, she slipped past a door that was not quite closed; an inch of space separated it from the doorjamb. Just as Peyton moved by, she heard the unmistakable sounds of a woman moaning. Shocked, she paused and listened intently, hearing another rattling moan. A deep, throaty echo that made her hair stand on end.

Suddenly deterred from the door she had been seeking, genuine concern welled within her and she took a step toward the cracked door, placing her hand on the panel as she listened. Just as she touched the aged oak, she heard another groan, low and mournful, and she instantly decided that something must be terribly wrong. Someone was in a great deal of pain. Forcefully, she shoved the door open with the full intention of helping.

But what she beheld shocked her beyond belief. A serving wench lay upon her back, her skirts hiked up around her waist as another female of rotund proportions went to work between her legs. It took Peyton a mere half-second to recognize Thia, her face pressed in to the wench's private parts, moaning with great pleasure as she stroked her long and hard with her tongue. Peyton could scarcely believe what she was witnessing; her throat tightened with bile or a scream, she could not be sure. But the one fact she knew for certain was that she had to leave as quickly as she had come.

Thia's head came up when she heard the wench gasp. Peyton stumbled back and tripped over her own feet, nearly landing on her bottom as her astonishment nearly incapacitated her. But as she struggled to maintain her balance, Thia was through the door and bearing down on her with the most horrifying gleam to her eye.

Thia was fast, but Peyton was faster. She rolled away from Alec's sister, scrambling to her feet. Thia snatched at her, snagging her gown and slowing her momentum, but Peyton yanked herself free and dug her heels into the floor with the full intention of out-running her pursuer. Unquestionably, Thia meant to do her serious harm and Peyton's chest swelled with panic; she had to make it to the safety of the grand hall.

As Peyton bordered on panic, Thia bordered on madness. Her brother's wife had discovered her secret and must be made to pay. She did not stop to wonder how she would explain Peyton's death to Alec; mayhap she would deny knowledge altogether. Whatever rationalization she formulated would come later; for now, she had an immediate need to silence the one person who could do her harm. Peyton was unable to get far before Thia threw herself forward and tripped, grabbing Peyton around the ankle. Peyton fell hard, smacking her head on the stone. Dazed but not senseless, she began struggling violently with Thia, kicking and punching as the woman attempted to enclose her in an iron grip.

Thia struck out and punched Peyton in the stomach, enough to knock the wind from her, but Peyton did not give in to the pain. Instead, she lashed out and raked her fingernails across Thia's plump face and drew blood.

"You bitch!" Thia's hand went to her bloodied cheek, to the wounds which would undoubtedly leave scars. Peyton, terrified, slipped out from underneath her and attempted to regain her footing.

But Thia was hell-bent on disabling her victim. She balled her fist and smashed Peyton on the back of the head, but her victim did not waver. Instead, Peyton tried to scratch her again, unsuccessfully, as she wobbled to stand. Thia thrust her big hands out to stop her but Peyton knocked them away, breaking free.

On her feet again, Peyton resumed her run down the hall with much less speed and a good deal more staggering. Thia, exhausted and bleeding, charged after her.

Toby suddenly appeared at the end of the hall, his blue eyes gazing at the struggling women with astonishment. Peyton saw him in front of her and dashed toward him, reaching him a split-second before Thia crashed into her from behind and grabbed a handful of luscious red hair. Screams and grunts filled the corridor.

Toby could scarcely believe what he was witnessing. He thrust his wide frame in between the two women, attempting desperately to unwind Thia's grip from Peyton's hair. All the while, Thia continued to slug at Peyton's head, sometimes making contact, and Toby was beside himself.

"Thia!" he bellowed. "Stop it! You will kill her!"

Thia wasn't listening to her half-brother. She continued to strike and strike until Peyton turned on her, lashing out with her foot and kicking her in the tender shin. Thia winced and loosened her grip, and Peyton drove her fist squarely into her pug nose.

Thia's grip relaxed and she fell backward, out of Toby's grasp. Peyton suddenly found herself free of the vise-like grasp and stumbled away, tripping, and landing on her knees. Toby moved to subdue Thia before she could attack Peyton again.

But Thia would not be controlled so easily. She swung her big fists at Toby, catching him in the mouth. He grunted, but easily reined in the wild woman. Peyton, meanwhile, was so shaken she couldn't seem to stand. She remained on her knees, trembling and dazed, as Thia resisted Toby's restraint.

Heavy boot falls sounded down the corridor, the sounds of men approaching from the direction of the grand hall. Peyton did not even look up; she was close to retching, trying desperately to gain a handle on her reeling senses. The first voice she heard was Brian's.

"God's Blood! What is going on?" Brian boomed, his big hands on Peyton's shoulders.

Peyton couldn't answer him; she began to cry and Brian looked to his frenzy-eyed daughter with shock. "Thia! What's happened?"

Thia seemed to be losing some of her madness as she realized her father was speaking to her. She ceased to grapple against Toby's iron grip and focused her small blue eyes on Brian.

"I....I..," she swallowed hard, struggling for a convincing reply. "She was spying on me!"

Peyton raised her head in a great frenzy of wild red hair. "I did no such thing! How dare you accuse me of subversion!"

Brian looked to Toby, who met his liege's gaze unwaveringly. "When I came upon them, Lady Thia was in pursuit of Lady Peyton. She has dealt her a serious beating."

Brian looked to Peyton and attempted to help her to stand, but Peyton was far too shaken to rise to her feet. Instead, she sat heavily on her bottom.

"Peyton, are you all right?" Brian asked seriously, baffled with the entire situation.

Peyton opened her mouth to speak, but sobs suddenly bubbled forth and she buried her face in her hands. "I want Alec!"

Brian removed his hands from his hysterical daughter-in-law and straightened, his hard gaze on Thia. "I would know what happened immediately," he slanted a gaze at his startled steward. "Find Alec. Now."

The man dashed off and Brian returned his focus to his daughter. "Answer me, Thia."

Thia was calming rapidly as she realized the gravity of the situation. It was obvious her father was not going to side with her, instead, choosing to side with the bitch. She flushed mightily.

"I told you, father. She was spying on me and tried to harm me."

Brian did not believe her for a moment, but he dutifully turned the question to Peyton. "My lady?"

Peyton removed her hands from her face, her gaze hot and angry on Thia. "I wasn't spying. I was looking for Alec and came across Thia…. in a room."

Brian's eyebrows drew together. "And? And what?"

Peyton focused on Thia's threatening stare, her terror being replaced by sheer anger and disgust. How could she tell Brian what she saw? She could barely think on it without becoming ill much less repeat the distasteful facts. As she struggled to find an answer, approaching boot falls distracted her attention.

Nigel and Colin stood in the hall, several feet behind Brian. Brian passed the men a glance, startled that they had not kept to the comfort of the grand hall, instead, choosing to pursue the sounds of struggle that had lured Brian from their company. The two were an unwelcome distraction and Brian impatiently focused on them.

"I apologize for the interruption," he said, although he did not mean it. Tensions were so high that Peyton and Thia's fight had actually provided him with a break. "'Tis nothing but a ladies' squabble. Retreat to the grand hall and I shall join you momentarily."

His request went ignored. Colin strolled forward and eyed the two women, the rake across Thia's cheek and Peyton's flushed face. "It appears to be more than a simply tussle, my lord." Much to Brian's dismay, his attention focused on Thia. "What's the matter, my lady?

Did she spurn your advances?"

Nigel snickered and Thia tensed in Toby's grasp, her face flushing a deep, startled red. Before Brian could lodge a strenuous protest, Peyton struggled to her knees. "Certainly you only have your own rejection experiences to relate to," she said breathlessly. "What occurs between the members of the House of Summerlin is none of your affair, Warrington."

Colin's face went taut with rage and he twitched in Peyton's direction, but his father stepped forward. "Nay, lad. She is Alec's wife."

Colin struggled with himself a moment, well remembering the beating Alec had dealt him earlier. Angry or no, he had no desire to provoke him again. Instead, he clenched his fists behind his back and glared at Peyton. Peyton met his gaze unwaveringly, although her head was swimming and her knees were weak. Somehow, her hatred for him was strength in and of itself.

"Where has your sister gone, Lady Summerlin?"

From one focus to another, the subject had shifted from Peyton and Thia's fight to Ivy's whereabouts. Peyton rose to unsteady feet, assisted by Brian. Her eyes were blades of sapphire, deadly and sharp.

"Out of your clutches, you vile bastard. Return to Wisseyham and rot."

Brian closed his eyes beseechingly a moment, wondering how such a beautiful woman could possess a razor-edged tongue. Although he would have liked to have said the very same thing, protocol and restraint prevented him from doing so. His grip tightened on Peyton, preparing to protect her from Colin's wrath.

But he never got the chance. Much to his shock and Peyton's as well, Thia tore herself free from Toby and thrust her meaty fist in Colin's face.

"You heard her, you misbegotten whoreskin," she seethed. "Return home. You are not welcome here."

Colin did not flinch as Thia planted herself in front of him, her chubby face threatening. Instead, he smiled humorlessly, a gesture which completely terrified Peyton. "I cannot without my intended. When I return, you will go with me."

Thia did not react immediately. Then, it was as if Colin had slapped all of the bravery from her body; she staggered back, her eyes seeking her father in disbelief.

Brian, however, was fully focused on Nigel. "That was never agreed upon, Nigel. I never intimated that I would consider it."

Nigel took his son's cue and stepped forward, a smug expression on his face. "You were given a choice, were you not? Ivy or Thia. Since Ivy is, shall we say, all but lost, you have apparently made your choice. Thia shall wed Colin."

"She will not!" Peyton was feeling stronger. It was odd that she should find herself defending a woman who had so recently tried to kill her; however, the common enemy seemed to join them as peculiar allies. No one, not even Thia, deserved such a fate.

Colin turned to her harshly. "This is none of your affair, Lady Summerlin. You told me to stay out of Summerlin concerns and I will demand you refrain from interfering in Warrington matters," he passed another distasteful glance at Thia before turning on his heel. "Have the contracts drawn up, Father. I wish to be done with this by the morrow."

Nigel watched his son march down the corridor before turning his attention to Brian. He shrugged callously. "You made your choice, Brian." With a lingering glance at Thia, he turned after his son.

For an endless, hanging moment, no one spoke. Peyton stared at the empty corridor, too shocked and dazed to respond. As she gazed into the dimly lit hall, a body suddenly appeared, walking towards her and Peyton knew even at a distance that it was Alec. He was the only man as tall as a god and as wide as a bear, his gait nothing short of a graceful swagger. Brian's steward scampered after him as they came into the light.

Alec did not look at anyone but Peyton. He reached out and snatched her from his father's grip, pulling her into a protective embrace. Peyton, still dazed and shocked, collapsed against him. Only when his wife was cradled in his arms did Alec dare to gaze at his father.

His voice was a growl. "I was told that there was some trouble. I would calmly ask what kind of trouble there was."

Thia couldn't answer; in spite of the obvious wound on her face, she turned away from her brother as if to ignore his question. Brian gazed at his son with a mixture of grief and concern. "A small tussle, Alec," he said quietly. "Nothing of concern."

Alec would not accept his simple explanation. Instead, he looked to Toby. "What happened? And no lies, or my wrath shall be swift."

Toby wasn't afraid of his older brother; at least, not truly afraid. But he did harbor a healthy respect for his strength and fighting abilities. Feeling trapped, he avoided Brian's piercing gaze and cleared his throat.

"A tussle, Alec," he said quietly. "I intervened before anyone was seriously injured."

Irritation growing at their evasive replies, Alec pulled Peyton's face from the safe haven of his chest and gazed deeply into her eyes. To his surprise, she smiled wanly and did not afford him the opportunity to put the same query to her. "I saw…. that is, I….I was spying on Thia," she whispered raspily. "She had every right to become angry with me."

Thia looked to Peyton in pure astonishment. Peyton met her gaze from the vise of Alec's hands, hoping that somehow the woman's bloodlust would fade when she realized Peyton was unwilling to publicly condemn her. Aye, she could have confessed, but she simply could not bring herself to repeat the disgusting facts. Mayhap if Thia saw that she was disinclined to reveal her secret, the tensions between them would ease. After all, Alec loved his sister a great deal. Peyton did not want to divide them, no matter what the circumstances.

Furthermore, Thia was in a good deal of trouble already with the Warrington betrothal. Before Alec could respond to her admission, she changed the subject. "Colin is demanding to wed your sister in Ivy's stead. You must not allow this."

As she hoped, Alec's attention was immediately diverted and his sky-blue eyes sought out his father with shock. "Is this true?"

Brian's lips possessed the familiar bluish twinge as he looked away from his son's intense gaze. He sighed heavily. "Thia should have been pledged long ago."

Alec dropped his hands from Peyton's face. "Have you gone completely mad? Pledging my sister to that bastard?"

Brian met his son's gaze, feeling distinctly weary. He had been an example of a weak-willed man within the past several days, giving his word only to refute it, making decisions only to change his mind. And Alec had witnessed all of his failings. Their clash not an hour before had been testimony to the fact that Alec no longer respected his father, and Brian was beyond devastated.

Gazing into Alec's eyes, he could read the contempt radiating from his son. But he was cornered; Nigel had made his demands known and he must comply, even if it meant betrothing his only daughter. He had no choice if the Summerlin name was to remain unblemished, no matter what Alec thought of him. Someday, mayhap, he would understand Brian's sacrifice.

"You have given me little choice in the matter," he said softly. "You married Lady Peyton and Ali has presumably married her sister. The Warringtons are demanding compensation."

"Thia is not compensation for my actions," Alec said hotly. "I shall not allow this."

Brian looked to his son, his expression considerably less tolerant. "You are not her father. I am, and I believe a match between Colin and Thia will be a suitable one. 'Twill bind the House of Summerlin to the House of Warrington, establishing close ties."

Alec listened to his father reason as if he were trying to convince himself that the union would be a beneficial one. But they both knew the words to be empty and desperate.

"I do not want to be married," Thia suddenly whispered, her face ashen. When her father reached out to touch her, she backed away violently. "I won't marry him. I…. I do not want him!"

"Thia, calm yourself," Brian said softly, eyeing her wound. "Let's have Pauly tend your cheek."

Thia staggered away from her father, batting his comforting arms away from her. "I do not want him!"

Alec left his wife to go to his distraught sister, pulling her into a crushing embrace. Peyton watched as Alec stroked his sister tenderly.

"Be calm, Moppet," he said gently. "I shall take care of you."

"I won't have him!" Thia renounced in a shaking voice. "I refuse to be made a peace offering!"

"Relax, love," Alec repeated soothingly.

"Thia, you will do as you are told," Brian said weakly, gazing at his grieving children. "We will all do as we are told."

Alec's eyes were blue flame. "Why did not you tell me the Warrington's had demanded Thia's hand for my actions?"

Brian met his son's gaze. "The choice was given to me before you whisked Lady Ivy away. I opted for the obvious selection, your wife's younger sister, since I felt Thia unprepared for a husband. You should have trusted me, Alec. I told you not to question my decision."

Alec's face glazed with disbelief. "And this is why? Because the Warrington's gave you a choice between Ivy and Thia, and you chose Ivy? Christ, Da, why did not you tell me from the onset?"

"Because it wasn't your choice to make."

Thia understood everything instantly; in spite of her peculiar nature, she was an intelligent woman. Her small blue eyes flew accusingly to her older brother. "You did this to me!"

Alec focused on his sister. "Unknowingly, Moppet. Believe me, had I but known the circumstances, I would never have acted so rashly."

Thia yanked away from him. "How could you, Alec! You are supposed to love me!"

"I *do* love you, Moppet," Alec reached out for his plump sister once again, but she moved away from him. "Please, Thia. Do not be angry with me."

Thia began to sob miserably. "I hate you, Alec. How could you?"

Alec caught his sister and brought her to him and she did not resist. "Do not cry, Thia. All will be well."

Peyton suddenly felt decidedly less benevolent towards her sister-in-law. A woman who had recently tried to kill her, whom she had lied for and protected, was cradled in her brother's arms as if she were a complete innocent. As far as Peyton was concerned, Alec should be comforting his wife who had suffered a complete whacking at the hands of the woman Alec was seeking to console. Warrington betrothal or not, the taste of jealousy was bitter on Peyton's tongue as she watched the tender scene. *I do love you, Moppet.*

Words she had never heard from him. Words she would probably never hear where they pertained to her. She realized how badly she wanted to hear them.

Incensed and bitter, Peyton turned away from the compassionate sight and moved down the corridor. She simply couldn't watch any longer, knowing that Alec loved his sister enough to tell her. Alec called after her, but she ignored him. She heard his heavy boot falls not a few seconds later, closing rapidly, and wasn't surprised when a massive hand snatched her arm.

"What's wrong? Where are you going?"

She jerked her arm from his grasp. "To my chamber to rest from nearly being beaten to death."

He eyed her in the dim torchlight. "What happened between you and my sister?"

Peyton was feeling stubborn and rejected. When Alec should have been seeing to her needs, he was intent on consoling his fat, disgusting sister and declaring his love for her. More unreasonable envy filled her.

"We fought," she said simply, still unwilling to divulge all of the distasteful details. "She was preparing to kill me, I think, but I doubt you would believe me. Go back to Thia and comfort her, Alec. I shall retire alone."

She turned again but he stopped her with a crushing grip on her arm. She winced, gasping when his other hand clamped down on her free arm and she was trapped before him. Sky-blue eyes glittered at her. "What's wrong with you?"

"Not a thing," she said evenly. "Let us say that I am glad my sister is out of Blackstone, lest you force her to wed Colin in Thia's place. I realize how precious your baby sister is to you. How much you love her. Now, let me go. You are hurting me."

His grip relaxed but he did not release her. Instead, his expression seemed to soften and he did not say anything for a moment. Peyton could almost read the fluctuation of ideas in his sky-blue orbs. "What did you see, Peyton?"

Her sapphire eyes widened with surprise. Her bitterness forgotten for the moment, she tried to pull free from his grip. "I…."

"Answer me."

She blinked, swallowing hard against his piercing gaze. "Why…. why do you ask what I saw?"

"Because you were about to tell me what caused the altercation before you changed your story. I know you well enough to know that you were not spying. Tell me what you saw that made my sister attack you."

There was no point in refusing to answer. Alec was the only person, aside from Ivy, that she felt she could confess to. Her only fear was the possibility that he would not believe her; after all, what she was about to say was shocking beyond reason. She would not have believed it if she hadn't seen it with her own eyes.

She relaxed in his grip somewhat, reluctant to meet his gaze. "Will you believe me if I tell you?"

"Without question."

Her resistance fled and she could feel the repulsion of her admission. "I went to look for you because you had been gone so long. I thought I could find a servant's entrance in the west wing so that I would not have to walk past the Warringtons or your father in the grand hall. I was moving down the corridor when I heard moaning. I swear to you, Alec, I thought someone was in pain. But when I opened the door, I saw…." she swallowed hard, ashamed and revolted.

"What did you see, love?" he encouraged gently.

She winced as if the memory brought a tangible pain. "I saw your sister with her face between a woman's legs," she whispered. "The moans were coming from Thia as she pleasured the serving wench."

Alec had known what her answer would be all along, but he still felt a bolt of nausea course through him. He knew he went pale as he pulled Peyton against his broad chest comfortingly, caressing her back. All of Peyton's opposition was vanished and she pressed against him, seeking his strength and comfort as if to block out the horrible vision.

"So she attacked you for discovering her secret," he whispered, voicing his thoughts aloud.

She nodded against his chest. "I am sorry, Alec. I would never lie about something like this. I was shocked and…."

"I know," he kissed the top of her head; slanting a gaze down the corridor, he could see the figures of his sister and father as Brian tried to calm the large young woman. "Did she hurt you? Thia is considerably more of an opponent than Ivy."

She managed a smile at the attempted humor, looking up to his beautiful face. "Not really. Ivy's stronger."

They grinned at each other a moment as Alec touched her hair, caressing her cheeks with his thumbs. It suddenly occurred to Peyton that he did not seem particularly upset by her revelation and her smile faded. "Are you not shocked by this? You do not seem overly concerned."

His smile faded, too, as his eyes roved her exquisite features. "I have lived at Blackstone most of my life. Sooner or later, the rumors will reach you."

"Then you knew?"

"I suspected."

She did not say anything for a moment, sympathizing with Alec's shameful secret. As the days progressed, it would seem that every passing moment brought new revelations of the Summerlin family, dark secrets and shameful stories that Alec hid behind an icy facade and an emotionless manner. She fleetingly wondered what else the proud family was hiding.

"So what now?" she asked softly, running her hand over his stubbled chin affectionately. "What are we to do?"

He sighed thoughtfully. "We return to St. Cloven tonight."

"What about your sister? She cannot wed Colin, Alec," Peyton said firmly. "You must do something."

"The woman attacked you and now you defend her?" he cocked a blond eyebrow.

"I am not defending her, merely stating a fact," she said softly. "You know that she cannot marry Colin."

He slanted a painful gaze at his sister, now in his father's arms. "I do indeed, but I do not know what I can possibly do to prevent the union, short of killing young Warrington. Unfortunately, my father is correct when he says that I am not her parent. As much as I hate to admit it, I fear that I am impotent in this matter."

"You were not Ivy's parent, either, yet you helped her," Peyton pointed out. "Surely you can think of something to help Thia."

"I was able to help Ivy because, technically, as your husband, I am your sister's guardian and may do with her as I please," his face was noticeably sorrowful. "I suppose I could do the same with Thia, but my father would not only disown me, he would probably have me killed. I have provoked the man beyond his limit with my intrusion."

Peyton was too concerned with Thia and the Warringtons to have given thought to the term "disown". She continued with her argument. "You are not meddling; you are simply doing what must be done. Why is your father so willing to give in to Nigel's demands? It's almost…. almost as if he is afraid of him."

Not strangely, Alec had been pursuing the exact same thoughts. It was as if Nigel intimidated Brian somehow, although Alec could not imagine why.

In fact, he had discovered a good deal about his father in the past several hours, traits he never believed the man capable of. It was as if the father he had known and admired all of his life was a grand facade, a product of an adoring young boy's admiration. He wondered if the Brian Summerlin he had loved and respected ever existed.

Brian began to move down the corridor towards them with Thia tucked against his torso. Toby, solemn and silent, followed. Alec watched, stone-faced, as his father approached. When Brian met his son's gaze, it was with the look of a beaten dog.

"I must attend the Warringtons," he said quietly. "Will you see to your sister's comfort?"

Peyton could sense a good deal of tension between Alec and his father. She deliberately avoided looking at Thia, instead, choosing to gaze at her husband.

"My wife and I are planning on leaving for St. Cloven immediately, as pursuant to our earlier conversation," he said coldly. "Since you have made it clear that I am no longer welcome at Blackstone, I am sure you will understand if I refuse to attend to your daughter."

Brian looked as if he'd been struck; his eyes took on a strange expression of grief. "You suggested that you depart this night for St. Cloven, not I. I never ordered you to leave."

"You did not have to. Your lectures and condemnations for my actions were enough."

Brian put his hand out beseechingly. "Alec, please. I was angry at the time and did not mean…."

"Aye, you meant it. Every word. Good life to you, Father," he glanced at his sister and a flash of anguish appeared in his sky-blue eyes. "Thia, you know where I will be should you ever need me."

With that, Alec led his shocked wife down the remaining length of the corridor and disappeared. He tried not to think of his sister in the hands of Colin Warrington, but his father had made it clear that his hindrance was unwanted. He was forbidden to meddle, discouraged from assisting. And according to his father, his punishment for aiding Ali and Ivy was long in coming for his repeated disregard of Brian's wishes. He was a man without an inheritance.

Alec knew he should attempt to help his sister, far more than his efforts to keep Peyton and Ivy from the Warrington clutches. Thia was his flesh, his only sister, and his heart ached for the plight he had brought down upon her. He cursed his father for lacking the faith to tell him of Nigel's ultimatum; Ivy or Thia. Had Brian been honest with him from the first, then he could have acted accordingly. Instead, he had unknowingly reduced his father's choice by one.

Aye, it was Brian's fault. Let him wallow in his own weakness, then. It was no longer Alec's problem to solve.

Her brother out of sight, Thia turned to look at her father questioningly, but Brian refused to meet her gaze. Instead, he hugged her tightly as if to break her.

"Come, Thia darling," he said hoarsely. "We must seek your mother and tell her what I have done."

CHAPTER THIRTEEN

PEYTON DIDN'T SAY a word as Alec loaded her onto her small palfrey, nor did she speak as he went about securing the caravan that would accompany them to St. Cloven. She continued to watch him closely, deeply curious as to what had occurred between him and his father. From the words that had been exchanged in the corridor, it was obvious that something severe had happened.

She'd not had the opportunity to ask him why he had been gone so long, leaving her alone to stew in her own fears, and after what had transpired with Thia, she had completely forgotten about his absence. But now, observing his cold manner and curt orders as he dealt with the servants, she would know what had happened between father and son.

She could stand her curiosity no longer. As Alec passed particularly close to her palfrey, directing a groom to better secure his Saracen stallion, she called out to him.

"Alec?" she hailed softly.

He turned sharply as if she had startled him, but his expression immediately softened. "What is it, sweetheart?"

She smiled weakly and politely beckoned him. Obediently, he complied and she immediately reached out to him. He took her hand and kissed it, although she could tell he was hurried.

"Are we to leave soon?"

"Aye, love. We are almost complete."

She cleared her throat, eyeing the large traveling party.

"Isn't your mother and father going to bid us farewell?"

His soft expression stiffened. "I do not think so."

He turned to move away from her but she gripped his hand tightly and he was forced to look at her. "Why not?" she asked softly. "Alec, what's happened between you and your father?"

He glanced over his group of horses and wagons. "Not now, Peyton. We will discuss it later."

She refused to let him off so easily. "Unless you have had bitter, awful words with them, I would like to bid your parents good-bye. They have been very kind to me."

"No," he said flatly. When she opened her mouth to protest, he cast her a beseeching look. "Not now, Peyton. Please. Do not press me at the moment."

She sighed heavily, with great disapproval, but complied. Alec kissed her hand again and released it, his focus returning to the impending journey. He hadn't taken two steps from her when Lady Celine suddenly exited the castle, her wide blue eyes focused intently on her son.

Alec froze, his gaze riveted to his mother. Before he could recover his surprise, Lady Celine crossed the bailey toward him with great determination.

"Where are you going?" she demanded loudly.

Alec moved towards his mother quickly. He would not allow family problems to be aired for the scrutiny of the world. He held out his hand to her, but she slapped it away angrily.

"Answer me, Alec. What's this nonsense I hear from your father?"

Alec was as emotionless as always superficially, but inside he felt like a five-year-old boy again. "Father has disinherited me. You will have to ask him for clarification."

"I did," she snapped. "He proceeded to inform me that you went beyond subordination this night, Alec. You defied him. What in the world would possess you to do this for a woman who is of no concern to you?"

Alec did not react, but he could only imagine how Peyton was feeling. "She is my wife's sister and, therefore, a great deal of concern to me. She and Ali have found affection and I could not stand by and watch my father ruin two lives."

Celine's eyes widened outrageously. "Ruin two lives? How dare you accuse your father of such injustice! As it is, you have ruined your sister's life as a result of your chivalrous loyalty to those who are of inconsequential concern. Ali and Ivy are nothing compared to blood ties."

Aboard her palfrey, Peyton turned away with tears in her eyes. But Alec faced his mother without emotion.

"Peyton is my wife, mother, and closer to me than all of the blood relations I have ever known. Her genuine unhappiness would have resulted from a marriage between her sister and the Warrington heir, and I will not stand for it. As Lady Ivy's legal guardian, it was my prerogative to do with her as I saw rightly over the desires of her liege. I was perfectly correct in my actions, only father is too stubborn to admit it. He is merely upset with the fact that I went against his wishes. Had he been honest with me at the first regarding the Warrington proposal, it is quite possible that we could have avoided all of this."

"'Tis not your place to demand explanations from your liege!"

"I did not demand an explanation, merely the truth. Father has himself to blame for Thia's predicament."

Celine's lip twitched menacingly. "How dare you turn the blame on your father. No one forced you to take matters into your own hands," her gaze drifted to Peyton's red head. "Or I am incorrect in that assumption? Did someone, in fact, demand you into action?"

"What I did, I did for the serenity of my own family purely by my own choosing."

Celine closed her eyes as if to ward off the thunderous headache that was sure to consume her. The circumstances of the day had sorely drained her strength and she simply could not believe the twist events had further taken. When she opened her eyes again to refocus on her son, her face was a darker shade of red.

"Then you are telling me, in essence, that you provoked your father's wrath for the happiness of your new wife, whom you have known for less than a week?"

Alec's only reaction to her scathing tone was to blink. "Aye."

Celine returned her gaze to Peyton, who was facing away from her. Alec could see that his mother was shaking terribly with anger and fatigue. "Did she ask this of you?"

"She did not."

Celine refocused on her son, her manner calming in spite of her increasing fury and disbelief. When she spoke, her voice was as menacing as Alec had ever heard it. "God help me, Alec, had I known that woman would turn you into such an idiot, I would have married her to Colin Warrington myself. Have you completely lost your sense of loyalty?"

Alec tensed ever so slightly. "Not at all. My wife comes first."

Celine's jaw twitched furiously and her eyes found Peyton once more. Before Alec could stop her, she voiced her outrage to his new wife. "What have you done to him?"

Peyton's head snapped to Lady Celine, tears coating her lovely face. Alec put his hand on his mother firmly and turned her toward the castle. "Not here, mother. Go inside and leave us alone."

Furious, Celine slapped her son harshly across the cheek. The resounding noise could be heard by all present and the entire bailey went abruptly silent. Peyton actually started at the sound, her tears forgotten for the moment as she waited for her husband's reaction.

But Alec did not react. In spite of his stinging cheek, he merely gave his mother a long look and turned back to his business. He resumed bellowing orders as Lady Celine stood in the center of the bailey, shaken and despondent to her very soul.

Even if Alec was ignoring her, Peyton wasn't. She liked Lady Celine a great deal and was crushed to realize that hard feelings had established themselves. As Alec's back was turned, she slid from her horse and timidly made her way toward Alec's mother. She simply couldn't leave with such terrible animosity filling the air.

"My lady," she whispered. "I…."

Celine whirled to her, startled to see that Peyton was nearly upon her. Her attention had been focused on her errant son, all but ignoring his wife. But before Peyton could continue, she held out a defiant hand.

"I will not hear you," she said angrily. "You who have turned my son against his family. I have not only lost a grandson this day, but my very own Alec. This is your fault! Go away from me!"

Peyton couldn't help herself; she started to cry again. Lady Celine had been so kind to her that she had almost come to think of her as a mother. To face her rejection was devastating. But far more than her own feelings, she was concerned with Alec; she couldn't fathom the possibility that his own mother would spurn him.

"Please, my lady," she said softly. "Be angry with me if you must, but not with Alec. There is no man more generous and kind in all of England, and he sincerely believed he was doing right for Ali and Ivy's sake. If you…."

"Not another word!" Celine snapped savagely. "I shall not hear you defend my son to me, you conniving wench. You coerced my son to the altar and now you have succeeded in convincing him to reject his family. Be out of my sight before I take a dagger to you!"

Alec was suddenly between them, his hands clutching his mother as he had never gripped a woman in his life. Celine gazed up into angry sky-blue eyes that she did not recognize, and fear immediately swelled in her breast. The eyes that blazed upon her were not the eyes of her beloved Alec.

"Were you a man, you would be drowning in your own blood for making such a threat. As it is, I shall thank you never to speak to my wife in that manner again," he released his mother as quickly as he had grasped her and turned to Peyton. "Mount your horse. We leave."

Without another word, Peyton did as she was told. She did not dare look at Lady Celine, fearful that she would be able to read the woman's hate in her eyes. When Alec reined Midas beside her a scant few seconds later, she was more than willing to retreat from the great bailey of Blackstone.

IT WAS LATE when they began their return trip to St. Cloven, and later still two hours into their journey. The Saracen stallion was not traveling well and Alec had to walk beside the horse to keep him calm. Midas, tethered to a wagon, snorted his disapproval to not be leading the caravan.

With Jubil in one of the wagons, Peyton found herself riding alone with Toby and several men at arms. In spite of his mother's anger, Toby felt compelled to accompany his brother to his new keep, if only for the fact that he knew Alec would sorely miss Ali's organizing presence. While Alec tended to other concerns, Toby would see to the security of his new keep.

In truth, he looked forward to the task; he'd not had a chance to prove himself to his brother with Ali's constant presence. He was eager to further establish his responsible nature by confirming to Alec that he was a mature, capable knight. Though it was never Alec's intention, Toby was positive his older brother still viewed him as an eager young lad with bucked teeth and a knack for trouble-making. Even if he was a fully grown man, Alec still saw him as his younger brother and Toby was certain the opportunity before him would sway his brother's opinion.

As the caravan traveled into the night, Alec was having better luck controlling the Saracen. The animal seemed to be calming somewhat and he was considering remounting Midas when a soft voice floated up beside him.

"Do you mind if I walk with you?"

He looked down to see his wife smiling up at him, the coarse road crunching under her delicate slippers. His first reaction was to sternly direct her back to her palfrey, but he found that he could not. It was nearly the first smiling face he had seen all day.

He reached out and took her hand. "Who allowed you to dismount?"

"Toby," she said. "'Tis amazing what a bit of sweet-talking can accomplish."

He raised a disapproving eyebrow. "Do not think to turn your feminine wiles on my younger, weaker-willed brother. You will ruin him."

She snickered. "I will not. But, in truth, he is terribly cute when he blushes. He turns red enough to ignite kindling."

Alec fought off a grin, gazing to the head of the column where Toby rode astride his chestnut destrier, dutifully leading Peyton's palfrey beside him. He shook his head. "You are an aggressive, terrible woman to take advantage of a noble knight. He'd do anything for you regardless of my wrath."

Her smile abruptly faded and she lowered her gaze, watching the road beneath her feet. Alec studied her bowed head and squeezed her hand gently. "What's wrong?"

She shook her head, preparing to evade his question, but she remembered well their mutually spoken requests of honesty. She swallowed and brushed at the threatening tears. "'Tis just…. that's what your mother called me."

His own smile vanished. Leaving the Saracen to nibble on his alfalfa, he whisked his wife across the moving caravan to where Midas was tethered. Deftly, he mounted her astride the plodding horse and bolted on behind her. With a clucking noise, he reined Midas to the very front of the column, away from the others.

Once alone, he kissed her head, her cheek, and the top of her ear. Peyton sighed raggedly, collapsing against him.

"I do not want you to fret over my mother's words," he said softly. "She was angry, a state which consumes her quite often, and she habitually says things that she does not mean. You must remember that."

"She hates me," she whispered.

He sighed deeply, hearing the song of a distant night bird. "Nay, she does not. She is simply overwrought with the turn of recent events."

Peyton did not say anything for a moment. "Did your father truly disinherit you?"

"So he says. That will remain to be seen."

"Is that why you were gone so long this evening? You said that you were merely going to see to your horses and nothing about speaking with your father."

"'Twas my intention to secure my Saracens and assemble a traveling party, which I did. The confrontation with my father was secondary."

"Confrontation?"

He snorted softly. "Indeed. After the lashing he'd been dealt by the Warringtons, it was inevitable that he would come after me with a vengeance. I half-expected the Warrington dogs to hound me as well."

"Why should they? They have Thia now."

He did not say anything for a moment. "Not if I can think of a way to release her from her bind."

"But what of your father? You said yourself he'd kill you if you interfered again."

"Figuratively. Well, mayhap literally. At any rate, I cannot allow my only sister to be swallowed up by those bastards." He did not say anything about her dislike for men, or how Colin's marital rights would be received by a woman who disliked the male species. But he couldn't help ponder the valid question. The only answers he seemed to come up with were ugly, violent scenarios.

The mood had grown far too heavy for Peyton's tastes and she could feel the weight of Alec's melancholy like a blanket. He was trying too hard to pretend that all would be well, eventually, when in fact a great rift had risen between him and his family. And through it all, she knew she was the cause.

Aye, everything he had done had been for her, she knew that. She'd never asked, nor had there ever been a spoken word between them on the subject, but she knew just the same. He said once that he would die for her. He would do anything for her. She believed him unquestionably.

She sat up, twisting slightly to look at him under the three-quarter moon. A faint smile creased her lips. "Were you given the choice, whom would you send to the Warringtons? Thia or me?"

He did not hesitate. "You."

"Is that so?" she raised an eyebrow.

He cracked a smile as she made faces at him in the moon glow, anything to splinter his rigid expression. She laughed softly when he crossed his eyes like a goon in response to her hideous expressions.

"I have caused you much trouble, my Alec. Mayhap I should present myself to the Warringtons as a peace offering and then all would be right between you and your family again."

His smile vanished. He pulled her against him, tightly, and she sighed deeply with his comfort. "You are my family."

High above them against the silk black sky, an owl soared across the moon.

☙

ST. CLOVEN WAS softly lit by a scarce few torches as the party approached. A few bellowed words from Alec to the sentries at the gate prompted the massive oaken panel to slowly groan open. And as the gate began to yawn wide for its new master, St. Cloven soldiers went scurrying inside the manse with news that Alec Summerlin and his wife, the Lady Peyton, were returned.

Alec had brought seventy-five men-at-arms with him from Blackstone, elite soldiers that he personally claimed, men who had fought with him and his father in the Holy Land. They were men who knew Alec before his vow had stilled his sword. The only knight he had brought was Toby, the others having sworn fealty to his father and were therefore required to remain at Blackstone. But one knight was all he needed as Toby took charge of the men with unmistakable authority and Alec was pleased with his little brother's fortitude.

Peyton was asleep in front of Alec when he rode through the gates, an unusual deep sleep. But she quickly roused when he gently shook her awake and Jubil was at her side when she dismounted Midas. Clearheaded, Jubil insisted on escorting the groggy Peyton inside while Alec saw to his men.

Gratefully, Alec was able to focus on the positioning of his sentries. With the Warringtons' fury, he wasn't at all sure that they would not try to take what they had been denied and he would not be caught unaware. In fact, as he watched his wife and her aunt retire to the great hulking manse of St. Cloven, he considered writing Edward to request more soldiers. He wanted to make sure Peyton and St. Cloven were safe.

After she disappeared inside, he forgot his wife for the moment and went about inspecting his keep. As Toby saw to the unloading of the wagon, Alec supervised the settling of his excitable Saracens and made sure Midas was livered. With the animals made comfortable, he moved on to the soldier's accommodations.

The team-house where the small force of St. Cloven was housed was a well-kept place, if not a bit cramped. Alec and Toby solved the space problem as his men settled in, and then the two knights proceeded to move about the entire perimeter of the keep to inspect the wall, her weaknesses, and her strengths. As Alec talked, Toby yawned, and Alec dismissed his sheepish brother with a slap to the back of the head. Alec knew it was late to be attempting a task that could be just as easily completed in the morn, but he was so excited to be home that he simply could not contain himself. His home.

He forced himself away from the fortified wall and on to the immediate tasks that could not wait until daybreak. When the caravan was completely disassembled and the wagon was on its way to the livery to be stowed, he decided to seek his bed for the remaining hours of the night.

The interior of St. Cloven smelled wonderful and warm, not at all like the stale halls of Blackstone. His former home possessed a distinct must, whereas St. Cloven smelled of cedar and fresh rushes, and he noticed the intricately worked cedar posts in the archway of the great hall and the large solar. In fact, nearly every room possessed a cedar door and related cedar work, and he inhaled the scent deeply. He remembered the smell from his childhood as peculiar and strong, but now he thought it to be delightful.

He heard footfalls behind him, whispers against the stone, and turned to face the approaching party. Jubil's fair face gazed up at him.

"Toby is in the chamber immediately at the top of the stairs," she told him. "I thought you would want him situated to protect the stairwell."

"Wise, my lady," Alec said quietly. "And where is my wife?"

"In your chamber, of course," Jubil said with a twinkle in her eye. "I doubt she is asleep. You'd better hurry before she comes looking for you."

The corners of his mouth twitched. "She would, wouldn't she? I have come to see that my wife is lacking in patience."

Jubil shrugged. "A trait that can be improved upon. Mayhap having a gaggle of children will force her to learn the attribute."

Alec nodded, glancing at the massive stone and oak staircase. "If we are indeed so blessed," he moved toward the steps. "Good sleep to you, Jubil."

His boot barely hit the bottom stair when he heard Jubil behind him. "You are already so blessed, my lord."

He couldn't help himself from halting his ascension, turning to peer curiously at the aged aunt. "And just how would you know that?"

Jubil smiled broadly, her blue eyes glittering in the dim torchlight. "Look at her, Alec. Can you not see that your seed has taken root? *Look* at her."

He had no idea what to say and did not dare to hope that Jubil spoke the truth. After all, it had only been a matter of days and there was no way Peyton could have known that she had conceived in that time. Thoughtfully, he mounted the remainder of the stairs and made his way to his chamber.

The master chamber was warm and dim, the light from the blazing hearth affording the only illumination. Alec entered the room quietly, his eyes grazing the surroundings; the bed was prepared and fresh rushes littered the floor. Closing the door softly behind him, he looked about for his wife.

She wasn't hard to find. Peyton stepped from the shadows clad in a shift made from the finest silk, spider-web thin, with ribbons of gold woven through it. It covered her completely from head to toe, yet obscured none of her beautiful body from his lusty gaze. One look at her and his mouth began to water.

"Welcome home, my lord," she said seductively.

He grinned, a nervous, excited gesture. "'Tis good to be home."

She moved into the light and all he could do was stare at her body though the screen of the transparent shift. "Christ, Peyton, you look…. magnificent."

"I should hope so," she purred, moving close enough to run her hand erotically from his narrow waist to his shoulder. "I have been waiting for you."

He grabbed the wandering hand and her with it. Peyton laughed softly as she found herself gripped against his mighty chest. His eyes blazed at her, the heat of his gaze searing her flesh and she licked her lips instinctively, waiting for his delicious mouth to descend upon her. He grinned when he saw her pink tongue flick about her lips, his great head dipping lower and lower.

"Wait no longer, then."

Alec suckled her mouth so hard that she was sure he had bruised her. She responded to him wildly, without reserve, and in little time they had made short work of his traveling tunic. The garment came off and Peyton couldn't take her mouth from his magnificent chest, lapping the salty musk from his skin and biting delicately at his nipples. She could feel his hands in her hair, the whispered inflections of her name riding on his breath.

With every passing moment, she grew bolder and bolder until she grasped his engorged manhood through his hose, stroking the length of it.

"Peyton…." he whispered.

"Nay, my Alec," she returned softly, pushing his hands away as they attempted to remove his breeches. "I shall do it. I shall do everything."

He was breathing heavily, watching the top of her head, feeling the molten liquid strands caressing his heated flesh. Gently, and a bit awkwardly, she released him from his breeches and lowered them to his knees. Without hesitation, her hot hands closed over his swollen organ and began to stroke it tenderly. He watched her, fascinated and consumed, as she inspected his manhood.

She continued to fondle him, her bravery growing. He waited impatiently for her to ask him for suggestions on how to fulfill his pleasure, but she seemed content to simply stroke him. For now, he was content with that as well. But his tolerance would not hold out indefinitely.

Which was why he was completely surprised when she lowered her head and stroked his manhood with her tongue, from the testicles to the ruby-red crown. He jumped at the action, grasping her by the hair and forcing her to look at him. His gaze bordered on rage.

"Where in the hell did you learn to do that?" he demanded hoarsely.

She grinned, embarrassed. "The cook's daughters are free with their advice. Ivy and I have learned much by listening to them."

His instant relief weakened him. His imagination had run wild in that split second, and he realized he was consumed with jealousy and rage when he thought of his sweet wife pleasuring her dead betrothed in the same manner. He could see Peyton's mouth coming to bear on the pulsing organ of a faceless knight and his possessiveness nearly devoured him. The alleviation at her admission was indescribable.

"I see," he rasped. "And what else did you learn listening to the trollops?"

Her grin broadened. "I did not truly learn anything, merely ingested for future reference. I have yet to actually attempt to practice."

He dipped his head low, kissing her fully on her ripe lips. "You may continue your practice."

She did, eagerly. When she realized she could turn him into a writhing mass of flesh simply by putting her mouth over the head of his manhood and suckling hard, she continued with her torture until Alec weakly begged for reprieve. She fully ignored his cries; before he realized it, she had maneuvered him into a chair and knelt between his legs, her hot mouth working him into a frenzy. With every stroke and every suckle, he was thrust further and further toward the point of rapture.

He was delirious; he wanted to bury his manhood deep within the recesses of her sweet body, but her mouth was ecstasy beyond words. With her hair splayed over his naked thighs and groin, he was incapable of summoning the effort to stop her onslaught so they could retire to the bed. All he could feel was Peyton's luscious mouth.

He erupted as she continued to suckle. First, she tasted the saltiness of his seed, and then she watched, fascinated, as he spent himself. The pearl-colored essence of life spilled onto her hand and she extended her tongue to taste it once again, gazing up into his eyes with great wonder.

"It tastes salty," she whispered. "Does it hurt when you spill?"

Weak and thoroughly spent, Alec entwined his great fingers into her silken tresses. "Nay, love, it doesn't," when she grinned, he seemed to snap out of his lethargy and scooped her into his arms. "You are a naughty, wanton wench, Lady Summerlin. How cruel. How terribly controlling. How lovely for me."

She laughed softly as he swung her to the bed, tossing her onto the mattress and descending upon her with his exquisite body. She continued to giggle as he kicked off his boots and restrictive breeches, but her laughter quickly turned to moans of pleasure as his mouth latched onto her earlobe and his hand closed over her breast possessively.

"Oh, Alec," she whispered as his fingers peaked her nipple. "Make love to me, darling."

He growled and his mouth left her ear to clamp down on a distended nipple through the thin silk. She groaned with pleasure, pulling at his short hair as he tugged insistently at her breast. His hands were consuming her, his strength finding release through his driven touch. The shift came off, somehow, she was not even aware; the very next thing she realized, Alec was fully aroused once more and driving his firm body into her swollen flesh.

His thrusts were deep, even, hard. Peyton planted her heels into the back of his knees and moved to meet his passion. She heard a throaty cry, not realizing that it was her own, as waves upon waves of delicious convulsions swallowed her whole. Alec had consumed her, digested her, until all that remained was a boneless, quivering form. His desire had rendered her a content, weak woman.

Alec found his own release again as Peyton's lusty body was wracked with spasms. His climax came so hard that he bit his lip, unaware of the pain yet totally cognizant of the pleasure.

Only when he moved to envelope her in his massive embrace did he taste his blood and he smiled wearily into the darkness. Christ, what this woman did to him.

He was home.

☙

THE NEXT DAY at St. Cloven dawned bright and temperate. Alec awoke shortly after dawn, as was habitual, and managed to disengage himself from Peyton without waking her. Moving from the massive bed, he donned his breeches and slipped into the hall, summoning a servant for hot water and food. The small bower next to the master chamber was virtually empty, and he proceeded to claim it for his private retreat.

He ate standing next to a lancet window, his gaze lingering on his new bailey as the sun rose. Washing quickly, he silently returned to the master chamber to retrieve his clothes, passing a tender glance at his wife. She was buried under the covers and he was only able to glimpse her wild red hair and half of her face. With a grin, he closed the door softly.

Clad in heavy breeches, thigh-high black boots and a durable tunic made from panels of black leather and black linen, he went about his new duties as lord of the keep. Toby met him in the great hall, greeting him amiably and voicing his approval for the liberal use of cedar. But in the same breath, Alec could read a strange confusion in Toby's eyes. He moved past the pleasantries.

"What's wrong?"

Toby tried to shrug off the question but he found he could not. In fact, he was glad Alec had asked and lowered his voice. "Aunt Jubil…."

"What about her?"

Toby looked decidedly uncomfortable and eyed the foyer beyond the hall. "I found her this morn…. well, she is not herself."

Alec put his hands on his hips. "What does that mean? Where is she?"

Toby gestured in the general direction of the foyer but thought better of sending Alec on to face the aged aunt alone. He motioned his brother to follow.

Alec was not surprised at the sight that greeted him in the small solar. In fact, confusion would have been a better term.

Jubil was hanging by her knees from an open beam, swathed from head to toe in a great cloak of black. Her faded hair hung askew and her blue eyes were closed. She was so still that she almost looked dead.

Toby eyed Alec as his brother moved into the solar, scrutinizing the woman with intense curiosity. He paced a complete circle about the hanging woman, peering closely at every aspect of her from ceiling to floor. He tore his gaze away from the dangling figure to pass a questioning glance at Toby, who merely shrugged helplessly. With that response, Alec returned his focus to Jubil.

"Jubil?" he said softly. "Can you hear me?"

Immediately, one eye popped open, studied Alec, and promptly closed again. "I am a bat. Can you not see for yourself?"

"Indeed. But why are you a bat?"

"Keen of hearing, sharp of smell. I must be a bat."

Alec put his hands on his hips, pondering her statement. "Is there a reason why you must be a bat?"

"I must hear. Leave me alone."

His brows drew together in puzzlement and he passed Toby a glance. His younger brother was watching Jubil with his usual fascination. "How long has she been like this?"

Toby shook his head. "I was up before sunrise and she was in this state when I happened upon her. Shall I summon your wife?"

Alec cocked an eyebrow. "Why? She shall simply become irritated," he moved away from Jubil, his gaze lingering on the older woman. "Leave her be. Make sure the servants do not disturb her."

Jubil heard the door close, and the faded blue eyes opened slowly. She stared into the emptiness of the room a moment, her mind cloaked with the venom of the monkshade.

"I must hear the danger approaching," she muttered feebly, for her ears alone. "I must be aware."

☙

UNDER THE COMMAND of his sergeants, the bailey seemed to be running smoothly enough. Men were manning the battlements as he had commanded and he was pleased to see that, so far, there were no wrinkles in his operation.

A harried groom approached him to announce that his Saracen stallion had endured a rough night and went on to suggest the addition of ale to the animal's water to calm him. Alec agreed, intending to administer the liquor himself, when a burly man approached him and bowed deeply.

"My lord?" he addressed timidly.

Alec fixed the man with his customary emotionless gaze. "Who are you?"

The man bowed profusely. He was a big man, with thinning reddish hair and small green eyes. "I am John Todd, the master brewer. I understand that the Lady Peyton returned last eve."

"My wife has indeed returned," Alec eyed the man with a degree of respect. "Is there a problem with the stores?"

"Nay, my lord, no problem to speak of," John assured him.

"But there is a batch of pale ale that is already ripe. Lady Peyton's approval is required."

Alec studied the man a moment longer as the weary groom still hovered beside him restlessly. "My wife will come to see you shortly. I shall summon her myself."

The master brewer bowed again. "Thank you, my lord, thank you."

When the fat man waddled away, Alec returned his attention the stable hand. "Let's tend to my vicious beast, shall we?"

The groom scurried after the long-legged master. "Vicious, indeed, my lord. He has nearly taken off my hand. Twice!"

Alec raised a disapproving eyebrow. "The first time should have been enough to warn you off. He is not to be trifled with."

"I was attempting to feed him, my lord," the groom replied with a touch of droll sarcasm.

Alec did not respond as they passed through an arched gateway in the wall and on to the protected stables.

☙

IN SPITE OF her long and strenuous night, Peyton arose shortly after Alec had left her. Taking her time, she bathed leisurely and dressed in a persimmon-colored surcoat that was nearly the exact color of her hair. Gathering her considerable mane of curls, she tied them loosely at the nape of her neck and went about with her plans for the day. And she had a load of them.

Driving the servants like a Roman emperor, she proceeded to have all of her father's items removed from the master wardrobe and replaced with Alec's things. Several strapping male servants brought in another wardrobe to house her possessions. The huge bed that had belonged to her father was stripped of its bedclothes and taken outside to be cleaned and re-stuffed with layers of straw and feathers. The more that was accomplished, the more she decided needed to be done.

The upper floor of St. Cloven turned into a clutter of displaced furniture and other items as the servants set about scrubbing floors and washing rugs and portieres at Lady Peyton's direction. But they were used to her dictatorial rule; she was an accomplished chatelaine and having been away from her home for so long strengthened her resolve to restore its perfection. With a new master in their midst, and a powerful one, the servants of St. Cloven were pleased to do her bidding.

Returning from the stables, Alec could see the cleaning commotion even from a distance and correctly assumed his wife to be at the head of it. With a faint grin, he made his way inside.

Peyton was standing in the middle of the upstairs corridor, expressing concern over the wearability of a particular woolen rug. He moved up behind her silently, only to grasp her firmly about the waist and plant a loud kiss on the nape of her luscious neck.

She started with surprise, but immediately relaxed into a radiant smile as he wound his thick arms around her torso and buried his face in her hair.

"Who is it?" she asked innocently.

He cocked an eyebrow. "Pray, Lady Summerlin, who else would greet you as I have just done?"

She pretended to think and he swatted her bottom with a trencher-sized hand. Laughing, Peyton whirled away from him as if to escape his wrath.

"No one has ever greeted me in that fashion, husband. Only you."

He rested his fists on his narrow hips. "Well and good for you," his gaze lingered on the hall in disarray. "What goes on here?"

"Cleaning," she told him. "I would make sure that your new keep is perfect."

He slanted her a glance. "With you residing within its walls, it could be nothing less."

She smiled prettily and lowered her gaze. He closed the distance between them, cupping her dainty chin in his hand. "Did you sleep well?"

She nodded. "Well enough. You were certainly up early."

"I had several things to attend to, and still more duties await me. But I wanted to bid you a pleasant morn."

She wrapped her arms around his thick neck and he lifted her off the floor with the power of his embrace. Sweet, lingering kisses filled the silence between them until Peyton shifted in his arms and he reluctantly allowed her to slide to her feet. As much as she would have liked to have relented to his fevered lips, she had more pressing things to attend to. And she fully intended to involve him.

"I would ask a favor before you return to your tasks," she took his hand and led him down the hall.

She took him to the chamber where she kept her paintings, the moody room awash with color and sorrow. Understandably, he was a bit wary, for their last visit to this room had resulted in a bitter argument. Moreover, it was the room where she kept reminders of her love gone by. Alec did not want to see of her love for another man.

The moment they entered the room, the black tides of jealousy swept him. His eyes avoided the brilliant displays of his wife's talent, instead, focusing on the broken joust pole in the corner. Somehow, he could visualize the strong young knight who had wielded the pole, a man who had kissed his wife, who had once been betrothed to her. The faded yellow and white colors of Sir James Deveraux took shape, molding into a vision of the fair-haired man who should have been standing in Alec's stead. Alec was glad he was dead.

Aye, he was glad. As selfish and distasteful as it was to be thankful for another's demise, he was nonetheless grateful. Had James survived his bout in Norwich, Alec would have never come to know the woman who had very quickly become the center of his world. He would have never known complete joy, or madness, sometimes one and the same. He would have never loved her.

Aye, he loved her.

The thought crept upon him so gently that he was not startled by it. In fact, he couldn't remember when he hadn't loved her. Gazing at his wife's red head as she moved across the room, he felt full of his feelings. They were subtle, yet so powerful that he couldn't remember when they hadn't been an integral part of his life. More than ever before, she meant the world to him.

But his love would never be returned. She had already informed him of that fact. Watching her move across the room, he hoped to summon the bravery to tell her of his feelings one day. One day when he was prepared for the biting sting of her rejection.

Peyton disrupted him from his train of thought when she stopped just shy of the twisted joust pole. When she turned to him, the smile was gone from her face.

"Would…. would you please remove these for me? I am afraid a servant would hurt himself on the broken pole. You are the only one qualified to handle it."

He took a hesitant step in her direction, his eyes studying the once-proud lance. "Where do you wish for me to put them?"

She passed a final glance at the reminders of her sorrow, of the tokens of her grief. The ache was still there, but as a melancholy memory and nothing more. The searing pain was vanished. Taking a deep breath for courage, she faced her husband.

"Burn them."

Surprised, his eyes focused on her. "Burn them? Are you serious?"

"Never more so," she moved toward him, curling her fingers around his massive forearms. "I do not need them anymore. Will you remove them for me?"

He gazed into her eyes, seeing complete sincerity. Would he remove the tokens of another man's love? Without hesitation. Tenderly, he patted her hand and moved across the floor, retrieving the pole as if it were made of feathers. The break proved awkward to manage, but he controlled it nicely.

With the bent pole in one hand and the leather scabbard in the other, he turned to his wife with the most wonderful of expressions. She could fairly read the depth of emotion in his eyes and it startled her; if she hadn't known better, she would have sworn the emotion was.... adoration.

"I shall dispose of them. You do not need them anymore."

The tears Peyton fought back as he quit the room were not those of sorrow. They were those of joy.

.... good-bye, James!

ALEC HAD THE pleasure of escorting his wife to the brewery after the nooning meal. Infinitely curious about the secretive brewing process Sir Albert had kept so closely guarded, a whole new world opened up before his very eyes.

He had seen the ale storehouse once before, but it was nothing compared to the sharp smell of the brick brewery. Well-protected and sunk deep into the rich English soil, the brewery was a fascinating place of copper tubs, presses, heat and stank. Peyton paid little mind to her surroundings as she went in search of the master brewer, but Alec was enthralled. He lagged so far behind in his curious observations that she paused so he could catch up to her.

She grinned at his interest. "For heaven's sake, Alec, it's just a brewery."

"I have never seen one before," he stated the obvious. "What's this?"

She looked in the direction he was indicating. "Those are vats of cooling mush. They've already been mashed and cooked and are awaiting yeast for fermentation."

He peered closely at the huge copper vats. "It looks like porridge."

"It is, basically. That batch will produce pale ale. It's simple barley."

He turned to her. "I know that St. Cloven produces four types of ale. Is each process unique to create a different end result?"

She began to walk and he followed, tightly clutching her hand. "The process does not differ, merely the ingredients. As I said, barley is used to create pale ale. For dark ale, we cook a mixture of roasted wheat, barley and molasses. With fruited ale, a recipe of apples, grapes, barley and molasses is combined. And the hearty ale, King Edward's favorite I might add, we combine roasted barley, roasted wheat, oats and honey."

He stared at her as if she had just recited the secret of life. "Christ, how do you remember this?"

She laughed softly. "I was born into it, my Alec. I should hope I would remember something."

Marveling at her knowledge, he gestured toward the great copper vats that were presently steaming with their contents. "Tell me something of the process. That is, if you feel you can trust me with the secret."

"The recipes are the secret, Alec, not the process," she responded to his droll comment. "Actually, the process is simple; the ingredients are mashed with water and cooked in the copper tubs you see. Then the mixture is cooled for at least a day and a night before cakes of yeast are added. In three days' time, the mixture ferments enough so that a head rises, and the head is skimmed away. Then, it is casked and stored for up to three weeks, depending on the strength of the ale."

"Amazing," he muttered, glancing about the bricked interior of the brewery. "I am married to a genius."

"Hardly. I did not invent the process."

"Nay, but you certain know your business. No wonder St. Cloven ale is the very best."

Feeling rosy with his adoration, she looked away shyly. With a faint smile, he brought her hand to his lips and kissed it, laughing softly when her blush deepened. "I know something of the ale process, too."

She looked to him. "You do? What?"

He looked rather pleased with himself. "I know that two hogshead equals one butt, and that four barrels equal one hundred and eight imperial gallons."

She shook her head slowly. "Really, Alec. Any drinking fool knows that."

He feigned injury. "I cannot help what I am. Certainly, I am not as intelligent as you. Pray be kind to me, madam, and my simple, drinking fool's mind."

She giggled, turning her attention back to the business at hand. "Are you going to help me determine the readiness of the pale ale?"

"Absolutely. In fact, 'twill be a duty I shall excel at."

They passed into the fermenting room and were immediately met by John Todd. The master brewer grinned broadly at Peyton, bowing purely out of habit. His eyes were warm upon his lady.

"My lady, how good to see you," he said sincerely.

"Thank you, John," she eyed Alec. "I understand you have met the new lord of St. Cloven?"

"Aye, we have met," John bowed to Alec, and Alec swore he'd never seen anyone bow so often in his whole life. The man was permanently bent at the waist. "A pleasure to see you again, my lord."

Alec nodded silently as Peyton delved into the subject at hand. "Last week's lot of pale ale should be ready for sale. I am worried that it has been aged over-long."

John led Peyton and Alec to an armored side door and they exited into the bright sunshine. "I do not believe so, my lady. After all, it has only been a week exactly."

"It was a week exactly last night. If the liquor takes on too much of the wood, it will be ruined."

"But it was casked in beechwood, which should discourage the added flavor," John said pointedly as they approached the massive storage barn.

Peyton's hair glistened like a raging fire under the brilliant sun, flickering wildly when she shrugged. "We shall see."

Alec listened in complete silence, vowing to learn all he could so that he would not be entirely ignorant when his wife brought up the subject of ale-making. After all, St. Cloven was his now, and as lord he should know something about the process.

The ale was ready. Almost over-ready, Peyton thought, but she ordered it distributed and sold. John Todd whipped the storehouse servants into an efficient frenzy and the casks of pale ale were lowered onto their sides and the seals broken. Alec watched intently as the liquid was delegated into various measurements for sale, all flasks and barrels emblazoned with the St. Cloven crest.

Alec studied the crest, considering minor changes to add his own House to the seal. Now that St. Cloven belonged to a Summerlin, it was only correct that the House be added to the emblem. A very minor change, to be sure, because the seal of St. Cloven was one of the most recognizable in England. If consumers were to make note of a major change, they might think the contents changed as well, and Alec would not risk the reputation of the liquor in such a fashion.

Great wagons were brought about for the transfer of the ale, men as well organized as any army as they began to load the product. Alec stood silently, studying every aspect of every job, watching the careful storage of the ale aboard the wagons and observing the rig drivers as they roped the barrels and packed straw around them to prevent damaging the goods.

The brewery steward who kept records of customers and payment brought Peyton a long list of taverns and private parties who were waiting for their shipment of pale ale. Peyton passed a glance at her husband when she saw Blackstone heading the list, but he did not catch her glance. Approving the tally, she moved to her husband as he watched the organized commotion.

Alec was enthralled with what was going on before him, furthermore involved when great barrels of newly-cooled hearty ale were brought in from the brewery and organized in to a specific corner of the storehouse. He watched curiously as the brewery steward's assistant scratched the date and time on one of the barrels. There was so much happening that it was difficult to keep track, but his sharp mind absorbed the chaos like a sponge. All of this was his.

It took him nearly an hour to realize Peyton was waiting for him to complete his observations. Enthralled as he was at the entire process, he'd lost track of time. When he became aware of her patient presence, he smiled sheepishly.

"I have never seen this before," he said with a weak grin.

"I am sorry to have kept you waiting."

"You did not," she wrapped her hands around his muscular elbow and smiled brightly. "But the last wagon is gone. Have you had enough of the brewery for one day?"

He returned her smile and shrugged, glancing about the empire he had acquired. The amazing process of ale making was still going on about him, a procedure refined by generations of de Fluornoys, now to be his. He could scarcely believe it all belonged to him. It almost made the pain of his estrangement bearable.

The dark sorrows that had constituted the previous day threatened him once again, almost stronger than before. But he fought back the grief, refusing to allow it to dampen his joy. Gazing down at the head of his wife, he knew he had finally found his place in life.

No longer was he the coward son, The Legend who had laid down his sword in dishonor. A disinheritance long in coming did not matter anymore. He did not need it.

He was Alec Summerlin, Lord of St. Cloven. Patting Peyton's soft hands, he led her out into the sunshine.

CHAPTER FOURTEEN

JUBIL WAS A bat for nearly a week. She continued to hang upside-down in the solar, shut away from the rest of the world as Peyton raged her irritation and then, finally ignored her. Alec went to the solar one evening after the meal and seated himself next to the hanging woman, pelting her with gentle questions as to why she must remain a bat. All she would tell him was that she must be made aware of the danger, and it puzzled him. He knew better than to ask Peyton for clarification; she thought it all a load of silly nonsense.

When Jubil finally descended from her cloud of toxin-induced visions, she could not walk and could barely speak. Toby had carried the woman to her bower where she proceeded to sleep for three days. In truth, Peyton was very concerned for her aunt and spent a good deal of time by her bedside in silent vigil, ready to offer watered ale or a bit of food should Jubil desire it. One moment she'd be terribly angry with her aunt for the self-abuse, but in the next moment she would pray for her recovery. She'd never seen Jubil so drained.

As Jubil recovered from her experience, Alec delved deeper and deeper into the workings of St. Cloven. His days were filled with ale-making and his Saracens, and his nights were filled with his wife. His life seemed to hinge on the bright red-gold head, eager to catch a glimpse of her as he went about his duties, more than eager to taste of her with a stolen kiss or a lingering embrace.

Peyton occupied every corner of his mind that wasn't busy learning about the ale process or focused on his foaling mare. There was so much to learn and be joyful of that he had little time to linger on the family he had left behind.

But linger he did. Sometimes at night after Peyton had fallen asleep, he found himself thinking on his sister's fate. Had she indeed married Colin? Or had his father shown an ounce of courage and denied the petition? God only knew how badly he wanted to contact his father, to apologize for actions he was not sincerely remorseful for committing. But he would apologize all the same, simply because he was sorry he had defied his father. He had never taken pleasure in the disobedience, but he knew in his heart that he had to do what was right.

Thrust into a new world he had fallen in love with helped ease the ache of separation from his tightly-knit family, but he still felt as if a piece of his life was missing.

The days were growing cooler. October was approaching and the winds of fall were upon them. The trees in the surrounding forests were changing with the season, turning colors of brilliant orange and yellows, and the animals were beginning to store their food for the winter.

One night, Alec and Peyton had spied a family of raccoons moving to a warmer hovel, and Peyton had taken delight in counting the five babies. He had simply taken delight in her, wishing he could summon the courage to tell her of his love. More than ever, his emotions for the woman were consuming and he cursed himself for not being strong enough to confess, strong enough to confront her rejection.

As fall deepened, so did his adoration for his wife and there were several times when he had literally bitten his lip raw in an attempt to keep from admitting his feelings. There were frequent moments when her gaze would scream of deeper emotion, a depth of caring he had never before witnessed, and he was quite content to believe that it was love. But he could not be sure.

Alec liked autumn. The days passed and he went about his usual duties, which now included shadowing the brewery steward to better understand his job. Moving across the bailey with the servant on his heels, he passed a glance into the nearby cluster of woods and noticed that some of the leaves were the color of his wife's hair. His mind wandered to Peyton for the hundredth time that day as the brewery steward, a thin man with the unlikely name of Job, rattled on about a delinquent account.

Increasingly disinterested with the steward's chatter, he began to seriously consider seeking out his wife for an afternoon encounter. But both men were abruptly cut short from their pressing thoughts when a shout erupted from the fortified wall.

Riders were approaching.

St. Cloven possessed no moat, nor portcullis within her broad walls, but the gate securing the complex was over a foot thick. The two heavy slabs of oak were already closed per Alec's command, since he did not feel comfortable with the bailey open and exposed, and he was therefore unconcerned with the manse's safety as he mounted the ladder to the narrow battlement. Joined by his sentries, he peered down the wooded road.

The south-facing thoroughfare was lined with brilliantly changing trees, but he could clearly make out one horse and two riders. It took Alec all of a split-second to recognize the charger; bounding from the wall, he sent a soldier running for Peyton.

Ali and Ivy were returned.

The heavy gates rolled open with a steady rhythm, yawning wide to greet her native daughter and new husband. Alec was standing at the gates as they rode in.

"Ali!" he shouted, motioning the gates closed before the destrier came to a halt. "You have returned!"

Ali brought his steed to a jerky stop, raising his visor with a dazzling smile. "My wife couldn't stay away. She hated France."

Alec put his arms up for Ivy, who slid into his brotherly embrace and pecked him dutifully on the cheek. She smiled brightly at him.

"Where's Peyton?"

"Probably breaking her neck on the stairs in her rushed attempt to greet you," he said drolly, but he was smiling. "You look ravishing, love. I see that married life agrees with you."

Ivy flushed prettily as Ali dismounted and put his arm around her affectionately. They gazed sweetly at each other. "She is my wife, Alec, in the eyes of God and England."

Alec looked puzzled. "What…. what do you mean?"

Ali's smile faded somewhat and he kissed Ivy on the forehead. "My wife would not be satisfied with a common-law ceremony, so we sailed to Calais and were married in a small monastery. 'Twould seem the French are more apt to accept a man of my color. They were more than happy to join us in matrimony."

Alec blinked, startled by the news. "You were married in a church?"

Ali looked a bit sheepish as Ivy gazed up at him in support. "I was willing to overlook my hatred of the religion in order to please my wife. She wanted to be married in a church, and we searched until we found a priest who would agree to baptize me into the religion. Simply because God does not recognize me as an English knight does not mean that he cannot recognize me as a Catholic husband."

A surprised pause was followed by a slow smile. Alec reached out and took Ali's gloved hand into his own, a handshake of friendship and congratulations. "My best wishes, Ali. You cannot know how glad I am to hear this."

Ali opened his mouth to reply but was thwarted when a loud shriek suddenly pierced the cool air of the bailey. Peyton, her red hair waving like a wild banner, raced from the manse like a madwoman.

Ali jumped back as she plowed into her sister, cries of welcome and grunts resulting from harsh embraces filling the air. Alec and Ali stood together, observing the touching scene between the two sisters.

"Christ, Peyton, do not break any bones," Alec admonished softly, grinning. "Let the woman breathe."

Peyton ignored him, but she did release her sister long enough to step back and take a good look at her. "You are back! Why have you returned so soon?"

Ivy thrust her left hand in Peyton's face; a gold and garnet band glittered brightly on the third finger and Peyton studied the ring with pleasure.

"We were married by a priest in France," Ivy said happily. "There was no reason to stay away. The Warringtons cannot dissolve a marriage performed by the church."

Peyton's mouth opened in surprise and glee. "You are truly married? How marvelous!" she hugged her sister tightly before turning to Ali.

The dark soldier was the recipient of a warm embrace from his redheaded sister-in-law. "Welcome home, Ali."

Ali was truly touched. For a man who had known rejection his entire life, it was enough to bring tears to his eyes. Although their initial reaction to the dark warrior had been moderately resistant and hardly surprising, Ivy and Peyton had differed from the rest of the female populace in that they had been able to move beyond the aesthetics. Never had he met women who judged him not by his appearance, but by what lay in his heart. As if his dark skin did not matter. They came to understand that he was a man like all the rest and his thanks went beyond words.

"Thank you, Peyton," he said softly.

Alec was smiling at his friend, knowing Ali's feelings all too well. As Ivy and Peyton had come to accept Ali, Alec had come to accept their approval without reservation. Once he had been hesitant, reluctant to believe their sincerity. But the hesitation was gone and he couldn't remember feeling such relief on Ali's behalf. It was better than he could have ever hoped for.

Just as the moment grew overly warm, Alec suddenly looked stricken as if a terrible thought had just occurred to him.

"Christ!" he boomed. "I just realized that you are my legal brother."

Ali mirrored his horrified look. "And you are mine. Alec, I do not know if I can show my face in public. I shall be the laughing stock."

While Ivy and Peyton giggled, Alec scowled and put his hands on his hips. "You insolent whelp. Being related to me is the answer to your prayers."

Ali snickered and put his arm around Ivy. "Sorry, Alec. My prayers have indeed been answered, but not by you."

Alec lifted an eyebrow in agreement and pulled Peyton into his embrace. "'Twould seem that God had been watching out for the both of us when he led the hideous Lady Peyton and her deformed sister to our doorstep those weeks ago."

"Hideous?" Peyton repeated with outrage.

"Deformed?" Ivy echoed on her heels.

"Aye, hideous and deformed," Alec insisted, looking between his wife and her sister. "I seem to remember women with white faces, blacked-out teeth, and circled eyes, acting like a pair of fools."

Peyton and Ivy looked at each other and grinned. "Ah, yes. Hideous and deformed," Ivy agreed.

Ali shuddered, as if remembering the appalling visions. "And I seem to recall a woman who picked her nose and scratched her arse like a man. Frightful."

Ivy pretended to slug him and he laughed his deep, throaty laugh. "My tactics were not too terribly frightful. They caught your attention, did they not?"

Ali cocked a black eyebrow. "Was that a sample of your feminine wiles? 'Tis no small mystery why you were unmarried at a proper age, then."

Ivy slapped at him again, much to Peyton's amusement. "Enough, Ali," Ivy commanded. "I am tired and wish to take a bath."

He fought off a grin. "Of course, sweetling. Care for company in your bath?"

"Mayhap later, darling," Ivy cast him a flirtatious glance, one that surprised and amused her sister and brother-in-law. However, the promise only served to inflame her eager new husband.

"Later?"

She nodded coyly, turning with her grinning sister towards the manse.

Ali could hardly wait.

LATER THAT AFTERNOON while Peyton and Ivy were otherwise occupied, Alec took Ali on a tour of the compound. His ebony friend was mightily impressed by the workings of the complex and Alec expressed an interest in having Ali solicit new customers. Although St. Cloven was hugely successful, it could be even greater with an overseas market. Pondering that very question, the two men paced the floor of the storehouse as another lot of fruited ale was brought in from the brewery to age.

"How did your father react to your disobedience, Alec?" Ali asked him softly.

Alec's head came up sharply and he focused on his friend. They had been speaking on foreign markets not a second before and now he found himself unbalanced with the change of subject. He wasn't sure he wanted to speak of it yet, even to Ali. "Then, I take it, you disagree that Ireland would be a profitable market?"

Ali smiled faintly. "Not at all. The Irish are extremely fond of liquor. But I agree that you are in a great deal of trouble. You have not mentioned your father once since I have arrived and I can stand it no longer. What happened?"

Alec stared at him a moment longer before turning away, raking his fingers through his short hair. "Christ, Ali, do we have to talk about this now?"

"We do," Ali said firmly, his smile fading. "What happened?"

Alec did not say anything for a moment. Then, he lowered his massive body onto a sturdy barrel and pondered his hands. "A bloody mess is what's happened. After my elopement with Peyton and my subsequent abduction of Ivy, my father saw fit to disinherit me. But there is so much more to it than that."

"What, my friend?" Ali pressed gently.

Alec threw up his hands in an irritated gesture. "When father changed his mind and dissolved your betrothal to Ivy, I questioned him as to his reasons. One minute, he was a staunch supporter of your union and in the next he was attempting to convince me that Ivy would be better off as chatelaine of Wisseyham. It was as if.... as if my father had been bewitched, somehow. I have never known him to show a weak moment, but suddenly he became a coward who went back on his word. I delivered Ivy to you because it was the right thing to do and I will never regret my decision. But what I did not know, or what my father neglected to tell me, was that Nigel Warrington had given my father an ultimatum; since I had married Peyton and presumable stolen his son's betrothed, Nigel bade my father to choose between Ivy and Thia for Colin's bride."

Ali, who had been listening closely, suddenly let out a hiss. "Which was why he appeared to have broken his promise regarding my marriage to Ivy. 'Tis only logical that he choose her over Thia, who shall probably never marry."

Alec shook his head. "She most likely already is, to Colin no less. I do not understand why my father did not trust me with Nigel's threat. Had I known, I most certainly would have made plans for my sister. As it was, I sealed her future the moment I took Ivy from Blackstone."

Ali drew in a long, cleansing breath as he digested the statement. "I do not understand why your father should be intimidated by Nigel Warrington. For that matter, I do not understand why your father would even deal with him. Your father is his liege, not the other way around. He acted as if the king himself had delivered the choice of brides."

"Warrington seems to be at the root of my father's bout with cowardice. The moment contact was established between Nigel and my father, submission and weakness constituted my father's character. It doesn't make sense to me, Ali. You know my father is nothing of the kind. At least, I never thought so."

Ali did not say anything for a moment. "Have you spoken with him since?"

"Nay," Alec shook his head regretfully. "And there was an ugly scene with my mother the night Peyton and I left."

Ali scratched his chin and pushed himself off the barrel that had been supporting his weight. Thoughtfully, he paced the straw floor. "I will send word to my father, then, and ask that he come to St. Cloven. He will be able to tell you what has happened since your departure."

Alec almost looked pleased, feeling relief that he would soon be discovering the fate of his family since his departure. In lieu of an emotional response, he rose on his long legs and clapped Ali on the shoulder as both men moved for the great doors of the storehouse. "I am glad you are here, my friend. I have missed you."

Alec did not want to talk about his problems anymore, which was fine by Ali. With all that Alec had sacrificed for his happiness, he was feeling tremendously guilty. He, too, was eager to change the subject.

"Do not kiss me," he warned sardonically.

Alec laughed heartily as the bright midday sun swallowed them up.

☙

OLPHAMPA ARRIVED AT St. Cloven three days later. Elegant Sula received Ivy as if she were her own flesh and blood, and even Peyton was blessed with a warm embrace. After a lengthy meal of fowl, mutton and boiled vegetables, the women retreated into a small solar to allow the men to converse.

Although Alec was perfectly willing to dance about with pleasantries before delving into the complex subject of his father, Ali was not. He rammed into the subject with the grace of a hurricane.

"I assume Lord Brian told you that he has disinherited Alec," he said in a low voice. "Has he reconsidered his stance? And what of Thia? Is she married to Warrington?"

Olphampa gazed steadily at the two men, drawing in a thoughtful breath. "As far as I know, he has not reconsidered his stance, although he has said very little on the subject. And as for Thia, she is not yet wed."

Alec looked surprised. "Why not?"

Olphampa poured himself more fruited water. "Brian pleaded for a 'grace period' by which to make arrangements, and also for the couple to become better acquainted. Thia and Colin have spent the time becoming accustomed to one another, although it is obvious that hostilities are growing," he eyed Alec hesitantly. "Alec, you know that I would never second-guess your father. He is a wise and generous man and I have known him the better part of my life. But this contract with the Warringtons.... even I cannot comprehend his reasoning. It's as if he is allowing Nigel to force him into compliance."

"I know," Alec said softly. "Ali and I were commenting on the very same thing. Would you have any idea why?"

Olphampa shook his head slowly. "Brian has not confided in me. But I see.... I see a fear in him when he looks at Nigel, an unholy horror. As if the man is a deadly threat."

Alec snorted, pouring himself more ale. "Warrington is not a threat. My father could snap the man's neck with two fingers."

Olphampa wagged a finger seriously. "Nay, Alec, not a physical threat. 'Tis more than that. A deeper, more devastating danger."

"What do you mean?" Alec asked, passing Ali a curious glance.

Olphampa sat back in his chair thoughtfully. His eyes were distant. "I do not know, Alec. I wish I did. Your father fears Nigel Warrington for reasons we may never know."

Alec rose, cup in hand. He pondered Olphampa's words, puzzled and worried. "Have you asked him?"

Olphampa shook his head, fingering his tunic. "Once. He avoided the subject as if I had asked him to pledge loyalty to the Devil. I never asked again."

Alec stopped his pacing and looked to the small black man. After a moment, he slammed his chalice to the table with a resounding clang. "I have had enough of this. Something is occurring and my father is lacking the simple courage to tell us. I have never known the man to have a cowardly day in his life until Nigel Warrington arrived," he jabbed his finger at Olphampa. "I am going to find out the reasoning behind this ungodly fear and do something about it. No man intimidates my father."

"And just what do you plan to do?" Ali asked quietly. "Call Nigel out in a duel? Burn down Wisseyham? Refuse him ale shipments? Think about what you are saying, Alec."

"I am," Alec snapped, his usual control loosened considerably. "I am thinking that Nigel Warrington has been too much of a problem and shall continue to be so until someone does something. He has harassed St. Cloven for years, he has been a party to rapes and unspeakable other crimes, and now he has my father whipped into submission for an unknown reason. I shall not tolerate his abhorrent presence any longer."

"What are you going to do?" Ali repeated his original question, eyebrows upraised intently. "Kill him?"

Alec paused a moment, turning to his ebony friends. His expression cooled considerably, like a man blessed with unquestionable confidence. "Hardly. I will not need to when I press Edward to confiscate Warrington lands and, in turn, annex the property to St. Cloven."

Ali and Olphampa looked at each other, surprised, before returning to their white-skinned companion. "Edward would confiscate all of England if you demanded it. You must be serious about this if you plan to contact our king."

"I am and I do," Alec said decisively. "I will not allow the Warringtons to destroy my family anymore than they already have. They must be neutralized."

"And thereby you hope to return to your father's good graces?" Olphampa asked softly.

Alec's confident stance wavered slightly and he lowered his gaze. "'Tis as good a start as any. Do you disagree?"

"Not at all. But you must do it before Thia weds Colin. If Edward confiscates the lands after they are wed, your sister will be in an even worse bind than she is already. She shall be the wife of a destitute," Olphampa stood on his short legs. "Were I you, young Alec, I would send a missive to London tonight and demand that Edward send word to Brian opposing the marriage between Colin and Thia. With the wedding postponed or dissolved, 'twill buy you time to petition Edward for the Warringtons' obscurity."

Alec nodded shortly and summoned a servant. As the woman went running for the brewery steward, he turned to his friends with regained confidence. "I do imagine Edward will be surprised to hear from me after all this time."

Ali smiled and returned to his ale. "His heart will probably stop from sheer shock."

"Christ, I hope not. I would hate to be indicted for murder."

Laughing at Alec's expense, Olphampa moved for the cedar-molded doorway that led from the great hall. "I must walk off your grand meal, Alec. Will you do me the honor of showing me your magnificent acquisition?"

The subject of Brian and the Warringtons faded as Alec took pleasure in displaying his new home.

☙

"HOW'S YOUR HEAD?" Ivy asked, smirking at her sister's discomfort.

"Awful," Peyton rasped, eyes closed as she slouched against the back of her chair.

Ivy laughed softly. "Jubil's willow potion is not helping?"

Peyton tore off the cold compress that she had been pressing to her forehead. "It tastes terrible and makes my stomach hurt. I have had this headache for four days and it has not gone away," she replaced the pack and sank even lower into the chair. "I think I am dying."

"Good," Ivy snorted, leafing through the book in her hand. "Now, shall I finish the story? Where was I?"

Peyton tossed the compress to the floor and stood up, weaving dizzily a moment. Ivy watched her with concern. "Now what?"

Peyton shook off her unbalance and moved for the door. "Nothing. I am going to paint for a while. Mayhap that will help my head."

Ivy's smile faded as her sister quit the room. Peyton wasn't feeling at all well; she hadn't been well for over a week. At least since she and Ali had returned to St. Cloven. The usually vital woman was sleeping longer and her fast temper was surely faster. Between the absence of appetite and the constant headaches, she had been a taxing companion. Alec, even though he had been very patient and sweet with her, had been preoccupied with his own problems and Ivy found herself with Peyton constantly, listening to the gripes.

Ivy returned to her book, puzzled with her sister's behavior and mystery illness. Even though she pretended otherwise, she was nonetheless concerned. She hoped Peyton's self-pitying prophesy wasn't unwittingly true.

Downstairs, Alec and Ali came in from the storehouse. Olphampa, sequestered in the solar with Sula playing a hearty game of backgammon, barely gave the two men a glance; he was terrified that his wife was close to becoming the victor. Alec and Ali grinned at the two latest residents of St. Cloven.

"If my father loses, he shall kill himself," Ali commented as they mounted the stairs.

"Your father takes his game playing too seriously," Alec replied. "Your mother is a highly skilled player; Christ, she can beat me."

Ali laughed softly as they reached the second floor. "Speaking of parentage, we haven't received a response from Edward as of yet and it has been six days. What do you suppose is keeping him?"

Alec shook his head. "I requested one hundred crown troops to reinforce my seventy-five. I expected to hear word on that particular solicitation, at least."

"Or a congratulations on your marriage. I cannot believe Edward would remain silent on that regard."

They reached the small ladies solar and were greeted by Ivy's blond head. Ali smiled at his wife as Alec's gaze perused the room. "Where's Peyton?"

"Fighting off a bad headache and a bad mood in her painting room," Ivy said, laying her book aside and focusing on her husband.

Alec nodded his thanks and quit the room in search of his wife.

Ali closed the door softly behind him, bolting it for good measure. Alone in the solar with his bride, there was no mistaking the seductive smile that spread across his face. Ivy matched his grin, reading his mind.

"Again, Ali? Now?"

The eager new husband nodded slowly, decisively. "Here and now."

ఆ

ALEC FOUND PEYTON seated in front of her easel, stroking the parchment delicately with a horsehair brush. Shades of yellow and black graced the vellum, so skillfully blended they appeared real. Alec stood behind her in silent appreciation for a moment, admiring his wife's talent.

"Sunflowers," he murmured. "'Twill be pleasurable to gaze upon during winter's bleak days."

"It's for your mother," Peyton said softly, expertly dabbing at her palette. "I thought she might enjoy them."

He put his hands on her shoulders, unnaturally large against her petite frame. He gazed at the flowers a moment. "She loves sunflowers."

Peyton worked on the shading, blending a mustard yellow into the paler yellow. "I know. She told me so."

His gaze lingered on the flowers a moment longer before he bent over and kissed the top of her head, releasing her shoulders to gain himself a stool. "How are you feeling today? Ivy says your headache has not retreated."

"It hasn't," she said. He noticed that she was particularly pale. "In fact, I do believe it is getting worse."

He touched her leg sympathetically, watching her as she worked on her painting. "Why do you not rest, then? The sunflowers will wait."

She snorted. "All I have done is sleep. I have never been so tired in my entire life."

"Do you suppose I should summon a physic? Mayhap you have caught an illness."

She shook her head, rinsing off her brush. "I shall be fine."

He stood up and shoved the stool aside. "I would feel better if you'd allow me to summon a physic. You are so pale, love, and you have hardly eaten in a week."

She dried her brush and rose, weaving slightly as her head swam. Alec reached out to steady her, concern etching his handsome features. When the swaying passed, he gathered her into his arms despite her weak protests.

"No more of this foolishness, Peyton. You haven't been feeling well for days."

She tried to squirm out of his arms as he swept her into the corridor. "I am fine, Alec. Put me down!"

He ignored her, instead, taking her to their chamber. Once inside, he set her carefully on her feet. "Get into bed. I am going to send Ali for the physic this instant."

She cocked an eyebrow at him, planting her bottom on the edge of the bed. She was fully preparing to stubbornly refute his assessment of the situation, but instead, she shrugged faintly. "I am not sick."

He rested his hands on his hips. "I beg to differ, madam. I have ignored your symptoms until this day, but I will not disregard them any longer. You will see a physic this day."

Peyton opened her mouth to argue. Suddenly, their bower door opened with a groan and Jubil stood in the archway, appearing somewhat stronger since her bout with the monkshade, but pale nonetheless. Alec frowned at the woman.

"Jubil, you will not enter our chamber without knocking."

Jubil stepped into the room. "I heard voices and knew that you and Peyton were not compromised. You do not usually talk through your lovemaking," she looked to her niece. "The child is announcing himself, is he not? You are ashen, sweetheart."

Peyton's eyes widened and Alec suddenly looked as if he'd been struck. The color drained from his cheeks and he looked to his wife, remembering Jubil's strange words not two weeks earlier. *Your seed has taken root.* Nearly choking on his tongue, he began to weave and his wife reached out a hand to guide him to the bed.

"Sit down, Alec, before you fall," she said, eyeing him anxiously. "Are you well, darling?"

He could only stare at her. "Me? Christ, Peyton, is Jubil speaking the truth?"

Guiltily, she eyed her aunt. "I.... I believe so. My menses are overdue."

"Two and a half weeks overdue!" Jubil announced. "I told you when we arrived at St. Cloven that your seed had found its mark, my lord. Did you not believe me?"

Alec was pallid, his sky-blue eyes like saucers. "I must confess, I did not. But.... Christ, Peyton, is this why you have not been feeling well?"

She sighed heavily, leaning against his arm as if her strength had suddenly fled. She should have been thrilled, but she was frankly too weary to muster the energy. "Aye. There's simply no other explanation."

Alec touched her head reverently, still reeling with the news. He was torn between berating her for failing to tell him the moment she suspected and complete, utter elation. The elation won over.

"A son?" he put his hands on her face, forcing her to look at him. "I am to have a son?"

She smiled wanly at his excitement. "Come late spring or early summer."

He couldn't speak. Lacking the words to express his surprise and joy, he clutched her against him with such powerful tenderness that Peyton's throat constricted with sobs. As tired and miserable as she was feeling in recent days, they were always close to the surface.

But Alec's unspoken demonstration of joy undid her. As she sobbed softly in his arms, Jubil continued to stand beside the bed and observe the touching scene.

"She carries the next Summerlin heir," she said softly. "Her safety is more important now than ever."

Alec glanced at the aged aunt. "What do you mean? She is in no danger."

Jubil looked particularly pale and drawn, and she pulled her shawl about her tightly. "There is a storm approaching. I can smell it."

She had spoken the same words a few days earlier when she had come forth from her trance. His expression was impassive. "So you have said, but you have failed to clarify yourself. Be more specific and I shall consider your advice."

Jubil seemed to falter a moment. She averted her gaze, moving to sit beside her weeping niece. Alec's eyes watched the woman intently. When she finally spoke, it was in a strangely quiet voice.

"I can smell a betrayal, murmurs of treachery upon the fall winds. An enemy where you least expect it."

"Who would do this? And, more importantly, why?"

"Why does one man betray another? For money, lands, revenge. All of these things are powerful motivators," Jubil touched Peyton's back comfortingly as her niece quieted. "All I can tell you is that this betrayal, this danger, will threaten your soul far more than your brother's death did. You must be alert, or you could lose your wife as well as your unborn son."

Alec unconsciously tensed as Peyton's weeping ceased. "Warrington?"

Jubil shook her head faintly. "I wish I knew. I can only tell you what I taste, or hear, or what the shades of the winds tell me. I cannot foretell the future as an exacting art, Alec. I can only warn you of what approaches."

In Alec's arms, Peyton wiped her eyes and twisted about so she could see her aunt. "Who told you of his brother, Jubil?"

Jubil smiled gently. "He did, sweetheart."

Alec's face was calm. "I never told you of Peter, Jubil. Someone else must have."

Jubil shook her head faintly. "You did not tell me in words, my lord. But there is a hollowness in your soul that reflects in your eyes. Only since you have met Peyton has the hollowness filled."

Alec stared at the woman a moment. Was she so perceptive, or had she merely heard the rumors? He wondered. Inevitably, his curiosity and sense of desperation got the better of him and he found himself focusing on another subject of more concern. If she were indeed so astute, then mayhap…. "My father hasn't been the same since this betrothal madness with Nigel Warrington. Can you…. sense anything?"

Jubil gazed at Alec steadily, pausing but a moment to collect her thoughts. As she spoke, she looked away from him. "I can sense nothing but turmoil within the House of Summerlin. Your father is greatly disturbed and it cloaks Blackstone like an evil fog."

In spite of his doubts, Alec found himself listening closely to her. Christ, he was so puzzled by his father's behavior that he was willing to listen to anyone for their insight. Even his wife's crazy aunt, who was so far proving to be less insane and far more wise.

"But why?"

Jubil shrugged, studying her hands. "I do not know, but I can only tell you what I have heard long ago."

Alec forgot all about Peyton's pregnancy for the moment. His attention was riveted to Jubil de Fluornoy. "What?"

Jubil felt his gaze and she rose from the bed as if it were too much for her to bear. "I have lived at St. Cloven all of my life, my lord. My brother Albert and I were the only children of Clive and Maeve. When I was young, I remember hearing my parents speak of a rumor regarding Sir William Summerlin, your grandsire. 'Twould seem that Sir William had fallen in love with a woman other than his wife and it was rumored that the suspect woman was Anne Warrington. Nigel's mother."

Alec did not say anything for a moment. "I have heard the same rumor, but I did not hear who the woman was. My grandsire had a wandering eye, so I was told."

"I do not believe that to be the case, Alec. Your grandsire was devoted to your grandmother as much as he could be, but she was a sickly woman with a heart of ice. Anne Warrington was a beautiful, vivacious woman married to a beast. Mayhap it was inevitable that dashing William and lovely Anne should find comfort in one another's arms."

Alec gently released his wife and rose, scratching his scalp thoughtfully. He peered at Jubil. "Do you suppose Nigel is blackmailing my father with that rumor? Threatening to spread more lies and gossip to damage the Summerlin honor?"

Jubil moved to sit by Peyton, refusing to look at Alec. "'Tis possible. But it is more possible that he threatens to bring forth an even darker secret."

"And what would that be?"

Jubil looked at him, then. Her faded blue eyes were as steady and hard as Alec had ever seen them. "That Nigel Warrington is your father's half-brother."

Alec's controlled facade vanished. He couldn't speak for a moment as Jubil's words pounded him. "You have heard this?" he managed to rasp.

Jubil could see his horror and nodded faintly. "I have. But it was a fleeting rumor, passed on by the servants. Most likely, it is a figment of ignorant imaginations."

Alec continued to stare at her in shock, finally putting a hand over his mouth as if to forcibly shut it. He turned away, pacing across the scrubbed floor aimlessly.

Peyton and Jubil watched him closely as his boots shuffled toward the window with absent echoes. He stopped a moment, contemplating the world beyond the lancet window before returning to his wife's aunt.

"Is it possible that Nigel has threatened to make this knowledge known?" he asked softly. "'Twould explain my father's severe change of character."

"As possible as anything," Jubil replied. "There is one way to find out; you must ask him."

Alec shook his head, turning away from the window. "He'd probably run me through. My father is so damn concerned with family honor and reputation that he'd explode if I even suggested such a thing."

"Then ask the black man," Jubil suggested softly. "He has known your father for many years. Mayhap he can help you. I can only tell you what I have heard."

Alec rubbed his chin thoughtfully. "I shall do that," his shock somewhat recovered, his soft gaze fell upon his wife. "I am sorry to have dampened your news with my preoccupation, love. I did not mean to suggest it was any less important."

Peyton rose stiffly, moving to embrace his slim waist. "You did nothing of the kind. Besides, I am not completely sure yet."

Jubil bolted to her feet and put her warm palm on Peyton's flat belly. "Have no doubt, sweetheart. You will continue the Summerlin line."

Peyton gave her aunt an impatient look but Alec merely laughed softly. "I choose to believe you, Aunt Jubil. My wife is refusing to face facts."

Peyton sighed heavily, leaning against her husband. "Mayhap so, but I cannot ignore my pounding head. I think I shall sleep until sup."

He kissed her sweetly. "I shall bring you sup personally and feed you every bite."

She grinned and he kissed her again. He would have surely liked to have stayed with her to celebrate their happy news but, due to her headache, he doubted she would have enjoyed the "celebration" as much as he would have. Furthermore, she most definitely would not have slept.

His gaze lingered on her a moment and he could not recall ever having loved anything as much as he had grown to love his wife. Not even Peter. She was his all, the center of his world, and he loathed himself for being too frightened to tell her.

She had told him once that she would never love him. And he had informed her that he did not require her love. That knowledge alone, words spoken during a turbulent phase in their relationship, was enough to keep him from voicing his feelings. He simply couldn't bear the rejection.

Bidding his wife a tender good-sleep, he escorted Jubil from their chamber as his mind refocused on the greatest paradox he had ever faced. His body and soul screamed to rejoice over the coming babe, but his mind was preoccupied with the possibility that his father was being blackmailed by dark family secrets.

True or not, he was horrified all the same and set out to find Olphampa.

Alec made it to the foyer before Toby came running in from the bailey, his fair face flushed with excitement. He did not afford his brother the chance to speak.

"Edward approaches!" he announced.

Alec's eyes widened. "What?"

Toby nodded his head like a wagging dog. "We have spied his dragon banner. There must be four hundred men approaching!"

"Christ," Alec hissed. "Where's Ali?"

Toby shook his head negatively as Olphampa and Sula exited form the solar, their black eyes round with surprise. Alec looked to Ali's parents.

"Olphampa, you will accompany me to greet our king," he ordered swiftly. "Toby, find Ali and send him to me. Sula, please help my wife prepare for our royal guests, if you would."

Urgency filled the air as everyone rushed to do Alec's bidding. Alec and Olphampa moved into the bailey of St. Cloven and Alec glanced about, wondering how in the hell he was going to house four hundred men.

"The king did not send word of his arrival?" Olphampa asked.

"Nay," Alec growled. "Christ, I am going to kill him. He is doing this simply to anger me. He likes to see me upset."

A corner of Olphampa's mouth tugged. "Why would he do this?"

"Because he likes to annoy me," Alec said accusingly, moving to mount the ladder to the narrow battlements. "He has always taken pleasure in seeing me riled because I show so little emotion."

Olphampa waited below as Alec scanned the road. Suspicions as to the true identity of the approaching party were swiftly quelled when Alec spat a curse and descended the ladder without benefit of the rungs. Gripping the vertical posts, he simply slid to the ground. Ali, with Toby on his heels, raced up.

"Edward is coming?" Ali asked, stunned.

"Edward is damn well here," Alec informed him, taking a deep breath to calm himself.

Ali grinned in spite of his surprise. "He did this simply to annoy you. No wonder we have not heard from him, Alec; he was already on his way."

Alec rolled his eyes knowingly as Olphampa chuckled softly. "Our king is very fond of you, Alec. If he has arrived without sending word ahead, then there must be a good reason."

"There is a good reason; he wants to irritate Alec." Ali suddenly let out a piercing whistle and several guards rushed toward him. He turned to the men swiftly. "Set up an honor guard of forty men just inside the gates. See to it, Hans, and be quick. Edward is upon us." He returned his attention to Alec. "We must make room for his horses, Alec. And what in the hell are we going to do with his excessive escort?"

Alec looked directly at Toby. "That will be my younger brother's responsibility. Toby, see to those problems as Ali and I take care of Edward."

Toby was off, pleased with the heavy responsibility and thinking that, mayhap, he had indeed proven his worth in the brief span of Ali's absence. Meanwhile, Alec had regained his careful control. He would not allow Edward the privilege of glimpsing his annoyance.

With a lingering glance at his manse, wondering how his wife was handling the unannounced arrival of the king, he returned his gaze to his companions.

"Gentlemen," he grinned, full of confidence and anticipation. "Shall we greet the king properly?"

Ali cocked a black eyebrow. "He would frown upon a barrage of arrows or a wall of flame, Alec."

Alec snorted. "I was planning no such greeting. Merely a friendly reception."

Ali laughed. "You may not slug him, either. Although Edward could easily take you on in a fight, I doubt he would take kindly to your display of irritation."

The corner of Alec's mouth dipped in a frown. "You have no faith in me, Ali."

Ali slanted his father a knowing glance. "I am speaking of a man who put dung in our king's bed."

"He did it to me first."

"But you were a new knight. 'Twas his right to humiliate you."

Olphampa shook his head. "Good King Longshanks is beyond practical jokes. I will hear no more of this treason."

A shout on the wall deterred them from their argument. Alec ordered the gates opened and found himself far more eager to see his old friend than he thought himself capable of.

Any contact between he and Edward over the past twelve years had resulted in uncomfortable pleadings for Alec to resume his knighthood. Now, with the wars in Wales augmenting, Alec would not be surprised if Edward again broached the subject.

In fact, he was sure of it.

CHAPTER FIFTEEN

"YOU WILL LOOK at me when I speak to you."

Thia was staring at the floor. When the subtle yet threatening words were spoken, she raised her head ever so slightly and fixed Colin with a heady glare.

He smiled thinly. "That's better. 'Tis better that we establish the rules before we are married, do you not agree? That way, there will be no room for error."

She ground her jaw. "What do you want? I have things to attend to."

"You mean women to chase," Colin cocked an eyebrow.

Thia's face mottled an ugly shade of red and she lowered her gaze in spite of his order. Colin's smile turned into a genuine gesture.

"Come now, Thia. You cannot believe that your secret was truly your own? You give little credit to the intelligence of those around you."

It was all Thia could do to keep from slapping the smug grin off his twisted lips. Deeply humiliated, her hands began to shake as she stared at the stone floor of her father's solar.

"You asked to meet with me privately. Say what you will and be done with it."

Colin observed the top of her dark blond head, her lovely hair the only beautiful feature on a woman who was otherwise quite homely looking. Arrogantly, he planted himself behind Brian's great desk as if he belonged there.

"Indeed," he folded his hands, examining the nails. "I have a proposition whose details will not leave the confines of this chamber. Do you understand this before we begin?"

Thia's head came up and she focused on him. "Nay. As you have pointed out, I am ignorant. Make yourself plain."

His eyes narrowed. "As I should have from the start. Thia, I am as displeased about this union as you are. I have made it no secret that I am marrying you simply as a duty and a difficult one at that. It's not you I want."

She wasn't following his reasoning. "As you have said. As you have all but shouted to the world. Please come to your point, if you can."

Colin did not deal well with disobedient women, and Thia had already proven over the past two weeks that she could push him into a rage. The wench was not only given to abnormal appetites, but she was mouthy and rude. And she was so strong she could have probably given him a good fight had their quarrels come to blows.

Brian and Nigel had spent a good deal of their time playing peacemaker between their children when they weren't battling each other. Within the past several days, Blackstone had become a bitter, uneasy place.

"I can indeed spell out my purpose, considering that is what it will take for your small mind to understand," he said cruelly, watching her jaw tick. "Lady Thia, you do not wish to marry me."

She cocked an eyebrow. "That is the first intelligent statement I have yet to hear you utter."

He forced a humorless smile. "That is because you have not been listening closely. 'Tis difficult to hear at all with your head buried between the legs of a wench," she did not flinch and he continued, somewhat perturbed that she had not reacted to his insult. "Considering that you do not approve of the proposed union, it would seem logical that you would do anything to be released from the obligation."

Caution gripped her. "Within reason."

His smile turned genuine. "Within reason," he repeated her words, mockingly, as he rose to stretch his long legs. Slowly, he paced toward the lancet window, pausing after a moment to face her. His eyes mirrored the evil within his soul. "You will help me destroy St. Cloven."

Thia's eyes widened. "What? I cannot…."

He held up a quieting finger, his voice loud enough to stop her protests. "I will relinquish my claim to you and you can frolic with the serving wenches happily for the rest of your life if you assist me in destroying St. Cloven."

Thia's face was white. Her first reaction was to condemn him, to deny him, but the prospect of finding a way out of the horrifying future her father had chosen for her was appealing. Too appealing. Gripping the arms of the chair with white-knuckled intensity, she eyed Colin warily.

"I will not destroy my brother."

"I did not ask you to. I merely asked for your assistance in destroying St. Cloven."

"St. Cloven is my brother's keep."

Colin fixed her with a look of such sinister proportions that it made her skin tingle. "It is only his property through his wife. I know you hold little love for Lady Peyton."

Thia relaxed somewhat, regaining a measure of composure. "She is a sly bitch and I hate her."

Colin sat on the edge of the desk, gazing down at her. "Enough to be rid of her?"

Thia's mind began to swirl, remembering the time when the very same thoughts had filled her mind. Good lord, she recalled plainly the very day in which she had sat in the grand hall listening to Nigel and her father tear at each other because of Alec and Peyton's marriage.

She recollected well the hatred she harbored for Peyton for causing such dissention by coercing Alec into marrying her. It was Peyton who had turned Blackstone into a battleground and the repercussions were still going on.

"Do you want her?"

Colin shrugged. "Not really. 'Tis the keep I want, but I have to be rid its mistress first. With his wife gone, your brother will most likely return to Blackstone and thereby leave the fortified manor vacant. My father will, in turn, petition for my supervision."

Thia sat back in her chair. "Why would Alec vacate the keep simply if his wife is no longer there? It's his keep now, not his wife's."

Colin gave her a condescending look. "Do you know nothing of the human character? 'Tis obvious your brother holds a good deal of affection for his wife and I would wager a great deal on the fact that he would not remain at the fortress simply because it would remind him of his dead wife at every turn. To be free of her memory, he would return to Blackstone to forget his grief."

Thia looked at him a moment. "It appears to me that there is more to this than merely being rid of Lady Peyton to obtain St. Cloven. I would venture that you are attempting to gain a measure of revenge against my brother for taking what you believe to be rightfully yours. That is your contention, is it not?"

"It is mine!" he suddenly spat. "It's always been mine and your brother had no right to take what was not his!"

Thia sighed, far calmer than she should have been. Clearly, she did not like the fact that she would be contributing to Alec's grief. She loved her big brother, but she was thoroughly convinced that he would be better off without the influence of his wife.

His grief would fade in time and he would marry again and forget all about the first wife who had alienated him from his family. Aye, he might even thank her someday for loving him enough to rid him of the red-headed leech.

It did not matter that Peyton had defended her against Colin's marriage demands. His brother's wife had led a strong opposition against Colin and, together, they had proved to be a most powerful force to reckon with. They had defended each other against the

Warrington bastard as if they had truly been sisters and in spite of her hatred, Thia had felt a strange bond with Peyton. The bond went beyond mere words or feelings. It cut deep. Peyton knew her secret.

Thia hated her for knowing her secret, a secret Colin was also privy to. Peyton had been presented with the opportunity to publicly admit Thia's private lusts, but she hadn't. Unlike Colin, she had tactfully kept silent.

She saw the opportunity to be free of her unwanted betrothal. That reality alone was enough to cause her to consider her priorities over Alec's. She did not want to be married to a man who took delight in humiliating her, who would force her to submit to his will in the bedchamber. That component in itself sent bolts of disgust racing up her spine; as reluctant as she was to harm Alec, she was selfishly thinking of her own needs. She almost did not care about her brother's feelings anymore, so long as she was free of Colin.

Her guilt was forgotten. But it was nonetheless difficult to spit out her agreement.

"What is it that you would have me do?"

Colin smiled, a genuine gesture. "Listen carefully."

Out in the hall, someone else was listening carefully, too. Paul Summerlin hovered near the door, listening to every word spoken. He knew he wasn't supposed to listen to the conversation of others; his parents had long chastised him for his bad habit. But it was part of his natural curiosity, an element of his pre-pubescent intelligence over which he had no control.

He had heard the words. Even with his limited capacity, he knew what Colin Warrington was suggesting was evil. And Thia was very bad for agreeing.

They were both very, very bad.

☙

EDWARD RODE INTO the bailey of St. Cloven grinning like a fool. Alec stood by, hands on hips, as King Edward I came to a halt aboard his gray destrier. Tall and lanky, his fair hair barely shadowed with gray at thirty-seven years of age, he dismounted his steed with grace. His gaze never left Alec's face.

In spite of his irritation, Alec couldn't help but grin. When Edward approached, he bowed deeply, only to find a hand thrust in his face. He took it.

"The Legend," Edward murmured appreciatively. "God's Blood, Alec, how long has it been?"

"Not long enough, Your Grace," Alec insulted his king softly. "I do not recall sending you an invitation to visit."

"Any missive from you is considered an invitation," Edward replied. "I came as soon as I could."

Alec cocked a blond eyebrow as Edward turned his attention to Ali. Long ago, the then Prince Edward had been one of the only men who had been able to see beyond the ebony skin, accepting Ali for his strength and fighting ability. He had come to appreciate the dark man's wit and intelligence and the fondness was still evident. "Ah, my black soldier. The years have been kind to you, Ali."

Ali bowed gracefully. "Thank you, Your Grace. 'Tis good to see you again. How is Queen Eleanor faring?"

"Well enough. She is expecting a child and unable to travel," he returned his focus to Alec. "And you. What's this that you have married without my permission?"

"Indeed, sire," Alec replied, his attention turning briefly to the ministers that had accompanied Edward. Men he had not seen in years who gazed back at him as if they were beholding God himself. A bit unnerved by the adoration, he returned his focus to the king. "My wife is inside, I am sure, having fits with your unannounced arrival. I shall leave you to soothe her irritation."

Edward snorted. "She is your wife, Alec. You calm the woman," his gaze traveled over the massive structure before him. "God's Blood. So this is St. Cloven."

Alec's proud gaze followed his king's. "The finest ale in all of England."

Edward nodded firmly, turning to Alec with a twinkle in his eye. "Does this mean I do not have to pay for my ale any longer?"

Alec cocked an eyebrow. "The price is double for you, sire."

Edward laughed heartily, clapping Alec on the shoulder. "I am weary, my friend. Let us retire to your hall and drink ourselves sick. We have much to discuss, you and I."

With a smile, Alec and the king crossed the bailey towards the expansive manse. Peyton and Ivy met them at the door, dipped low in a customary display of respect. It did not take a trained observer to note the quaking hands and quivering knees, indicative of their level of shock as the King of England entered their home. Had their faces not been parallel with the ground, their surprise would have been easily interpreted.

Edward eyed the two women but before he could demand to know which was Lady Summerlin, Alec reached out and pulled Peyton to her feet.

"Sire, may I introduce you to my wife, the Lady Peyton Summerlin."

Edward looked Peyton over from head to toe. Much to Alec's amusement, Peyton was as white as plaster and her eyes were so large with shock that he actually thought they might pop from the sockets and roll across the floor.

"A pleasure, Lady Summerlin," Edward said after a moment. "Alec has delightful taste in women."

Peyton nearly choked on her own tongue as the king took her hand. In lieu of a complete seizure, her cheeks suddenly flushed a dull red and she lowered her gaze. "Thank you, Your Grace. Welcome to St. Cloven."

The corner of Edward's lips twitched, noting her horror and Alec's mirth over his wife's pallor. "I am pleased that your husband was gracious enough to invite me to his home, considering I was excluded from the wedding," he cast Alec a long glance before allowing his gaze to rove the great foyer of the fortified manse. "I would greatly enjoy coming to see this grand ale empire for myself."

Peyton looked to her husband, who reached out and took her hand, gently, from Edward's grasp. "My wife and I would be delighted to escort you on a tour."

"Do you have to come?" Edward cocked a disappointed eyebrow.

Alec chuckled, tucking Peyton's hand into the crook of his elbow. "I am afraid so. My wife has a nasty temper and I fear for your safety."

Edward shook his head reprovingly at Alec, but Peyton was mortified at her husband's jest. Moving beyond the insult dealt to Lady Summerlin, the king turned his attention to the elaborate entryway and the strong smell of cedar. Alec was eager to show off his most prized possession, next to his wife.

As Alec took the king and his retainers on an in-depth tour of the bottom floor of St. Cloven, Peyton clung tightly to her husband, hardly daring to believe that the King of England was treading the floors of their beloved home. Ivy and Ali followed at a distance, as did the rest of Edward's retainers as Alec displayed his remarkable manse. Edward seemed intent on questioning Peyton, who was gradually overcoming her shock. Eventually, she took over the tour and presented a most charming, intelligent picture of the perfect chatelaine, as befitting The Legend's wife. Silently by her side, Alec couldn't remember ever being so proud.

A tour of the second floor inevitably brought them to her painting room. Suddenly very self-conscious, Peyton attempted to close the door and divert the king's attention, but he was not so easily duped. He had caught a glimpse of color, wonderful color, before Lady Summerlin had moved to shield his view. The tantalizing glance had been enough to intrigue him.

"What is this magnificent place?" he demanded softly, moving past Peyton and into the chamber.

"My painting room, Your Grace," Peyton replied as Alec came up behind her. He patted her shoulders gently as Edward milled about, studying the pieces of parchment with great interest.

"Did you paint these?" he asked seriously.

Before she could reply, Alec spoke. "An extraordinary talent, would not you say?"

Edward was scrutinizing a landscape scene. He raised his head to glance from the lancet window facing east, and then returned his focus to the vellum. He shook his head in wonder.

"Magnificent," he murmured. "You have captured the eastern horizon perfectly. The colors of sunrise are masterful."

Embarrassed for an entirely new reason, Peyton blushed faintly at his praise. Alec patted her shoulder proudly as if to confirm that his same observations had not been merely those of a loyal husband.

"Will you sell this to me?" Edward focused on her, almost demandingly. "I must have this. In fact, I see several paintings that I would like to purchase."

Peyton was stunned. She turned to Alec helplessly, unsure of how she should answer. Certainly, she was flattered, but there was tangible fear in having her personal paintings displayed at Windsor for all to see. Her paintings were her release, emotions captured from her soul. She did not want her soul displayed for public analysis.

Alec read her hesitation. "We can certainly discuss the possibility, sire, although I must say that I am uncertain as to whether I want my wife's talent exhibited publicly."

"God's Blood, why not?" Edward demanded, looking to the half-finished sunflowers. "Alec, if my wife had half the talent that your wife displays, I would exhibit her ability all over the damn country. How can you be so selfish?"

Alec gripped Peyton's hand gently. "For the simple reason that she is my wife and I do not wish to share her with all of England. And the paintings are a part of her."

Edward raised a disapproving eyebrow. "I choose to ignore you," he focused on Peyton, moving to take her hand. Gently, he tore it from Alec's grasp and tucked it firmly into the crook of his elbow. "You and I have much to discuss, Lady Summerlin. I should be mightily proud to have your paintings exhibited at Windsor. Mayhap we could add another legend to the House of Summerlin."

Peyton allowed the king to lead her from the chamber, turning to glance at Alec, Ivy and Ali as they brought up the rear.

"Another legend, sire?" she inquired politely.

"Indeed, my lady. The legend of your magnificent artwork," he gazed at her. "Haven't you heard of your husband's own legend?"

She nodded faintly. "A little. He is quite modest."

Edward laughed loudly as they reached the stairs. "Then he has changed a good deal."

ଓ

PEYTON SAT THROUGH a wonderful meal. Alec introduced her to the small group of men who had accompanied Edward; Anthony Bek, the king's secretary, Robert Burnell, his chancellor, and the Earl of Gloucester, Gilbert de Clare. Peyton was overwhelmed once again to be in the presence of such powerful men, but she soon calmed with their easy manner. In fact, as awed as she was of them, they seemed even more impressed with Alec.

The earl was determined to occupy all of Alec's time, grilling him endlessly on his life for the past twelve years. He appeared to be a nice enough man, but Peyton rapidly grew impatient at his attempts to monopolize Alec. Across from her, the king and his chancellor were focused on tasting a new ale Alec himself had devised a recipe for.

He had yet to come up with a name for the nearly-black liquid, but the general opinion seemed to be one of approval. Peyton hadn't tasted it yet; for the past week, any attempt to taste ale had led to gagging, which left Ivy, Ali and Alec in the delightful position as official tasters. She trusted Ivy far more than her male counterparts; if it was good enough to get drunk by, it met with their endorsement.

Olphampa and Sula had kept a discreet distance since Edward's arrival. Even though they sat at the same table with the king, they took seats at the far end and seemed more intent to serve than to enjoy the company. Ali had to continuously insist his parents sit and enjoy their meal, going so far as to become angry with his mother when she tried to pour him more ale. Ivy, playing the mediator, bade her husband to be silent and allow his parents to assist if they were more comfortable doing so.

The one person who had been conspicuously absent from the beginning had been Jubil. Peyton and Ivy had been too caught up in the king's arrival to lay search for their aunt, and a servant had returned shortly after the meal had commenced to inform Peyton that Jubil was not in her rooms. Puzzled but unconcerned, Peyton continued to enjoy the evening.

Until Jubil showed herself. One look at her aunt told Peyton that she was flying again and she cast a panicked glance at Alec as the woman entered the room. Jubil's face was slack, her eyes bright, as she made her way toward the table.

"Christ," Alec muttered, leaping to his feet.

Swiftly, he moved to intercept the older woman, who merely smiled at him dreamily. "Sweet, sweet Alec," she murmured. "Peyton's Alec."

Alec smiled weakly and turned the woman around. But not before Edward caught sight of her.

"A relative, Alec?" he asked casually.

Alec paused, Jubil clutched in his grip. "This is the Lady Jubil de Fluornoy, my wife's aunt. She is.... not feeling well."

Edward, half-drunk with fine ale, eyed her. "She appears well enough. Bid her join us."

Seated down from the king, Peyton shook her head faintly, fearfully. Alec caught her silent pleas.

"I am afraid not, sire. Lady Jubil should not exert herself."

Edward shrugged, not particularly caring if the woman joined their meal or not. Thankfully, Alec quickly hustled the woman to the door.

"Do you know the story of the Trojan horse, Alec?" Jubil whispered.

"Aye," he said shortly, interested in returning the woman to her chamber.

Jubil was nearly dead weight in his arms, leaning against him. "Beware of Greeks bearing gifts. Beware of the threat from within."

Alec heard her words, but he wasn't listening. He half-carried her up the stairs, only to be met by Toby. The young knight, having recently returned from seeing to the king's troops, had just finished changing into a clean tunic to join the festivities.

But Alec had other plans for his brother. He thrust Jubil at him. "Take her. Return her to her chamber and post a guard. I do not want her near the dining hall in her condition."

Toby took the woman upon him and, as always, was awed by the woman's mysterious powers. He gazed at her, the delicate face and faded blue eyes, as she smiled up at him.

"Darling Toby. You love your brothers terribly, all but one. You hate him with a vengeance."

Toby's brow furrowed as Alec waved his hand at the two of them as if to resign Jubil to the care of the angels; he had no time or desire to deal with her. As his brother retreated down the stairs, Toby assisted Jubil back to her chamber. The older woman kept her empty gaze on him, making him nervous and curious at the same time.

"'Tis a terrible thing to be a bastard," Jubil whispered as Toby dumped her onto the mattress. "How fortunate that Lord Brian should accept you so."

Toby did not reply. He did not like to be reminded of his roots and he moved for the door, trying his best to ignore the woman who held such a peculiar fascination for him.

"Do you hate your natural father as well as his son?" she asked, her eyes half-lidded.

Toby stopped, his irritation rising. "I do not know my natural father. Go to sleep, my lady."

Jubil's eyebrows rose slightly. "Have you no clues as to who has fathered you?"

There was something in her voice that made Toby nervous. He

paused in the half-open door, eyeing Jubil as if she were about to spout forth curses damning him to eternal hell. His common sense told him to leave before it was too late, but the urge of a fatherless boy demanded to hear her through.

"What is it that you know?"

Jubil propped herself up on an elbow, her gaze clouded. "Have you never asked your mother, sweetheart?"

Toby shook his head, his only answer. Jubil smiled a drug-relaxed gesture and patted the bed beside her, motioning for him to sit. With the greatest hesitation, he did as he was asked.

"Your mother loves you," she said softly, running a finger up his broad arm seductively. "So does Lord Brian, in spite of your shaming circumstances. Look into your heart, sweet Toby. Do you truly have no clue as to who your natural father is?"

Toby gazed at her with veiled terror. Slowly, he shook his head. Jubil smiled faintly, her warm hand caressing his shoulder. "So strong. So young. So unlike your cursed family roots."

Toby felt the heat from her massaging hand like a roaring blaze. He wanted to pull away, but it was as if he lacked the strength. He could do naught but sit and stare at the woman. His mouth worked nervously as he tried to respond and when he spoke, it was forced and breathless.

"Who, Jubil? Damnation, tell me what you know!"

Jubil tore her gaze away from his powerful young body and fixed him in the eye. "Give me what I want and you shall have your answer."

His eyes widened as he realized what she meant. He swallowed hard, his gaze unsteadily raking over her body. Although she was old enough to be his mother, she did not lack for physical beauty and the prospect, strangely, did not disgust him. In fact, if he thought about it, his ideas had not been much different since the day they'd met. He'd always held an unusual interest for the sorceress.

His gaze returned to Jubil's pale blue orbs. Without a word, he began to remove his clothing. Jubil watched, biting her tongue between her teeth, as he stripped off his tunic to reveal a magnificently trim torso. Before he could move to his breeches, she leapt up from the bed with a cry of passion and sank her teeth deep into the flesh of his abdomen.

Toby grunted with the pain and surprise, knowing that the woman had drawn blood. His first reaction was to pull away from her, but the very moment his hands touched her silken blond hair he found himself pressing her face against his flesh. The harder he pressed, the harder she bit.

"Christ," he gasped, more aroused than he had ever been in his entire life.

Jubil grinned, pulling her mouth away from the swollen bite. Breathing heavily, Toby watched as she licked the wound, lapping up the pin-points of blood that her teeth had created.

Gazing into Toby's astonished, flushed face, her soft hands moved for his breeches.

"You will not forget tonight, sweet Toby," she rasped, freeing his thick manroot with a crow of delight.

"I expect I won't, Jubil," he replied raggedly.

One hand cupped his testicles reverently while the fingers of her other hand embedded themselves in the cleft between his buttocks. He grunted with fevered pleasure as her hot mouth closed over the crown of his manhood.

Toby was closer to dying from sheer ecstasy than he ever thought possible. Lust such as he had never known bolted though his big body with aching force, weakening him to the point of collapse.

"Christ!" he exclaimed in a harsh gasp, feeling himself peaking.

Her mouth still on his throbbing organ, Jubil smiled. "Nay, sweetheart, not Christ. You may call my Cybele."

☙

PAUL HAD BEEN waiting and waiting for Colin. He knew that Colin liked to take an afternoon ride, usually meeting one of the serving wenches in the stables beforehand. But today Colin was late and there was no wench waiting for him in the shadows of the livery. Paul stood by a huge pile of straw, waiting still.

Just when he thought he might have to seek Colin another time, a recognizable blond head caught his eye. Tall and muscular, Colin made his way toward the stable dressed in heavy leather garments. As he approached, Paul twitched nervously. He did not like the bad man.

Colin did not say a word to Paul, but passed him a curious glance as he headed for the stable. Paul, his palms sweating, dashed to intercept him.

"I would speak with you," Paul said quietly.

Colin stopped impatiently. "Speak to me? About what? What could you possibly have to say to me, simpleton?"

Paul did not react to the insult; his diminished capacity afforded him little feeling in the area of humiliation. Instead, he fought hard for much-needed bravery. "I heard you telling Thia that you wanted to hurt Lady Peyton."

Colin's eyes widened immediately. "You…." quickly, he glanced about. Grasping Paul by the sleeve, he yanked him into the dim recesses of the stable.

Paul jerked himself free of the iron grasp, stumbling over a stool and struggling to regain his footing. "I heard you. If you hurt Lady Peyton, I shall tell my father."

Colin's reactive instinct was to strike the man senseless, but he uneasily refrained. It would not do to strike his future brother-in-law and, someday, his liege. Swallowing his shock, he struggled to remain calm.

"I am not going to hurt her," he said evenly, moving toward the dense man. "I simply…. I want to surprise her, and I need Thia's help."

Paul shook his head hard, backing away. "That's not what you said. I heard you tell my sister that you wished to exact revenge."

Colin was advancing, slowly and steadily. "You misunderstood, Paul. I would not hurt your brother's wife."

Paul swallowed, back-stepping as the taller man stalked him. He knocked over a bucket, tripping over the handle and wildly kicking it away. He did not like the gleam in Colin's eye. "You said you were going to kill her and I won't let you. She is too lovely and…. and I like her. She is kind."

"You won't let me?" Colin raised his eyebrows. His footfalls were slow, deliberate. "And just how do you plan to stop me?"

Paul was unaware that he was backing himself into a dead end. Behind him, his father's massive charger was tethered in his stall because the animal had a tendency to bite at everything that moved. A black hood covered the horse from his ears to his nose, purposely blinding him to the grooms who tended him.

"I told you," he said in a thin voice, bumping into the wall of the stall as he continued to backtrack. "I am going to tell my father what you said."

"Why haven't you told him already?" Colin asked softly.

Paul swallowed hard; his terror was gaining a handle on his composure and he gasped when he nearly tripped over his own feet. Colin kept moving toward him and Paul was sure the man was going to strike him, or kick him, or worse. Beads of sweat began to form on his oily brow, realizing too late that confronting Colin Warrington with the information had not been a wise decision.

"Why?"

Paul's eyes were wide at the repeated question. "Because…. I wanted to exact your promise that you would not harm her. I thought I could convince you to leave her alone."

"You intended to blackmail me?" Colin cocked an eyebrow, a thin smile on his lips. "My, my, Paul. How grown-up of you to resort to blackmail."

Paul knew vaguely what blackmail meant and realized that, indeed, that was what he had meant to do. It wasn't until this moment that he realized there was a word for what he was trying to accomplish, and his bravery made a weak return.

"Then you had better promise that you will not harm Lady Peyton," he said firmly. "'Else I shall tell my father, and he shall be angry with you."

A few feet behind Paul, the warhorse began to quiver. Colin could see over Paul's shoulder that the horse smelled the men approaching. Silk-smooth nostrils flared and slender ears piqued, listening. The closer Paul drew unknowingly, the more excited the horse became.

A flash of evil crossed Colin's mind. It suddenly became clear how he could rid himself of the impending threat without taking the blame. His lips creased with a sinister expression.

"I promise, Paul," he said quietly, advancing still, maneuvering Paul towards the charger's stall. "I swear that I shall not harm Lady Peyton."

Paul's sweaty face washed with instant surprise. "Truly?"

Colin nodded slowly. "Truly."

Paul stopped his back-peddling a mere foot in front of the open stall, but Colin continued to advance. When he was nearly upon the simple man, he smiled benevolently. "You and I are to be brothers, are we not?"

Paul nodded eagerly. "We are. I should like another brother since Alec has left."

A degree of hatred rippled across Colin's face, but it was quickly gone. Instead, he held up his arms as if to hug the smaller man. "I will be a better sibling, I promise. Embrace me, brother."

Paul, eager and innocent and trusting, put up his arms. Instead of drawing him into his embrace, Colin planted his hands on Paul's shoulders. Instead of clasping him against his breast, he shoved as hard as he could.

Instead of living to a ripe old age, the heir to the House of Summerlin met his death beneath the hooves of a startled destrier. Colin watched and smiled, unconcerned with the splatters of blood that rained against the walls of the stall. When a massive hoof came down on the weak human skull, Colin turned away and leisurely strolled from the stable.

The heir was dead.

CHAPTER SIXTEEN

"ALEC, BEFORE WE go any further, I demand to know what this nonsense is regarding your sister's wedding," Edward demanded, already into his fourth tankard of St. Cloven hearty ale. "Why did I have to stop the wedding?"

Alec, beside Peyton, held his wife's hand tightly. "For several reason I should be happy to explain, Sire. But tell me; did you send word to my father instructing him to postpone the wedding immediately, as I asked?"

Edward belched loudly. "I did. I told him I wished to attend the ceremony and forbade him to commence until I was able to travel to Blackstone. However, I never indicated when, exactly, I would be available; therefore, I would assume plans are on hold indefinitely."

Alec sighed with relief, squeezing his wife's hand. "Thank you, Your Grace. I am grateful."

Edward grunted into his tankard. "I do not know why I should do this for you when you have never done a damn thing for me. You have repeatedly denied my requests to lead my army and I have no idea why I should leap up to grant you a favor."

Alec grinned faintly as Peyton leaned against his arm, her sapphire-blue eyes gazing at him adoringly. "Then you shall not like to hear what I have to say. Mayhap we should discuss it in the morning when you are sober, Sire. You never could hold your liquor."

Edward raised his eyebrows at the challenge. "Is that so? I shall have you know that I can drink you into your grave any day of the week, Summerlin. How dare you insult me."

"'Twas no insult, Sire, but a fact," Alec's grin broadened as he glanced at Anthony Bek's smirking face.

"Insult me no more," Edward commanded. "Tell me why it was necessary to postpone your sister's wedding."

Alec's smile froze, faded. "Because I will not allow her to wed Colin Warrington. The contract must be terminated because I plan to obliterate him."

Edward's jovial mood fled and he fixed Alec with a questioning gaze. "Is that so? Why, may I ask?"

Alec's face was emotionless. "Because the man and his father have been harassing my wife's family for the better part of thirty years. They have seen fit to raid the small village within the fiefdom, raping women and young girls, and murdering small children. Their mere presence on this earth is an abomination to the human race and I, for one, am anxious to be rid of them."

Edward was listening intently in spite of his drunken haze.

"This has gone on for thirty years? God's Blood, why haven't I heard of this Warrington clan?"

Peyton answered for her husband. "'Tis a large country, Your Grace. You cannot be expected to know of every feud and disagreement within her boundaries. The conflict between the Warringtons and the de Fluornoys began thirty years ago when my grandfather cleared several acres of forest in order to use the land for growing barley. It was neglected land until my father and grandfather sought to make use of it. When the Warringtons discovered that the de Fluornoys planned to make a profit from the land, they rose to dispute the boundaries between St. Cloven and Wisseyham Keep. Even though their records could not prove conclusively that the disputed lands were within their territory, unfortunately, St. Cloven could not prove that they held title, either."

Edward rubbed his chin thoughtfully. "So they took to harassment to force you to relinquish your claim?"

Peyton nodded. "Thirty years' worth, Your Grace."

The king let out a slow, weary sigh. Alec slanted Ali a gaze and silent words passed between the two. Edward was generous, but he was not foolish. More than likely, he would play his advantage and Alec cringed at the thought. Alec wanted something; so did the king. He knew, without a doubt, what proviso Edward's reply would contain.

"And if I grant your request, Alec, and arrest the Warringtons for crimes against England, do you intend to annex all of their lands?"

That had been Alec's original intention. But gazing into Ali's black eyes suddenly gave him an idea. "Nay, Sire. I would have Ali assume the fiefdom of Wisseyham. He would be an excellent lord and neighbor. Moreover, he is my brother-in-law and we would forge a powerful alliance."

Both Ali and Ivy looked shocked until Ivy turned to her husband with a hopeful grin. Edward watched them both, mulling over the possibilities. It did not take him long to come to a conclusion.

"Agreed," he said softly, turning to fix Alec in the eye.

"I will dissolve your sister's betrothal and arrest the Warringtons as you ask, but with one stipulation. That you return to my service and help me subdue Llewellyn ap Gruffydd."

Alec did not react, but Peyton's eyes widened. She did not dare look at her husband, surely knowing what his answer would be. After a moment, Alec smiled thinly.

"Ever shrewd, Edward. You stop the marriage between my sister and the Warrington bastard, turn their confiscated lands over to Ali, and in turn you wish for me to help you defeat the Welsh prince."

Edward, suddenly fully sober, cocked an eyebrow. All of the humor had fled from the conversation, the comfort and warmth. Abruptly, it was tense and uncomfortable, and no one dared to twitch a muscle as Alec and Edward stared at each other.

Currents of emotions played upon the warm, stale air, enveloping all present. Peyton felt the uncertainty and squeezed Alec's hand encouragingly, distressed when he did not respond to her gesture.

"You are fully aware of my vow," Alec said in a low voice.

Edward was the first to avert his gaze. "No one is more aware of it than I, Alec. But that was twelve years ago. Surely you have resigned yourself to Peter's death by now. You must go forward with your life," he suddenly slammed his tankard against the table. "I have waited twelve damn years to come to grips with your mistake and I refuse to wait any longer. You want something from me, Alec, and I want something from you. Will you do this for your king, or will you continue to live your life in self-pity? I have always believed you to be made of stronger character than that."

Peyton's eyes were wide enough to pop from her skull. She swallowed hard, her gaze moving between Edward and her husband. Alec, however, hadn't changed expression. He was still smiling faintly at his king, although it wasn't a humorous smile. Edward, irritated and full of alcohol, rose unsteadily to his feet and jabbed a long finger at Alec.

"You would expect me to do you a favor, yet you have no intention of reciprocating. God's Blood, Alec, I won't lift a finger to grant your requests unless you agree to help me. I need you, Alec. I need your sword!"

Alec's eyes glittered. "I will have to discuss this with my wife."

Edward turned from the table, throwing up his arms in a gesture of resignation. "By all means, Alec. Discuss it with your beautiful wife and let me hear of your answer. I shall not ask again. If you deny my request this time, then you can consider your ties to the throne cut. You will no longer exist to me."

Tears welled in Peyton's eyes. She refused to sit by while the drunken monarch humiliated her husband. She leapt to her feet before she could control herself, fully prepared to defend him against the king.

"You cannot speak to him in such a manner," she sobbed. "His father has disinherited him, his mother hates him, and still he is trying to do what is best for them by eliminating the Warringtons. How dare you threaten to destroy your friendship."

Alec reached up and grasped her by the arms. "Sit down, love. It's all right."

She whirled to him angrily. "Nay, it is not all right. You have given up everything and still the king threatens to take away more," she refocused on Edward, her sobbing lessened as she wiped the tears from her cheeks. "Wasn't Alec's strength and reputation enough for you in the Holy Land? My God, he killed his own brother trying to protect your approach to Acre. He has sacrificed everything in the name of the crown and still you have the gall to berate him as a weakling."

Edward stared at her as Alec gently pulled her to sit. He tried to comfort her, but she would not let him. She continued. "Sire, Alec has nothing left but St. Cloven and a bad-tempered wife. You have stripped him of his dignity by reaming him in front of his colleagues and peers, and now you would destroy your friendship? I do not know if I can respect a king who resorts to intimidation and threats to gain his wants. I thought you loved Alec."

Edward did not reply for a moment. His half-lidded gaze never left her. "My lady, your husband means more to me than you can possibly know. There is not a fighting man in England who has not heard of The Legend. What he has just heard from my lips is nothing he hasn't heard before; in fact, I believe I say something similar every time we meet. I have been threatening to disregard him for the past twelve years; obviously, I have no intention of following through on my warning. I am sorry to have upset you so."

Alec's smile returned as his gaze moved between Peyton and the king. His massive arm was around her shoulders, watching her expression as Edward explained his actions. He could see, however, that she was not entirely convinced and he kissed her tenderly on the cheek.

"Edward rants and raves habitually, sweetheart," he murmured. "'Tis nothing new."

Peyton sniffled loudly, lowering her gaze to wipe daintily at her dripping nose. As the realization of Edward's words settled, she calmed somewhat. But she was still grossly upset with the king for berating Alec for all to see.

"'Tis new to me, and I do not think I like it," she sniffed again, wiping the remainder of her tears away in a lady-like gesture. Her sapphire blue eyes found Edward once more. "I would appreciate it, Sire, if you would ream my husband outside of my presence. I shall not stand to see anyone browbeat Alec but me."

A flicker of a grin creased Edward's lips. "Understood, my lady," he cocked an eyebrow at Alec. "But my offer stands firm. Help me with Llewellyn and I shall rid you of the Warringtons."

Alec sighed deeply, thoughtfully. "I have not wielded a sword in twelve years. I would probably cut my head off."

It was the first time since Peter's death that Edward interpreted what he considered to be an affirmative consideration to his pleadings. A response he never actually thought to receive. His eyes widened and he actually gripped a chair for support. "God's Blood, Alec…. do you mean you will consider it?"

Alec thought a moment. Then, he looked to his wife's open expression. God, she was so beautiful, so intelligent. Fiercely protective of him. For twenty-one years, he and Peter had protected and defended each other. And then he had killed his brother. Cancerous guilt had been a part of his daily life since that fateful event.

Until he had met his wife. She absorbed the guilt, the pain, creating within him a healed wound that was stronger than the wings of angels. It took him a moment to realize that the guilt had left him the very moment he'd married her. Without the guilt, there was no longer any reason to maintain his vow.

For the first time in twelve years, he realized Peter's death was an accident. And for the first time in twelve years, he understood what had happened and why. He suddenly found himself missing the feel of a sword in his hand.

Peyton had done this for him. She had healed him. Christ, how he loved the woman.

"I shall consider it," he whispered, still gazing into Peyton's eyes. Her instant smile warmed him like a bolt from heaven.

Across the table, Ali dropped his head and said a swift, silent prayer of thanks. When he looked to Alec again, his smile lit up the room. Olphampa and Sula clutched each other thankfully, never believing they would live to see the day when Alec Summerlin would again bear a sword.

The joy that infiltrated the room moved from person to person, each lost to their own fantasies of The Legend returned to life. It was a miraculous moment for all to witness.

But Edward wasn't smiling like the rest of the group. He was still reeling with surprise. Anthony Bek rose slowly, the only occupant of the table seemingly immune to joyous shock.

"Twelve years of prayers have been answered, your grace," he said to Edward. "The Legend still lives."

As if realization suddenly dawned, Edward grinned. "Llewellyn doesn't stand a chance. With his brother David siding with me, he is already at a distinct disadvantage. But with The Legend leading my armies, Wales shall be mine. I can taste victory already."

Alec's gaze was even. "I merely said I would consider it. I haven't pledged my services yet."

Edward slapped at the chair happily. "God's Blood, Alec, you might as well have. A promise of consideration is as good as an agreement in my view," he passed a joyful glance at Anthony and Gilbert de Clare. "I knew this trip would be fruitful. Did I not say that before we left Windsor? Did I not tell you that The Legend would return?"

Gilbert nodded slowly. "Aye, Your Grace, you did. But Alec is correct; he has not yet consented. As he said, he must ask his wife."

All eyes suddenly riveted to Peyton and she felt the weighty stares as if she alone were to decide the fate of England. But her gaze, her adoration, shone only on Alec. She understood just how monumental his decision was and did not take it lightly.

"My lady?" Edward encouraged hopefully.

She smiled into Alec's eyes, reaching out to trace a finger over his smooth, sensuous lower lip. "'Tis his decision, your grace. I cannot make it for him. But if he chooses to resume his knighthood, my support is with him." *And my love.*

Across the table, Ali rose to his feet. "As I recount my oath of loyalty, as well. Where Alec goes, I go, be it at St. Cloven or the Welsh border."

Alec heard Ali's words, but he was far more caught up in Peyton's sensual touch and loving gaze. Her fingertips were caressing his cheek, his chin, and he nearly forgot about the question looming over their heads. Every man and woman in the room was waiting for an answer, as if the entire future of the civilized world depended upon it.

Though consumed with his wife, he was not senseless. His mind was working furiously, weighing the possibilities, the liabilities, and the entire situation. His reasoning came to bear and the answer he sought emerged, like the brilliance of the sun released from the shielding clouds.

Alec knew that his destiny was at hand. As Peyton's fingers moved over his lips, he kissed them sweetly and rose to his feet. Six and a half feet, two hundred forty pounds of English knight focused on his king. The power, the force radiating forth from the man, was beyond believing; as if, somehow, the man were myth and human combined. Strength bestowed by the gods filled his limbs, feeding credence to the reputation.

Time froze for a moment. Peyton felt it; they all did. The Legend was restored.

"I would be honored to return to your service, Sire," Alec said unwaveringly. "But I would prefer not to lead your armies at the moment and, considering Llewellyn is not an impending threat at the moment, I do not see that my presence in London is imperative. I should like to remain at St. Cloven until the birth of my son, and then I shall be more than happy to join your army at Windsor."

Edward had to sit down. Twelve years of pleading, begging and threats had finally come to an end and he was weak with the overwhelming knowledge.

"You cannot possibly know how glad I am to hear you say that, Alec," he said hoarsely. "God has answered my prayers."

Alec glanced down at his wife. "And mine."

The Legend had returned.

☙

"YOUR SON WILL not be born until April or May," cradled in Alec's naked embrace, Peyton was nearly asleep.

Alec's eyes were closed as well, the end result of a most strenuous love-making. "And I doubt Llewellyn will choose to revolt during the harsh winter months. By the time spring thaws the ground, my son will be in my arms and the Welsh prince will be planning his strategies. There is plenty of time yet."

She snuggled closer, smiling sleepily. "Edward was surprised, wasn't he? I thought he was going to swoon when you agreed to resume your knighthood."

Alec turned on his side, capturing her in a tight embrace in preparation for slumber. "Did you see Ali's face? I thought he was going to weep like a woman."

She sighed deeply, relishing his warmth. "I am so proud of you, my Alec."

He smiled into the darkness, yet in the same moment, a hint of uncertainly clawed at him, second-guessing his decision. But he knew, clearly, that he had made the correct choice. The doubts he felt were a natural part of a most enormous resolution.

Peyton's supple, nude body was pressed against him as close as she could go. His heat was lulling her into a delightful slumber as she felt his massive hands drift over the swell of her white buttocks. Surely there was nothing more wonderful than her husband's delicate touch, a gentleness she had experienced from the very first day he had held her in his arms. A power that filled her, a strength that possessed her soul.

A strength that would soon be leaving for a date with destiny. The Welsh border beckoned her husband and Peyton's eyes lurched opened with that thought. As delighted as she was with the resumption of his knighthood, the heavier emotions of longing and fear began to plague her. The longer she lay enveloped in his massive arms, the more potent they became.

"What will I do when you are gone, my Alec?" she whispered, clutched against his magnificent chest. "Who will be here to hold me?" *Who will be here to love me?*

She had told him once that she would never love him and he had acted indifferently to the suggestion. Now, more than ever, she wanted to declare her feelings, but knowing he cared not for her love prevented her from hazarding the venture. She would not tell him what he was unwilling to hear. But, Good Lord, how she ached with the want to tell him everything. Especially now.

Alec's held her tightly, staring off across the darkened room. "You will have my son to hold," he said after a moment. "Moreover, you are entirely selfish in your thinking. What am I going to do without you to quarrel with or make love to? I shall be entirely lonely."

"You will have Ali."

"Somehow, it's not the same."

She giggled. "Nor will it be for me. Your son and Ivy simply cannot fill the void."

He put his hand under her chin and lifted her eyes to meet his serious gaze. "Do you not want me to go? I will not leave if you do not want me to."

Her eyes widened. "Of course you must go! Never imagine for one moment that I do not want you to fight for Edward. I am so proud of you, my Alec. I never thought that you would lift a sword again."

He touched her cheek gently. "Nor did I. Since I have met you, I have done a great many things that I never thought to do."

She looked at him a moment. "Do you plan to tell your father of your decision?"

He averted his gaze, studying her hair, the sweet curve of her face. "Someday. Mayhap the same day I tell him of his grandson."

"You plan to wait that long? Truly, Alec, do you not think your father will want to know this most incredible turn of events?"

He shrugged faintly, his eyes on the swell of her breasts.

"He shall want to know. But I am not sure when I plan to tell him. Mayhap tomorrow. Mayhap in ten years. I simply do not know."

He was still aching with the estrangement and she did not push him. As much as he tried to pretend that she and St. Cloven were his life, she knew he was still hurting a great deal.

Seeking to lighten the dampening mood, she cocked an auburn eyebrow tauntingly. "Any regrets, my Alec?"

He looked entirely serious. "Christ, where to begin?"

She pinched him lightly and he laughed, pulling her close. As she burrowed against him in preparation for sleep, his smile faded. Any regrets? Only one. That he would be separated from her for an indeterminate amount of time when he joined Edward's cause. Already, he knew the isolation would drive him insane. Christ, he loved her so. He cursed himself yet again for being too weak to tell her.

Peyton had fallen asleep when sentries sounded the alarm from the battlements. With nearly four hundred crown soldiers housed within the grounds of the fortified manor, Alec was unconcerned as he carefully disengaged himself from his wife and went to the lancet window, peeling back the oiled cloth to gaze over the compound. Below, there was a heightened level of activity, but nothing that warranted panic. One of the gates had been opened and he could see a single horse and rider surrounded by his own elite guard in the center of the bailey.

Moving from the window, Alec donned his clothing and was in the process of pulling on his boots when a faint knock rattled his door.

Toby stood in the archway, half-dressed in a disheveled tunic, hose and boots. "A lone rider, Alec. From Blackstone."

Alec's eyebrows rose faintly. "Blackstone? Christ, what's he doing here at this time of night?" Suddenly, his face paled and his eyes widened. "Oh, Christ.... my father. Something has happened to my father."

Toby could read the panic in Alec's face and quickly sought to calm him. "The rider says that your father sent him, Alec. Nothing has happened to Lord Brian."

Alec visibly relaxed. "Thank God," giving his sleeping wife a final glance, he moved into the corridor and closed the door softly. He found himself passing a second glance at Toby's unkempt appearance, uncommon for the usually-polished knight. "What in the hell happened to you?"

Toby looked as if he did not understand his meaning. Then, he glanced down at himself and noticed faint blood spots staining the midsection of his tunic. He ran his finger over the area. "Oh.... I guess I cut myself."

Alec frowned and attempted to lift the garment. Toby protested weakly and tried to move away, but Alec was far superior in strength and ended up in a wrestling match with his younger brother.

"Damnation, Toby, hold still!" he snapped, shoving the man against the wall. "Let me see what you have done!"

"'Tis nothing, I tell you," Toby tried to yank the tunic free from Alec's grasp.

Alec put an elbow against Toby's chest to slow his struggles, knocking over a chair in the process. Perturbed, he grabbed Toby by the neck.

"Cease your wrestling, boy, or I shall bind you hand and foot," he snarled. "What in the hell do you not want me to see?"

A perfect set of teeth marks appeared in the weak light. Alec's very perplexed look met with Toby's guilty expression.

"What is this?"

Toby averted his gaze. "A bite. What does it look like?"

Alec's eyebrows rose and he refocused on the wound. "That's not merely a bite, Toby. Someone tried to have you for supper. Who did this?"

Irritated, Toby yanked from his brother's grip and straightened his tunic. "I am a grown man, Alec. What I do is my own business."

Alec folded his thick arms across his chest. "And I never said otherwise. You are not into peculiar sexual thrills, are you? I can tell you from experience that you might end up seriously injuring yourself."

Toby cocked an eyebrow at his brother. "You can tell me this as fact?"

Alec shrugged faintly. "I was young once and eager to sample anything remotely erotic."

Toby raised an eyebrow. "Does your wife know that?"

"She does not, and you will not mention it lest I castrate you the hard way," his gaze turned to that of genuine concern. "What happened?"

Toby absently touched his abdomen, moving his gaze to the floor. "I.... oh, hell. Jubil bit me."

Alec nearly keeled over with shock. His eyes widened and his arms uncross. "Jubil bit you?" he clapped a disbelieving hand to his forehead. "Christ, I do not want to know anymore," he turned away, pretending to storm down the hall when he suddenly whirled on his heel and was back in Toby's face. "Jubil bit you?"

Instead of cowering in fear of his brother's anger, Toby faced him openly. "She did. And other things."

Alec's mouth gaped open, and then promptly shut. Suddenly, his eyes twinkled. "Did you.... take her?"

"Several times."

Alec's mouth was open again, but there was a curve to the corners. "You.... several times? Christ, Toby, she is old enough to be your mother!"

Toby scratched his neck thoughtfully. "Your point being?"

Once again, his mouth closed and Alec blinked thoughtfully. "Nothing, I suppose," he said slowly. "Except.... I will not allow you to make a sport out of her. She is my wife's aunt and a respected member of the family. Do you comprehend me?"

"Indeed," Toby nodded. "And who says I intend to make a sport out of her? I.... well, I just might marry the woman."

Alec's shocked expression was back, greater than before.

"Marry her?" he repeated, then rolled his eyes as if unable to believe what he had heard. Grabbing his brother about the neck, he started down the corridor. "You and I must have a talk, Toby. You do not marry the first woman who pleasures you beyond reason. You may believe yourself in love with her simply because she has made you mindless with erotica but, believe me, that is not love."

Toby allowed his brother to lead him away. "I never said I was in love with her. What I do with her is my affair and there is nothing to say on the matter."

Alec cocked an eyebrow. "Aye, there is a good deal to discuss, but now is not the time. I have a messenger from Blackstone waiting for me and I shall not be distracted."

Toby did not say anything more, unable to decipher the confusion he was feeling and unwilling to discuss it further at the moment. Since the first instant he had beheld Jubil, he'd been in the grip of something powerful, something he had been unable to resist. Something he could not put into words and he was glad Alec had not pressed the subject. He wasn't sure exactly how to answer.

Alec released him from his grip when they hit the stairs and he silently, pensively followed his brother out into the courtyard.

The damp night air was filled with smoke from the torches as Alec approached the messenger. He recognized the man as one of his father's household soldiers, and the warrior saluted him smartly.

"Greetings, my lord," the soldier said formally. "I bring a message from your father, Baron Rothwell."

"My father is well?" Alec couldn't help himself from asking; he'd frightened himself with thoughts of his father's demise and wanted a bit of simple reassurance.

"Aye, my lord," the soldier replied, eyeing Alec hesitantly for the first time. "Would you prefer that I deliver the message in private?"

Alec almost demanded that the man spill his message immediately and be gone, but something in the soldier's expression made him pause. Without a word, he beckoned the man to follow.

Ali met him in the foyer, passing an eye over the familiar soldier. Alec led Ali, Toby and the soldier into the small solar and closed the door softly. As Toby lit an oil lamp, Alec faced off against the messenger from Blackstone.

"What is it?"

The messenger did not hesitate. "Your brother Paul was killed in an unfortunate mishap earlier this day. As the new heir to the barony of Rothwell, your father requests your presence at your brother's funeral the day after tomorrow."

Alec did not react for a moment, but Ali and Toby passed astonished glances. "How did Paul die?" Alec asked, his tone considerably more subdued.

"He was apparently attempting to ride your father's destrier and the horse trampled him, my lord," the soldier replied quietly. "Your sister's betrothed discovered the body in the stall."

"Warrington?" Alec's jaw suddenly developed a tick. He slanted Ali a disbelieving gaze before returning his attention to the soldier. "So my father requested my company at the funeral, did he?"

"Aye, my lord," the soldier nodded firmly. "And your mother sends her warmest regards to you and your lady wife."

Alec's gaze rested on the man a moment longer before turning away, moving pensively towards the wide oak desk that used to belong to Albert. Ali and Toby watched him closely as he digested the news, wondering if he were going to refuse outright to all questions posed.

When Alec reached the heavy piece of furniture, his focus trailed across the surface, lost in thought for the moment. Eventually, he sat heavily in the hide-covered chair behind the desk.

"You will return to Blackstone this night and inform my father that my wife and I will attend my brother's funeral as requested," he said quietly. "Be gone with you."

The soldier faltered a moment, expected to carry a much longer, far more emotional reply, but saluted sharply and spun on his heel. When the door closed behind him, Toby let out a sharp hiss.

"Paul hated horses!" he blurted. "There is no possibility that he would have been anywhere near Lord Brian's charger!"

Alec did not reply for a moment. "I am particularly interested in the fact that Colin Warrington discovered his body," slowly, he looked to his ebony friend. "Mere coincidence, mayhap?"

Ali shook his head decisively. "Paul was terrified of horses. I cannot ever recall seeing him in the vicinity of the stables," he lowered his muscular body onto the edge of the desk. "Something is very wrong here, my friend."

Alec drew in a deep sigh. "Wrong indeed. My brother is dead and his body is discovered by a man of sinister character."

Ali met Alec's gaze a long, contemplative moment, as if they could read one another's thoughts. "I wonder if Colin was the last person Paul saw on this earth. Is it possible they shared a conversation, an argument? Even if Colin actually killed Paul, strangulation or stabbing would have been obvious. The messenger said your father's charger killed your brother, which means there must have been no outward signs of murder."

"Unless Warrington beat him to death and put him in the stall to make it look as a mischance," Toby said in a low voice.

Alec sat back in his chair pensively. "Murdered by Warrington, who then conveniently places his body in the stall to make it appear as an accident," he drummed his fingertips against one another. "Assuming this presumption is true, the question remains; why did he kill Paul? Surely he did not consider my brother a threat."

"Not in the physical sense," Ali said. "Mayhap Paul saw something that he should not have. Or mayhap he did something extremely offensive."

"Offensive enough to kill?" Alec shook his head, the realization of his brother's death beginning to settle. "Paul was no more a threat than a mere child. I cannot imagine what he could have possibly done to warrant his own death."

Ali did not say anything; he, too, was beginning to feel the loss of Paul as the shock of the news wore in. "We attend the funeral in two days. Mayhap we shall come across our answers then," he rose from the desk and turned to face Alec. "You, however, have been handed a great inheritance this night. Congratulations."

Alec looked at him as if the thought had not yet occurred to him. "As I recall, my father disinherited me not three weeks ago. And now I am heir to Blackstone?" he shook his head. Then, he chuckled. "And my mother. Sending her warmest regards to me and my lady wife. It would seem that she has had ample time to regret her harsh words to us."

"She'd kiss your arse if it would appease you," Ali snickered. "Your mother has the fastest temper and the fastest mouth in all of England. She most likely regretted her slander the moment she issued it."

Alec smiled faintly, thinking on the estrangement that had infected him for weeks. Anger and concern for a father who was apparently a weakling, puzzlement over the entire Warrington situation. Was Paul's death another example of the power Nigel Warrington was presumably exercising over his father, over the entire House of Summerlin? As pleased as he should have been that his parents had apparently forgiven his actions, he was nonetheless deeply perplexed with the falling of events.

But one thing was certain; he had lost another brother and although he and Paul had not shared a companionable relationship, he was naturally grieved. But he could not dwell on the fact that his only remaining full-brother was deceased, not when there were far too many other anxieties occupying his attention.

Ali clapped him sympathetically on the shoulder, breaking him from his train of thought. Alec glanced up at his friend, who was focused on Toby. The young knight stood against the wall, his handsome face drawn with sorrow. "I am sorry for you as well, Toby. You and Paul spent a good deal of time together," Ali said softly.

"We used to fish sometimes," Toby said vaguely.

Ali wisely decided to leave the brothers to their own thoughts, giving Alec a final pat before moving towards the cedar door. His hand was barely to the latch when he heard Alec's voice behind him.

"Ask Toby about his love bite."

He thought he hadn't heard correctly. He turned to Alec curiously, wondering how a statement like that became mixed up in the grieving process. But Alec was looking at Toby, a dull twinkle in his sky-blue eyes.

"How inappropriate, Alec," Ali scolded quietly. "We are mourning your brother's loss and I consider your remark improper at best."

Alec sighed and stood his full height slowly, wearily. "Ali, you know that my brother and I were never close. Paul was more of a distant relative than a brother, and I shall mourn his loss as such. But nothing more. Were you or Toby to perish, then I would mourn your deaths for the rest of my life, as with Peter," he eyed his younger half-brother. "Since I do not feel like dwelling on my brother's death until there is something I can do about it, for my own sake I choose to lighten the mood. For Christ's sake, I am tired of grieving. Toby, show Ali your love bite."

Ali shook his head in resignation, knowing Alec's explanation to be correct. But he stopped short of concurring to alleviate the heady mood. "Do not show me, Toby. I do not care about it, nor do I wish to see it."

Alec cocked an eyebrow. "Jubil did it."

Ali's eyes flew open wide and he yanked up the young knight's tunic. "God's Blood! She did not merely bite you, man, she *ate* you!"

The bite was purple and swollen, and Toby flinched when Alec touched it. "She must be half-wolf," Alec remarked.

Ali's black eyes glittered with mirth. "I am curious to know what else she did to you."

Toby looked sheepish and Alec put his arms around his brother's wide shoulders. "I was quite astonished to realize my little brother is no better than the rest of us. I believe he needs our experienced advice."

Ali suddenly thrust himself forward, embracing Toby as one would a lover. "God's Blood, Toby, I never knew. I think I am in love with you."

Toby yanked himself free of the two taunting men. "Too late, Ali. You had your chance."

Alec and Ali were grinning mischievously, closing the gap between themselves and Toby, and backing the young man into the wall. "Jubil, is it?" Ali queried seductively. "I am surprised. Your tastes usually run to the petite young women from the village that comprises your admiring throng."

Toby groped for the door latch, opening the door to escape just as Alec slammed it shut.

"Do not leave yet," Alec purred. "You told me you might marry the woman. Well?"

Toby pursed his lips irritably. "I said might. *Might!*" he snatched at the door latch again and yanked it open, wedging himself in the archway when Alec tried to close it again. "And I think it's terrible that you should disregard Paul's death so easily. Instead of mourning properly for the man, you choose to taunt me instead."

Alec's expression softened somewhat. "Were I not teasing you, I would most likely be riding to Blackstone, determined to receive answers to our assumptions," he said quietly. "You as well as Ali know that I have spent the majority of the past twelve years grieving. No one grieves more deeply than I do. But I explained my reasons to Ali regarding my relationship to Paul and I shall not repeat them. I am, however, deeply distressed with the circumstances regarding his death. I suppose lightening the mood helps me deal with the overwhelming situation."

Somewhat appeased, Toby lowered his gaze uncertainly, rubbing at his bite. Alec, his humor fading, opened the door wide and put his hand on the young man's shoulder. "I think, mayhap, it would be best if you return to Blackstone immediately and comfort mother. The woman has lost two sons and I expect she would like to see her remaining sons as soon as possible."

Toby nodded, albeit hesitantly. His first reaction was to refuse for two reasons; firstly, he was becoming far too infatuated with Jubil and their blossoming relationship and was eager for another encounter, if for nothing more than to further explore the attraction between them. The sexual magnetism was obvious; it was the emotional aspect he was more concerned with. And secondly, mayhap more prevalently, she had yet to divulge the promised information of his heritage.

Upon reflection, he wondered if she truly held the key to his past. Mayhap she has simply hinted to the fact to obtain what she wanted from him which, in fact, turned out to be what he wanted from her as well. But he would do what was asked of him; family came first, and his raging emotions secondly. Perplexing as they were.

Ali moved past the brothers and into the foyer, feeling his fatigue and eager for sleep. "When do you wish to leave for Blackstone, Alec?" he asked as he reached the stairs.

Alec scratched his scalp, passing a glance to the lancet window facing the bailey. "Christ, there cannot be more than two hours until sunrise. I would like to leave by early afternoon."

Ali nodded shortly. "I shall inform my family. We will be ready."

Alec watched his dark friend mount the stairs, turning to Toby after a moment. "Are you well? You and Paul were fairly close."

"I am fine, truly. Just a bit shocked, I suppose," Toby moved for the stairs. "I shall change clothes and ride to Blackstone. Is there any message you wish me to deliver to Mother?"

Alec gazed at his fair-haired brother a moment. "Nay," he said softly. "I shall be seeing her soon enough."

Toby took the stairs and disappeared into the bowels of the upper story. Alec continued to stand in the doorway, his sky-blue eyes dark with speculative thought.

There was a murderer among them. He knew who it was, and he was determined to know why. The same bastards responsible for his father's cowardice were responsible for his brother's death, although he knew not how at the moment. And a separation that promised to dissolve his relationship with his parents was apparently on the mend. He knew without a doubt that Peyton was included in their merciful disregard.

He leaned his head wearily against the doorjamb, wondering how so much could happen all in the space of a day. Too much, too quickly, too violently.

It was enough to set his head to spinning.

Chapter Seventeen

THE MASSIVE BIRD of Prey standards were flapping in the cool breeze underneath the brilliant blue sky. As the party from St. Cloven drew closer, Alec drank in the sight of his black-stoned birthplace, a myriad of emotions filling him. Above his head, Edward's dragon standard flanked the length of the column. The king, beside Alec on his charcoal charger, was engaged in conversation with his secretary while Ali rode to the rear in full armor, silent and strong. The mood was somber, quiet.

Peyton, Ivy and Jubil rode in a wagon in the middle of the column, well protected by both Alec's and Edward's guard. Even though the day was bright and the temperature moderate, Peyton could not have been more miserable. Adding to her perpetual headache was the compounding discomfort of constant nausea, and traversing the bumpy roads of Cambridgeshire did nothing to ease her distress. In fact, dying would have been preferable.

But they were traveling for a reason, and a powerful one at that. Alec had woken her with the news of Paul's passing, almost adding as an afterthought that he was now heir to the Rothwell barony. Peyton had been torn between grief and delight as the tender moment between them rapidly turned heated, but the mood was cut short when she promptly vomited the contents of her stomach into the nearest basin. All thoughts of Blackstone were shoved aside as her misery returned and Alec had laughed softly with sympathy. She had thrown a shoe at him.

As he rode with the king, Alec kept glancing over his shoulder to his wife, lacking any color whatsoever as she swayed on the wagon seat in rhythm to the forward motion. Dressed in a luscious blue gown that matched her eyes, even her lips were ashen. He would have preferred to have ridden in the wagon to comfort her, but he thought it best that he ride with the king in a show of loyalty. They were a quarter of a mile from Blackstone when Ali rode up beside him, raising his visor at the sight of the mighty stone fortress.

"Do you think the Warringtons will still want to have me arrested for thievery?" he asked, although his eyes were twinkling. "I did, after all, steal Colin's intended."

Alec cocked an eyebrow. "It would never stand at trial because the contract between Ivy and Colin was purely verbal. Were your marriage common-law, I would be somewhat concerned. However, the two of you are legally wed and there is naught the bastards can do about it."

Ali laughed softly at the Warrington's expense. Sobering, he slanted Edward a glance, several feet away. "When is Edward planning on arresting them?"

Alec kept his eyes trained ahead on the approaching bastion. "We were discussing that very subject over the morning meal while you were still frolicking in bed with your wife. Edward plans to send men into the village of March where most of the Warrington crimes occurred for the purpose of obtaining sworn testimony. Even if one girl comes forward with her story, Edward swears it will be enough to arrest Nigel and Colin and confiscate their lands. Unfortunately, the discovery process will take time and until then, he will delay my sister's wedding indefinitely."

Satisfied, Ali's black eyes met with the looming sentinel of Blackstone thoughtfully. "What about your father? Do you still plan to confront him regarding Nigel's blackmail?"

Alec sighed heavily. "With Paul's death, I do not think now would be the correct time. My father has lost his heir and his grandson within the same month and is sure to be brittle. But we shall see what the situation warrants."

"To learn of your return to the knighthood and his unborn grandchild should ease his aching spirits," Ali said encouragingly. "I suggest you inform him as soon as possible. The man is in desperate want for a bit of good news."

Alec grunted his agreement, passing a glance at his wife. "All he will have to do is look at Peyton and see that she is pregnant. I have never seen anyone so ghostly pale."

Ali turned to look at the women in the wagon. "To compare her to Ivy is night and day. All my wife does is eat, eat, eat."

Alec looked sharply to his friend, who laughed heartily and nodded his head. "It would seem that our children are destined to grow up together, as we did."

A smile of pure pleasure creased Alec's lips. "I did not know! Peyton did not tell me!"

"That is because Peyton doesn't know," Ali said quietly, still grinning. "Ivy was only sure herself yesterday."

Alec reached out, shaking Ali's hand in a gesture of complete happiness and friendship. "Congratulations, my friend. God has been good to us both."

Ali's smile faded. "You know I never had much faith in God, or the church. Mayhap.... mayhap had I not experienced the disappointments, I would not have known the joy I feel now. I know without a doubt that God brought Ivy to me and now has blessed me with a child. It makes all of life's failures pale by comparison."

Alec sobered, too. "Why do you think I agreed to resume my vows? My bad-tempered, aggressive wife has accomplished a feat no other man or God has managed; she has healed me. I am whole again, Ali, no matter what comes. She shall always mean the world to me."

Ali watched his friend, the tenderness of his expression.

"You love her deeply."

Alec averted his gaze, wrestling with his inner feelings. How could he admit a love for someone who did not return the sentiments? He may have been deeply, completely in love with his wife, but he did not lack for self-protection. "She…. she is my world." It was as close to a confession as he could come.

As they drew closer to Blackstone, the sentries on the battlements sounded their approach and the great gates began to crank open. Crimson-clad guards poured from the opening, lining the bridge as the king and Alec approached.

Alec felt a sense of relief as the familiar bailey enveloped him. Somehow, he had imagined that it would have changed in his absence as if to disorient the errant son. He was pleased to see he had been wrong. As he dismounted his charger, his gaze suddenly fell on a wild vision of silk rushing from the castle.

"Alec!" Celine cried. "My God! You have come!"

Alec barely had time to stand before his mother was slamming into him, collapsing in a heap of frantic sobs. Ali rushed from his own mount, helping Alec support his hysterical mother.

"All is well, mother," Alec whispered gently, embracing the woman in his massive arms. "I have returned."

"My boy, my little boy," Celine sobbed. "I have missed you so."

One of Alec's men helped Peyton from the wagon. She approached cautiously, unsure if she should show herself to the frenzied woman. After their last exchange she was understandably wary, but her natural instincts wanted desperately to comfort the woman who had been so kind to her.

She came to a halt several feet away, her own eyes filled with tears for the woman's loss. Alec held his mother tenderly, nothing like the angered son who had left Blackstone those weeks ago. Peyton remembered that he had told her of his mother's habitual temper fits; quickly roused, quickly forgotten. Apparently, all was forgiven between mother and son and she was deeply grateful. She hoped the same mercy applied to her.

She did not have to wait long. In the midst of her turmoil, Celine caught a glimpse of blue satin from the corner of her eye and turned her full attention to the beautiful woman with the gorgeous red hair. Without hesitation, she opened her arms to her.

"Come here, Peyton dear," she said softly. "I have not seen you in weeks."

Tears on the surface, as they were these days, Peyton joined her mother-in-law in her weeping, thankful that their harsh words had been forgotten and sympathizing with her grief. Lady Celine had both arms around Peyton, squeezing her tightly, while Alec enfolded them both within his massive embrace. Ali discreetly stepped aside, moving to Ivy and Jubil several feet away.

"All will be well, Mother," Alec repeated, his lips against Peyton's head. "We have returned."

Celine released Peyton long enough to look her in the eye, her soft hands grasping the young face. "How dare you stay away so long," she whispered, wiping at her daughter-in-law's tears. "Not a word, nor a message. I should spank the both of you."

Peyton sniffled loudly, her eyes wide with confusion. "But... we thought...."

"We have been very busy, Mother," Alec interrupted. His mother's anger was forgotten so quickly that she probably couldn't truly remember their argument; she was most selective in her recollections. When Peyton looked at him, perplexed, he simply smiled tenderly. "We have been busy creating another heir for the House of Summerlin."

Lady Celine's eyes widened with understanding and she burst forth again in sobs, this time of joy. She threw her arms around Peyton, causing the woman to begin weeping anew. Alec smiled, a weary gesture, his relief evident.

Edward and his retainers were standing by respectfully, pretending to disregard the touching scene. Alec caught a glimpse of his king and immediately moved to pry his mother and wife apart.

"Mother, our good king has come to pay his respects," he turned

Celine in Edward's direction. "Kindly greet him and then you may return to strangling my wife."

Celine, composing herself as a proper lady would, shot her son a reproving look. "Another remark like that and you shall know the true meaning of strangulation," she moved towards Edward, the model of a perfect chatelaine. Her knees gave way in a practiced curtsy. "Welcome, Your Grace. Please forgive me my emotional display. I… 'tis only that…."

Edward cut her off gently. "No need to apologize, my lady. I quite understand."

She smiled as she came up from her bowed gesture. "We had no idea to expect you so soon, Your Grace."

Edward received her warmly. "Nor I, my lady. I was visiting your son when I heard of Paul's unfortunate accident. Please accept my sympathies."

Celine nodded graciously. "Thank you, Sire. If you would be so good as to come inside."

As his mother led Edward toward the castle, Alec was suddenly aware that his father had not come out to greet them. Or Toby, for that matter. Celine and the king were engaged in pleasant conversation and he would not interrupt to demand trivial answers. Instead, he turned to Ali.

"See to dismantling the caravan and then take the ladies inside," he grasped Peyton by the shoulders and kissed her tenderly on the forehead. "Go and rest, love. I shall seek you shortly."

"Where are you going?" she demanded.

He seemed preoccupied. "To find my father. And to make sure the Warringtons are corralled during Edward's visit."

He stormed off, jogging across the compound and entering the castle through a smaller door. Peyton watched him wistfully.

Ivy came up behind her as Ali went about disbanding the men. "So we have returned to the den of vipers," she said softly.

Peyton cocked an eyebrow. "The Summerlins are not vipers."

"I did not mean the Summerlins. I meant the Warringtons."

Peyton's gaze lingered on the black-stoned structure. "Alec will see that they do not bother us."

"What about his fat sister?" Ivy wanted to know. "She hates you, too. After that incident with the serving wench…."

Peyton glanced at her sister, recollecting that she had told her of the most distasteful event some weeks back. As always, she and Ivy had no secrets and she had sought reassurance that she had handled the situation correctly. She wanted to make sure that if Alec's sister was intent on maintaining their hateful relationship, it would not be because of something Peyton did, or did not do. At the time, she had handled the circumstance as she saw rightly. Ivy had agreed.

"I can only pray that she has gotten over it," she replied after a moment. "I should not like to be fighting her off at every turn."

Ivy cocked a severe eyebrow. "Do not forget, darling. I am with you now. She won't come within a foot of you."

Jubil sauntered up beside them, looking amazingly lovely. Her faded blond hair was attractively arranged and her gown was clean and pretty. Her eyes were remarkably clear for a woman who had been entranced only the night before.

But her expression was taut. Peyton observed her aunt curiously. "What's wrong, Jubil?"

Jubil shook her head faintly, her eyes never leaving the black castle. "Something is not right."

"What's not right?" Ivy asked.

Jubil pulled her shawl about her tightly as if to ward off a growing apprehension. "I smell a good deal of darkness. It's everywhere."

Ivy sighed sharply. "Are you flying again?"

Jubil shook her head firmly, much to their surprise. "Nay, little goats. Not today. What I smell can be sensed without the aid of a potent."

The two women turned their attention to the massive structure. "What kind of darkness, Jubil?"

When their aunt did not answer, they turned to her with concern. Jubil was riveted to the bastion; suddenly, she shuddered involuntarily and turned away.

"You have got to leave, Peyton," she whispered sharply. "You must demand that Alec return you to St. Cloven. 'Tis not safe for you here."

Peyton and Ivy passed curious glances. "Why?" Peyton demanded softly, feeling herself being unwillingly pulled into her aunt's anxiety.

Jubil inhaled deeply, her eyes closed as she attempted to regain some of her composure. But the talons of uneasiness refused to release her. Since the very moment they set foot inside the keep, she had been buffeted by the turbulent grasp of terror.

"Beware of the threat from within," she suddenly whispered, sounding very much like the crazed woman they had come to expect. However, the insanity was not drug-induced this time. It was real. "The threat, Peyton, the threat! You must leave!"

Peyton went to her aunt, wrapping a comforting arm about her shoulders. "There is no threat, Jubil. Alec will protect me."

Underneath her grasp, Jubil was shaking. She suddenly grabbed her niece by the arms, pushing her toward the gates. "Go, Peyton. Run home. Run home, sweetheart!"

Peyton tried to pull herself free of the insistent grasp.

"Stop pushing, Jubil. I am not going anywhere."

Ali, in the midst of disassembling Alec's elite guard, saw what was transpiring and left the duties to a senior sergeant. He came upon the two women quickly.

"What's amiss, ladies?" he asked.

Peyton was having difficulty dislodging her aunt's hand from her arm until Ali broke the grasp. "Jubil's exhausted. Can we retire now, Ali?"

He opened his mouth to reply when Jubil suddenly turned on him, sinking her nails into his mahogany flesh. "She must leave, Ali. 'Tis not safe for her here!"

She had drawn blood, but he did not flinch as he disengaged her claws. "She is safer with Alec than with God himself, Jubil. Come, let's get you inside."

Jubil was quivering terribly. Peyton and Ivy passed concerned glances, wondering if their aunt wasn't having a mental breakdown as a result of years of imbibing potions. With Ali firmly on one side and Ivy on the other, they began to move Jubil toward the castle.

Jubil did everything but drag her heels. She pleaded, she coaxed, and she threatened. Still, they refused to listen to her. Peyton's life was depending upon what she was able to sense and distress overwhelmed her when she realized they were not taking her seriously. The only person who ever remotely listened to her was nowhere to be found, and she began to beg to speak to Alec.

Still, they refused to listen. Peyton's life was in serious jeopardy and no one believed her.

No one.

Her sense of desperation consumed her.

By the time they reached the cool innards of Blackstone, Jubil had worked herself into such a state that the moment she smelled the damp must, she fainted dead away in Ali's arms.

ALEC HAD PRECEDED his mother and the king into Blackstone by several minutes, ample time to locate his father. Although his mother hadn't mentioned his father's mental state, a suspicion nagged at him, so much so that he had to find his father personally to quell his own apprehension.

His first destination was his father's solar. As he passed through the servant's corridor and into the grand hall, several familiar faces greeted him. The servants looked shocked and pleased to see Alec, but he brushed past them without acknowledgement. By the time he hit the foyer, he heard a familiar voice calling to him and paused in his serious quest. Toby was moving toward him from the kitchens.

"Where's my father?" Alec demanded. "Edward's here, for Christ's sake."

Toby appeared fatigued. "Upstairs, in his private sitting room," in his hand he carried a tray with bread and watered berry juice. "I was bringing this to him."

"What's the matter? Why did not he greet us?"

Toby sighed wearily. "Lord Brian has been drunk since Paul's body was discovered yesterday. Mother is beside herself dealing with your father's sorrow and Lady Rachel's grief."

Alec relaxed slightly, closing his eyes briefly in a sorrowful gesture. "Where are the Warringtons?"

"In your father's solar," Toby said quietly, passing a glance in the general direction. "Nigel acts as if he owns the damn place."

Alec expression turned menacing. "No longer," he growled. "I have had enough of this. Put down that tray and come with me. I may require your strength."

Toby followed his larger, stronger brother across the foyer. The two of them burst into the solar with the force of a gale storm, rattling the castle to its very foundation as they threw open the heavy oaken door.

Nigel was seated behind Brian's desk, leisurely sampling a fine bottle of wine. Near the lancet windows, Colin slanted the two intruders an intolerant glance.

"Do you not know how to knock, Summerlin?" he demanded.

Alec was closer to losing his temper than he had come in a long time. He moved into the room, his handsome face tight with fury and his gaze hot enough to burn. An unfortunate chair happened to be in his way; he destroyed the furniture with a kick, tossing the shattered remains aside and nearly taking off Toby's head in the process. His fury, his disgust, was palpable.

Nigel leapt to his feet. Even Colin's arrogant expression faded; he knew firsthand that Alec's strength could be devastating and had no desire to experience another round.

"What do you do, Alec?" Nigel demanded, giving the man a wide berth. "How dare you burst in here and…!"

"This is my father's solar, to be mine when I inherit the barony, and

I shall do anything I damn well please," his voice was like thunder. "I have had enough of your presence at Blackstone. You have all but destroyed my family and I shall not stand for it any longer. Whether you leave this place by casket or by horse, 'tis all the same to me. But I want you out."

Nigel stared at him. His face was pale, but his expression held. "Your father is the only one who can order us to leave. And he shall not do that, not until your sister weds my son."

A second chair met with Alec's furious fists in an obvious display of displeasure, sending both Colin and Nigel ducking for cover. "Your son will not wed my sister, foremostly because I refuse to allow her to marry a murderer. Tell me, Colin; what did Paul see or hear that caused you to take his life?"

Near the lancet windows of the small room, Colin's eyes widened at Alec's presumption. "You are mad, Summerlin!"

Alec clenched and unclenched his fists. "Not at all. You see, I know for a fact that Paul was terrified of horses. Never once have I seen him near the stables and considering you found the body, it would lead me to believe that perhaps you lured him there. Or placed him there after you killed him. What did he happen upon, Warrington? My patience wears thin."

"I did not kill him," Colin denied staunchly. "I was going for a ride when I happened to discover his body. I have no idea why he was in the stables."

"You are lying," Alec advanced on the man. "Shall I wring it from you?"

"You will not touch him!" Nigel threw himself in front of his son. "How dare you make threats!"

Alec raised a well-defined blond eyebrow. "I never threaten. As you can see, I fully intend to carry out a promise. Your son killed my brother and I will know why."

"Alec!" came a great booming voice.

The occupants of the room turned abruptly to see Brian standing in the solar's elaborate archway, his face pale and his body unkempt. Alec turned his full attention to his father, shocked at his appearance.

"Da?" he whispered. "You look terrible!"

Brian was beyond drunk; he was a living, breathing cask of liquor. He staggered in through the door, nearly tripping over his feet as he moved. Alec reached out to steady him, his face glazed with horror at his father's demeanor. Brian clutched his son, his drunken face washing with a desperate expression.

"My only living son," he murmured, touching Alec's cheek. "My heir. Alec, my beloved boy, you have returned. I did not think you would."

Alec was mortified, his carefully controlled facade crumbling. He managed a quivering smile as he attempted to guide his father to an unbroken chair. He knelt before Brian, his entire body awash with sorrow and remorse. All of the anger and confusion he had felt towards the man within the past several weeks was suddenly gone, the deep love he had always felt filling him tenfold.

"I am here, Da," he said softly, his throat tight with emotion. "I shall not leave you again. I swear it."

Brian stroked his son's face as if rememorizing the features, never wanting to let him go. Tears were in the great brown eyes.

"Paul is dead, Alec. Peter is dead. There is only you. You are all I have."

Alec swallowed hard, feeling as if his heart were being shredded by the force of his father's sorrow. He grabbed the man's hands, enfolding them within his own. It occurred to him that he'd never seen his father drunk. The man before him was not the same man he had known for thirty-two years. The change began to take place shortly after the arrival of the Warringtons, as he had always suspected. He realized that if any more changes were to take place within his father's troubled soul, it would kill him. The Warringtons would murder yet another Summerlin.

Refocused on his fury, he rose to his feet, still clutching his father's hands. The expression he turned on Nigel and Colin was deadly.

"What in the hell have you done to him?" he hissed.

Nigel gazed at Brian impassively. "He has done it to himself."

"Like hell!" Alec roared. Brian's hands fell from his grip and the man nearly tumbled from the chair with the sudden movement. In two long strides, Alec was upon the father and son Warrington. With one man in each massive hand, he slammed them both against the wall in macabre unison. Toby moved in to support his brother, but he could see quite clearly that Alec did not need his assistance. He could hold two grown men at bay easily.

"What have you done to him?" Alec repeated through clenched teeth. "You are killing him!"

Soft, indistinguishable voices suddenly came from the foyer and Toby bolted into action. Moving quickly for the open solar door, he slammed it shut just as Celine and Edward entered the keep. Alec waited until the voices faded before returning his attention to the men within his grasp. Nigel was struggling; Colin was not.

"Now," Alec growled, forcing himself to calm with the king in such close proximity; he did not want Edward to hear him lose control. "I will demand two answers from you. Colin, you will tell me why you killed my brother. And Nigel, you will tell me what it is that has my father acting like a gutless fool. I am waiting."

Colin was the first to speak. "Release us, Summerlin. We cannot supply you with answers we do not have."

Alec's grip on Colin's neck tightened and he fixed him with a pointed look. "You hold quite a few answers, my friend."

Colin opened his mouth to refute, but Alec slammed him against the wall so hard that he bit his tongue. Nigel yelped, genuine fear clutching at him. Alec was apparently intent on doing them great bodily harm while Brian sat like a simpleton. Nigel knew their only chance lay in the drunken baron.

"Tell your son to release us, Brian," Nigel said loudly, firmly. "Do you comprehend my meaning?"

Brian remained slumped like a dullard for several moments. Then, slowly, as Alec dealt Colin another heavy slam, Brian grasped what Nigel had inferred. It was enough to bring him to his feet.

"Release them, Alec," he said hoarsely.

Alec ignored his father, disregarding the blood that trickled from Colin's mouth as he reaffirmed his stance. "Well, Colin? Spill your guts before I do it for you."

"Alec!" Brian demanded, more forcefully. "I said release them!"

Alec remained focused on Colin. Then, slowly, he turned to his father. "Why?"

Brian looked confused. He put his hand against his desk to steady himself, all the while searching for a reasonable answer in his alcohol-soaked mind. Why?

"Because.... because I demand it," he said weakly. "I shall not allow you to bully our guests."

"Guests?" Alec repeated with disbelief. "They're goddamn vultures! If you weren't so drunk or so frightened, you'd be able to see that."

"Do not speak to me in that manner!" Brian boomed unsteadily. "You are still my son, Alec, and you will do as I say!"

Alec gazed at his father as if he were looking right through him. His features took on a curious look. "What is it about these jackals that has you running like a coward?"

Colin suddenly brought up his knee and caught Alec in the abdomen. Alec grunted with shock and pain, releasing his hold on the younger man but maintaining his grip on the father. Colin, not at all a weakling, caught Alec in the face with a sharp blow, snapping his head severely.

Head spinning, Alec released Nigel and cocked his arm, driving his fist into Colin's jaw. As the younger Warrington went flailing backward, Toby jumped into the melee and clobbered him with a blow to the back of the head.

Nigel was screaming murder as Brian, fighting for lucidity, attempted to prevent Alec and Toby from killing their nemesis. But his weak actions were in vain, for between the two large men, Colin was dangerously close to losing his life. The only reason preventing Alec from snapping his neck was the fact that he wanted answers to Paul's death.

The solar door suddenly flew open and Ali charged in, yanking Toby away from the chaos and fully intent upon aiding Alec as he plowed into Colin. He had heard the scuffling sounds upon entering the foyer with the ladies and his intuition told him Alec was in the midst of the struggle. As always, he would be at Alec's side whatever the situation and had nearly ripped the door from its hinges in his haste to reach his friend.

In the doorway, Peyton and Ivy stood in horror as Jubil struggled to recover from her recent fainting spell.

"Alec!" Peyton cried.

Barely aware of Ali's presence, Alec was fully cognizant of his wife's voice. His head came up sharply, focusing on her beloved features. Only when he read the terror on her face did he slow his actions.

Toby, his knuckles bloodied, pulled the women into the room. Closing the door softly, he bolted it this time. The chaos that had filled the small solar not a moment before was suddenly vanished, bringing about an eerie, heavy silence.

Peyton stared at Alec as if he had suddenly gone mad. Across the room, Nigel was twitching with fury and fright.

"I told you," he said to Brian. "I warned you!"

Brian did not respond, but Alec rose to his feet threateningly. "And I warned you. I am seeking answers, Nigel, and I fully intend to have them."

Nigel was ashen as he focused on Alec. "Is that what you seek, Legend? Answers? Very well, then. I shall give you what you seek."

Brian abruptly came alive, his face mottled with terror. "No! I forbid you! I have done everything you have asked, Nigel, everything! I forbid you to go back on your word!"

"I have given you no word," Nigel snarled, turning to Alec once more. "Answers, did you say? Gladly."

"No!" Brian roared pathetically, his hands gripping his hair as if to pull it from his scalp, his anguish a palpable entity. There was not a person in the room who was not visibly moved by the man's agony. His obvious terror.

Alec glanced at his father with great concern. "What is it, Da? What in the hell would upset you so?"

Ali, rising from his crouch over Colin's unconscious form, tried to push Brian into a chair. But Brian would not respond, instead, he seemed to be slipping deeper and deeper into horror. Peyton had been frozen with shock from the moment she had entered the room, but hearing Brian's pitiful bellow jolted her from her trance and she moved swiftly to comfort the man. He attempted to ignore her, too, but her firm, soothing voice eventually permeated the cloak of his panic.

Alec watched as Peyton and Ali lowered Brian into a chair. Only when his father was seated did he return his attention to Nigel.

"Tell me now or I shall rip your heart out." It was not a threat. It was a pledge.

Nigel was calming in spite of Alec's vow. With a gesture that could only be described as an arrogant shrug, he moved from his position against the wall, toward Alec.

"It is your father's fault that I am forced to divulge this information. Had he controlled you better, it would not have been necessary," he glanced at Brian, paled faced and blue lipped, before continuing. "You said you wanted answers. What precisely do you want to know?"

Alec was so tense he was literally quaking; over his shoulder, Brian emitted another piteous groan of denial. In a flash, Alec remembered his conversation with Jubil and prepared himself for the lies and rumors that would come spouting forth from Nigel's thin lips. Bracing himself.

"Why is my father so afraid of you?"

Nigel raised an eyebrow. "Most likely because I can destroy the House of Summerlin in one blow."

"How?"

"By divulging the fact that he and I are half-brothers. I am your uncle, Sir Alec. Your illegitimate uncle, the result of your grandsire's lust for my mother."

Alec's brow furrowed, unconcerned. "That will destroy the House of Summerlin? You will have to do better than that."

Nigel's smug expression faded. He had been positive Alec would fly into a frenzy as he digested that small measure of reality, but apparently, Alec was unfazed. In fact, he was beyond unfazed; he appeared undaunted by information that would have brought most men to the border of shock at the very least. But Alec Summerlin appeared… bored.

In a reversal of roles, Nigel found himself shocked as a result of Alec's calm acceptance. He was seized with the desire to damage the emotionless man, whatever it would take. As Colin began to come around, spitting teeth and blood, Nigel demanded satisfaction. The shock turned to madness. They would all pay.

"I would think that would be enough, but I see that I must disclose additional realities before you understand the gravity of the situation," he suddenly focused on Peyton. "Your betrothed was killed in Norwich over a year ago, was he not? By a spear tipped joust pole? I can tell you for a fact that it was not an accident. De Fortlage was well paid for his role as an assassin."

Alec could take a verbal attack on his family, the implied threats of infidelities and deeper behaviors. But he would not tolerate an assault on his wife. His thinly held control snapped and he growled, taking provocative steps towards Nigel when soft hands were suddenly gripping him. He stopped immediately as Peyton pressed her sweet body against him in order to halt his advance.

Peyton could feel Alec quivering beneath her hands. Truth was, she was shaking, too. Although she was reeling with shock, she would not allow Nigel to visibly upset her. Especially with Alec and Brian so volatile. When she was positive Alec had ceased any further forward movement, she turned to the older Warrington with a careful calm.

"I would assume, then, that you initiated the murder?" she asked steadily.

Nigel shrugged vaguely. "Poor knights are always in need of additional coinage. With Deveraux moldering in the ground, I was able to press Colin's suit for your hand. 'Tis only right that a de Fluornoy marry a Warrington and end the feud that has lasted for decades."

Peyton was nearly ill with what she was hearing, but she maintained her calm facade if only for Alec's sake. "Since your raids and harassment failed, you resorted to murdering an innocent man to seek vengeance on St. Cloven?"

Nigel snorted. "Deveraux wasn't an innocent, I assure you. The man has two bastards in King's Lynn, mayhap more. He never wanted you; 'twas St. Cloven he wanted. Feud or no feud, it's what I wanted, too. Even your husband, I would wager. Your keep is far more beautiful than you could ever be."

Peyton's knees weakened, but she fought it. As cruel as Nigel's words were, she wasn't overly astonished by them. She knew St. Cloven to be a prize; she'd always known. Nor was she shocked to hear of James' bastards; it wasn't an unusual occurrence, although she would have hoped he would have remained celibate out of respect for their betrothal. But the mention of his personal disregard for her feelings disturbed her.

It wasn't true! She and James had loved one another, once. It seemed like an eternity past. At least, she thought she had loved him. Whatever the feelings they shared, they had faded into the recesses of her mind and she refused to be become upset by Nigel's remarks. James was simply was no longer an issue. He hadn't been an issue since the day Alec had kissed her.

She felt Alec squeeze her shoulder comfortingly, bringing her back into the present. The only matter of import was her feelings for Alec. Whether or not he had married her simply to gain St. Cloven was not a concern. Although it may have been his initial reasons for marrying her, she knew they shared a very special bond between them – an unborn child. *And my love.*

She fixed Nigel with an unwavering gaze. "Then I would thank you for shaping my future, Nigel. Had you not killed James, I would have never loved Alec."

Alec's heart soared skyward on the wings of angels, scarcely believing what he had heard in the midst of their swirling hell. *She loved him!* Christ, he'd experienced so many emotions this day that he doubted one more would have been any different from the rest. But he was wrong; with the rainbow of emotions he had experienced, Peyton's declaration of love trumped everything. Christ, how he loved her.

He enfolded her in his arms, wishing he could tell her everything he was feeling. But Nigel Warrington's smug expression and his father's pants of grief prevented him from becoming too emotional. Instead, he forced himself to deal with the issue at hand, albeit with less conviction than before. It had almost been worth all of the agony and sorrow to hear his wife's confession.

"Is there anything else you wish to reveal?" he asked quietly, feeling the scale tipping in his favor. "Any other revelations to upset and shock us?"

Nigel's advantage was slipping. Two major disclosures had barely raised an eyebrow and he was struggling to maintain his edge. God's Blood, he had as much as admitted to a murder and the results had been worthless. He had to make Brian pay!

The entire room was focused on him; Brian, the black beast, all three de Fluornoy women, Alec, and Toby. His palms began to sweat with sheer panic until another, last ditch attempt demanded release.

....Toby!

"Just one more," he said, smiling thinly. "I understand Toby has never been told of his roots. Allow me to introduce myself, Sir Toby. I am your father, and the man you so recently thrashed is your half-brother. You, dear boy, are the result of a liaison between your mother and myself."

Toby's eyes widened, giving Nigel the reaction he had failed to procure from Alec or Peyton. He stumbled back, his eyes flying to Brian, silently demanding answers. But Brian refused to meet his gaze, and Toby knew without a doubt that Nigel spoke the truth.

Open-mouthed, he returned his focus to Nigel. "You? How… how… oh, God…."

Jubil had been huddling by the door with Ivy in stunned silence throughout the entire exchange. But when Nigel focused his venom on her sweet Toby, she thrust herself forward and clasped the young man protectively.

"Easy, sweetheart, easy," she whispered soothingly. Toby was ashen with shock as he turned to her, but she simply smiled. "It matters not. You are a noble Summerlin, not a Warrington. You have always been a Summerlin."

Toby stared at her, the pain of disbelief in his eyes. "Is…. is that what you were going to tell me?"

She maintained her smile, touching his face tenderly. "Would you have believed me?"

He shook his head unsteadily. "How did you know?"

Peyton and Ivy watched with astonishment as Jubil kissed him tenderly. The air between them, laced with shock though it might be, was charged with sexual tension.

"I have lived in this barony my entire life, sweetheart. Eventually, you hear everything there is to hear. Although you favor your mother greatly, you possess Nigel's eyes. Eyes of blue steel."

Toby rested his forehead against Jubil's. His face was transforming from shock, to pain, to fury as he came to grips with his roots. Jubil murmured soft words to him, easing his shock, forcing him to calm. But Nigel did not afford him the opportunity to complete the process.

"Satisfied, my son?" he mocked. Somewhat fortified by Toby's unguarded reaction, he turned to Alec. "And you, Legend. Are you satisfied? Do you have the answers you seek?"

Alec was gripping Peyton fiercely, knowing that as long as they held together, nothing in the world could harm them. Peyton had always made him strong, but knowing she loved him fed him with the power of the heavens. Toby was controlled in Jubil's embrace as Ali moved to his wife, drawing her against him. They were all whole, strong, and unbreakable.

He glanced over his shoulder to his father, still slumped in the chair. Their eyes met and Alec smiled weakly. Brian's bluish lips returned the gesture.

"Is that what you were afraid of?" he asked softly. "I am hardly bothered by it. You really should have told me yourself and saved Colin the beating."

Brian closed his eyes and two fat droplets pelted his pale cheeks. His huge hand batted weakly at the tears. Weakly, he nodded once.

"I would assume, then, that this was the reason why you changed your mind about the betrothals? Because Nigel threatened you with the release of dark secrets if you did not bend to his will?"

Again, Brian nodded. Alec's heart was breaking for the fear the man must have suffered. "All is well, Da," he whispered, returning his attention to Nigel confidently. "The House of Summerlin is still standing."

There was no mistaking the look of defeat on Nigel Warrington's face.

CHAPTER EIGHTEEN

NIGEL WAS UNDER house arrest for having confessed to arranging the murder of James Deveraux. Colin, recovering from a severe pounding at the hands of Alec and Toby, was confined to his rooms. Alec never did receive a straight answer from him regarding Paul's death, but he had not given up hope. There would be another time, another place.

Brian had recovered to the point where he was able to take sup with Edward and the rest of his family. Peyton's pregnancy was all he could speak of and he kissed his daughter-in-law affectionately with every opportunity, much to her delight. All of the quarreling, the animosity, the anger that had constituted their lives since the day Peyton and Alec had been introduced was gone. She was part of their family.

It was hard not to celebrate their joyous reunion when, in fact, the very reason for their visit was a funeral. Lady Rachel had not joined the meal, as was proper since she was in mourning, but Peyton could not help but think of the plain woman who had not only lost a child, but her husband as well. Even though she did not know Rachel beyond a mere acquaintance, her grief on the woman's behalf was nonetheless deep.

Pondering the subject of sisters-in-law, Peyton was fully aware that Thia had made herself scarce since their arrival. Brian and Celine were so excited about her pregnancy and the visit of the king that they had not mentioned their daughter and Peyton hadn't thought to ask. Not that she particularly cared, but she was curious all the same.

"Would you look at Jubil?" Ivy, on her left, elbowed her sister in the ribs. "She and Toby haven't taken their eyes off one another!"

Jolted from her thoughts, Peyton passed a casual glance at the older woman and her young knight. It was enough to set her to grinning. "I knew Toby was fascinated by her, but I had no idea he was interested in her," she whispered in reply. "Jubil is forty-two years old!"

"And Toby is twenty-three," an impish gleam suddenly appeared in Ivy's eye. "I wonder if they've…."

"No more," Peyton put her hand up sharply, distracting Alec from his conversation. She smiled sweetly at her husband until he returned to his attention to Edward. "Do not say anymore, Ivy. I cannot think of Jubil in those….terms."

Ivy giggled. Ali, diverted with his wife's snickers, broke off his conversation with Anthony Bek. As Ali and Ivy lost themselves in private conversation, Peyton sank back in her chair with a chalice of boiled fruit juice in her hand. She was far lighter of spirit than she had been in some time, immensely pleased that all had worked out to a joyful ending. Nigel and Colin were defeated, Thia was scarce, Alec was now heir of Blackstone, and everyone was happy.

She sighed contentedly and Alec squeezed her knee, still conversing with Edward. It was amazing how in-sync they were with one another; hearing only each other, sensing what others would miss. He knew she loved him and he had seemed pleased with her admission, and although he had not responded in the like, his soft gaze and tender touch told her what his lips could not seem to form.

On Edward's left, Brian was engaged in an intense conversation with his son and the king. Peyton watched the man a moment, his color and vigor seemingly returned. It occurred to her that, to her knowledge, her husband had not informed his father of his most monumental decision. After all, the man had a right to know, did he not?

Setting the chalice to the table, her lovely hands clutched her husband's massive arm as she politely invaded the men's conversation.

"My most humble apologies for interrupting, my Alec," she said softly, making sure she had Edward's and Brian's attention as well. When Alec smiled warmly at her, she returned the gesture. "Have you told your father of your future plans?"

A blond eyebrow raised and he seemed to falter slightly. "Nay, love, I have not had the opportunity as of yet."

"Goodness, Alec, you should have shouted it to the rafters the moment you entered Blackstone," she chided gently, fixing Edward with her sapphire gaze. "And you, Your Grace? You have not seen fit to inform Lord Brian of Alec's decision?"

Edward grinned at her. "Nay, my lady, I have not. That is Alec's privilege, although I am growing weary of waiting. I should like to declare my joy before I burst."

"Joy?" Brian repeated, looking between the three of them. "I do not understand. What could possibly be more joyful than a new grandson?"

Peyton and Edward looked to Alec. After a moment's pause, he smiled weakly and grasped his wife's hand. "I have agreed to help Edward subdue Llewellyn."

All of the color left Brian's face. His mouth opened with shock, his brown eyes wide. "You.... you are to resume your service?"

Alec's smile widened. "Edward demands that I lead his army or he shall throw me in irons," he could read his father's surprise and sought to explain his choice. "I have so much in this life – beautiful wife, a profitable keep, my family and friends. What happened with Peter was.... an accident. I have never believed that until now, but now that I fully understand my mistake there is no longer any reason to waste the talent God has given me. My one regret is that it has taken me twelve years to realize it."

Celine was listening. Seated next to Brian, it had not been difficult to hear her son's softly spoken confession. Immediately, her eyes swam with tears and she clutched Brian's hand tightly.

"My dear Alec," she murmured tightly. "We have prayed for as many years that you would recover from your grief. Our joy is beyond what mere words can express."

Brian was still staring at his son, but he had managed to close his startled mouth. "Are you serious, Alec? You have recanted your vow?"

"Aye," Alec nodded sincerely. "Are you pleased?"

Brian put a disbelieving hand to his head, wiping at the sweat as he attempted to compose his thoughts. "My God, Alec, I have waited twelve years to hear you say that. I.... I simply cannot believe it."

"Believe it," Peyton lay her head on Alec's arm affectionately. "The Legend has returned."

"Here, here!" Edward suddenly boomed, raising his chalice high. Immediately, the entire table was silent and goblets were raised in response. "The Legend lives!"

The table repeated the shouted salute, congratulating Alec and Peyton, Brian and Celine. Edward grinned as Alec accepted the tribute with a degree of modesty.

Only Brian seemed overcome with the news. Aye, he was joyful, but he was also remorseful. He had lived the past twelve years waiting to hear those uttered words but, suddenly, he was sorry to hear them for purely selfish reasons; Alec was his only remaining son. He couldn't help but wonder if his heir would meet death on the Welsh border at the hands of the rebelling prince.

He did not want Alec to die. He almost wished he had never agreed to resume his knighthood. But he kept his feelings to himself and tried to show a measure of happiness, for Alec's sake. Deep down, however, his heart ached for what the future might hold for the heir of Rothwell.

ꕥ

THE DOOR TO Colin's room swung open, spilling forth Thia. Colin eyed the woman as the door shut softly behind her.

"You summoned me?" Thia demanded.

"You took long enough. I take it you were in the grand hall, drinking yourself ill alongside our king?"

Thia cocked an eyebrow. "I was not. I have no use for Edward, and I have especially no use for the company he keeps."

"Your beloved sister-in-law?" Colin smirked. "What about your brother?"

A flash of pain crossed Thia's thick features. "He is busy with his wife at the moment. Mayhap I shall seek him later when he is alone. I have no desire to meet up with the bitch."

Colin snorted, wincing when the pain in his face bloomed with the action. Instantly, his mood was darker.

"Your brother did this to me," he growled. "All because of her. Do you realize that?"

"I do."

Colin's shadowed eyes glared daggers, slicing through Thia's flesh, bone, soul. She could nearly feel the physical pain, like the ache left where her brother's companionship used to be. All because of her.

Colin rose unsteadily. "I am, for all intent and purposes, a prisoner."

"There is but one guard on your door, a household guard. He did not say you were a captive."

Colin turned away thoughtfully. He paced the length of the small chamber, trying to ignore the ache of his head as he concentrated.

His father was a prisoner, most likely slated for execution in light of a murder confession. He himself was very nearly a captive, his future unclear. The grand plans that had been so carefully cultivated were spinning out of control, dissolving, as the Summerlins and the de Fluornoys triumphed once more. Whether the dispute be over unsettled lands or questionable parentage, 'twould seem that the Warringtons always ended as the losers.

He wasn't even sure if his betrothal to Thia was still viable. For that fact, he knew he needed to act quickly and decisively if he was going to accomplish the ultimate act of vengeance upon the Houses of Summerlin and de Fluornoy. Even if his father had failed, he himself would not.

He could devastate both families in one swift action, one swift death. The Warringtons would triumph in the end, as was their duty. But he had to act now.

He turned to Thia. "You will take me to the stables. Tell the guard that you are taking me downstairs to join the festivities; I care not the excuse used so long as he allows us to leave together."

"To help you escape? Why in the hell should I do that?"

Colin's jaw ticked as he crossed the floor towards her. "I shall not be escaping alone, foolish bitch. After you leave me in the stables, you shall return to the dining hall and lure your brother's wife to the stable yard. I shall take care of her from there."

Thia raised an eyebrow. "Abduct her? What about my brother?"

Colin thrust a finger at her. "That will rest on your shoulders, lady. You must convince your brother that you merely wish to speak to his wife on the pretense that you would end the hostilities between you. Being a loving brother, he shall trust you to a private conversation while he remains in the hall."

Thia swallowed, knowing surely that all trust would be destroyed between her and Alec should she deceive him in such a fashion. If trust was lost, then there would be no hope of regaining the relationship they once shared before the introduction of his hated wife.

For the first time, she began to reconsider her reasons for being rid of Peyton. Were they really valid enough to warrant something as potent as murder? Mayhap, with time, they could learn to tolerate....

"Well?" Colin broke into her thoughts roughly. "Do you understand what you are to do?"

She fixed him with an uncertain gaze. "And if I refuse? I could run straight to Alec with your plans, you know. He'd surely kill you."

The blue veins on Colin's temples throbbed. When he spoke, his tone was low and controlled. "If you do, I shall tell Alec that you were responsible for Paul's death. I shall tell him that I personally witnessed you push Paul under the chargers hooves, and out of fear that my testimony would not be believed, I kept silent."

Thia's eyes widened. "You would not dare! He would never believe you!"

"Are you willing to take the chance? With the animosity and brutality you have already displayed toward his wife, do you think Alec would believe you incapable of murder?"

Thia was beginning to quake with fear. "What do my actions towards his wife have to do with Paul's death?"

Colin crossed his arms smugly. "You tried to kill his wife because she discovered your 'secret'. What if Paul discovered the same mysteries, only did not have the fortune to escape your wrath? I could convince them of your barbarous act, Thia. Have no doubt."

Her mouth opened in outrage. "It's a bloody lie!"

Colin made a sweeping motion toward the door. "Take your chances, then. I invite you."

Thia was shaken to the core. Unfortunately, Colin made sense and she was torn between refusing to help him abduct Peyton and following through simply to avoid the embarrassment and controversy that was sure to arise as a result of his libelous blackmail.

She turned away from him, her mind and soul being ripped in two by her indecision. Thia was not evil; she was brash, aggressive and rude, but she was not a sinister character. The desperation resulting from an unwanted betrothal was sucking her deeper and deeper into a bottomless hole; the further she sank, the harder it was to climb free.

Aye, she wanted to be rid of Peyton. The fact had already been established. But her conscience was gaining the upper hand against her will to be done with her brother's wife, even as the force of self-preservation fought for control.

She did not want her secret to be known. As much as she regretted what she must do, she must preserve herself above all.

Thia was shaking when she turned to Colin once more. Her gaze was guarded. "I shall do as I agreed as long as you swear to me that there will be no marriage between us, and that you shall not leave a trace of my brother's wife. He shall never know my part in this."

Colin smiled faintly, thinking of simple Paul as he attempted to blackmail him with what he had overheard. He could easily kill Thia as well; but, somehow, he rather liked the fact that they would share a dark secret between them. It would make her far more receptive to his desires in the future, as she would hold the future baron's ear.

"That is the bargain," he said quietly, fixing her in the eye. "Now, my lady. You will get me out of here."

ଓ

PEYTON WAS SO drowsy she could barely keep her eyes open. Pulled against Alec's warm torso as he conversed with Edward and Brian, her head resting on his massive shoulder, it was all she could do to remain lucid. But she was losing the struggle; Alec's delicious heat combined with his deep, soothing voice had a hypnotic effect on her and she yawned more than once, trying desperately not to be rude. She did not realize that Celine was well aware of her plight.

Alec's mother rose from her chair and made her way to Alec and Peyton. A sharp nail tapped her son on the shoulder.

"You have been so busy chattering that you have failed to notice your wife's exhaustion," she chided softly. "Release her, Alec. I intend to put her to bed myself."

Appalled at his lack of consideration, he faced his wife full of concern. "Are you well, sweetheart? I did not mean to ignore you."

She smiled as Celine frowned. "You are a rude, insensitive man," his mother admonished. "I shall deal with you after I have settled your wife."

Peyton laughed softly. "Truly, my lady, Alec wasn't being rude in the least. I am more comfortable in his arms than anywhere else."

They smiled tenderly at each other as Celine practically lifted Peyton to her feet. "Come, dear. You belong in bed, resting."

"She shall not be resting after I join her," Alec mumbled into his cup.

Peyton giggled as Celine pinched her son on his rock-hard bicep. "Enough, Alec. I demand you leave your wife alone. You have done your duty; now allow her to complete hers unhindered."

He laughed then; a loud, obnoxious snort. "Duty, did you say? I would hardly call it a duty. And if you think I am going to leave my wife alone for the next eight months, you are out of your…."

Celine slapped him on the shoulder this time, interrupting the conclusion of his sentence. Ali, seating on the other side of his wife, heard the statement and chuckled heartily, lifting his tankard in agreement to Alec's assertion. The two men snickered and snorted as Celine grew more outraged.

"Louts, the both of you. I shall not have it," she had Peyton by the arm, pulling her away from the table. "Come along, Peyton dear. You must be positively ill with fatigue."

"Hold, Mother," Alec rumbled, setting his goblet to the table. Wiping his mouth, he rose to his full height and stepped around his chair. Peyton saw the look in his eye, having seen it many a time before. Always before he made love to her.

His smile broadened as he approached his wife. Peyton returned his smile, her heart thumping madly against her ribs as his massive arms encircled her slim torso. In spite of Lady Celine's pleas of control, Alec bent his wife over backward and kissed her so passionately that the entire room went mad with approval.

Alec heard the roar of favor, lost in the depths of Peyton's honeyed mouth. He could feel his mother slapping weakly at his arm, demanding he unhand his pregnant wife. But he ignored her, indulging himself in a kiss seldom used outside of the bedchamber. It was a farewell, an invitation, a promise until he joined her later.

He was grinning as he released her. Peyton, flushed and dazed, returned his gesture.

"God's Blood, Alec. No wonder the woman is pregnant," Edward quipped, joining the laughter at the table.

Celine spanked her son across his taut buttocks as she grasped Peyton once more, assisting the blushing woman from the room. Alec resumed his seat, his warm gaze lingering on the brilliant red head until the foyer beyond swallowed her.

Christ, how he loved her. Had his mother not been standing in such close proximity, he would have told her so. Well… mayhap.

… coward.

By the time Peyton and Celine reached the stairs, their arms were linked companionably and they were laughing softly at Alec's display. In truth, Celine wasn't appalled by the lack of control; she thought it wonderful that Alec had married a woman he was so entirely smitten with. Soft conversation bounced between them as they mounted the stairs.

"Mother?" came a soft voice from behind.

They both turned to see Thia standing at the base of the stairs, her heavy face amazingly calm. Peyton instinctively tensed as Lady Celine, well aware of the animosity between her daughter and Alec's wife, faced her daughter pleasantly.

"What is it, Thia dear?"

Thia swallowed hard in the first display of uncertainty Peyton had ever seen from her. She seemed subdued, repressed somehow.

"I was… was wondering if you would allow me a moment's privacy with Peyton," she said quietly. "I… I would like to speak with her."

Her question was entirely respectful and Peyton's natural defenses faltered slightly. She sounded utterly sincere and Peyton wanted desperately to believe that, mayhap, she was attempting to extend a measure of reconciliation.

Celine glanced at Peyton. "I do not think so, dear. Peyton is very tired and was just about to retire. Mayhap tomorrow would be a better time."

The Thia that gazed up at them looked nothing like the brash, belligerent woman Peyton had become acquainted with. Her expression was almost pleading.

"I was hoping to speak with her tonight," she said, clearing her throat loudly. "You see, Lady Peyton and I have not been on good terms since her arrival and I have had time to think…. I would like to speak with her for a few minutes, mother. Please? I shan't keep her overlong. Just time enough to say what I must."

Celine and Peyton exchanged glances. "Are you up to it, my lady?" Celine asked her gently.

Peyton wanted nothing more than to be at peace with all of Alec's family. She wasn't suspicious of Thia's motives in the least; if the woman was willing to talk out their differences, then she would stay up all night if that was what it would take. She was more than eager to forgive and forget their rocky beginning.

She smiled at Thia. "Of course. I would be delighted."

Celine smiled as well. She knew that the two women could mend their shortcomings and was thrilled that Thia was making a peace overture. She knew her daughter well enough to know that she was a reasonable, honorable person.

Or so she thought.

"Very well, Thia," she moved away from Peyton and descended the stairs. "I shall leave you ladies alone."

With a lingering smile, she turned for the dining hall until a call from Thia stopped her.

"Do not mention our talk to Alec, mother," she said with as much innocence as she could muster. She was terrified that somehow she would betray her true motives, still reeling with surprise to have come across Peyton without her husband tailing her. It would make what she had to do far easier. "He knows we haven't gotten along and I fear he shall try to interrupt us."

Celine did not hesitate. "I understand."

Peyton and Thia watched Celine disappear into the dining hall. When the woman was gone from view, they faced each other with a degree of uncertainty.

"Where would you like to go?" Peyton asked softly.

Thia cleared her throat again, nervously. Her palms were sweating profusely. "I… I thought someplace private. Like the stables."

"The stables?" Peyton repeated. "The solar is private. And closer."

"And someone can interrupt us, like my meddlesome brother. If he comes looking, I want him to search for awhile and allow us our time together."

Peyton grinned, slowly descending the stairs towards her sister-in-law. "He is meddlesome, isn't he? Pushy, too."

In spite of her nerves, Thia couldn't help but grin. "And arrogant. And loud."

Peyton laughed, feeling better than she had in weeks. She was absolutely positive that she and Thia would grow to be very chummy if they could only spend a few moments together, getting to know one another.

"And he has the manners of a goat. Do you know that he and Edward had a competition to see who could belch the loudest the very first night the king arrived at St. Cloven?"

This time, Thia laughed. "That's nothing. He and Ali and my father used to sit in front of the hearth on cold winter nights and attempt to out-fart each other. The solar would smell of rotting bodies for days afterward."

Peyton laughed uproariously, moving for the door that led to the bailey. "Disgusting. And your mother allowed this?"

Thia opened the door to allow Peyton to pass through. "Better. She would bolt the door from the outside and not let them out until morning. They very nearly suffocated."

Peyton convulsed with laughter the entire walk across the bailey. When they reached the nearly-deserted stable yard, Thia silently led her into the same bank of stalls where Alec had first made love to her. She entered the warm stable, reliving the sweetest of memories as Thia drew her deep inside.

"I hope you do not mind that I insisted on such privacy," she said quietly. "I thought it would be better this way."

"And you are correct. I agreed with everything you said about Alec. And more." She settled herself on a large bale of pressed hay.

Expectant silence filled the dim livery. Peyton gazed at her sister-in-law, waiting for the woman to begin speaking. But Thia seemed very ill at ease, not at all comfortable. Peyton took the silence for natural nervousness.

"I am glad you suggested that we talk," she said after a moment. "You and I have not exactly been on pleasant terms and I have always been sorry. Alec thinks so much of you."

Thia felt as if Peyton had driven a dagger into her heart. She wanted to curse and reject the woman in one breath and declare her apologies with the next. Her inner turmoil bubbled like a simmering cauldron, simply waiting for the heat to increase and induce an explosion. She was positive Peyton would be able to sense her treachery.

"He is my only living brother," she whispered lamely. "I think… I love him a great deal."

"As do I," Peyton agreed fervently. "Which is why I want things to be right between us, Thia. I do not want to live the rest of my life at odds with you."

"I know," Thia nodded, fidgeting with her skirt. "I… I suppose I was envious of you when you first came to Blackstone, because I could see the way Alec was looking at you and I thought mayhap he would forget about me. He has always been my dearest friend."

"I realize that. But you were so terribly hostile that I naturally reacted in the same manner simply to protect myself. I never meant for it to go as far as it did."

Thia cocked an eyebrow, much in the same fashion as her older brother did. "You mean when I nearly beat you senseless? I can honestly say that I wanted to kill you, Peyton. Mayhap I would have if Toby hadn't come along when he did."

Peyton wasn't uncomfortable with the declaration; she had suspected as much. "You fight fairly well. As it is, I have had ample practice against my own sister and was able to defend myself," when Thia cracked a thin smile, she continued. "I will be completely honest and tell you that I wasn't spying on you. I was looking for Alec and got lost. It was never my intention to invade your privacy."

Thia scratched her neck nervously, avoiding Peyton's gaze. She could barely speak on the subject that had been a part of her life for so many years. "No one knows. At least I thought no one knew," she met Peyton's gaze guiltily. "Did you ever tell Alec the real reason behind our fight?"

Peyton's smile faded. "No," she said without hesitation. So what if it was a lie. She could see that Thia was terrified of her brother discovering her true lifestyle and had no desire to damage their fragile peace. Later, Alec himself could explain to Thia that her choice in lovers made no difference to him.

Thia lowered her gaze, moving toward the stalls and drawing Peyton's attention away from the shadow lingering in the recesses. Colin had been with them since they had first entered the livery, but the longer they conversed, the more Thia was in favor of telling Peyton to run for her life. The violent internal struggle increased rapidly.

"Alec was betrothed once before," Thia said, diverting the subject in an attempt to mask her anxiety. "A very powerful family; the de Courtenays. But after he killed Peter and refused to bear arms, the family petitioned the church and had the contract dissolved. 'Twould seem that they did not want a coward in the family."

Peyton looked surprised. "He never told me."

Thia shrugged. "It was a long time ago."

Peyton examined her hands thoughtfully. "Was he… did he care for his betrothed?"

Thia pursed her lips, remembering. "I was only seven or eight years old at the time. As I recall, Lady Genisa de Courtenay was a very pretty girl who was mad about my brother, but he showed little interest in her. In fact, I have never known him to show much interest in a woman until he met you."

Peyton was fortified by the reassurance that Alec had never possessed feelings for another woman. Slowly, she rose from the bale of hay and wandered near the stable door, gazing out across the compound.

Behind her, the shadow moved closer. Thia saw Colin moving toward Peyton and was seized with panic; God, how she wanted to tell the woman to run! Colin made eye contact with her and she nearly swallowed her own tongue, biting off the scream that rose within her throat.

Run, Peyton, Run!

"Have you spoken with Alec since our arrival?" Peyton asked softly, unaware of the lurking danger behind her.

"Nay." *Run, Peyton, Run!*

Peyton smiled, gazing up at the three-quarter moon. "We are expecting a child late spring. He is convinced it is a boy. I think all men want boys. Personally, I think a girl would be a lot less trouble."

Dear God, Thia thought wildly. *She is pregnant*! How can I allow this to happen…? "The world would be a far better place without men in it," she stammered. "I am pleased to hear of your fortune."

Run, Peyton, Run!

Colin loomed closer. Thia saw with horror that he clutched a large club, or blade; she couldn't tell in the dim light. Terror swept her as she wondered if he was intent on killing the woman before her very eyes.

"I prefer to think of it as a gift from God," Peyton replied softly, feeling the soft autumn breeze caress her face. "With the expectation of the child, I would like to hope that Alec will completely recover his grief and his dignity. He has suffered so."

Thia closed her eyes tightly as the image of Colin passed before her. She knew, mayhap better than anyone, just how deeply her brother had suffered. He had agonized and died a thousand times over since Peter's death. She had to admit that Peyton had healed her brother tremendously, returning him to the man that had existed only in legend. If Alec were to lose the very reason for his existence, The Legend would die forever.

Her struggle ended as her conscience emerged the victor. She could remain silent no longer.

"Run, Peyton!" she suddenly screamed. "*Run*!"

Peyton started violently. She gave in to her first reaction, which was to turn questioningly to Thia. As her eyes beheld the rotund woman, she saw a shrouded figure raise an arm high into the air. There was something clutched in the dark hand, something she couldn't see. But in a sickening instant, the arm came down and Thia went crashing to the dusty, chaff-covered floor of the stable.

Peyton did not think. She whirled on her heel, fully preparing to run for her life. But she never had the chance; in a flash of searing pain and bone-jarring force, her world dimmed, danced, and finally vanished.

☙

BACK IN THE dining hall, Jubil suddenly let out a piercing cry and crumpled to the floor in the throes of agony.

CHAPTER NINETEEN

ALEC RETIRED TO his chamber well after midnight. The room was dark and he did not bother to light the taper. Silently removing his clothes, he eased himself into an empty bed.

"Peyton?" he reached for the flint and lit the candle. As the room came into view, he could see that he was quite alone.

Puzzled, he got out of bed and glanced about the room curiously, as if expecting Peyton to be huddled under a chair or in the wardrobe. Donning his hose and boots, he threw open the door.

The corridor was vacant, dimly lit by dying torches and smelling heavily of smoke. He stormed down the hall, turning the corner and coming to pause in front of the door to his mother's bower. He rapped loudly on the door until a perturbed figure opened the panel.

"This had better be important, Alec," she growled, smoothing at her mussed hair. Alec glanced over her head, seeing his father lying innocently in bed. Normally, he would have laughed himself ill. But at the moment, he was too preoccupied.

"You took Peyton to bed this eve," he said shortly. "She is not in our chamber."

Celine's eyes widened and she seemed to falter terribly. "She is not in your chamber?" she repeated weakly.

Alec cocked an eyebrow. "I have no time for this. Where's my wife, mother?"

Celine began to breathe rapidly and a white hand clutched her throat in confusion. "I…. I do not know," suddenly, her eyes filled with tears. "That was well over three hours ago!"

"I realize that. Do you know where she might be?"

Celine was seized with a budding horror. She had been reluctant to leave Peyton in Thia's company simply for the fact that the last time the women had met, they had managed to injure each other substantially. She had put her faith in Thia's sincere manners, mayhap too much faith. Mayhap she had believed only what she wished to believe, that Thia was intent on a reconciliation. Mayhap she had been wrong.

"I…. are you sure she is not in your chamber?" she asked feebly. Her hands were beginning to shake.

Alec cocked an eyebrow. "I am not an idiot, Mother. I think I would have seen my own wife within the confines of our bower."

Celine suddenly sobbed, a hand flying to her mouth. "I do not know where she is. Oh, Alec, something must be wrong!"

Alec sighed heavily; he hadn't meant to upset his mother with his harsh manner. He had no idea that the tears in Celine's eyes were the result of her guilt as his manner softened. "Nothing is wrong, I am sure. Return to bed, mother. I shall see if Ivy knows where she is. Mayhap she couldn't sleep and is simply walking about."

Celine watched her son turn down the hall. After the briefest hesitation, she called out to him.

"Alec?" she moved toward him timidly. "I lied to you, dear. I did not take your wife to bed as I said. I…. I left her with Thia."

"You *what*?" Alec roared. Even as Brian bound from the bed and made haste to his wife's side, Alec was descending on her with a fury neither parent had seen before. "How could you have left her with Thia when you know… oh, *Christ….*"

He spun on his heel, racing the length of the corridor and disappearing around the corner. Celine, her eyes spilling over with tears, yelled after him. "Thia wanted to apologize to her, Alec! I saw no harm in…," she suddenly clutched her husband. "Go after him, Brian. Rouse

Ali and Toby. If Thia has done something to Peyton, I fear..!"

Brian was already lumbering after his son as fast as he could go.

THIA WASN'T IN her chamber, either. Alec turned the entire fortress inside-out in search of his wife, never thinking to search the Warrington rooms. Edward, Toby, Ali, and the rest of the household joined in the search for the two women and Alec's panic was increasing by the moment. When they searched the wine cellar and still found nothing, he began to border on hysteria.

Ali remained his rock. Alec was virtually incapable of forming a rational idea beyond his thoughts of Peyton and it was Ali who organized the soldiers and sent them on a search of the grounds. Two hours before sunrise, several of Edward's guard came jogging into the grand hall where most of the searchers had congregated before proceeding on to other areas.

"My lord!" the sergeant called to Alec. "We have found one of the women in the stable and she is badly injured."

Alec nearly vomited from sheer nerves. "Which lady? What color is her hair?"

"Brown, my lord," the soldier said, breathing heavily as a result of his run. "One of your men has sent for the castle surgeon."

Alec thundered out of the room with the rest of the search party on his heels. Barreling across the bailey and into the stableyard, he did not slow his pace until he reached the indicated stable wing. The same stable where he had first made love to his wife.

At the end of the livery he could make out a few figures illuminated by an oil lamp. He stormed up on Pauly and several soldiers as they huddled over the still form of Thia.

Alec did not stop there; he shoved one of the soldiers aside and knelt beside his sister.

"Moppet," he whispered. "What happened? Where's Peyton?"

Thia twitched and moaned, rolling her eyes open. "Alec?"

In spite of his wildly surging nerves and shaking hands, he touched her head tenderly. "I am here, love. Where's Peyton?"

Thia closed her eyes and swallowed hard. Her entire head was sticky with blood and Alec wondered horrifically if his wife had had a hand in her injury. He simply wasn't thinking rationally.

"He…. he was going to kill her," she whispered. "I couldn't let him do it."

Alec clenched his teeth so hard that he bit his cheek. "Who, love? Where is she?"

She opened her eyes again, her expression dazed and open. Pauly waved a hand in the midst of her line of sight; her eyes refused to focus. He did it once more and still received no reaction. Passing a glance at Alec's ashen face, he moved toward his medicament bag.

"Answer me, Thia."

Thia swallowed again. "Where are you, Alec?"

Consuming grief and anguish clutched at him, claws of pain ripping his soul to pieces. Brian, his massive body quivering with the agony of his child's fate, knelt beside Alec and placed a hand on his daughter's bloodied head.

"Alec is here, darling, as am I," Brian murmured through his tears. "Where's Peyton?"

She closed her eyes wearily. "C….Colin was going to kill her. I tried to warn her."

Alec was visibly jolted. He rocked back on his heels and leapt to unsteady feet. Before he could issue commands, Ali was already in motion and within seconds, Toby and several soldiers were racing for the castle.

"Colin is under guard," Alec mumbled, like a man losing his mind.

Ali's gaze was full of concern. He'd never seen Alec come remotely close to an emotional breakdown and was deeply distress. Thia was dying, Peyton was missing, and Alec was on the brink of collapse. Edward, exhausted and unkempt, put his hand on Alec's shoulder.

"We will find her, Alec," he mumbled. "Have faith."

Alec did not have any faith left. Nor did he possess hope, or joy, or feeling of any kind. He was only able to feel a degree of grief he hadn't felt since the very moment he realized that he had killed his brother. Deeper, even.

Colin was gone. The soldier on guard informed them that Thia had escorted her betrothed to the grand dining hall earlier in the evening and, considering the man wasn't technically under house arrest, the soldier had no choice but to let him go. Thia had assured the man that Edward had requested Colin's company.

Alec was nearly overwhelmed with the growing clues that, mayhap, Thia had been a party in Peyton's disappearance and not simply an innocent victim. But he couldn't dwell on the growing evidence, not yet; he had a wife to find.

Before he could draw another breath, Alec was at Nigel's door, into the room, putting his massive hands around the man's neck as Edward and Ali attempted to pull him free. The grunting, the sounds of struggling emanating from the chamber, filled the castle.

Nigel was turning blue as Alec hovered over him, not the least bit concerned with the man's discomfort. "Your son has abducted my wife. Tell me where he has taken her."

Nigel could barely breathe much less speak. "I.... I do not know! I wasn't aw.... aware of his p-plans!"

Alec squeezed harder and Nigel gurgled loudly. Ali had stopped trying to pry the man's hands free; it was an impossible feat.

"If you kill him, you will never have your answers," he murmured into Alec's ear. "Bargain with him, man. Deal with his greed."

Alec's grip did not loosen. Then, slowly, he relaxed and Nigel spilled to the floor in a coughing heap. Alec loomed over him like the Angel of Death.

"I have no time for your games," he growled. "You will tell me what I want to know and I, in turn, will ask Edward for leniency for your case."

Nigel propped himself up on an elbow, rubbing at his throat. "I told you, I did not know of his plans," he eyed Alec. "But if you wish for me to help you, a pledge for leniency will not be sufficient."

Alec glanced at Edward. The king gazed emotionlessly at Nigel for a moment before turning away. "Grant him his freedom if he will help you find your wife, Alec."

Nigel, wide-eyed, watched the king lumber for the door, the characteristics of a weary man. When he should have been asleep, he was in the midst of a critical crisis. Edward knew for a fact that if something had happened to Lady Summerlin, he could completely disregard Alec's pledge of service. He suspected, more than likely, that Alec Summerlin would cease to exist and he was willing to do everything in his power to prevent the probability.

"Tell me," Alec diverted Nigel's attention away from the king. "Where would Colin take her?"

Nigel rose to unsteady feet and staggered to the nearest chair, still rubbing at his throat. As much as he loved his son, he was a selfish man. He saw freedom looming before like water before a thirsting man and he was drawn to it. Above all, he must preserve his own life and he was not ashamed that he was about to betray his only son.

Above all, he must survive. The battle against St. Cloven and Blackstone was already over, he would admit. But it did not mean that he had to become a casualty. Arrogance vanished, he would tell them everything he could.

"I truly do not know," he said hoarsely, thinking. "Certainly, he would not return her to Wisseyham, knowing it would be the first place you would search. More than likely, he has taken her someplace where you would never find her."

Alec's face was ashen, taut. "He plans to kill her?"

Nigel met his gaze steadily. "If she is already dead, he must find a suitable place to dispose of the body. If she isn't dead, then he surely intends to kill her."

Alec's jaw ticked furiously. "You are his father. Where do you think he will take her?"

Nigel thought a moment; betraying his son had been easier than he had anticipated and he felt no remorse. After all, he hadn't told Colin to abduct that woman. If his son's foolishness got him killed, Nigel certainly wasn't to blame. He cleared his throat, rubbed at it.

"He has always held a fascination for the Fens," he said.

"The Fens?" Ali repeated sharply. "North of Guyhirn?"

Nigel nodded slowly, thoughtfully. "Once, when he was a lad, his old nurse used to weave a tale of Druid priests dumping the bodies of sacrificial victims into Wicken Fen because the ground absorbed the corpses and left no trace. Colin always held a strange interest in Wicken Fen because of it. If I were he, that is where I would go."

"Wicken Fen is the other direction, south of Ely," Ali said quietly. "We can make it there in a few hours."

"He already has a four hour lead on us," Alec murmured dully, his gaze lingering on Nigel one last time. "Are you reasonably certain he would take her to Wicken Fen?"

"As sure as I can be," Nigel said. It was the truth.

Alec had no other choice but to trust him. But, strangely, he did not feel the hopelessness he had felt only moments earlier. Now, at least, he had a clue to Peyton's whereabouts.

"You will not be granted your freedom until my wife or your son, or both, are found," he said, turning for the door. "If your information proves to be false, you will die on the block."

Edward had already quit the room, with Alec close behind. Only Ali lingered a moment, his thoughtful gaze on Nigel. Passing a glance into the empty corridor to make sure Edward and Alec were well out of earshot, he closed the door softly.

Nigel eyed him warily. "What is it that you want, black beast? I have told you all I can."

Ali cocked a slow eyebrow. "So you have said. I wonder, however, if you did not have a hand in this."

"Does the color of your skin inhibit your intelligence? I told you I did not."

Ali stared at the man for a long, heady moment. Their gaze locked, absorbed, intertwined. Then, Ali slowly unsheathed the broadsword at his side. Nigel recognized his very own sword, confiscated not five hours earlier.

Nigel almost looked amused as the weapon came forth. "Do you think to threaten me?"

"Nay," Ali said softly. "I think to kill you."

Nigel's eyes rounded, slowly, as he realized that Ali meant what he said. "I have told you all I know. Alec promised me my freedom!"

It was Ali's turn to smile. "And I shall provide it. The freedom of your soul from its earthly confines."

Nigel scrambled away from the stalking soldier. "You cannot! The king will…."

"The king will commend my actions. 'Tis something that should have been done long ago," he took two swift strides and was upon the sweating man, gripping his tunic with an iron fist. "For what you have done to Brian, to Alec, to my wife's family, you are about to pay with your life."

Nigel could feel the cold steel against his gut and began to twist like a fish out of water. "You have no right!"

"No right?" Ali's eyebrows rose. "I beg to differ, my lord. 'Tis my right to repay the Summerlins and the de Fluornoys for their kindness and loyalty by destroying their most grievous nemesis. I will not think of the insults you have dealt me as I drive your sword into your soft innards. What I do, I do for them."

There was no time for Nigel to reply as steel met with flesh, blood, and guts. Ali drove the sword deeper than he ever imagined it could go, feeling the rush of pleasure, of vengeance, of relief. Even when the broadsword exited Nigel's back, still he thrust as his buried sense of retaliation found its release. For all of the years of torment and cruelty, he was finally dealing a measure in return and was not the least bit remorseful.

Nigel represented the very worst England had offered to her adopted son and Ali was content to seek revenge for himself. For the

Summerlins, for the de Fluornoys. He thrust until he could thrust no more.

When a Warrington soldier came to retrieve his lord some time later, he was not surprised to find Nigel's body impaled against the wall by his massive, gore-covered broadsword. With his reputation ruined, his life a disaster, certainly there was only one honorable way out of his predicament.

It was a most peculiar, painful suicide.

ᘛ

ALEC MET UP with his father in the dining hall. Brian and the remainder of the search party, including Ivy and Jubil, had congregated in the hall and were unenthusiastically sampling the early morning meal.

"Where is my sword and armor, Father?" he demanded quietly.

Brian rose from his chair, his eyes wide. "Did Nigel tell you where Colin has taken Peyton?"

"He thinks mayhap Wicken Fen. I need my equipment."

Ali entered the hall behind Alec, wide-eyed and breathless. Ivy immediately leapt to her feet, rushing into her shaking husband's arms. Perplexed at his state, she turned her questioning gaze to him but he merely smiled, putting his fingers against her lips to silence her inquiry.

Alec glanced over his shoulder at his friend to make sure he was present, but that was the extent of his attention. He did not seem to notice the blood stain on Ali's mail. His focus immediately returned to his father.

"Well?"

Brian did not hesitate. He marched purposefully from the room with Alec, Ali, Toby and Edward in pursuit. A few other retainers followed at a distance, knowing that The Legend was about to become whole once again. There wasn't a man or woman in the room that wanted to miss the rebirth.

Brian took his son into a seldom-used wing, the same wing where Thia and Peyton had nearly killed one another. The faint light from the rising sun was beginning to seep through the lancet windows, bathing the black stone a warm pink as Brian stopped in front of an old door and shoved it open. The sense of urgency was growing more profound by the moment.

The room was vacant for the most part, with the exception of a massive wardrobe against one wall and an unused bed. Brian went immediately for the wardrobe.

"I have kept it here since the day you discarded it," he threw open the doors to the cabinet. "Do you remember that day, Alec? 'Twas the day you returned prematurely from the Crusade. You rode into the bailey, dismounted, and shed every piece of armor on the spot. You never touched it after that."

Alec nodded faintly, his eyes glued to the contents of the wardrobe; as if suddenly revealed from the realm of the gods, his armor gleamed weakly in the faint light. Magnificent, perfect, and untouched for nearly twelve years. He felt the familiar power flooding him as he stared at the protection, remembering both the glory and the pain.

The entire room was still as Alec stared at his armor. Brian, smiling faintly at his son's expression, moved toward the small bed.

"I did not want to put your sword in the wardrobe," he said quietly, fumbling with the linen covers on the mattress. "I wanted to make certain your blade was well protected should you ever decide to use it again."

Alec moved forward as if in a trance, touching the breast plate of his armor. The Summerlin crest glimmered brilliantly against his touch, silently greeting the man called The Legend. Alec could feel the strength of the armor against his fingertips, the promise of might feeding his sagging spirits. The armor that had been a physical part of him for four solid years.

From the corner of his eye he could see that his father's eager movements had come to a halt. He turned his attention from his armor in time to see Brian moving toward him, a massive shaft of metal in his hand, over five feet in length. An instrument of death, of freedom, and of life – his sword.

Alec stared at the broadsword he hadn't seen since he had killed his brother with it. Brian had commissioned the sword made for his son when the lad was just sixteen, a sword so heavy and massive that seasoned knights used to laugh at the tall young squire for daring to master such an outrageous piece of equipment.

Christ, he remembered the sword with every cell in his body. His palms began to sweat and his entire body tingled strangely as his father extended the pommel of the sword as if offering his son the Holy Grail.

Alec gazed at the hilt before him; intricately detailed, inlaid with four sapphires the size of small eggs. The leather on the pommel was undamaged by age, still supple and strong. The blade itself was possibly the most terrifying ever designed; one side was as sharp as a razor, meant for a quick kill. The opposite side was grooved like the teeth of a portcullis, serrated fangs of death. The sole purpose was to bring a lingering, painful demise.

It wasn't just any broadsword; it was The Legend's blade by which he had earned his reputation. It was the Gateway to Death.

"Take it, Alec," he heard Ali whisper.

He wanted to. Christ, it was as if the sword had eyes, pleading with him to grip it once again and become whole. He could look deep into the eyes of the sword and see his greatest battle yet to come....sapphire-blue gems, like the sapphire blue eyes of his wife. He knew at that moment that the sapphires set deep into the hilt had been chosen sixteen years ago with a purpose. They were Peyton's eyes, and he was hesitant no longer.

His massive hand shot out, snatching the blade from Brian. Immediately, he could feel the recognizable power of the sword filling him, the wordless welcome as weapon melded with master. Alec ran a finger along the razor-smooth edge of the blade, drawing blood and unaware of the injury. He saw blood, but it wasn't his. It was Colin's.

Warm beams of light from the rising sun filtered into the room, reflecting off the massive broadsword. Alec turned the blade back and forth in the light, watching it gleam, feeling the oneness between Legend and Sword. Knowing that between the two of them, Peyton was halfway home.

Naught else mattered at the moment; Edward, the Welsh, Blackstone, or St. Cloven. Alec realized that all of the battles he had ever fought in were a practice for the main event – the redemption of his soul, the reclamation of his wife. All else paled by association. There was nothing more important than the woman he loved.

Brian, driven to blinding tears by the sight of his son holding his sword once more, sniffled loudly and waved wearily to the populace of the room.

"Allow Alec to dress, if you would," he began to herd them from the chamber. "The man has no time to waste."

When the room was clear, only Ali and Toby remained to help Alec with his protection. Ali tried to take the sword from him so they could commence with the acquisition of armor, but Alec refused to let it go. He hadn't held the weapon in so long that he was content to relish the feel of it in his hand.

Grinning, Ali began to help Toby with the leg plates and chain mail.

ꟾ

COLIN KNEW THAT Peyton was gravely injured. The blow to her head had split her scalp, and probably her skull. Leaving Thia for dead, he had pitched Peyton onto the back of a sturdy warmblood and squeezed out of the servant's entrance built into the outer wall of Blackstone, an exit he had become acquainted with during the weeks he had been a guest of Baron Rothwell. In the dark, his ride to freedom had been an easy one.

His initial destination had been Wisseyham. Although he knew it would be the first place Alec would come in search of his wife, he paused long enough at his ancestral home to gather some necessary items, including a secondary sword and pieces of armor to replace the newer items that had been left at Blackstone. He had no idea where he would be going and wanted to make sure he was prepared for any eventuality.

When he remounted his steed and set off again, Peyton had not yet regained consciousness. Riding north towards the coast and The Wash, he began to ponder in earnest where he should go to deposit her body. If the blow to the head did not kill her, he would surely slit her throat and be done with her in that manner. His sole purpose was to kill her; no ransom, no demands, no torture. As he had told Thia, his one and only desire was to see the heiress to St. Cloven dead. Generations of Warringtons demanded it.

He would kill her and throw her into The Wash. To the north of The Fens, it was a vast expanse of ocean that….suddenly, he recalled a story he had heard when he was a small lad. Thinking of The Fens had brought the tale to mind. 'Twas an old story of Wicken Fen, a place where Druids used to deposit their dead. It was a place where bodies were never recovered.

Suddenly, he wasn't so sure that disposing of Peyton in The Wash was an intelligent idea. After all, sooner or later her body would wash up on shore. And with her obvious red hair, eventually, Alec would catch wind and identify her. He did not want the evidence of his murder turning up on the white sand shores of The Wash.

But in Wicken Fen, she would never be found. No evidence, no proof for her desperate husband to cling to. Without proof, Alec Summerlin would have no definitive reason to seek out Colin and dispense justice.

After all, with Thia dead, there was no one to confirm that Colin abducted Peyton. For all they would know, Colin had merely escaped his confinement and had ridden off into oblivion.

There was no definitive link between him and the fate of Thia and Peyton. After he disposed of Lady Summerlin, he would ride south to London and catch a barge to Calais. He could assume another identity in France, mayhap pose as a wealthy earl, and marry well. Summerlin would never find him.

With a sense of purpose, Colin turned his mount south for Wicken Fen.

ꕥ

OVER THREE HUNDRED pounds of flesh and metal entered the grand hall of Blackstone. Brian looked up from his porridge and his jaw dropped. The chalice in his hand clattered to the floor. He couldn't ever remember seeing a more terrifying, omnipotent sight.

It was The Legend as if he had never left them. His armor and mail, polished to a high sheen, caught the weak torchlight and reflected the illumination like bolts from Heaven. All in the massive gallery were touched by the daggers of power, blinded by them, striking them speechless with awe. The Legend was in their midst.

Alec, ignorant of the reverence, raised the visor of his helm and focused on his father.

"I ride south to Wicken Fen," he said in a commanding tone. Edward ran an approving eye over his warrior. "God's Blood, Alec. I do not think I have ever seen anything quite so intimidating. Hell, man, I am frightened simply looking at you."

Alec couldn't muster the energy for their usual banter. His mind, his body, was focused on but one thought. "I am taking Ali and Toby with me, if for nothing more than to protect Peyton while I take care of Warrington. I would ask your permission to acquire their services."

"By all means, Alec," Brian swallowed the food in his mouth before he choked on it. "They belong to you. Sworn to me or not, they have always belonged to you."

Flanking Alec on either side, Ali and Toby were dressed to the hilt in gleaming armor and mail. Ivy, seated beside her aunt, left her seat to go to her husband and brother-in-law. Alec glanced at the woman, his thinly-held control nearly crumbling when he saw the tears in her eyes.

"You will…. you will bring her back, won't you? No matter how you find her?" she whispered, falling into Ali's embrace.

Alec's breathing quickened, but he forced himself to calm; he had only been able to maintain a handle on his emotions by convincing himself that his wife was still alive. He simply could not entertain the alternative.

"I shall return her, Ivy," he said in a tone that warranted no contradiction. Then he turned to his father once more. "How is Thia?"

Brian swallowed hard, his expression washing with grief.

"Pauly says her skull is broken, and she cannot see. But she lives, although Pauly seems to think she will not survive the day. Your mother is with her."

Alec's jaw ticked. "Thia was an accomplice in all of this. I do not know if I can forgive her, but I shall pray for a painless end to her suffering."

"I tried to warn you but you would not listen," Jubil whispered. "I tried to tell you, Alec. Several times. I tried to tell you to beware of the threat from within, to beware of Greeks bearing gifts. But you ignored me."

For the first time in hours, Alec's emotionless facade faltered. "You weren't clear, Jubil. Your warnings were too vague for me to contemplate any action."

"But I warned you!" Jubil leapt to her feet, agitated and filled with grief. "I told you I smelled danger, but you did not listen! All I could do was inform you of my suspicions, of the troubles whispered upon the winds. There was no way I could tell you for fact that your sister would be the Trojan Horse to your destruction."

Alec swallowed hard, well remembering the mumbled warnings of a crazy woman. Christ, he should have listened to her. She had been right all along, about everything, and he hadn't paid her the heed deserving of her skills. He continued to stare at the woman helplessly as she approached him.

"I spoke to your mother of Thia's overture and, suddenly, all became clear to me. Thia's gift was the promise of peace. She promised peace between Peyton and herself, and lured your wife into a trap. She was the Greek of my prophesy, Alec. 'Twas her gift you were to be wary of."

His expression flickered with pain. "Had I but known."

Jubil grasped him gently by the arm, her manner relaxing as she gazed deeply into sky-blue eyes. "Peyton is your Helena," she murmured. "You would walk through fire to retrieve her, you would sanction the deaths of thousands if only for a glimpse of her sweet face. She is your Achilles Heel, Alec, the Keeper of your Soul. You have always known that."

He closed his eyes against her earnest face, feeling the impact of her words like a thousand hammer blows. He lost his breath, caught it, and refocused on the older features.

"I have always known that," his whisper echoed, hypnotized by her piercing stare.

"And you love her more deeply than you ever thought possible."

He let out a choked sob, completely ignoring the room full of people watching him. Tears sprang to his eyes, glistening on his blond lashes as he looked to Jubil as if she held all the answers.

"I love her more than life," he echoed faintly.

Jubil smiled faintly and patted the powerful knight on his stubbled cheek. Tears dripped from his lashes and onto her hand.

"Do not weep, sweet Alec," she murmured. "You may be The Legend, but Peyton's love had made you immortal. Go and find your wife."

He sighed raggedly, wiping at the tears that were blinding him. "Is....can you sense if she is still alive?" He almost couldn't bring himself to ask.

Jubil paused a moment, staring deeply into his eyes. Then, slowly, she brought her hand to her lips and licked the tears that had touched her. "Aye," she replied softly. "She lives still."

Alec took it as a promise from God. Without another word, he spun on his heel and quit the room, leaving an entire hall of royalty and commoners alike reeling in his wake.

CS

TWO HOURS AFTER sunrise, Wicken Fen came into view. A massive expanse of bogs, reed-filled swamps, and other beautiful but undesirable elements, it was teaming with wildlife and bramble.

Colin entered the parklands from the northern outskirts, intent on finding the very best spot to discard his load. Taking his leisure time about it, as his manner had been unhurried since leaving Blackstone, he picked his way deeper and deeper into the fen.

It never occurred to him that he was being pursued. Even if his escape had been discovered by now, there was no one to tell where he had gone. A trip to Wisseyham would happen upon servants who had not seen their master return; he had been very careful to keep himself concealed from the few serving wenches they employed, and he certainly had not brought Peyton into the open expanse of the bailey. The horse, and Peyton, had remained concealed in the woods.

Furthermore, it never occurred to him that his father would have betrayed him by giving Alec Summerlin suggestions as to where he might have gone. His father knew nothing of his plans; therefore, he would have been unable to provide Alec any assistance. Never in his wildest dreams would he have believed that his father had not only betrayed him, but had known his son well enough to guess his destination. It was frightening to imagine that father and son thought so very much alike, evil in every fashion. It never occurred to him that for every moment he lingered, Alec Summerlin was closing the gap.

The sun filtered in through the canopy above, increasing the humidity of the air surrounding him. The smell of his dirty horse and moldering leaves filled his nostrils and he was suddenly quite eager to be done with his deed. Far over to his left, he could see a swampy bog that extended nearly as far as the eye could see.

He made it as close to the bog as he could before his horse became stuck in the mud and could go no further. Turning the horse around, he managed to rein the animal to more solidified ground before dismounting.

Peyton was still unconscious. He pulled her off the mount like a sack of grain and deposited her under the nearest tree. Taking the time to remove the saddle from his horse and provide the animal with a bit of water, he then proceeded to dig about in his saddlebags for his dagger. She wasn't dead yet; he had to kill her and be on his way.

The dagger was long, perfect to complete the deed in one stroke. He wiped at the blade, examining it, thinking ahead to the meal he would ingest tonight at a fine inn and lingering on his approaching voyage. He'd never been to France and looked forward to the adventure.

The sun was rising steadily and Colin was eager to get on with what he must do. Moving to Peyton where she lay prostrate under the tree, he knelt beside her.

The dagger rested in his hand. "So sorry, love. Well, truthfully, I am not. Your family has be a thorn in the Warrington's side for many years. 'Tis only right that the crisis come down to you and I as the surviving heirs," he traced the red hair with the sharp tip of the dirk, watching the light play off the strands. Beautiful as it was, he still wasn't remorseful in the least. "Have a grand time in hell, my lady."

The blade caught the sunlight with sinister elegance as Colin raised it high. Peyton's white neck was open and exposed, making a perfect target that beckoned to his twisted sense of revenge. He heard the call, as he was about to answer.

But he never had the chance to follow through. Suddenly, a balled fist caught him in the groin and the brief moment of shock that followed was pursued by pain such as he had never known. It felt as though his testicles had been driven into his throat. Sparks of agony sent him face first into the soft earth of the fen.

Peyton rolled away from him, nauseous and dizzy, and thoroughly sick. But she was awake, and alive, and she intended to remain so, no matter what it took. The last few uttered words of his speech had roused her, primed her for the battle that lay ahead. Fear was virtually unknown; the basic instinct for survival was all she could feel as her muddled senses attempted to orient themselves.

As she struggled to her knees, a rotted branch met with her hands.

Shaking like a leaf, she clutched the branch and charged the fallen Colin with the full intent of beating him dead with it.

Colin took two severe blows to his head before he managed to raise his hand and dislodge the weapon. Undeterred, Peyton kicked him in the thigh and pounded him with her weak hands, but he nearly captured her and she scampered into the underbrush, shrieking and gasping like a madwoman.

Peyton had no idea where she was. The ground beneath her was lurching and swaying, and it was all she could do to maintain her footing. Around her, unfamiliar trees loomed and the very earth she stood upon seemed intent to suck her under. Her delicate green slippers were instantly wet and dirty.

But she kept moving, away from Colin and away from his insane ideals of family and vengeance. She stumbled over exposed roots, scraping her knees and drawing blood, but still she kept moving. She had to put as much distance as she could between Colin and her unborn child.

She clutched her stomach, wondering if the babe had suffered during her ordeal, wondering if she would do more damage with what was yet to come. Hot tears stung her eyes and the bile in her throat gagged her, but still, she kept running. It was run or die.

She burst through a thicket of brush, having no idea where she was going, only knowing that she had to find help. She tripped over something she did not notice, and ended up on her hands and knees. Beneath her hand, a sharp thick stick was partially lodged into the damp ground. With a grunt of effort, she yanked the weapon free and resumed her panicked run.

With a roar, Colin was suddenly in her path and she screamed, barely avoiding his vicious grasp. She whirled away from him, finding new strength in the fear that was flushing her veins, and tore a wild path through the growth as he staggered after her. His groin injury was hindering him greatly as he pursued.

Peyton could hear him following, cursing and snorting as he stumbled through the bramble. Her head was clearing a bit even if her stomach was still churning, and she was beginning to think more clearly. Dodging behind a thick tree, she doubled back through a cluster of thick underbrush and emerged on the other side.

Still clutching the sharp wood, she found a large branch that would do quite nicely in wreaking severe damage on Colin's skull. Peyton crouched low to the ground, trying to quiet her breathing so she could hear her enemy. So she could hear Death as it approached. Colin was about, somewhere, and she was intent on harming him before he could do her mortal damage. He might have been larger and stronger, but she was more intelligent. She would win this battle. She had to.

"Peyton!" Colin shouted. "I know you can hear me! Show yourself and I shall be swift with my justice. If I have to hunt you down, I shall make you suffer. I swear it!"

Head clearing, stomach settling, Peyton remained still and silent. Colin stomped about, moving away from her as he went about his search.

She waited until he moved off before attempting to follow. Stealthily, she pursued the storming, cursing man, making certain to remain far behind him and out of sight. Coming through a particularly thick patch of brush, she tore her slipper on a prickly branch and nearly tripped.

Irritably, she ripped the shoes off her feet and tossed them aside. The ground beneath her feet was freezing, but she ignored the discomfort. It was minor to the overall situation.

The sun overhead provided limited light within the heavy canopy of trees. Colin was backtracking, returning to his steed, and Peyton stayed within the sheltering cover of the undergrowth as she followed his movements.

When it became apparent that Colin was intent on waiting her out, eager to take advantage of a movement or a mistake, she sat on her bottom in the brush and refused to budge. If he was going to wait, then so was she.

Wait for death to claim one of them.

CHAPTER TWENTY

THE SUN TRAVERSED the afternoon sky with painful slowness, reminding Peyton with every passing second of her discomfort and hunger and fear. But as long as she held Colin in her sights, she could ignore the obvious in lieu of self-preservation. Nothing mattered but keeping him at bay until she could move away from him, unheard. She began to pray fervently for nightfall, knowing that her only chance to escape him would be while he slept.

Colin was leaning leisurely against a tree, the evil-looking dagger clutched in his gloved palm. Absently, he hacked at the bark of the tree, pondering the bog before him. Peyton sat, still as stone, and watched every move.

"Peyton?" he suddenly called. "I know you are out there, listening to me. Watching me. How does it feel, knowing it will only be a matter of time before you die?"

He was met with the chirp of birds, the singing of the wind through the trees. Smiling as though he were laughing at a clever remark, he pushed himself off the tree and turned toward the overgrowth. Peyton swore he was looking right at her.

"Do you know that my father took your crazed aunt's virginity?" he said carelessly, trying to provoke an angry response. "Several years ago, in fact. He found her eating leaves in the forest and took his pleasure with her. That is what your aunt does, isn't it? Eat leaves and brew witches potions? There's not one person in the barony that believes she is sane."

The echo of his own voice greeted him. He maintained his thin smile and paced about, hacking at anything he came close to with the dagger he clutched.

"And your husband. Oh, excuse me. I meant *The* Legend," he sneered mockingly. "Strange that a coward should carry such a prestigious title. He is certainly not worthy of such a reputation. From what I have heard, he fled the Crusades in terror and returned home to breed horses and master needlepoint."

In the bushes, Peyton was red with fury but she was wise enough to know that Colin was attempting to lure her from her safe haven and she struggled to keep her mouth closed.

But it was growing increasingly difficult. The ground was cold and her feet were frozen, her head ached terribly and her stomach was quivering. Her exhaustion, fed by her other symptoms, threatened to overwhelm her. She wondered darkly if she would be able to stay awake long enough to escape him.

"I even heard rumor once that he and Ali were lovers," Colin leaned against the tree again, picking his teeth casually. "As Thia possessed strange tastes, so did her brother. His tastes run to dark meat. Tell me, Lady Summerlin, have you been forced to share your husband with his black bitch?"

Peyton nearly lost her composure then. She bit her lip so hard to keep from replying that she sampled her own blood. Still, she kept silent. She had no choice.

He laughed softly and dug into his pack, bringing forth cheese and bread. Peyton caught sight of the food and realized she was starving. He ate loudly, enjoying every bite, and Peyton's eyes stung with tears as she watched and listened. Her misery was growing by the second.

Misery for herself. Misery for Alec. She'd never told him she loved him, not once. True, she had confessed her feelings to Nigel and Alec had heard her, but she'd never told him face to face. She was desperate to see him again, to tell him how she had always loved him. She couldn't remember when the irritation ceased and the love began, for it seemed as if she had loved him from the start. If God would only grant her the opportunity to hold him one last time, she would be content for all eternity.

The sun galloped across the bright blue expanse of sky, approaching late afternoon. Nightfall would soon be upon them and Peyton began to seriously worry about her stability. Her fatigued body was beginning to scream for release and she knew it would only be a matter of time before her mind would no longer be able to control the physical need. But for as long as she was able, she would fight. Tears spilled down her cheeks as her hand moved over her belly, comforting the child within. God help her, her son would grow to know his father. Her own selfish reasons aside, she had to live for the unborn heir.

Night was nearly upon them. Peyton's limbs were frozen from hours of sitting upon the wet, cold ground and her eyes were attempting to gain a measure of rest. The lids would droop closed, only to be startled open again by Peyton's inner sense of self-preservation. Colin had not moved from his post by the tree, and she would make sure that she kept him in full view until he succumbed to the exhaustion they were both experiencing.

She prayed that Colin would find his rest first. She wasn't sure how much longer she could remain strong. But her exhaustion eventually proved to be too much for the new mother to take – sleep claimed her and she was hardly unaware of the state. She was unaware when she crashed softly to the ground, unaware when Colin rose, his ears piqued at the faint sound. She wasn't aware when he began to hunt for her in earnest, stalking her like a cat. She only became aware when someone grabbed her by the hair.

Instantly awake, Peyton let out a howl that reverberated off the trees. Colin had her by the hair, pulling her from her protective thicket, scratching her tender white flesh as he dragged her through the thorns and branches. His grunts of effort mingled with her screams, filling the fen like an eerie symphony.

Peyton was full of vigor, of fight. She swung her fists at him, kicking and biting and aiming for his soft groin or his neck. He struck at her, feebly, for it was difficult to strike and maintain his hold on her hair. She was a wild thing, an animal fighting for survival, and Colin was amazed at the strength she exhibited.

Nonetheless, he managed to pull her out into the clearing that overlooked the bog. His dirk was lodged in the tree trunk and he struggled toward it, dragging his fighting quarry across the cold, dark earth. Peyton dug her heels in, driving her fists in to his soft abdomen when he moved too close to her. Gasping, he slapped her across the face.

She slapped him back, and kicked him, and screamed and cursed and howled like an unearthly being. She knew he was moving for the dagger wedged into the tree and she used all of her strength to keep him from reaching it. It did not matter that he was nearly pulling her bald; the loss of a chunk of hair was insignificant to the loss of her life.

Colin was stronger and larger and, inevitably, was gaining ground towards the tree. Peyton had resorted to scratching, drawing blood on the hand that gripped her hair as he cursed and slugged at her with balled fists. Still, she did not give up. *She had to fight.*

It took a small eternity of screaming and fighting, but he managed to drag her close enough to the tree where he was able to touch the hilt of the dagger with his fingertips. His arm was extended as long as it could go, straining, pleading, begging to acquire the instrument of murder. He could almost reach it.

Colin was so involved in his quest that he failed to hear the approaching thunder. Peyton was so caught up in her struggle that she neglected to feel the trembling of the ground. All she knew was that her frozen feet were numb, her body was near collapse, and she had bloodied her hands fighting Colin.

Distant thunder rolled across the fen, lured by the loud screams of a desperate woman. The advance of myth, mortal, and man combined. The Legend had arrived.

Colin was the first to realize the advance. He paused suddenly, his senses failing to believe what his eyes were undeniably envisioning. The largest knight he had ever seen was bearing down on him, flanked by two equally large warriors. They were laden down with so much armor that it was impossible to distinguish any identifiable characteristics other than Death.

Colin knew who they were. Somehow, some way, Alec had found them. His mind was whirling with frenzied thoughts, coming so fast and furiously that he barely had time to grasp them. For the moment, he could barely comprehend anything other than being rid of the banshee within his grasp. It did not seem to matter than Alec would witness his action; all that mattered was being rid of her. The last punishment would be handed out and Alec would witness it.

Colin stopped attempting to drag Peyton by the hair. Instead, he balled his fist and swung as hard as he could, catching her in the temple. Peyton collapsed, falling against him. The ground shook underneath his feet as he swept her into his arms, struggling with every ounce of strength toward the murky bog.

ଓ

ALEC SAW HIM carrying his wife's limp form toward the bottomless muck. Midas was already moving as fast as he could go, but still, Alec drove his spurs into his silver sides until they bled. He had to make it to her. Christ, he was so close he could taste her and he refused to succumb to the wild panic that was threatening. But even as he raced toward the two figures, he knew he would not be in time.

Peyton hit the muddy water of the bog with a loud splash. A second later, Alec was upon Colin as the man raced back toward his charger, desperate to retrieve his blade. Toby and Ali immediately reined their destriers at the edge of the muddy pit. Ali dismounted first and started to plunge into the cloudy water when Toby halted him.

"You do not know how deep it is!" he shouted. "Give me your hand!"

Ali grasped the extended gauntlet, plunging feet first into the muddy mess. He sank up to his thighs, desperately searching underneath the surface for a scrap of cloth, a bit of hair, a hand. *Anything.* But his urgent grasp met with leave and twigs, and he continued to descend as the water level moved up to his groin, his hips, his waist. Deeper and deeper he went and, still, there was nothing. No sign, no Peyton.

He let go of Toby's hand and tore off his helm, tossing it to the shore. He was vaguely aware of Alec shouting his name, but he ignored him. He had to find Peyton.

Armor and all, Ali dove underneath the surface of the bog.

ALEC CAME TO rest beside Colin's charger. In spite of the fact that he hadn't worn armor in twelve years, he moved with the grace of a cat, as if the plates of metal were an insignificant drain on his incredible strength. Sword unsheathed before Midas had come to a halt, he dismounted the steed with unparalleled agility and charged toward his fumbling nemesis. Colin barely had time to move into a defensive position before Alec brought his sword down in a crushing strike.

The blow sent Colin to his knees. The horses danced about as he scampered underneath his mount in an attempt to escape The Legend's wrath. Alec kicked the horse aside and charged after his enemy, his mind torn between Ali's rescue and his own attempt to exact vengeance. He thought he shouted to Ali, once, but he couldn't be sure. Colin was up in an offensive stance and Alec found himself fully focused on the challenge.

It did not matter that Alec hadn't wielded a sword since he had gutted his brother in the heat of battle. From the moment he had reclaimed his weapon it was as if it had never left his hand. As if it were a physical extension of his body. When Colin attacked him with a strong downparry, Alec responded with a swift movement of his own that sent Colin reeling into a thicket of holly.

Alec followed him into the brush, desperately torn between his wife's rescue and the justice he must dispense. He knew, for his own peace of mind, that he must do what was necessary. He would have to trust his wife to Ali and Toby.

As he trusted them with his own life, he would have to trust them with Peyton's. At the moment, there was no other alternative.

Alec wasn't in the mood to test his dormant skills. He was determined to bring about a quick kill and when Colin regained his footing, Alec plowed into him with unearthly power. Thrust, parry, thrust, parry.... on and on it went. The very air trembled with the collision of their might.

Colin was powerful and Alec was somewhat surprised that he had been able to hold him off thus far. Not many people had lasted so long against The Legend. But Colin's skill was of little consequence; Alec used his intelligence, something Colin had been unable to do in his fright, and managed to corner the man into a particularly thick portion of bramble. It was a stroke of tactics, of pure skill. Of sweet revenge.

Colin realized too late what Alec had done, and in his panic, worked himself into a fighting frenzy that merely succeeded in weakening him further. Alec merely went through the movements, meeting Colin's thrusts, knowing the end was near. He could have waited for the man to simply tire himself out, but he did not want to wait.

Colin lashed out with a skilled thrust, which Alec met deftly. Using his power, he shoved his opponent backwards and both swords ended up wedged into the bark of a thick tree. Colin grunted out of fright and frustration, attempting to dislodge his weapon even as Alec held it firm. The Legend was in control.

"You will answer a question that I put to you yesterday, Warrington," he growled. "Did you kill my brother?"

Colin was quivering with adrenalin as he gazed upon the fearsome helm. "A moot point, Summerlin."

"Untrue. Whether or not you did, it makes no difference, for you shall die regardless. But I would know just the same."

Colin's jaw ticked as he struggled with futile effort to extricate his sword. Realizing the endeavor was useless as long as Alec held him firm, he exhaled sharply. "I did not kill your brother. Your father's horse did."

The eyes behind the closed visor glittered. "What does that mean?"

Colin had nothing to lose by confessing. "Your idiot brother had the misfortune to overhear my conversation with your sister regarding my plans for abducting your wife. When he confronted me, I silenced him by shoving him under the hooves of the charger. Satisfied?"

Alec stared at him, his stomach lurching as his suspicions were confirmed. "Thia knew of your plans?"

Colin was in no mood to carry on a conversation. "Aye, she did indeed. I told her I would dissolve our betrothal if she helped me destroy St. Cloven. She did not want me, I did not want her, and she was willing to do anything to be free."

Alec did not react outwardly, but inside, he understood Thia's desperation and cursed her at the same time. "You coerced her, you bastard. All to destroy St. Cloven."

Colin yanked at his blade, managing to somewhat dislodge it. "Nay, Summerlin," he grunted. "All to destroy the de Fluornoys!"

Colin freed his blade, shoving Alec back with a kick to his armored groin. Colin's sword arced upward and Alec suddenly saw the opportunity he had been looking for.

It was too easy, too unworthy of The Legend's reputation, but he was in no mood to confirm his fame. In a fraction of a second, he reversed the sides of his blade, moving from the razor edge to the serrated side. In the next half-moment, he went down on one knee, below Colin's aim, and brought the sword straight across.

Blade met with flesh, bone, vital organs, and blood. In a signature stroke, Alec has sliced Colin in two clean halves.

ᘓ

ALI NEVER SAW the battle or the final stroke. He was struggling through mud and zero visibility in search of his sister-in-law. As the seconds passed, his panic increased, and twice he'd had to come up for air. Toby, on shore, was overwhelmed with horror.

On his third dive, Ali was ready to scream with helplessness. He couldn't locate Peyton in the spot she had been dumped, and his anxieties were threatening to destroy his control. Further and further he swam, deeper and deeper, dragging his gloved hands long the bottom of the bog until a slip of material met with his hand. Hope soared as he yanked hard on the material, attached to a weighty anchor.

As fast as was possible in the heavy water, he pulled her against him. His lungs were near bursting with need for air but he ignored the pain, the heat welling within his chest. It was nothing compared to the stale air saturating Peyton's chest, draining her life away. Struggling with every fiber in his body, he persevered to overcome personal agony and threatening unconsciousness to bring Peyton to the surface of the deadly bog.

When his face met with the fresh, icy air, his painful gasping sounds brought Toby plunging into the water. Ali couldn't manage to speak; he did not have to. Toby was already yanking Peyton from his arms and thrusting her onto the shore.

As Ali clawed his way onto dry land, Toby turned Peyton on her side and pounded on her back to evacuate the water from her lungs.

"Breathe, Peyton, breathe!" he rasped. "Goddammit! Breathe!"

Peyton was ghostly gray, covered with mud and leaves. Her luscious red hair was caked with muck as Toby brushed it out of her face, clearing her mouth of debris. Again, he pounded her on the back.

"Oh, God, *breathe!*"

Behind them, the sounds of the swordfight had grown eerily still. But neither man was aware of anything but the still form on the ground as Ali crawled closer, barely recovered from his own near-drowning.

"Again, Toby!" he gasped. "Do it again!"

Toby pressed firmly on her stomach, bringing up water and bile, before pounding her again. He repeated the process two or three times when Alec was suddenly by his side, shoving him out of the way.

"Peyton!" he shouted. "Peyton, my love, my dearest love, you have got to breathe!"

Ali managed to push himself to his knees. "T….turn her on her back," he instructed in a hoarse voice. "You must get air into her lungs!"

Alec, a hair-breadth away from full-blown panic, did as he was instructed. He smoothed the dirty hair from her face, whimpering softly as he gazed into her gray face. "Breathe, love, please. Christ, Peyton, breathe!"

"Blow into her mouth," Ali coughed, wiping the muck off his face. "Put your lips on her mouth and blow."

Alec did not hesitate. Clamping his lips over her sweet mouth, he blew hard. As Ali encouraged him onward, he kept blowing. He did not know if he was doing any good, but at least he was doing something to aid her. Anything to bring her back to him.

He stopped blowing for a moment, watching Peyton's chest to see if she had resumed breathing on her own. After a few seconds, she remained still and his sense of despair immediately overwhelmed him.

"Christ…," he desperately touched her face, her body, her dirty hair. "Oh, God, Peyton. Do not leave me. Not when we haven't yet begun to live," his hand was at her face, gripping her chin with his massive fingers. Suddenly, the pain of it was too much to take and he slapped her gently as if that action would bring her out of her state. One slap led to another and before he realized it, he had slapped her twice, hard, across her beautiful face.

"Do not leave me!" he cried, his voice cracking. One moment of slapping turned into another of desperate embraces, clutching her against his hard chest as tightly as he could. "I forbid you to leave me, do you hear? You have made me whole, sweetheart. Without you I am nothing. Christ, do you hear what I am saying? I need you! I love you more than life!"

Toby's face was in his hand, hiding the tears that were coursing down his cheeks. Ali, having regained his breath and strength, knelt on the other side of Peyton's body.

"Lay her down, Alec," he encouraged firmly. He could see that Alec was beyond rational thinking. "Let me try."

"No!" Alec sobbed, his face in her dirty hair. "She can't leave me, Ali. I will not live without her!"

"If I am successful, you will not have to live without her," Ali said firmly, gently. "Lay her down!"

After a moment's hesitation, Alec tenderly lowered his wife to the ground, kissing her sweetly as he released his hold.

"Oh, Peyton...." he whispered, kissing her again. "Do not leave me, sweetheart. I love you."

Ali gently pulled him away, moving to resume blowing air into Peyton's lungs. As he put his hands on her face and hovered over her lips, she suddenly let out a violent cough.

Ali let out a whoop of surprise and barely managed to turn her on her side as she commenced vomiting water. Alec, overcome with astonishment, began gasping like a dying man as Ali thumped Peyton on the back to aid her in clearing her lungs.

"Peyton!" Alec cried, nearly pushing Ali over in his attempt to be near his wife. "Can you hear me, love? Peyton?"

Peyton vomited until there was nothing left. Air, rushing into her lungs, sent stabs of pain radiating throughout her body. Vaguely, she could hear Alec's voice and Ali's low laughter, but beyond that she was incapable of sensing anything else. She thought she was dreaming... or dead.

Last she remembered, she had been struggling with Colin. And now.... she truly had no idea what had happened, or where she was. Mayhap, in fact, she had dreamed the whole event with Colin. Or mayhap she was simply insane.

However, she had heard one thing clearly; Alec told her that he loved her. Somewhere in the mists that had fogged her mind, she had felt a stinging pain to her cheek and she had heard an unashamed declaration of his love. Then there had been this man...a man with golden red hair. He seemed to know her, for he had been smiling openly. Strangely, she did not fear him. As he moved toward her through the mists, tall and broad and handsome, she realized there was something very familiar about him. His voice, rich and deep, distinctly informed her that it was not yet her time. She thought she had dreamt him, too.

Alec's voice reached her again, panicked and pleading. The tall man seemed to hear it, for a wistful look came to his eyes. Then, he put his hands on her shoulders and turned her away from the warm, bright light that had been intent on luring her. She had gazed at him questioningly but he had merely smiled and gave her another brotherly shove. Then she heard Alec's voice again, telling her that he loved her.

It had been enough to bring her back from the light beckoning her towards everlasting peace. A glance over her shoulder had showed the red-headed man once last time, his smile faded into a pensive gesture. His sky-blue eyes had reached out to her.

"Tell Nubs there is nothing to forgive, Peyton," he said.

And then she had come back.

"Alec?" she rasped; talking as well as breathing was mayhap the most painful experience of her life.

His hands were on her face, clutching her as if he were afraid she was intent upon leaving him again. "I am here. Christ, Peyton, can you hear me?"

She slipped into a coughing fit, agonizing with every breath. "Where…. where I am?"

His tears were falling freely, pelting her pallid cheek. "Safe, love. You are safe."

She swallowed hard, trying to calm her breathing. Slowly, the sapphire blue eyes opened and Alec nearly collapsed when they focused on him. His lip quivered and Peyton shushed him softly.

"Do not cry, my Alec," she whispered. She tried to raise her hand to him but was far too weak; he saw her feeble attempt and grasped her hand, holding it against his cheek fervently.

He closed his eyes against her frail, cold hand as his tears coursed warm paths over their flesh. "I thought you were lost," he whispered.

She managed a very weak, very pale smile and closed her eyes. "Not hardly. I.... I had to live long enough to hear you tell me of your love."

He kissed her hand eagerly. "'Tis more than love, sweetheart. Much, much more. You are my life."

She started to respond when her smile suddenly vanished and her eyes opened again. "Where's Colin?"

Alec kept her hand clasped to his cheek, his red-rimmed eyes steady. "Dead."

She coughed again. The pain, though still there, was fading. She seemed to be looking at him strangely. "You are wearing your armor?"

He smiled weakly. "It's almost too small. I fear I have grown in twelve years."

Ali and Toby chuckled softly at Alec's expense, remembering that they had almost been unable to secure the protection about his wide shoulders. Alec had not only grown upward, but he had also gained pure muscle and power since he last wore it. Before long, he would have to have a new suit commissioned.

She smiled in response to the low chuckles, her fingers gently caressing his cheek. "You look every bit The Legend. Welcome back, darling."

His smile faded as his tears returned. Choked, he kissed her palm tenderly, worshiping the feel of her warmth. "I would say the same to you," he murmured.

The setting sun bathed the fen in a golden glow, kissing the earth with a fading warmth. As Alec gathered his wife into his arms, he couldn't dwell on how very close he came to losing her. He was desperate to return her home, where she belonged, and put this episode far behind them.

"Tell me of your brother, Alec," she whispered as he moved toward his destrier.

He paused, confused. "I will later, love. I promise."

"Tell me now," she could barely speak.

Alec reached Midas and gently handed his wife to Ali before vaulting onto the saddle. Ali lifted Peyton up to him as if she were made of the most fragile glass while Toby covered her with a traveling cloak to ward off the evening's chill.

"Tell me, Alec."

He gathered his reins. "What do you wish to know?"

She did not say anything for a moment. "Was he very tall, with golden-red hair?"

"Aye, I told you he had red hair."

"And his eyes were sky-blue, like yours?"

He nodded faintly. "Why?"

She opened her eyes, gazing up at his helm-clad head. "He told me it wasn't yet my time."

He looked at her, then. "*Who* told you?"

"Peter," she whispered. "He told me it wasn't yet my time and helped me return to you."

Alec didn't say anything. He continued to stare at her, wondering if her experience had somehow damaged her mind. However, there was just the smallest part of him that was somehow willing to believe her. He hadn't listened to Jubil and it had nearly cost him everything. Mayhap Peyton had indeed seen something in the great beyond.

He forced a gentle smile. "You are sure it was Peter? I cannot be positive that my brother made it to Paradise. More than likely, he is paying for his sins as Lucifer's minion."

She smiled, feeling weak enough to sleep for a thousand years. "He said something else, something strange. He told me to tell Nubs that there was nothing to forgive."

Alec's face drained of all color. He stared at his wife, his mouth agape, and she caught his astonished expression immediately.

"What's the matter?"

"You…. what you said," he whispered in a tight voice. "Christ, Peyton…. he mentioned Nubs?"

"Who is Nubs?"

He could barely speak. "Me," he breathed. "'Tis a nickname my brother gave me when we were children because I used to chew my nails until they were bloody nubs. Only Peter called my by that name."

She smiled and reached up a frail hand to touch his face. Shaken, he kissed her fingers. "He really said that?"

She nodded slowly. "He said there was nothing to forgive."

He blinked and tears glistened on his thick lashes. He was so choked with emotion that he could not speak. Had he been hesitant before, there was no lingering doubt that Peter had indeed appeared to Peyton as she drifted in the realm between life and death.

Only Peter would have humiliated him by mentioning an embarrassing nickname. Only Peter would have known how very much Peyton meant to him, breaking whatever bonds confining him to the Netherworld to help her return to her frantic husband. As Alec had taken from him, only Peter would have given his brother his life back.

He clutched Peyton tightly, kissing her forehead tenderly as she dozed against his chest. The world around him, though fading in the weak light, was bright and new.

"I love you, sweetheart."

"I love you, too, my Legend."

EPILOGUE

1283 A.D.

THE EARLY MORNING sun had barely crested the horizon as a single rider pounded down the road toward the fortified manse of St. Cloven. The early May weather was beautiful and clear, quite wonderful after the harsh winter England had suffered through.

The rider was laden down with hundreds of pounds of armor, well-used. The horse, a silver charger of magnificent heritage, kept steady pace as St. Cloven came into view. Up on the battlements, the shouts from sentries filled the damp morn.

The heavy gates swung open, welcoming the master returned. Sir Alec Summerlin reined his massive steed into his bailey, barely giving the animal a chance to slow before he was dismounting. Immediately, he was met by several men.

"Where's my wife?" Alec demanded breathlessly.

The soldiers were grinning like fools. "Inside, my lord, with your mother and father," answered one.

Alec had the answer he sought. Without another word, he charged head-long into the cool interior of his manse.

Jubil was the first familiar face he saw. Greeting her with a distracted kiss, he patted her swollen belly fondly. "How much longer, love?"

"Too long," Jubil growled. "Where is my errant husband? He was supposed to return with you. Do not tell me he is still on the damnable

Welsh border!"

"Toby is at Blackstone," he held up a hand to silence her when she opened her mouth to protest. "He shall be along shortly. 'Twould seem he has a surprise for my son, something he has been working on himself, and wished to retrieve it."

Jubil smiled. The woman hadn't touched any of her medicaments or potions in nearly a year and had never looked so young or beautiful. At forty-four years of age, she had recently entered into her first marriage and was expecting the miracle of her first child shortly. Content for the first time in her life, she had all but given up her mysterious ways. Alec only knew he had never seen his brother happier.

"He made the babe a little cart, with wheels, so Peyton can push him around," she said fondly. "He is ever so proud of it."

Alec grinned, moving for the stairs. "Is Ivy here?"

Jubil shook her head. "She is still at Wisseyham. Her babe is due any day and Pauly refuses to allow her to travel. She is a sight, Alec; Ali is going to have his hands full with her until this child is born. All she does is eat and cry."

Alec paused on the steps. "Ali is still with Edward. He is helping the king design a string of fortresses along the Welsh border to protect and manage Wales. Edward has always recognized Ali's talent and swears he cannot do without his greatest architect. In fact, he has taken Ali off the front lines entirely and commanded him to devote all of his time to the construction of these bastions."

"Truly? That's wonderful, of course, but Ivy will have his head if he is not here in time for the birth of his child."

"I understand, but at the moment Ali is in the middle of constructing his greatest fortress yet. 'Tis called Caernarfon Castle, the most massive thing I have ever seen. Most impressive."

Jubil cocked an eyebrow. "I hope you can explain that to Ivy before she rips your tongue out and shoves it up your nose."

Alec moved to unlatch his helm from his breastplate. "I do not intend to explain anything to her," he gave her a thin, humorless smile.

"I shall send mother instead."

He mounted the stairs and moved down the corridor, his excitement growing with leaps and bounds. The last he saw of his wife, she was very pregnant and very hysterical. As much as he wanted to be present at the birth of his son, Llewellyn and his brother David, after betraying Edward's trust, had rallied a full-scale rebellion against the English crown. Alec had been forced into service far sooner than he had hoped.

Leaving his stricken wife had been the hardest thing he had ever had to do. As the fighting lasted through March and April, he waited eagerly for word from St. Cloven announcing the arrival of his child. Then, when the fighting seemed to be easing around the first of May, the long-awaited missive had come. His son, healthy and whole, had arrived.

He'd ridden night and day to make it to Peyton's side. As eager as he was to see his son, he was far more eager to see his wife to make sure she had come through her ordeal unscathed. Childbirth to him was a miraculous, frightening thing, and he had been absolutely terrified that Peyton would somehow suffer in the event. But God had blessed him with a healthy son and a recovering wife, and he had never been more grateful for anything.

As he passed down the corridor lined with Peyton's paintings, he found himself smiling as he remembered how difficult it had been to convince her to display her portraits. She had staunchly balked at the suggestion until one night, after she had fallen asleep, he and Toby had nailed nearly two dozen of her paintings to the walls of the upstairs corridor. Peyton had awoken to her openly-displayed talent and had promptly slugged her husband in the jaw. But the exhibitions of her skill remained.

He passed by her painting room en route to the master chamber when, suddenly, something inside the room caught his attention. Retracing his steps, he peered into the chamber.

A familiar red-head greeted him. Facing away from the door, Peyton was seated in front of her easel, delicately shading the vellum before her. His heart surged wildly into his chest at the sight of his wife, more love than he could ever express flooded his veins. Far more involved in his silent approach, he failed to notice the picture she was painting until he was nearly upon her.

It was a portrait of a man with red-gold hair. Alec nearly swallowed his tongue when he found himself staring into a perfect likeness of his dead brother.

"Peter!" he gasped.

Peyton started violently, dropping her brush and spilling her paints. But the spill and the brush were forgotten as Alec immediately took her in his arms and silenced her sobs of amazement with his joyful kisses.

"You spoiled your surprise!" she whispered, responding to his fevered lips with her usual abandonment.

"I care not," he murmured against her mouth. "All I am concerned with is you, and my son. Christ, Peyton, it's been so long."

"Nearly three months," she gasped as he suckled her lower lip. "Too long, my Alec. Thank God you have returned to me whole and sound."

His kisses slowed, being replaced by reverent caresses, meaningful gazes. "And I thank God that you have come through the birth of our son uninjured. I think I was more frightened for you than you were for me."

Her hair was pulled away from her face, revealing the beautiful features as she gazed into his eyes. How could she tell him that his son had been born blue, the cord wrapped around his tiny neck? Recollections of Rachel's dead child had haunted her since the day she had witnessed the event; fortunately, her son had recovered. He was perfect, as was his father.

"It was not as difficult as I had been told. Jubil gave me an ergot potion for the pain and the entire birth was over in three hours." A slight omission of certain facts. She knew, without a doubt, that he would not have taken the whole of it well.

"Three hours?" his eyebrows rose in surprise. "Christ, woman, I have had stomach aches that have lasted longer."

She giggled and he kissed her teeth, her nose, her chin.

"Where is my son?"

She made a wry face. "Where else? The only time I am allowed to hold him is when I feed him. The rest of the time, your mother and father fight over him. Truly, Alec, you would have thought I birthed the Christ child."

He grinned, helping her to rise slowly. "Are you supposed to be out of bed yet? You gave birth less than a week ago."

"I am fine," she said, avoiding his question as they moved for the door. Pauly had told her to stay in bed for three weeks; naturally, she disobeyed. But she did not want Alec to know, not just yet, for she knew he would insist that she take to her bed immediately. She wanted a few precious moments with him before he forced her into confinement.

She paused in the archway, returning her attention to the portrait she had been painting to divert his focus away from her. "You recognized your brother immediately. I must have a very good memory."

His gaze rested on the perfect likeness. "'Tis as I remember him. As if he had never left. Christ, you are amazing."

She smiled. "Your mother cries every time she sees it. I suspect you will have quite a fight on your hands when it is finished. Your mother has already declared her want for it."

He touched her face, kissing her cheek tenderly. "I will share it with her. But I shall not share my son. Take me to him."

Peyton curled her hand into the crook of his arm and led him, albeit stiffly, down the hall. There was a smaller chamber directly next to the master bedchamber, a room Alec had once claimed as his personal retreat. Peyton, however, had made it into a nursery.

The door was open and they could hear soft voices floating upon the warm air. Pausing in the doorway, Alec drank in the sight of the room; his father was seated in a large, comfortable chair, a small bundle cradled in his arms. His mother hovered over Brian, cooing sweetly at the swaddled parcel. And Thia, seated by the window and folding linens, was gazing at the wall with sightless eyes and telling her parents how foolish they were acting.

Alec had to smile at his sister; he and Peyton had long since forgiven the woman and Peyton had even gone so far as to demand that she reside with them at St. Cloven. Alec suspected that Peyton felt a certain amount of guilt for her misfortune, misplaced though the blame might be. But Peyton insisted there was no guilt involved; Thia was a good deal like Ivy and she missed her sister terribly after she and Ali had moved to Wisseyham. Somehow, Thia helped heal the void.

The two women had become the best of friends and Peyton had been delighted to discover that Thia's delicate palate for ale matched her own. Peyton had been unable to tend her duties as the official ale taster during her pregnancy, duties which Thia had taken on gladly. Although Colin had robbed her of her sight, it had not dampened her spirits and she had melded into the life at St. Cloven admirably.

He snapped out of his train of thought when Peyton tugged at his arm. His parents were cooing and carrying on so that they did not notice when Peyton and Alec stepped into the chamber.

"I would hold my son, Da," Alec said softly. "That is, of course, if you can pry him out of your arms."

Faces stricken with surprise, Brian and Celine faced their mighty son. Thia dropped the linen she was folding, her sightless eyes turning toward the source of her brother's voice.

"Alec!" Celine cried, rushing into his crushing embrace. "We heard the sentries but did not look to see if it was you!"

"No doubt," he snickered. "How could you possibly divert your attention away from my son for even one moment?"

"It's difficult," Brian agreed, his eyes twinkling. "My son The Legend. Tell me; how goes the Welsh border?"

"Calming," Alec could not take his eyes off the wrapped babe. "Fighting in Snowdonia has proved more difficult than expected, but victory shall be Edward's."

"With The Legend leading the army, there was never a doubt," Brian said proudly, his eyes soft. "We have been reading the missives from Ali. He swears it is as if you had never been without a sword in your hand. If Llewellyn possessed an ounce of intelligence, he would surrender before you cut him in half, too."

Alec grinned faintly. "*Diolch.*"

Peyton peered strangely at him. "What does that mean?"

"It means 'thank you' in Welsh." In the corner, Thia stirred and drew his attention briefly. "*Shwt mae*, Moppet. How go my ale stores?"

Thia cocked an eyebrow. "Are you attempting to prove your masterful use of the Welsh language? I refuse to answer you unless you address me in English."

He laughed softly. "I simply asked how you were, love."

She cracked a smile, relenting. "Well enough. Your private recipe ale is doing exceptionally well, by the way, although your wife has yet to taste it."

Peyton made a face. "I cannot stomach ale. It still makes me gag."

Alec grinned, his attention turning once more to his son. All other thoughts faded; he had waited long enough. "Give him to me."

Celine immediately took the child from Brian to allow the man to stand. Alec took his place in the large chair, armor and all, and held out his hands expectantly.

Peyton smiled and took her son from Celine, tears of joy brimming in the sapphire blue depths. Cradling the babe, she began to unwrap him for presentation to his father. The mood of the room went from sharp joy to one of muted, expectant awe as the Legend was to meet his legacy.

"You have not yet asked me his name," she murmured to her husband.

He looked confused. "I thought we agreed on Christian?"

"We did, and I fully intended to call him by that name," the blankets fell away, giving Alec a tantalizing view of chubby little arms. "But the very moment he was born, I gazed upon him and suddenly, I couldn't name him Christian. He.... he did not look like a Christian."

"He did not *look* like a Christian?" Alec repeated. "I do not understand."

She gazed up at him before the final wrap fell away. The tears in her eyes had found their way down her cheeks and her smiling lips trembled.

"You will."

The last of the swaddling fell away and Alec felt his limbs grow weak. Peyton held the babe up for display, a chubby, round, perfect little boy with his father's handsome features, his mother's sapphire blue eyes and red-gold hair – Uncle Peter's hair. Alec stared, fascinated, unaware of tears that had found their way onto his cheeks.

"Peter," he whispered.

Peyton laughed softly, placing the little boy in his father's arms. Celine protested softly, packing blankets around the babe to protect him from the cold armor.

"Peter Albert Brian Summerlin," Peyton said softly, touching the tiny red head. "There was simply no other name for him, my love. I can see that you agree."

Little Peter stared at his father, his big blue eyes crossed and out of focus. Alec gazed at the tiny infant, feeling more love and contentment than he ever thought possible. After a moment, he grasped his wife's hand and kissed it tenderly.

"Thank you," he whispered.

She smiled, touching his cropped blond hair, relishing the feel of her husband underneath her palm. He was whole, returned, and gazing upon the result of their consuming love. The babe in his arms was the outcome of adoration that spanned the ages.

But to Alec, it was more than that. Suddenly, he found himself staring into the evidence of his brother's spiritual existence. God had not only forgiven him his most heinous offense, he had bestowed him with unimaginable blessings.

As Alec had taken away, so had he given back. Tiny Peter Summerlin was living proof that Alec had the power of life as well as death and he knew, without a doubt, that his brother was still with him. The circle of life continued.

The Legend was immortal.

☙ THE END ❧

Author's Note

The House of Summerlin is connected with Beast. Sparrow Summerlin is a secondary character in Beast.

Beast

For more information on other series and family groups, as well as a list of all of Kathryn's novels, please visit her website at www.kathrynleveque.com.

ABOUT KATHRYN LE VEQUE

Medieval Just Got Real.

KATHRYN LE VEQUE is a USA TODAY Bestselling author, an Amazon All-Star author, and a #1 bestselling, award-winning, multi-published author in Medieval Historical Romance and Historical Fiction. She has been featured in the NEW YORK TIMES and on USA TODAY's HEA blog. In March 2015, Kathryn was the featured cover story for the March issue of InD'Tale Magazine, the premier Indie author magazine. She was also a quadruple nominee (a record!) for the prestigious RONE awards for 2015.

Kathryn's Medieval Romance novels have been called 'detailed', 'highly romantic', and 'character-rich'. She crafts great adventures of love, battles, passion, and romance in the High Middle Ages. More than that, she writes for both women AND men – an unusual crossover for a romance author – and Kathryn has many male readers who enjoy her stories because of the male perspective, the action, and the adventure.

On October 29, 2015, Amazon launched Kathryn's Kindle Worlds Fan Fiction site WORLD OF DE WOLFE PACK. Please visit Kindle Worlds for Kathryn Le Veque's World of de Wolfe Pack and find many action-packed adventures written by some of the top authors in their genre using Kathryn's characters from the de Wolfe Pack series. As Kindle World's FIRST Historical Romance fan fiction world, Kathryn Le Veque's World of de Wolfe Pack will contain all of the great story-telling you have come to expect.

Kathryn loves to hear from her readers. Please find Kathryn on Facebook at Kathryn Le Veque, Author, or join her on Twitter @kathrynleveque, and don't forget to visit her website at www.kathrynleveque.com.

Made in the USA
San Bernardino, CA
29 November 2016